TO HAVE AND TO HOLD

By the same author

ANNE BENNETT

To Have and to Hold

HarperCollins*Publishers*

HarperCollins*Publishers*
77–85 Fulham Palace Road,
Hammersmith, London W6 8JB

www.harpercollins.co.uk

Published by HarperCollins*Publishers* 2006
1

A catalogue record for this book
is available from the British Library

ISBN-13: 978 0 00 722599 6
ISBN-10: 0 00 722599 7

This novel is entirely a work of fiction.
The names, characters and incidents portrayed in it are
the work of the author's imagination. Any resemblance to
actual persons, living or dead, events or localities is
entirely coincidental.

Set in Sabon
by Palimpsest Book Production Limited, Polmont, Stirlingshire

Printed and bound in Great Britain by
Clays Ltd, St Ives plc

*To my eldest grandchild and only
granddaughter Briony Wilkes
with all my love.*

CHAPTER ONE

Carmel was positively mesmerised by the bustling docks at Belfast. She could barely wait to board the mail boat anchored in the dock, fastened tightly to the solid concrete bollards with ropes as thick as a man's forearm. Yet still the boat moved ever so slightly and Carmel tingled all over as she wondered how it would feel to be aboard that vessel and moving out into the open sea.

Just a little later she stood at the rails and watched the shores of Ireland disappear. She felt not homesickness, but relief, and she gave a defiant toss of her head that set her auburn curls dancing, while the excitement shone in her flashing dark brown eyes as the boat ploughed its way through the waves. Many were sick as the boat listed from side to side, including the nursing nuns that she was travelling with, but Carmel discovered her sea legs and explored the mail boat from end to end.

She was quite disappointed to leave the boat in Liverpool, yet as she and the nuns boarded the train for New Street Station in Birmingham, her insides turned somersaults with excitement – and a little trepidation. From the station she would be taken to the nurses' home attached to Birmingham's General Hospital where she would live for four years. She could barely believe that she was really here at last, and just as far from her family as she had wanted to be. She had known she wouldn't feel free of her father's dominance until she reached the shores of Britain. From now on, she decided, her life was to be her own. She would start the same as all the other probationers and no one need know about her earlier life at all. She would try to scrub it from her mind and forget it had ever happened.

But as the train rattled over the rails, taking her to her new life, she allowed herself to remember with great relief all she was leaving behind, like the abject terror her brutal father had always induced in her till she didn't know that there was any other way to feel, and regarded herself as worthless and of no account.

She would never forget her horrifying schooldays, especially that awful day when she was about seven, when Breda Mulligan, the post mistress's daughter, had pushed her face close to Carmel's and said, 'My mammy said I am not to play with you because you are dirty, smell bad and have nits in your hair.'

It had all been true. Carmel remembered then how the other children had formed a circle around her and chanted tunelessly in the school yard, 'Carmel Duffy has nits in her hair, nits in her hair, nits in her hair.' Time and again she had tried to break out of the circle, but the children held firm and pushed her back in. Even now, years later, she recalled crying with helplessness and fear. As the tears had trickled down her dirty face, they mingled with the snot from her nose that she wiped away with the sleeve of her ragged cardigan. 'Filthy, snotty Duffy,' Breda had cried with disgust, and they had all taken up the call. Eventually, one of the teachers, Mrs Mackay, had saved Carmel, scolded and scuppered the children and took Carmel inside to clean her up, but the damage had been done.

After school, the children had been waiting for her, but Mrs Mackay had anticipated that and she left her down at the house. House, huh, more like a shack – and Carmel had been mortified at her teacher glimpsing the hovel she lived in.

Once, Carmel imagined, the small cottage walls had been whitewashed and the thatch thick, but long ago the neglected thatch had had to be removed and lay in a sodden, rotting heap beside the house. The only roof they had then was of corrugated iron, and the sides of the house were reduced to bare stone. The shabby and ill-fitting door was hanging off its hinges, one of the grimy windows covered with cardboard after her father, in a rage, had put his fist through it, and outside was a sea of mud. Carmel wanted to curl up and die with shame.

After Mrs Mackay had told her mother why she had brought Carmel home, her mother, Eve, had waited only until Dennis left the house before boiling up a large pan of water on the fire. She scrubbed Carmel from head to foot, kneading at her hair until her scalp tingled, and then washed her clothes in the water and dried them before the fire.

It made no difference: it was too much fun hounding

someone for any of the bullies to want to stop, and if they were inclined to, Breda would invent some other taunt so that Carmel began to dread going to school. In the end, Mrs Mackay suddenly found she had many jobs to do inside at lunchtime with which she needed Carmel's help, and when she found the child had arrived with no dinner, which was usually the case, she would always say she couldn't finish her own and share it with her.

Small wonder Carmel had loved her with a passion and worked like a Trojan to please her, thereby achieving more than anyone expected. She never had one friend, however, because of the reputation of her drunken, violent father, Dennis. The townspeople had the whole family tarred with the same brush. Dennis had an aversion to work of any kind, so that the family were forced to live on charity and were dressed in shabby cast-offs. Many in Letterkenny would shake their heads over the way the children had been brought up and mutter to themselves that, with such a start, what sort of a turnout would the children make at all, at all?

Carmel was the one who had to run the gauntlet every week, doing the shopping for her mother, paying for it with the vouchers from St Vincent de Paul, which were given to the poor of the parish, shaming her further. She would see girls of her own age wandering arm in arm about the town and she had ached to be accepted like that, but she knew that would never happen. She didn't even look like them, with their clean, respectable clothes, socks and shoes.

However, she refused to lower her head to those disparaging people. It was hard to retain dignity when your dirty feet were bare and your clothes were on their last legs, but Carmel would raise her chin defiantly and hold their sneering gaze with eyes that flashed fire

'Do you see the set of that one with the insolent look on her and her head held high, as if indeed she has anything at all to be proud of?' she heard one women remark, as she passed her in the street.

'Aye. I'd say they would have trouble with that one,' her companion replied.

'And not that one alone, I'm thinking. There's a whole tribe of them back at that shack of a place.'

'Aye, and what else can you expect after the rearing they've had?'

One by one, the townsfolk waited for the Duffy children to go to the bad. But Carmel had a champion in her teacher, Mrs Mackay. Yet, they both knew that there was neither the money nor the will in the Duffy household to keep a child at school a minute longer than was necessary, however intelligent she was.

As Carmel neared fourteen, Eileen Mackay approached her sister, who was a nursing nun, known as Sister Frances, in Letterkenny Hospital, and asked if there might be an opening for the girl.

'Only as an orderly just,' Sister Frances said.

'There isn't anything else, anything better that she might train for?'

Sister Frances shook her head. 'Nothing. But I will take the girl on, if she is agreeable, and we'll see how she shapes up.'

Carmel shaped up better than Sister Frances could have believed, and it was obvious she loved the work and the patients loved her. Her touch was firm yet gentle, and her voice calm and low, soothing to the apprehensive.

Within a year she was taking temperatures, helping to dress wounds, wash and feed the frail and helpless, and encourage those who were able to get out of bed to do so. Frances began to wonder how they had ever managed without her.

Carmel was too wise a girl to long for something she couldn't have, but one day, when she had been at the hospital almost two years, she admitted to Frances that she would have loved to have had the chance to go into nursing. Sister Frances knew that she make a first-rate nurse so she asked the advice of her fellow nursing nuns at the convent.

'Few of us had secondary education,' one said, 'but our training and such was done through the Church. She wouldn't think of taking the veil herself?'

Frances thought of Carmel and the light of mischief that often danced in her eyes, and she said, 'I should very much doubt it. Just as I am convinced Carmel would make a very good nurse, I know too that she would make a very bad nun.'

'Pity.'

'There is an exam they can take,' said another. 'Of course she might need coaching to pass it. How old is the girl now?'

'Sixteen.'

'Then you have two years to lick her into some sort of shape,' the nun said, 'for they'll not touch her at all until she is at least eighteen.'

'Put it to her and see what she says,' another advised. 'She might not be willing for all the hard work.'

However, Frances saw how Carmel hugged herself with delight and knew that that hard work wouldn't bother her a jot if it was moving her a step nearer her objective. 'This isn't a foregone conclusion,' the nun said. 'You do realise the exam is likely to be quite hard?'

'Would you help me with the work?' Carmel asked.

'Of course,' Sister Frances said. 'But your parents . . . your father . . .'

'Is to know nothing about it.'

'Carmel, I—'

'Sister, you have already said it is not a foregone conclusion that I pass the exam,' Carmel said. 'Maybe I won't even get that far. What is the point of telling my father now?'

Frances could see the logic of that and agreed to say nothing for the time being. That evening, when Carmel explained she was on a special training course at the hospital and would be later home at least two nights a week, her mother just accepted it. Only her father asked if she'd get more money because of it.

'Hardly,' she snapped. 'It's a training course. You just be grateful that you aren't being asked to pay for it.'

'You watch your mouth, girl, and the way you talk to me,' Dennis growled. 'You're not too old for a good hiding and don't you forget it.'

Carmel held her father's gaze. Let him yell and bawl all he liked. She was going to be a nurse and master of her own life. Marriage, with children and all it entailed, was not the route she would take. No, by God, not for all the tea in China.

She had seen one aspect of marriage in the bruises her mother sported often, and she was well aware what happened in the marriage bed. It usually began with her mother pleading to be left alone, and then the punches administered, but it always finished the same way – with the rhythmic thump, thump, thump of her parents' bed head against the wall and the animal grunts of her father, which were perfectly audible over the background noise of her mother's sobs.

'Mammy,' she had said one day, seeing her mother sporting yet another black eye and split lip, 'how long are you going to put up with Daddy slapping and punching you whenever he has the notion? Stand up to him, for once in your life, why don't you?'

'Look at me,' Eve demanded, standing in front of her daughter. 'What match am I for your father? Jesus, I'd sooner do battle with a steamroller. I'd likely come off less damaged.'

Carmel knew her mother spoke the truth, for there was little of her, but her husband was built like an ox. Carmel had inherited her mother's fine bones and slight frame, but Eve was now scrawny thin because she often ate less than a bird so the children could eat a little better, while Carmel, though still slender, got a good meal each day at Letterkenny Hospital. Knowing Dennis Duffy and his love of the drink, whether he had the money or not, Sister Frances had arranged for the money for Carmel's meals to be taken out at source, so that once a day at least she was well fed. But even so, Carmel and her mother together would be no match for Dennis Duffy.

'Then tell the priest,' Carmel said.

'I did,' Eve admitted. 'Just the once, after the first baby was stillborn and I put that down to the beating I had received the day before.'

8

'And?'

'The priest told me I married the man of my own free will, that I married him for better or worse, and he couldn't come between a man and his wife,' Eve said bitterly. 'I was eighteen, and I didn't bother telling him that it was not my free will at all, and that I had not cared a jot for Dennis Duffy. My opinion had never been asked. My marriage had been arranged by my father in exchange for a parcel of land the Duffy family owned. Think of that, Carmel. A bare green field was prized more highly than me, and that meant I could not appeal to any of my family for help either.'

'God Almighty!' Carmel said, for she had never heard this before. 'Does the priest know that sometimes Daddy near kills you and the weans are petrified rigid of him?' she demanded. 'You won't go across the door if Daddy marks your face. Maybe you should. Let the priest and the townspeople know the manner of man he is altogether.'

'I'd die of shame, Carmel.'

'Mammy, it isn't you that should be ashamed. It's him,' Carmel said fiercely.

Eve shook her head. 'Don't keep on, Carmel,' she said. 'Anyway, the answer from the priest would likely be the same.'

Carmel knew her mother was probably right about that, for the priests seemed in collusion with most of the men of the parish. Did she want a slice of that? You had to be joking.

As for children . . . Eve had eight living children, two she had miscarried and two more were stillborn. Carmel had seen how tired she had become with each pregnancy and how each birth had near tore the body from her. Carmel had been helping the midwife at the last few births and had seen the agony of it all etched on her mother's contorted face and the way she had chewed her bottom lip to try to prevent the screams spiralling out of her, lest her husband hear and be vexed at her making a fuss.

She wanted none of that either, nor the rearing of the children after it. God, hadn't she had her fill of children, helping bring up the seven younger than herself?

'I don't want to train in Derry or Dublin,' Carmel told Sister Frances that first evening as they settled to work.

'Why not?'

'My father could still reach me if he felt like it.'

'But surely—'

'I want to go to England,' Carmel said. 'I don't care where. I would just feel much safer with a stretch of sea separating us.'

The nun had developed a healthy respect for Carmel and knew she spoke the truth. The man could take a notion to just bring her home and there would be nothing then that Carmel could do; her chance would be gone. Better by far to have her well out of the way from the beginning. Sister Frances had an idea germinating in her head. She said, 'Don't get your hopes up, Carmel, but when I was at the convent school just outside Letterkenny, I was great friends with a girl called Catherine Turner. She wasn't a Catholic, but her father had work in Derry and favoured a convent education for his daughter. We were both mad keen to nurse, but while I left the convent at sixteen to enter the Church and do my nursing training that way, Catherine stayed until she was eighteen. By then, her family had moved to Birmingham and she began her training there.

'We vowed to keep in touch and compare the different paths our lives had taken, but the training was intensive and in the end it dwindled to a Christmas card with a scribbled note inside. However, I know that she is a matron at a place called the General Hospital in Birmingham, and from what she says, I understand the hospital runs a training school for nurses. It would be marvellous if she would consider you, because our order has its own hospital in Birmingham called St Chad's, and the sisters from there would be at hand to keep an eye on you.'

She smiled at the face that Carmel pulled. Sister Frances knew full well what that expression said: that she neither wanted nor needed anyone to keep an eye on her. However, Birmingham was a large city and she would be miles from home. Sister Frances imagined that the hospital was much larger and possibly more impersonal than the small county hospital she had trained at and the only one she had any experience of. She said, 'And you can pull a face, my girl, but it is a big thing to go so far at such a young age. I will write to Catherine tonight and see what's what. I'm going to talk no more about it now, for we have a heap of work to get through.'

From the day Carmel had started at the hospital and Sister Frances had a glimpse of the life she led, she had advised her not to tell her parents of the wage rises she had been given. Her conscience had smote her about this, for surely it was a sin to deceive parents? But then Dennis Duffy didn't act like a good and concerned parent. Both she and Carmel knew that however much she took home it would not benefit any but Dennis Duffy. Carmel also understood that she would not stay under the roof of a drunken bully for one minute longer than necessary, and that to escape from him she needed money. So every week Sister Frances took the money Carmel gave her and put it in the Post Office. Soon there was more need than ever to save, for the reply came from Catherine Turner. Sister Frances handed Carmel the letter to read.

> Normally, I would not entertain taking a girl on until I had interviewed her, but I trust your judgement and so I will bend my own rules and take her on provisionally. I will arrange to see her as soon as she arrives. She will initially enter the preliminary training school for a period of six weeks, receiving basic instruction in Anatomy, Hygiene, Physiology and the Theory and Practice of Nursing. At the end of this period, there will be exams, which the candidates must pass in order to be admitted to the hospital as probationary nurses for an initial period of six weeks. There is no payment for the first three months and after that, the salary is £20 for the first year, £25 for the second, £30 for the third and £40 for the fourth year. A list of requirements Miss Duffy will need to bring will be sent at a later date.

'What sort of requirements? I haven't much money, Sister Frances,' Carmel said in dismay.

'Haven't you been saving for the last two years, and

will have two more years before there is anything much to buy?' Sister Frances said. 'Don't fall at the first hurdle.'

'I don't intend to fall at any hurdle,' Carmel said almost fiercely.

'So you're still as keen as ever?'

'Keener, if anything, now I know it might actually happen.'

Nearly two years later, in June, Carmel stood before her father and told him of the exam that she had taken behind his back. She also told him that she had passed it with flying colours and that meant she could start her training to be a nurse in a hospital in Birmingham, England.

She had known that, at first, anyway, her father would protest, for didn't he protest against every mortal thing as a matter of course? She knew too her father's protests were usually expressed in a physical way. He wasn't the sort of man anyone could have a reasoned discussion with. His fists or his belt usually settled any argument to his advantage.

But Carmel was more determined than she had ever been about anything. She had borne the thrust of his anger more than enough and she'd had as much as she was prepared to take.

'He'll never agree to it,' Eve warned her daughter that first evening when her father was out of the house. 'Sure you must put it out of your head.'

'I will not!' Carmel shouted defiantly. 'He's not thinking of anyone but himself as usual. He's not objecting to me going because he is going to miss me at all. Huh, not a bit of it. All he'll miss is the beer money I have to tip up every Friday night.'

'Hush, Carmel, for pity's sake,' Eve said, in an effort to soothe her daughter's temper before Dennis came back, for she was worried what he would do if Carmel stayed in this frame of mind and spoke out, as she was wont to.

Eve's words, though, just stiffened Carmel's resolve and she refused to let the matter drop, though she knew she was sailing nearer and nearer to the wind. Her mother begged her to stop, to give in, and her younger brothers and sisters looked at her in trepidation, mixed with a little awe, especially her brother Michael. At sixteen, he was nearest to her in age and he told her he would rather tangle with a sabre-toothed tiger than his father.

Eventually, Dennis snapped. Carmel had known he would and though she was scared, she knew it probably had to come to this for her to get her freedom from his tyranny. She groaned as her father's fists powered into her face, almost blinded by the blood falling into her eyes and so dazed from the blows raining down on her, she fell to her knees. She screamed as her father grasped a handful of her curls and dragged her to the bedroom. Holding her fast with one hand, he loosened his belt with the other. The belt whistled through the air and when it made contact with her skin, ripping easily through the thin fabric of the dress she wore, she thought she would die with the pain of it. He hit her again and again, until the agonising pain was relentless and all-consuming, and she thought he would kill her.

It was the combined efforts of Michael and her

mother that saved her, although she hadn't been aware of it at the time, hadn't been aware of much. She languished on the mattress that did as a bed for three days while Eve settled Carmel's sisters – twelve-year-old Siobhan, seven-year-old Kathy and the baby, Pauline, who usually shared the mattress – on the floor on a heap of rags lest they hurt her further. Eve then sent eleven-year-old Damien to the hospital with a note saying Carmel had a cold. Carmel didn't protest. She felt truly ill and in tremendous pain, and was glad she hadn't got to try to move. At least she was semi-protected from her father.

The fourth morning, though, she heaved her painful body out of the bed and began to dress.

'Where d'you think you are going?' Eve asked, but quietly, lest she wake Dennis.

'To see Father O'Malley.'

'Ah, no,' Eve protested. 'Surely not. Not with your face the way it is.'

'Aye, Mammy,' Carmel said. 'He needs to see it. Know what sort of a madman I have for a father.'

Eve bit her lip in consternation, but Carmel was right. The priest was horrified at the extent of her injuries. He left her in the capable hands of his unmarried sister, who acted as housekeeper to him, and went down to the Duffy house to have strong words with Dennis.

According to Eve, who heard the whole exchange and reported it back to her daughter, Dennis said the girl was disobedient and had been deliberately provoking him. 'And,' he went on, 'did you know of the exam that that bloody nun Sister Frances was after encouraging Carmel to take, and this without any knowledge, let alone permission being given? Surely to God such secrecy and deceit is not to be borne if a man is to be master in his own house and can not be blamed for chastising his own flesh and blood.'

The priest, however, remembered Carmel's injuries and said maybe it might be better if she was away from the home for a little while, until things settled down.

Carmel stayed the night in the priest's house and the next day, Father O'Malley went to see Sister Frances and she told him about Carmel's love of nursing and the exam she had taken to enable her to attend the nurses' training school in Birmingham, under the jurisdiction of her friend Catherine Turner, who was the Matron there. Together they went to see Carmel.

Sister Frances noted the girl's split lip, grazed, bruised cheeks and black eyes, and when she saw the careful way she sat and held herself, she knew it wasn't just her face her manic father had laid into and made such a mess of. Her eyes filled with tears and she was ashamed that she had let Carmel cope with breaking her news on her own. She knew the manner of man that Dennis was – why hadn't she gone with the girl to explain and taken her out of the house that same night?

She turned to the priest and said, 'Surely, Father, you can see Carmel cannot go back home after such a beating? And what is wrong with training to be a nurse? It is a very noble profession and Carmel is a natural. She has worked extremely hard, passed the stiff examination and, of course, has much practical experience to draw on too.'

'This is all very well,' the priest said, 'but you say she wants to train in Birmingham, England, when we have

16

perfectly good hospitals in Derry. I would understand any parent's concern at the thought of their young daughter going so far on her own.'

'My father has never had one minute's concern about me,' Carmel cried. 'All he cares about is himself and always has done. I wouldn't be far enough away from him in Derry.'

'I've been to see the father, given him a stern talking-to,' the priest said stiffly. 'He says he knows he went too far and it will not happen again.'

Carmel gave a humourless laugh. 'And you believe him?' she asked, adding, 'Of course you do. But, you see, I don't, Father. This isn't the first time that I have been beaten, but it is going to be the last, the very last, and if you won't help me, or let Sister Frances help me, then I will do it on my own.'

The priest was clearly uncomfortable. He knew he should point out her duty to her parents, but it was hard to do so and look upon the handiwork of one of those parents.

'And Carmel won't be totally on her own in Birmingham anyway, Father,' Frances said. 'Four of our nursing sisters are leaving in September to take up posts in our own hospital of St Chad's in the very same city and they could all travel together. They all know Carmel well and have worked with her on the wards at Letterkenny. They would be there if she should have need of them at all.'

Her eyes slid across to Carmel's as she spoke but this time Carmel pulled no face. She was no fool and knew that this information would act in her favour, especially when Sister Frances went on to say, 'And I have already explained that the matron who the young nurses are accountable to is an old friend of mine. I'm sure that she would keep a weather eye on young Carmel too. I don't think anyone needs to worry on that score.'

'Do you really want to do this nursing?' Father O'Malley asked Carmel.

'More than anything in the world,' she said.

The priest saw the light shining behind Carmel's eyes at the thought of it, but he also saw the determination there and he knew if she was thwarted in this, then she might just do what she threatened and take off on her own. If something should happen to her then, he would never forgive himself. He had known Carmel since the day she was born and the teachers had never said she was bold or naughty, just very bright and tenacious. He knew that in this instance he had to give Carmel her head, and with his blessing.

Carmel continued to stay at the priest's house. The housekeeper was kindness itself to her, seemed determined to fatten her up and nursed her battered body tenderly.

A week later, when Carmel's face was almost back to normal, she went with Sister Frances to the medical supplies shop in Derry armed with the hospital list. They had to buy six white linen belts, two plain print dresses, fourteen aprons, eight pair of cuffs, six collars, one pair of silver-plated surgical scissors, two named clothes bags and four pairs of black woollen stockings. Carmel also needed to take two dusters, one pincushion, one pin tray and one physiology book by Furneaux. She would never have been able to buy all she needed if it hadn't been for the generosity of the hospital staff who had had a whip-round for her. There was even enough left to buy the regulation lace-up Benduble shoes, which were fifteen shillings and nine pence a pair, but which Sister Frances said would see her right through her training.

That night Carmel packed all her purchases in the case Father O'Malley had lent her and knew that the die was now cast. Here she was on her way. It was September 1931 and Carmel Duffy, at eighteen years old, was off to live her life the way she wanted to. All she had to do was look out for New Street Station and let her new life begin.

CHAPTER TWO

At New Street Station Carmel said goodbye to the nuns. She was sad to leave them, for they had been kindness itself to her, but they had their own transport arranged to St Chad's on Hagley Road, which they said wasn't far from the General Hospital.

'Now you will be all right?' the oldest of the nuns asked.

Suddenly Carmel felt far from all right, but she told herself sharply that it was no time for second thoughts, so she answered firmly, 'I will be fine. I am to be met, the letter said so.'

'If you are sure . . .?'

'Yes, I am, honestly. You just go. You are keeping the taxi waiting.'

She watched them walk away and looked around the noisy station, trying to drink it all in. All around her trains were clattering, their brakes squealing and steam hissing. The platform was thronged with people, some talking and laughing together, others rushing past her with strained faces. Porters, their trolleys piled high with suitcases, warned people to 'Mind your backs, please,' and a little man selling newspapers from a cupboard of a place advertised them constantly in a thin, nasal voice that Carmel couldn't understand a word of. Above this cacophony a loud but indistinct voice seemed to be advising people what platform to go to and what train to catch, though the words were as incomprehensible as the news vendor's to Carmel.

Carmel no longer felt apprehensive, but thrilled to be a part of such vibrancy, so much life. Soon she was approached by two girls about the same age as herself.

'Are you Carmel Duffy?' the one with short bobbed black hair and laughing brown eyes asked. 'Do say you are.'

Carmel gave a brief nod and then, before she had the chance to reply further, the other girl went on, 'The home sister, Sister Magee, said we could come and meet you because we will be sharing a room. She told us you were coming all the way from Ireland. Gosh, I think that's jolly brave. I bet you are tired after all that travelling and I bet you see a difference here from where you come from. Course, I am a brummie born and bred, and so—'

'Do wrap up, Jane, and let the poor girl get her breath,' said the other girl with a laugh. She looked at Carmel and said, 'We only met yesterday and I already know that Jane Firkins here can talk the hind leg off a donkey, as my grandfather used to say.'

'Only making her feel at home,' Jane protested. 'Friendly, like.'

'Yeah, but you've got to give her space to speak,' the other girl said, and extended her hand. 'I suppose you *are* Carmel Duffy?'

'Aye, um, yes,' Carmel said, shaking hands and noting

the other girl had dark blonde hair in waves, pinned back from her face with grips and a band of some sort. Her eyes were more thoughtful than Jane's and dark grey in colour.

'I'm Sylvia,' the girl said, 'Sylvia Forrester, and you have already met Jane.'

'Yes,' Carmel said. 'And we will be sharing a room?'

'That's right,' Jane put in. 'There are four of us and so there will be another one, called Lois something, but she isn't arriving until tomorrow.'

'Anyway,' Sylvia said, 'let's not stand here chatting. I bet you are dropping with tiredness.'

Carmel suddenly realised she was. It had been the very early hours when she had left the priest's house that morning carrying the case packed with the hospital requirements and also with the clothes Sister Frances had let her choose from those collected to send to the missions. Carmel had been surprised at what some people threw out. 'I am tired,' she admitted.

'Who wouldn't be?' Sylvia said sympathetically. 'Come on. Let's head for the taxis.'

Carmel was very glad the girls were there, taking care of everything, and when they were in the taxi and driving through the slightly dusky evening streets, she looked about her with interest.

'The General Hospital is only a step away from New Street Station really,' said Sylvia, 'and so close to the centre of the town it's not true. Jane and I walked here to meet you, but it is different if you have heavy bags and cases and things.'

It seemed only minutes later that Jane was saying. 'This is Steelhouse Lane, called that because the police

22

station is here, and the nurses' home is on Whittall Street to the left just here.'

However, the taxi driver didn't turn into Whittall Street straight away because Sylvia asked him to drive past the hospital first so that Carmel could have a good look at it. It was built of light-coloured brick that contrasted sharply with the dingy, grim police station opposite. Carmel was stunned by the sheer size of the place, which she estimated would be four times or more bigger that the hospital at Letterkenny. She felt suddenly nervous and was glad of the company of the friendly girls beside her.

A few moments later, Carmel was out on the pavement scrutinising the place that would be her home for the next four years. It was built of the same light bricks as the hospital, large and very solid-looking.

Jane led the way inside. 'Our room is on the first floor,' she said over her shoulder to Carmel, and Carmel followed her, hearing the chatter of other girls and passing some on the stairs. There seemed a great many of them and it was strange to think that in a short space of time she would probably know every one.

Then she was standing in the doorway of a room and Sylvia was saying, 'What do you think?'

Carmel stepped slowly inside and looked around. The floor was covered with mottled blue oilcloth, light blue curtains framed the two windows and beside each bed was a dressing table and a wardrobe.

For a split second, she remembered the room where they had slept at home. The bed had been a dingy mattress laid on the floor and she had been squashed on it together with Siobhan, Kathy and even wee Pauline, who wasn't yet a year old, while coats piled haphazardly on the top did in place of blankets. There were no curtains at the begrimed windows and an upended orange box housed their few clothes. Now her sigh was one of utter contentment.

'Your bed is either of those two by the door,' Jane said. 'Sylvia and I have nabbed the two by the window.'

'Just at this moment I wouldn't care if my bed was out on the street,' Carmel said. 'It looks terribly inviting.'

Sylvia laughed. 'You will have to wait a bit,' she said, glancing at the clock on the wall. 'The bell for dinner will go any second.'

The words had barely left her mouth when the strains of it could be heard echoing through the home. Carmel quickly removed her coat, hung it in the wardrobe, pushed her case under the bed and followed the others streaming, with hurrying feet and excited chatter, down the stairs towards the dining room.

The good wholesome food revived Carmel a little, although she was still extremely tired. She was quiet at the table, glad that Sylvia and Jane were there to keep up the conversation because she didn't feel up to talking, laughing and being polite to those she hadn't got to know yet.

Later, up in the room, she confessed to the other two what a relief it was to be there.

'You don't worry that you might be homesick?' Jane said.

'There is not a doubt in my mind that I will never miss my home,' Carmel said. 'As for wishing I was back there, no thank you.' She gave a shiver of distaste.

'Ooh, I might wish that sometimes and quite easily,'

Jane said, 'especially when Matron's on the warpath. Our next-door neighbour was here five years ago and said she was a targer.'

'Our matron could be strict,' Carmel conceded. 'She was fair, though.'

'Did you work in a hospital then?'

'Aye. I was a ward orderly in Letterkenny Hospital, which was near where I lived,' Carmel said. 'Our matron had a thing about hospital corners on the beds and she was a stickler for having a tidy and uncluttered ward. But I was good at the bed-making and I like order myself, so we got on all right.'

'Did she suggest you going in for nursing?'

'No, that was Sister Frances, the nun I worked with mostly,' Carmel said. 'Matron did support me, though, when she knew about it.'

'You didn't lose your heart to any dishy doctors then?' Jane asked.

Carmel laughed. 'There weren't any. I think ugliness or at least general unattractiveness with a brusque bed-side manner were the requisites for any job there.'

'Well, I hope it's not the case here,' Jane said with a slight pout of discontent.

'I thought you came to learn nursing, not hook your-self a husband?' Sylvia said scornfully.

'No harm in combining the two ambitions and seeing what comes first,' Jane said with a simper.

Carmel laughed. 'You can do all the hooking you wish,' she said. 'I won't be any sort of threat to you, because I won't be in the race.'

'What do you mean?'

'I don't want a husband – not now, not ever.'

The other two looked at her open-mouthed. 'Not ever?' Sylvia breathed.

'You can't honestly say you want to be an old maid all your life?' Jane cried incredulously.

'Oh, yes I can, because that's exactly what I want.'

'But why?'

Carmel shrugged. 'Let's just say that what I have seen of marriage, children and all so far has not impressed me one jot.'

'Your mom and dad, I suppose?' Sylvia asked.

'Aye,' Carmel said, 'in the main, but there were others I knew who were downright unhappy. I want to be my own person without relying or depending on someone else, and to have no one leaning on me.'

'You can't go through life like that,' Jane said. 'It's so sad and lonely-sounding.'

'Yeah,' Sylvia agreed. 'And just 'cos your parents didn't hit it off, what's that got to do with you and your life? I mean, Carmel, if you could see mine . . . Fight like cat and dog, they do, and always have done, but I will be ready to take the plunge when I'm swept off my feet.'

'And me.'

'Well, I wish you the well of it,' Carmel said.

'But, Carmel—'

'The thing is,' Carmel said, 'you don't really know anything about a man until you marry him. That has been said to me countless times.'

A yawn suddenly overtook her and she gave a rueful smile. 'Sorry, girls, I am too tired to be fit company for anyone tonight. I will have to leave my unpacking till the morning. Thank God I had the foresight to put all I would need for tonight in the bag.'

As Carmel padded down the corridor to the bathroom in her bare feet, Jane whispered to Sylvia, 'D'you think she really means it about men and that?'

Sylvia shrugged. 'Sounds like it, but she is only eighteen.'

'Yeah. Likely change her mind half a dozen times yet.'

Carmel was woken the next morning by the ringing of a bell and for a moment or two was disorientated. Then the previous day and all that had happened came back to her. She felt her whole body fill with delicious anticipation and she could barely wait for the day to start.

The system of the bells had been explained to her and other new arrivals after dinner the previous evening. She knew she had twenty minutes between the first bell and the second, when she was supposed to be in the dining hall. The clock on the wall told her it was twenty to seven and she knew it would take her all her time to wash, haul something suitable and as uncreased as possible out of the suitcase, make her bed and arrive in the dining hall on time and so she slipped out of bed quickly.

The other two had barely stirred and she made straight for the bathroom, delighting in hot water straight from the tap and plenty of soap and soft towels. She was invigorated by her wash and returned to the room in a buoyant mood to see Sylvia up, while Jane still lay curled in her bed with her eyes closed.

In fact, Jane was so hard to rouse, Carmel feared they would all be late. To try to prevent this, she ended up making up Jane's bed, to enable Jane to have time to dress herself.

'It is good of you,' Jane told her. 'I've never been my best in the morning.'

'You'd better work on it,' Sylvia told her grimly. 'Neither Carmel nor I is here to wait on you.'

'I know. I'm sorry.'

'Come on,' Carmel urged. 'Look at the time. The next bell will go any second.'

The girls scurried from the room, arriving in the dining hall just as the strains of the piercing alarm were dying away. Carmel's stomach growled and she knew she would be glad of the breakfast, which she soon found out was thick creamy porridge with extra hot milk, and sugar to sprinkle over, followed by rounds of buttered toast and cups of strong tea.

She had never had such a breakfast, and remarked to a girl beside her that she would be the size of a house if she ate like that every day. The girl looked at Carmel's slender figure and smiled.

'I doubt that,' she said. 'I think it is more the case of keeping your strength up. From what I was told, they run every morsel of food off you. I mean, have you seen any fat nurses?'

'No,' Carmel had to admit, 'And I'm too hungry anyway not to eat.'

The last of the probationary nurses were arriving that day, and for this reason the others were free until one o'clock, when they had to report to the lecture hall. Some of the girls, including Jane and Sylvia, went to the common room, but Carmel, mindful of her case not yet unpacked, was going to attend to it when the home sister hailed her.

'Are you Carmel Duffy?'

'Yes, Sister.'

'The matron would like a word.'

'Yes, Sister.'

The matron wore a dark blue dress, covered with a pure white apron. The ruff at her neck seemed as stiff as the woman itself. Her grey hair was scraped back from her head so effectively that her eyebrows rose as if she were constantly surprised. On her head was perched a starched white matron's cap. Her eyes were piercing blue and they fastened fixedly on Carmel as she bade her sit at the other side of the desk.

'Sister Francis thinks highly of you,' Matron began.

What could Carmel say to that? 'Yes, Matron,' sounded the safest option.

'And I have further endorsements from the matron at Letterkenny Hospital, detailing your suitability to be taken on this course, and a character reference from your parish priest.'

'Yes, Matron.'

'What I want to make clear to you, Miss Duffy, is that I broke the rule of interviewing you before accepting you, even so far, because of the friendship of someone in the same field as myself whose judgement I trust. You are not and will not be treated as a special case.'

'No, Matron,' Carmel said. 'I truly hadn't expected to be.'

'As long as that is firmly understood.'

'Oh, yes, Matron.'

'You may go, Miss Duffy. And I am glad to see,' she added, 'that you have the regulation stockings and shoes.'

As Carmel scurried from the room, Catherine smiled. She knew more about Carmel Duffy than the young woman realised, because Sister Frances had told her all about her background and the type of home she came from. She had gone on to say that the child and young woman that she had known for four years had remained untainted by this and had the ability and will to make something of herself. Catherine liked the sound of Carmel Duffy and had been impressed with what she saw, but because Frances had also said she hated talking of her family and in particular her father, she had asked no questions. Anyway, she had the girl's testimonials, and all Matron really was interested in was whether Carmel would make a good nurse.

Unaware of the matron's thoughts, Carmel, glad that quite painless interview was over, returned to her room to find a girl, still in her outdoor clothes, looking a little lost.

'Hello,' Carmel said. 'You must be Lois.'

The girl's sigh of relief was audible. 'Yes,' she said, extending her hand. 'Lois Baker.'

'And I'm Carmel Duffy.'

'No secrets about where you come from,' Lois said. 'Your accent is lovely, and what gorgeous hair.'

'Thanks,' Carmel said, liking the look of Lois too, with her dark brown curls and merry brown eyes.

'Where is everyone?'

'Well, we've not long had breakfast,' Carmel explained, hauling her case from beneath the bed as she spoke. 'We haven't got to report for duty until one o'clock in the lecture theatre, and most of the girls have gone into the common room. I only arrived last night myself, though, and was too tired after the meal to unpack so I'm doing it now. I'm not sure when I'll have a spare minute again.'

'Good idea,' Lois said. 'I'll do the same.'

As Lois hauled her case up onto the bed as Carmel directed her to, she said with a wry smile, 'I find it hard to believe I am here at last. There were times I didn't think I would make it.'

'Nor me,' Carmel said. 'Did your father object too?'

'No, it was my mother,' Lois said. 'She kicked up a right shindig about it. In fact, if it hadn't been for Daddy and his support, I wouldn't have made it.'

'Why did she object?'

'Well, she's an invalid, you see,' Lois said. 'At least . . .' she wrinkled her nose, 'she's supposed to be an invalid. I have my doubts. Well, more than doubts because I have caught her out a time or two. She's not half as helpless as she makes out.'

Carmel couldn't quite believe that anyone could act that way. 'Are you sure?'

'Oh, I'm sure, all right, but . . . well, what can I do? All the years I was growing up, it was impressed upon me – on all of us – that Mummy wasn't very strong. You get sort of conditioned. I have a brother and a sister both older than me and they got away in time so there was just me left.'

'What about your father?'

'Daddy is marvellous and he said I should run while I had the chance. Now he pays a woman, an ex-nurse, to come in and see to Mummy.'

'Is your father rich to be able to just employ someone like that?'

'I don't know,' Lois said. 'I've never thought about it.'

'What does he do?'

'He's a department manager in Lewis's.' Then, at the perplexed look on Carmel's face, Lois went on, 'It's a big store in the city centre, bigger even than Marshall & Snelgrove. D'you know how Daddy got around my mother in the end?' Carmel shook her head and Lois continued. 'Told her that I was training as a nurse so that I could look after her more effectively.'

'And will you?'

'Not likely,' Lois said determinedly. 'She is a slave-driver and not averse either to giving me the odd hard slap or pinch for little or nothing at all. She behaves better with other people. Daddy has the patience of Job with her – with everyone, really. He is a wonderful person. What about you?'

Carmel was laying the pin cushion and pin tray on the dressing table as the letter had directed her to but her hands became still at Lois's question. She didn't want to bring the details of her former dirty, gruesome existence and the deprived brothers and sisters she'd left behind into this new and clean life.

She gave a shrug. 'I may tell you about myself some other time,' she said. 'But if you have finished your packing, we'd best go down and meet the others.'

'I'm all done,' Lois said, snapping the case shut. 'What do we do with the cases?'

'Leave them on the bed,' Carmel said. 'That's what I was told. The porter or caretaker or whoever he is comes and takes them away later.'

'Right oh, then,' Lois said. 'Lead the way.'

*   *   *

The lecture theatre was in the main body of the hospital, which was connected to the nurses' home via a conservatory. Outside the room it was fair bustling with noise as Carmel, Jane, Sylvia and Lois congregated there with everyone else.

'Out of the way!' said a grumbling voice suddenly. 'Bunching together like that before the door. Ridiculous! Get inside. Inside quickly.'

Carmel had never heard the words 'lecture theatre' before, never mind seen inside one and she surged inside with the others and looked around in amazement at the tiered benches of shiny golden wood that stretched up and up before the small dais at the front.

The woman's entrance into the room had caused a silence to descend on the apprehensive girls. The woman spoke again. 'I am Matron Turner and when you refer to me, you just call me Matron. Do you understand?'

'Yes, Matron.'

'Remember that in future and now I want you all against the wall,' Matron said.

Carmel found herself next to Jane. 'Now prepare to face the firing squad,' Jane whispered, and Carmel had to stifle her giggles with a cough, bringing Matron's shrewd eyes to rest upon her.

She found fault with many of them and when she got to Carmel, the girl wasn't surprised to be told her hair was too wild and frizzy. 'You will have to do something with it,' she said. 'You'll never get your cap to stay on that bush. Our standards are high,' Matron's voice rapped out, 'and hygiene is of paramount importance. Hold out your hands.'

Wondering why in the world they had to do that,

Carmel nervously extended her hands and tried to still their trembling as the woman walked up and down inspecting them.

'Before going on to the ward, your hands must be scrubbed, and before you attend a patient, and between patients,' the matron said. 'Nails must be kept short at all times and dirty nails will not be tolerated. And,' she went on, fixing the students with a glare. 'if you have been prone to bite your nails in the past – a disgusting habit, I might add – then you must stop. A nurse cannot run the risk of passing on the bacteria in her mouth to a sick and vulnerable patient. I hope that I have made myself clear.'

Again came the chorus, 'Yes, Matron.'

'We expect high standards. If you have come here as some sort of rest cure, then you are in the wrong job. The hours are long and some of the work arduous. You must understand that from the outset.

'Before you even start a shift, your bedroom must be left clean and tidy at all times,' the matron continued, fixing them all with a gimlet eye. 'This shows that you have refinement of mind, clean habits and tidy ways. If you are careless or slovenly, then these same attributes will be carried on to the ward, and let me tell you,' she added, 'I will not have any slatterns on my wards.'

'No, Matron,' chorused the girls in the pause that followed this declaration.

'You are on the brink of entering a noble and respectable profession and this must be shown in your manner at all times. There is to be no frivolous behaviour in wards or corridors and, of course, no running at any time. No nurse is to eat on the wards, there is to be no jewellery worn, nor cosmetics of any sort, and the relationship between nurse and patients must be kept on a strictly professional level. There is to be no fraternising with the doctors either, and no nurse is to enter any other department without permission. Is that clear?'

'Yes, Matron.'

'Now, you are each required to have a medical examination, as the list of rules explained, so if you make your way down to the medical room you will be dealt with alphabetically.'

'Phew, she must have been practising that sort of attitude for years,' Jane remarked when the matron had gone.

'I know one thing,' another girl put in, 'the army's loss is our gain. God, wouldn't she make a first-class sergeant major?'

'Oh, no,' Lois said. 'She wouldn't be happy unless she was a general.'

'You're right there,' the first girl conceded, and there were gales of laughter as the girls left the room.

That night, after being declared fit and healthy, Carmel examined her hair ruefully. The matron was right about one thing.

'How the hell am I going to get any sort of cap to stay on my head under my mass of hair? After the initial six weeks I'll have to wear one,' Carmel lamented.

Jane gave a hoot of laughter. 'It will be like getting a quart into a pint pot,' she said.

'Let's not be so defeatist about this,' Lois said. 'Your hair will have to be put up, and surely that is just a matter of a thousand Kirbigrips or thereabouts?'

'Come on, then,' Jane said. 'Let's try it.'

With the combined efforts of Jane, Lois and Sylvia, and using all the grips the girls possessed, Carmel's hair was finally up, or most of it, though tendrils of it had already escaped. Carmel felt the rest of it pulling against the restraining grips, threatening any moment to break free. She surveyed herself critically in the mirror.

'It won't do, will it?' she said. 'Even if I had the time to do this every morning and could manage it without help, I have the feeling it would burst out and cascade down my back as soon as I began work.'

'Oh, can you imagine the matron's face if that happened?' Sylvia said.

'And her comments,' Lois added.

'I'd rather not think of either,' Carmel said drily. 'The woman would probably scalp me into the bargain.' She released her hair and lifted the curls critically. 'It will have to come off,' she said. 'It is the only way.'

'It seems such a shame when it's so lovely and thick,' Lois said. 'But I do see what you mean. I'll do it for you, if you like. I was a dab hand at cutting my mother's.'

'Well, I'd rather you than Matron,' Carmel commented grimly, 'and I suppose it had better be done sooner rather than later.'

Despite Carmel's spirited words, she felt more than a pang of regret as the Titian curls fell to the ground. Lois, though, didn't just hack the hair off, but took time to shape it. The other girls were impressed.

'Years of practice,' Lois said. 'My mother hasn't been able to visit a hairdresser for some time and Carmel's hair is so soft and luxuriant, it's a joy to work on.'

Jane laughed. 'Whatever you say,' she said. 'It's

another string to your bow. If ever the wish to tell Matron where to go overcomes you totally, then at least you can take up hairdressing, I'd say.'

'I'll keep it in mind,' Lois said grimly, 'for I'd do anything rather than go back home again to live.'

'Let me see what you've done,' Carmel demanded. 'Your keep talking about it and it *is* my hair.'

'It's lovely,' Jane said, as Lois went for the mirror. 'Truly lovely. You lucky thing.'

Carmel looked at her reflection and couldn't help but be pleased at what she saw. As the waves had been shorn, it had taken the weight from the head so the rest had sprung into curls that encircled her head and framed her face. The result was very pleasing indeed.

Carmel had never been encouraged to think of herself as pretty or desirable. She had neither the money, clothes nor even the time to make the best of herself, so until she arrived here she had never thought much about her appearance at all.

But now she saw that the face reflected in the glass looked quite pretty, and much of that was because she was smiling.

'You have done a wonderful job,' she said to Lois, full of admiration. 'I look a different person.'

'Yeah, but just as stunning,' Jane commented glumly. 'What chance have we got of attracting the chaps when you look like you do?'

'You have a free playing field as far as chaps go,' Carmel told her. 'For as I said, I want no truck with any of them.'

'You didn't mean it, though, did you?' Sylvia said. 'I mean, we've all said that in the past when we have been let down or something, but it doesn't last.'

'Believe me, this is more deep-seated than that,' Carmel said. 'And I have never gone out with a either a man or a boy to give them any opportunity to let me down.'

'Never?' Jane and Sylvia said, incredulous and in unison.

'Nor have I,' Lois admitted. 'Mummy would never have allowed it. I was barely allowed to leave the house for any reason.'

'Oh, I see we shall have to take you two in hand,' Jane said. 'For neither of you knows what you have been missing.'

'That's right,' Sylvia said. 'You'd better believe it. We are going to teach the pair of you to live.'

'I told you—' Carmel began.

'Shut up,' Jane said. 'We're not talking fellows here, we are talking about girls having fun.'

'Oh, well, in that case . . .'

'How else will we be able to withstand the dreaded matron?' Jane remarked.

'Oh, how indeed?' Carmel agreed with a smile, and the girls burst into laughter.

CHAPTER THREE

Carmel knew from talking to others that she was one of the few there who had left school at the statuary leaving age of fourteen and was not kept on till sixteen, or even later. Despite the excellent tuition from Sister Frances that had enabled her to pass the exam, she worried that she wouldn't be able to understand the classes and would make an utter fool of herself.

However, she saw much of what she was taught was common sense and she enjoyed the first six weeks, despite the long hours. The working day began at 7.15 a.m. and didn't end until 8.30 p.m. Anatomy, Physiology and Hygiene were taken by a sister tutor in the lecture room. Senior doctors used the same room to teach the theory of nursing in their specialist subjects, and so the students learned about ear, nose and throat problems, ophthalmics, gynaecology, midwifery, paediatrics and how to care for post-operative patients. They had many visits to the wards to observe what they had been told about in action.

They visited a sewage farm too, in order, Carmel supposed, to see the benefits of cleanliness in the hospital and for a similar reason they went another day to

Cadbury's to view their ventilation system. The place Carmel liked most, though, was Oozels Street, where they had cookery classes so they could manage the special diets some patients might have.

Both because of fatigue and lack of funds, most girls tended to stay close to the hospital during their free time in the early weeks, despite their proximity to the city centre. There was nothing more frustrating, Carmel thought, than looking into shops when a person hadn't a penny piece to spare to buy anything, or smelling the tantalising aroma seeping out from the coffee houses when there wasn't the money to sample a cup. Most of the girls were in the same boat, though some, like Lois, had an allowance, but she didn't make a song and dance about this.

The Hospital was well aware of this, and organised whist and beetle drives for the girls, and they were promised a dance nearer to Christmas. They often met up in the common room to chat or play dominoes or cards. Carmel hadn't a clue at first, but she quickly caught on and was soon a dab hand at rummy or brag. Often the four friends would just go back to their room, Carmel and Lois feeling incredibly fast as they experimented with some of the cosmetics that Jane and Sylvia had or tried out different hairstyles on one another.

Sometimes they would just chat together. It was soon apparent to the others that though they would talk freely about their families, Carmel never mentioned anything about hers and she neatly side-stepped direct questions. They knew she wrote dutifully to her mother every week for she had told them that much, and to the nun Sister Frances, whom she seemed so fond of. She received regular replies, but never commented about anything in the letters.

As far as Carmel was concerned, her life began when she entered the nurses' home. Despite her lack of money, a state that she was well used to anyway, she was very happy, and couldn't remember a time when she had felt so contented. Warmed by the true friendship of the other three girls, she didn't want to be reminded of the degradation of her slum of a home, and certainly didn't want to discuss it with anyone else.

In fact, she often found it difficult to find things to write to her mother about. Sometimes the letters centred around the church she now attended, St Chad's Cathedral. She wasn't the only Catholic studying at the hospital, although she was the only one in the first year, and they all had dispensation to attend Mass on Sundays. Fortunately St Chad's was only yards from the home, on Bath Street, which was at the top of Whittall Street. The first time that Carmel saw it she was impressed by the grandeur of the place, though she had to own that for a cathedral it wasn't that big, and very narrow, built of red brick with two blue spires.

She had made herself known to the parish priest, Father Donahue, but he already knew more about her than she realised. St Chad's Hospital was primarily a hospital for sick or elderly Catholic woman and Father Donahue called there regularly to hear confession, administer communion, tend or give last rites to the very sick or dying and sometimes took Mass in the chapel for the nuns and those able to leave their beds.

The four nuns who had travelled to Birmingham with Carmel had told the priest all about her and the type of home she had come from. Father Donahue never mentioned this to Carmel, but it gave him a special interest in the girl and he always had a cheery word for her. She would write and tell her mother this, and about the nuns in the convent that she visited as often as she could and who always made her very welcome.

Eve's replies told Carmel of her father still raging over what he called 'her deception'. Carmel knew what form that raging would take and that her mother would bear the brunt of it. She would hardly wish to share that with anyone, or what her deprived siblings were doing and the gossip of the small town she was no longer interested in.

One Sunday morning, as Lois watched Carmel get ready for Mass, she suddenly said, 'My Uncle Jeff is a Catholic.'

'How can he be? You're not.'

'No. He's married to Dad's sister, my Aunt Emma, and she turned Catholic to please Jeff. The boys have been brought up Catholic too – the dishy Paul and annoying Matthew.'

'Dishy Paul?' Carmel echoed.

'I tell you, Carmel, he is gorgeous,' Lois went on. 'He is tall and broad-shouldered and has blond hair and beautiful deep blue eyes and he only has to go into a room to have all the girls' eyes on him.'

'Sorry,' Carmel said, 'that is exactly the type of man I dislike most. I bet he is well aware of that and totally big-headed about it.'

'That's just it, he isn't,' Lois maintained. 'I think that it is something to do with the family being so down-to-earth – well, Uncle Jeff, anyway. I mean, he owns a large engineering works and they have pots of money, but you would never know it.'

'And so Paul is going to have the factory handed to him on a plate?' Carmel said, in a slightly mocking tone, all ready to dislike this so perfect cousin of Lois's.

'No,' Lois said, 'Paul doesn't want it. He's training to be a doctor. Ooh, I bet he will have a lovely bedside manner,' she said in delight. 'When they let him loose I should imagine at least half of the female population will develop ailments that they have never suffered from before.'

'You are a fool, Lois,' Carmel said, though she too was laughing. 'No one can be that charming and good-looking.'

'Paul is,' Lois said adamantly. 'I tell you, if only we weren't first cousins I would make a play for him myself. Paul has everything I admire in a man and I am not talking money here either. He even speaks French like a native. I mean, I learned French but mine is very schoolroomish. Jeff was half French and when Paul and Matthew were little, their French grand-mother was alive and lived not far away and they would natter away to her in her native language. After she died, Uncle Jeff said he didn't want the boys to lose the language, so Paul studied for two years at the Sorbonne.'

'Where's that?'

'A university in Paris. Matthew will go too next year.'

'You don't like him so well.'

'He's all right,' she said. 'I suppose he is handsome too, in a manner of speaking, but he is a poor shadow next to his brother and he's the one going to inherit the factory as Paul doesn't want it, though Uncle Jeff says he will have to start on the shop floor and work his way up, so he will know every aspect of the trade.'

'I think that is a jolly good idea.'

'Me too,' Lois agreed.

The six weeks passed quickly as the days were so busy. The four room-mates were delighted to find they had all passed their exams at the end, and with good marks too. Now they could go down on to the wards like proper nurses.

They began at seven o'clock each day and, with short meal breaks, continued until eight o'clock at night with one day off a week.

Each day, the ward sister would read the report left by the night sister and allocate work to be done that day by the senior and junior staff nurses and probationary nurses alike. Carmel was first under the direction of Staff Nurse Pamela Hammond, whom she estimated to be in her late twenties. Her grey eyes were kindly, and from around her cap, tufts of dark blonde hair peeped. She worked hard and expected her probationer to do the same. As hard work was second nature to Carmel, the two got on well.

In the early days it seemed to Carmel and her friends that they cleaned all day long, unless they were helping serve drinks or meals. They cleaned lockers, bedsteads and sluices. The rubber sheets of the incontinent had to be scrubbed daily and left to hang in the sluice room, bedpans were scalded, and at the end of each day, all dirty laundry had to be folded, counted and put in linen bags to be taken to the laundry. The girls were usually too weary even to talk at the end of a shift and only fit to fall into bed, particularly when they also had to attend lectures in their scant free time away, which they did after the initial six weeks on the wards were up.

Although it didn't help the weariness, Carmel found the day passed quicker and far more pleasantly once she saw the patients as people. She had done this before in Letterkenny, though many had been known to her at least by sight, maybe from Mass or in the shops. She found if she thought that even the unappealing tasks she was doing were for the patients' comfort and well-being that gave everything more of a purpose. Also it was pleasant to chat to them as she was working, and many said they loved her lilting accent.

The preliminary six-week period was over just before Christmas. Carmel offered to work through because she had nowhere to go. She had been asked by each of her flat mates in turn to go to their homes for Christmas, but though she know the girls well, she didn't know a thing about their families and was nervous of descending on anyone at such a family time. Anyway, the hospital was always short-staffed at Christmas and extra hands were always welcome.

Carmel enjoyed the dance put on for the girls. She could do none of the dancing herself, but she wasn't the only one, and she liked the music and to see people enjoying themselves. Unfortunately the girls had to dance with one another as there were no men present, and the evening came to an end altogether at nine-thirty. The singing of carols with the other nurses and the concert put on for the patients on Christmas Eve she thought she enjoyed more than they did, for she had never seen or done such things before.

The next morning Carmel slipped out to Mass before beginning her shift on the ward, which brought home to her the true meaning of Christmas once more. She felt at peace with the world as she returned to the hospital.

After the Christmas period was over, Carmel was introduced to the experience chart, which the sister had to fill in and which she explained was deposited with the matron each term so she could see the progress of each probationer at a glance. So over the next few days Carmel watched as the more experienced nurses showed her how to read a thermometer, to dress a wound, make up a poultice, roll a patient safely and give a bed-bath. Though she had done some of these things alongside Sister Frances, she said not a word about it.

The new year of 1932 wasn't very old when all the room-mates had to do their annual block on night duty. All probationers once a year had to do almost three months on nights. This involved the girls moving out of the nurses' home to rooms above the matron's offices, which were quieter so that they could get some sleep in the day. Sleep was desperately needed as the girls worked from 11 p.m. until 8.15 a.m. for twelve nights followed by two nights off duty. So it wasn't until the end of April, after their spell of night duty was over, that all four girls had a Saturday completely free.

'We shouldn't waste a whole Saturday off,' Lois said gleefully after breakfast.

'I suppose you would consider it a total waste if I suggested spending my day off in bed?' Carmel said wistfully.

'Yes I would, so don't even bother thinking that way,' Lois said firmly. 'Come on, Carmel. What's the matter with you? I want to show you around Birmingham, take you to my dad's shop, show you the Bull Ring.'

'All right, all right,' Carmel said, giving in, 'but the other two might not want to go gallivanting around the town.'

'They'll be fine,' Lois said confidently, but Jane and Sylvia were difficult to rouse, impossible to motivate and point-black refused to go anywhere for a fair few hours.

'But the day will be gone then.'

'Good,' said Sylvia.

'Where do you want to go in such a tear anyway?' Jane asked.

'To town, the Bull Ring and that.'

'Are you mad?' Jane said. 'Haven't we seen it all a million times? It can wait until we feel a bit more human.'

'Carmel hasn't seen it.'

'Well, show it to her then,' Sylvia said irritably.

'All right then,' Lois said, conceding defeat. 'Why don't you meet us for lunch in Lyons Corner House on New Street?'

'Make it tea and I'll think about it,' Sylvia said with a yawn. 'I want a bath and to wash my hair and there's homework to do first, and so until then let a body sleep, can't you?'

'All right,' Lois said. 'We can take a hint. We know when we're not wanted.'

As they walked up Steelhouse Lane a little later, Carmel wondered what was the cheapest thing Lyons Corner House sold because she hadn't the money to go out to eat. She would have to impress that on Lois as soon as she could.

'Right,' Lois said, taking Carmel's arm, 'if we were to walk up Colmore Row as far as the Town Hall, then we can go for a toddle round the shops and have a bite to eat in Lyons before we tackle the Bull Ring. What do you say?'

'I say, I can't really afford to eat out, Lois,' Carmel said uncomfortably.

'My treat.'

'No, really.'

'Listen,' Lois said, 'Daddy sends me an allowance every month and I have hardly spent any of it. I have plenty to treat my friends.'

'Even so . . .'

'Even so nothing,' Lois said airily. 'Come on, this is Colmore Row now.'

The road was long and wide with tram tracks laid the length of it. Carmel's eye was caught by an imposing building on her right. It had many storeys, supported by pillars, and arched windows. 'Snow Hill Station' was written above the entrance.

'There are three stations in Birmingham,' Lois said, taking in her gaze. 'The one you arrived in was New Street, this is Snow Hill and the other one is called Moor Street down Digbeth way. We'll be nearly beside it when we are down the Bull Ring. But that is for later.' She pointed. 'If you look across the road now you will see St Philip's Cathedral. See, it's no bigger than St Chad's.'

It was grand, though, Carmel thought, taking in the majestic arched, stained-glass windows. There was a tower above the main structure and a clock set just beneath the blue dome above it. All around the church were trees and tended lawns interspersed with paths, with benches here and there for people to rest on. Carmel thought it a very pleasant place altogether and would have liked the opportunity to sit and watch the world go by.

However, Lois was in no mood for sitting. She led the way up the road, and after a short distance it opened out before a tall and imposing building of light brick.

'Our own Big Ben,' Lois told Carmel with a smile, pointing to a large clock in a tower at the front of it, 'known as "Big Brum" and this statue here is of Queen Victoria.' She led Carmel over to look at the statute of the old and rather disgruntled-looking queen.

'And that truly magnificent building in front of us is the Town Hall you spoke about?' Carmel asked.

'The very same.'

'It's huge!' Carmel said, approaching the marvellous structure. 'Look at the enormous arches on the ground floor and those giant columns soaring upwards from it, and all the carvings and decoration.'

'You never really look at the place you live in,' Lois said. 'And I am ashamed to say that, though I knew all about the Town Hall, I've never truly seen its grandeur until now. It's supposed to be based on a Roman temple.'

'Gosh, Lois,' said Carmel in admiration. 'What a lovely city you have.'

Lois was surprised and pleased. 'You haven't even seen the shops yet,' she said.

'Well,' said Carmel, 'what are we waiting for?' She linked arms with Lois and they sallied forth together.

* * *

Carmel came from a thriving town, a county town, which she'd always thought was quite big, but she saw that it was a dwarf of a place compared to Birmingham. The pavements on New Street, on every street, were thronged with people, and she had never seen such traffic as they turned towards the centre where cars, trucks, lorries and vans jostled for space with horse-drawn carts, diesel buses and clanking, swaying trams.

Carmel had never see a sight like it – so many people gathered together in one place – had never heard such noise and had never had the sour, acrid taste of engine fumes that had lodged in the back of her throat and her mouth. The size of the buildings shocked her as much as the array of shops or things on offer. Some of the stores were on several floors. Lois had taken her inside a few of these and she had stood mesmerised by the goods for sale, by the lights in the place, the smart shop assistants.

Some of the counters housed enormous silver tills, which the assistants would punch the front of and the prices would be displayed at the top. Carmel had seen tills before, but none as impressive as these. Best of all, though, were the counters that had no till at all. There the assistant would issue a bill, which, together with the customer's money, would be placed in a little metal canister that was somehow attached to wires crisscrossing the shop. It would swoop through the air to a cashier who was usually sitting up in a high glass-sided little office. She would then deal with the receipt and, if there was any change needed, put it in the canister and the process would be reversed.

It was so entertaining, Carmel could have watched it

all day. But Lois was impatient. 'Come on, there is so much to see yet. Have you ever been in a lift?'

No. Carmel had never been in a lift and when Lois had taken her up and down in one, wasn't sure she wanted to go in again either.

'I'll stick with the stairs, thank you,' she said.

Lois grinned. 'I'll take you to some special stairs,' she said, when they were in Marshall & Snelgrove. 'See how you like them.'

Carmel didn't like them one bit. 'They are moving.'

'Of course they are.' Lois said. 'It's called an esca-lator.'

'How would you get on to it?' Carmel said. 'I prefer my stairs to be static.'

'Where's your sense of adventure?' Lois demanded. 'It's easy, even children use them. Come on, follow me.'

Carmel did, stepping onto the escalator gingerly and nearly losing her balance totally when the stair folded down beneath her foot. All the way to the next floor she didn't feel safe, but still she felt proud of herself for actually doing it.

'They have escalators in Lewis's too, where Dad works. You remember me telling you?' Lois asked. When Carmel nodded she added, 'Well, that is where I am going to take you next.'

Carmel thought Lewis's at the top of Corporation Street a most unusual shop altogether. It appeared to be two shops on either side of a little cobbled street called The Minories, though Lois said they joined at the third floor.

Carmel gazed upwards. 'I can see they join some-where.'

'The fifth floor is the place to be,' Lois said. 'It's full of toys.'

'Toys?'

'Yes, but toys like you have never seen. Before my mother took to lying on a couch all day long and moaning and groaning, she'd bring us to town sometimes and we always begged to go to the toy floor. I have to go again, if only to see if it has the same fascination now that I am an adult.'

With a smile, Carmel agreed to go with Lois so that she could satisfy her curiosity, but she didn't expect to be much interested herself. What an eye-opener she got.

The first thing she saw were model trains running round the room, up hill and down dale, passing through countryside, under tunnels and stopping at little country stations where you could see the streets and houses and people. Then they would be off again, changing lines as the signals indicated.

'It's magical, isn't it?' Lois said at her side. 'I used to watch it as long as I was allowed.'

Carmel could only nod, understanding that perfectly.

There were other toys too, of course, when Carmel was able to tear herself away – huge forts full of lead soldiers, or cowboys and Indians. There were also big garages with every toy car imaginable and a variety of car tracks for them to run along.

Another section had soft-bodied dolls with china heads and all manner of clothes nice enough to put on a real-life baby, and the cots and prams and pushchairs you would hardly credit.

'Did you have toys like these?' Carmel asked Lois.

'No,' Lois said. 'Our stuff was basic, nothing like these magnificent things.'

Carmel wandered around the department, mesmerised. Teddy bears, rocking horses, hobby horses, spinning tops, skipping ropes with fancy handles, jack-in-the-boxes and kaleidoscopes were just some of the things she knew her little brothers and sisters would love. There were giant dolls' houses, full of minute furniture and little people that would thrill the girls. And she so wished she could buy her brothers a proper football, for all they had to kick about were rags tied together, or the occasional pig's bladder they begged from the butcher in the town. And wouldn't they just love the cricket sets and blow football, and they could all have a fine game with the ping-pong.

The only thing the Duffy children had to spin was the lid of a saucepan, and their toys were buttons, clothes pegs, or stones. Any dolls were made of rags. Carmel felt suddenly immeasurably sad for her siblings, but even worse, she also felt guiltily glad that she was no longer there to share their misery.

'Well,' said Lois, 'I don't know about you, but I am ready for my dinner and Lyons is as close as anywhere.'

'Are you sure you can afford it?'

'Don't start that again,' Lois said. 'We have already discussed it. Come on quick for my stomach thinks my throat is cut.'

Carmel realised she too was hungry and her stomach growled in appreciation when just a little later a steaming plate of golden fish and crispy chips was placed before her. Both girls did the meal justice, and Lois sighed with satisfaction as she ate the last morsel.

'Ooh, that's better,' she said. 'It's amazing how a meal revives you. I was feeling quite tired.'

'So was I,' Carmel said. 'But I have enjoyed today, for all that. You have a very interesting city here, Lois.'

'You know,' Lois said. 'I have never really thought that before. What do you say to us exploring the Bull Ring now?'

'I say lead the way,' Carmel said, and the two girls left the cafeteria arm in arm.

The Bull Ring astounded Carmel. There were women grouped around a statue selling flowers, such a colourful and fragrant sight, though she had to shake her head at the proffered bunches for she hadn't enough spare money to buy flowers.

The hawkers, selling all manner of things from their barrows, swept down the cobbled incline to another church that Lois told her was called St Martin-in-the Fields, though there were precious little fields around, she noted. It was however, ringed by trees, its spire towering skyward.

Everywhere hawkers shouted out their wares, vying with the clamour of the customers. One old lady's strident voice rose above the others. She was standing in front of Woolworths, which the two girls were making for, and she was selling carrier bags and determined to let everybody know about it.

'Woolworths is called the tanner shop,' Lois said.

The two girls wandered up and down the aisles, looking at all the different things for sale for sixpence or less.

'Everything is just sixpence?' Carmel asked in amazement.

'Oh, yes,' Lois said with a smile. 'Though some say that it's a swizz. I mean, you do get a teapot for a tanner, but if you want a lid for it that is another tanner and a teapot is not much good without a lid, is it?'

'No,' Carmel agreed. 'But I don't know that that is not such a bad idea. After all, it is usually the lid breaks first. I would be very handy to be able to get another and all for just sixpence.'

'Well, yes,' Lois conceded. 'That's another way of looking at it, I suppose. Come on, I want to take a dekko at Hobbies next door.'

The window of Hobbies was full of wooden models of planes, cars and ships of all shapes, sizes and designs. Carmel was amazed at the detail and size of them.

'My brother would spend hours in here,' Lois said. 'They sell kits, you know, to make the things you can see, and Santa always had one in his sack that he would drop off ready for Christmas morning.' She wrinkled her nose and went on, 'I can smell the glue even now. It was disgusting.

'Now,' she said, turning away from the shop, 'I think the Rag Market is the place we'll make for next, down by the church. Watch out for the trams. They come rattling around in front of St Martin's like the very devil and there might be a couple of drayhorses pulling carts too.'

'Drayhorses I have no problem with,' Carmel said. 'I'm used to horses, but those trams frighten the life out of me. I will give them a wide berth, never fear.'

Lois laughed. 'You'll soon get used to them,' she said, but Carmel doubted she would. She'd seldom seen anything so scary.

Once inside the hall, there was a pervading odour. 'What's the stink?' Carmel asked Lois. 'It's like fish.'

'It *is* fish, left over from the weekdays when this place is used as a fish market,' Lois said. 'But never mind that. This is the place where bargains are to be had.'

Carmel thought it a strange place, for while some of the goods were displayed on trestle tables, others were just laid on blankets spread on the floor. She was very interested in the second-hand stalls where she saw many good quality clothes being sold comparatively cheaply, and she thought she would bear that in mind in case she needed anything another time.

She could have spent longer in the market, for such unusual things were being sold there. She stood mesmerised by the mechanical toys a man was selling. Catching Carmel's interest, he wound up a spinning top.

'On the table, on the chair, little devils go everywhere,' he chanted. 'Only a tanner. What d'you say?'

What Carmel would have liked to have said was that she would take four or five to send home to her wee brothers and sisters. She could imagine their excitement, but instead she turned her head away regretfully. 'I'm sorry. I haven't the money to spare.'

'Your loss, lady.'

'Come on,' Lois urged. 'I want you to see Peacocks. You can buy almost anything there, and we must go to the Market Hall before we leave.'

When they were outside the Rag Market a far more pleasant smell than that of stale fish assailed Carmel's nostrils and she sniffed appreciatively.

'That's the smell from Mountford's, where they're

cooking the joints of meat,' Lois said. 'Makes you feel hungry, doesn't it?'

'Not half.'

They passed the shop, where there was the tantalising sight of a sizzling joint on a spit turning in the window. Carmel felt her mouth water. It would be at least another hour before she ate anything, for she and Lois were not meeting the others until five and it was only four o'clock.

'Come on,' Lois urged. 'Let's go and see around Peacocks. I used to love this too when I was just a child.'

Peacocks was packed – Lois said it always was and Carmel could well see why, for the store had such a conglomeration of things for sale, clothes and toys as well as anything you would conceivably need for the house.

Outside Peacocks, a hawker had a stall selling fish. 'What am I asking for these kippers?' he demanded. 'A tanner a pair, that's what. Come on, ladies, get out your purses. You won't get a bargain like this every day.'

Because of the press of people, the girls had reached the steps leading up to the gothic pillars either side of the door into the Market Hall before Carmel noticed the men. They were shabbily and inadequately dressed, their boots well cobbled, and the greasy caps rammed on over their heads hiding much of their thin grey faces. They all had trays around their necks, selling bootlaces, razor blades, matches and hairgrips. Carmel felt a flash of pity for them, and as soon as they were in the Hall and out of the men's hearing, asked who they were.

'Flotsam from the last war,' Lois told her. 'They can't get proper jobs, you see. I mean, there is little work anyway, but some of these men couldn't do anything hard or physical, because many are damaged in some way from the war, shell-shocked perhaps, or suffering from the effects of gas. There is one man comes sometimes and he's blind and led along by a friend, and another with only one leg.'

'It's awful,' Carmel burst out. 'And so unfair. These men have fought for their country – surely the government should look after them now.'

'Of course they should, but when has that made any difference?'

'Yes, but—'

'Look,' Lois said, 'this is your first experience of this, but I have seen them there for years. You get almost used to it, though if I have any spare cash I will buy something because I do feel sorry for them. But if we get upset, it won't change things for them, will it?'

And of course it wouldn't. Carmel saw that and she took her lead from Lois. In the Market Hall there was much to distract her, anyway, for, like the barrows outside, stalls selling meat, vegetables and fish were side by side with junk and novelty stalls and others selling pots and pans, cheap crockery, sheets and towels. However, for Carmel the main draw was the pet stall.

She had never owned a pet, and though she would have loved a cuddly kitten of her own, or a boisterous puppy to take for walks, she knew there had been barely enough food for the children, never mind an animal. She'd never have taken a defenceless animal near her father either, for she thought a man who would beat his wife and children without thought or care, wouldn't think twice about kicking an animal to death if the notion took him.

There were rabbits and guinea pigs in cages, and twittering canaries and budgies that Lois spent ages trying to get to talk. Carmel had never heard of a talking budgie and was inclined to be sceptical. However, just as Lois was maintaining that some budgies did talk and she had an aunt who had owned such a bird, there was a sudden shriek and a raucous voice burst out, 'Mind the mainsail. Keep it steady, lads. Who's a pretty boy then?'

The milling customers laughed and the stall owner went into the back to bring out a parrot that neither Lois nor Carmel had noticed.

'There,' Lois said with satisfaction. 'I told you that some birds can talk.'

'You said budgies could, not parrots,' Carmel contradicted. 'I knew about parrots, though I had never heard one until today.'

'Even budgies . . .'

However, Lois didn't get to finish the sentence, because someone beside her suddenly said, 'It's nearly five o'clock.'

Carmel put the kitten she had been holding back in the box, and stood up, brushing the straw lint from her coat. 'We'd better get our skates on,' she said. 'The other will be there before we are.'

'No, wait on,' Lois said. 'If we are a few minutes late, they won't mind. They can have a cup of tea or something.'

'But what are we waiting for?'

'The clock,' Lois said, pulling Carmel to the front of the stall. Everyone was suddenly still, Carmel noticed, and gazing up at the wooden clock on the wall, watching the seconds ticking by. And then the hour was reached

59

and three figures, like knights and a lady, emerged to strike a set of bells to play a tinkling, but lilting tune. Carmel was as enthralled as anyone else.

'Oh, it's lovely,' she cried, when the strains of it had died away.

'It wasn't always here,' Lois said, as they walked outside again. 'It was first put into an arcade up Dale End way, but my dad said that the arcade went out of business through lack of custom. He told me the man who made the clock was never paid the full asking price and he is supposed to have put a curse on it and that was why the arcade in Dale End had to close. That is hardly going to happen here, though, to the thriving Market Hall. You saw that for yourself today.'

'Yes I did,' Carmel agreed. 'But I can't help feeling sorry for the man who made the clock not getting the money for it. It's a magnificent piece of work and must have taken him ages and ages – and then to be diddled like that . . .'

'You're all for the underdog, aren't you?' Lois said. 'First the old lags on the market steps and now the poor clockmaker. I've never ever given that man a minute's thought.'

'I don't like unfairness.'

'No more do I,' Lois said. 'Only now that I am nearly grown up I see that there is unfairness everywhere, and as individuals there isn't much we can do about it. The poverty of this place, which I imagine is repeated in most cities, would really depress you if you let it. You sometimes have to rise above it, even if you care desperately.'

Carmel said nothing more, for wasn't that just what she had done – risen above neglect, poverty and the downright tyranny of her home and left the others to manage as best they could? She had cared while she was there, for all the good it did, but when this means of escape had been handed to her, she had grasped it thankfully and pulled herself up. She had no intention of letting herself go back to that sort of situation ever again and so without another word she followed Lois to meet the others.

CHAPTER FOUR

Carmel was surprised when, after a very substantial tea, Jane and Sylvia elected to go back to the Bull Ring when Lois asked them what they wanted to do for the evening.

'Is there any point?' Carmel asked. 'I mean, won't everywhere be closed now?'

Sylvia laughed. 'Not tonight,' she said. 'Tell you, girl, you've not lived till you see a Saturday night down the Bull Ring.'

Carmel wasn't convinced. Lois had mentioned both the music hall and cinema, and Carmel would have given her right arm to see either. Though free tickets sometimes came for the probationary nurses, Carmel had always refused any invitation for she felt she hadn't the clothes for such outings. Now though, she would have put up with the embarrassment of that to have an evening out with her special friends.

'After all, the night is mild enough,' Jane remarked.

'Yeah,' Sylvia agreed. 'Might as well make the most of it. We can go to the pictures or music hall another time, when the weather isn't so kind to us.'

Only Lois saw the brief flash of disappointment cover

Carmel's face. 'Do you mind?' she said. 'Is that where you want to go too?'

Carmel had never had friends before. Because of the type of home she came from, she had never had anyone to link arms with and whisper confidences to, or go out to the socials at the chapel with. And she wasn't going to risk damaging the relationship developing between her and the others by going against them now. So she said, 'I honestly don't care where we go. It is all new to me, don't forget, so everywhere is an adventure.'

The dusk had deepened as they made their way back to the Bull Ring and Carmel saw that around the barrows, and in other strategic points, there were spluttering gas flares, slicing through the darkness and making the whole place look a little like a sort of fairyland, and as different from the Bull Ring in the daytime as it was possible to be. And then in the shadows cast by the lights, Carmel spied some beshawled women lurking, many with babies in their arms and surrounded by raggedy children with bare feet, arms and legs like sticks.

'What are they doing here?' she asked, appalled.

'Waiting for the hawkers to virtually give the stuff away,' Sylvia said. 'They do that at the end of the day and those poor old buggers go home with some scrappy meat and overripe veg and look like they have won a king's ransom.'

'These are the real poor that I mentioned earlier,' Lois said. 'They are always here of a Saturday and you can just stand here all night and stare at them, which will either make them feel more ashamed, or else angry, or you can do them the dignity of pretending you see nothing amiss and come about with the rest of us.'

'I'm sorry,' Carmel said. 'I never thought of it that way.'

'Watch out!' called Jane, who was a little way in front. 'The stilt walkers are coming.'

The crowds parted to let past the incredibly tall men, dressed in exceedingly long black trousers, striped blazers and shiny top hats. They doffed their hats to the people, who threw money into them.

'Just how do they do that?' Carmel asked.

'Who knows?' Jane said. 'But they're good.'

'Carmel, you have seen nothing yet,' Sylvia promised.

'Jimmy Jesus is getting up on his soap box,' Lois called.

'Jimmy Jesus?'

'The old fellow with the white beard,' Lois pointed.

'Is that his real name?'

'No,' Lois said. 'Don't know if anyone actually knows what his real name is. But that is all I have ever heard him called, 'cos as well as the way he looks he spouts on about the Bible, you see.'

'There's usually some fun when the hecklers start,' Sylvia said. 'I don't know about the rest of you, but I'm not ready for a sermon just yet a while.'

'Me, neither,' Jane declared. 'Let's take a look at the boxing.'

Carmel didn't say, but she hated the boxing, where a big bruiser of a man challenged those in the crowds for a match. 'Knock the champ down and you win five pounds,' his promoter urged from the corner.

Carmel thought the champ, with his build, his beefy

arms, legs like tree trunks, small, mean-looking eyes and belligerent features reminded her of her father.

'I'm not surprised that no one has taken him up on the offer,' she said.

There were a fair few men in the audience, but none seemed anxious to take up the challenge, though they hung about for a little while.

'It's early yet,' Sylvia told her. 'Wait till they've sunk a few jars in The Bell. The weediest ones will think they can take on the world then.'

'Have anyone ever laid the champ out?'

'Are you kidding?' Jane said, as she steered Carmel away. 'Do you think they would be offering five pounds if people were likely to win it? Mind you, we have seen quite a few of the challengers spread their length on the sawdust.'

'Ugh, it's horrible.'

The others laughed at Carmel's queasiness, but kindly.

'I'll bet you'll think this just as bad,' Jane said, and Carmel thought that she was right for as they turned the corner, there was a man lying on a bed of nails. He had very brown and oily skin and there was a lot of it to see, for he had few clothes on, just something wrapped around his head that Lois told her was a turban and what appeared to be a giant nappy on his lower half. As the friends watched in horrified fascination, two girls stepped forward, shed their shoes, and stood one his chest and one on his abdomen. The man made no sound and he seemed not to either feel the girls' weight, nor the nails they could clearly see were pressing into his skin.

Eventually, the girls got off and money as thrown into the bowl by the nailed bed by impressed onlookers. The man got up and came over to the nurses.

'Any of you lot like to try? Promise I won't look up your skirts.'

'Carmel might fancy a go,' Jane said with a smile at the repugnance on Carmel's face.

'Carmel would not – oh, no, definitely not,' Carmel declared vehemently. 'I think it's just, well, just awful.'

The man shrugged as Lois pulled her away.

Carmel wasn't that keen on the man tied in chains either, but was quite willing to stay around to see he got free in the end and was unharmed, though the others eventually got fed up.

'He won't even try until there is at least a pound in the hat, and that could take ages yet,' Lois said.

'Have you ever seen him get out?'

'No, I haven't personally.'

'I have,' Jane said. 'But just the once.'

'How?' Carmel asked, for the man was trussed up like some of the chickens she had seen hanging from butchers' stalls earlier that day.

'I don't know,' Jane admitted. 'He had a cloak around him. Didn't take him long, I do remember that. People say it's a swizz, but you can examine the chains and all if you want. He doesn't mind.'

'Well, I don't fancy waiting around any more tonight.' Sylvia said. 'And the musicians will be setting up soon, I should think.'

'Music,' Carmel said. 'That's more my kind of thing.'

'Oh, you'll like it, all right,' Lois said. 'It's from your neck of the woods – the first stuff they play, anyway –

jigs and reels and that, and then they go on to the songs from the music halls that everybody knows.'

'I don't.'

'You will when you've been here a bit,' Sylvia put in.

They went past the stilt walkers, still striding effortlessly around the market, and past Jimmy Jesus again, urging the people to repent and then their souls would be as white as the driven snow, washed by the blood of the Lamb. There were a few catcalls from some of the lads and a bit of jeering, but generally people seemed to tolerate the man very well. Carmel was glad, for she thought he had a very gentle voice and manner about him.

By now the accordion players were just setting up in their corner.

Lois said, 'I don't know what's the matter with me, after that tea and everything. I must have worms because I could just murder a baked potato.' She indicated a little man nearby with an oven shaped not unlike Stephenson's Rocket, which Carmel had seen pictures of.

'It's just because you can smell them,' Sylvia said. 'They always smell lovely, I think.'

'I don't care what it is,' Lois said, 'I am buying one anyway. Anyone else want one, or are you going to let me be the only pig?'

'Let me buy one for each of you,' said a male voice suddenly.

Lois swung around. 'Paul!' she exclaimed, and gave the man a hug before introducing him to her friends one by one. 'Sylvia, Jane and Carmel, this is my cousin Paul.'

'God,' said Jane in an aside to Sylvia, 'why haven't I got cousins like that?'

67

'Having them as cousins is no good,' Sylvia replied, as the man in question and Lois went over to the hot potato man. 'Did you see that dazzling smile he cast your way, Carmel?'

'I can't say I noticed,' Carmel said.

'You must be flipping blind then,' Jane put in. 'I really don't know what's the matter with you.'

'I've told you, I'm not interested in men.'

'God, Carmel, you must be mad,' Sylvia protested. 'I'd be turning somersaults if a man as dishy as that one smiled at me like he did you.'

'Well, that's you, isn't it?' Carmel retorted. 'I don't feel the same, that's all.'

'Carmel, we're not talking of marrying the man, just having a bit of fun, and no harm in that either,' Sylvia said. 'After all, none of us can get married for years anyway, if we want to finish our training.'

'Oh, I don't know,' Jane said. 'It depends on whether a better offer comes along. A man like that wouldn't have to try very hard to entice me from the charming clutches of Matron.'

The girls laughed but talk about Paul had to cease there, for he and Lois were approaching. Carmel found the potato surprisingly tasty. The music was good too and made her foot tap. The only thing that spoiled it for her was seeing the shambling women, clutching their spoils, children trailing behind them, leaving the market as the hawkers began packing away.

She turned her face resolutely away from the sight and didn't mention it at all lest the others be irritated by her. They tried to get her to show them a jig or a reel, but she would never show herself up like that and especially not with Paul's eyes fastened on hers so intently.

By the time the music-hall songs were being played, the hot potatoes were all eaten and everyone was belting out the songs, Paul had somehow arranged it so that he was right next to Carmel. He might as well have been invisible for Carmel took no notice of him at all.

Eventually, in a lull between tunes, he said, 'I believe you and my illustrious cousin are room-mates?'

Jane, hearing this, gave Sylvia a nudge, she nodded and they moved forward into the crowd, taking Lois with them.

Carmel answered, 'That's right.'

'And this is your first visit to the Bull Ring she said?'

'Yes.'

'Well, what do you think of it?'

Carmel shrugged. 'It's all right.'

Paul smiled. 'Just all right?'

'What d'you want me to say?' Carmel cried. 'It's good. I've enjoyed it.'

'Have you anything like this where you come from?'

'No, not really.'

'You hail from Ireland, Lois said?'

'That's right?'

'Which part?'

'Why do you want to know?'

Paul was nonplussed. He wasn't used to having this reaction, especially from girls. He shrugged. 'Just interested.'

'Why?' Carmel demanded. 'You don't even know me.'

'Maybe I was trying to get to know you.'

'I don't see the purpose of it.'

'It's just . . . it's what people do, that's all.'

'It's not what this person does,' Carmel snapped. She looked around frantically for the others, but found herself somehow positioned at the edge of the group with other people in front of her, separating her from her friends. Everyone was singing with gusto about it being a long way to Tipperary.

Paul, though taken aback by Carmel's response to his innocent questions, was not one for giving up easily, especially with a girl as lovely-looking as Carmel. He thought maybe she was shy and so he drew her away from the group slightly and said, 'Please don't be offended. I really meant no harm. It's just that I am interested in people. It's partly why I want to be a doctor, I suppose, and with you in the same line of work, as it were, and a room-mate of Lois's, I just thought it would be nice to get to know you a little better.'

'So now you know I'm not worth the effort.'

Paul gave a slightly hesitant laugh as he said, 'Surely, Carmel, I should be the judge of that?'

'No,' Carmel said. 'I should. I really have no wish to talk to you further and I want to rejoin my friends.'

That wasn't so easy, however, because there was a body of people in front of her that she couldn't push past and so she stood awkwardly on the edge of the group with Paul beside her. He was wondering how in heaven's name he could break down this delicious-looking girl's reserve, but Carmel had many secrets in her past she had no intention of sharing with a virtual stranger.

The musicians finished and began tidying away. Carmel sighed. Now perhaps she could meet up with the others and they could all go home, away from this irritating man and his constant questions, but as she thought this, the strains of a brass band could be heard in the distance and she lifted her head to listen.

'That's the Sally Army playing "Jerusalem",' Paul told Carmel, seeing her interest.

'Sally Army?'

'Salvation Army I mean really,' Paul said. 'But you would hardly knew about those either, coming from Ireland. They come here every Saturday evening and collect up all the hungry and destitute, the sort of person you or I would cross the street to avoid, for they are usually none too clean and alive with vermin. The Salvation Army don't seem to care about that, and they will take these people back to the Citadel, which is what they call their headquarters, and give them hot broth and bread, and try and find the especially vulnerable a bed for the night.'

It happened just as Paul said. From the minute the Salvation Army swung into view, singing with all their might, tramps began emerging from every corner.

However, some of the crowd had begun to melt away and Carmel was able to push past the rest and rejoin her friends again. Unseen by Carmel, Lois raised her eyebrows quizzically at her cousin and he shook his head slightly.

Jane was saying to Carmel, 'D'you want to stay and sing some more?'

'I don't know any of these,' Carmel said truthfully as the band announced they would be singing 'The Old Rugged Cross'. 'I'm ready to call it a day if you are.'

'But the night is young yet,' Paul said. 'How about a drink to round it off?'

Alone, Carmel would have refused. She had a horror of drink and drunks and pubs, but she wasn't alone and it wasn't totally her decision to make.

Paul turned pleading eyes on Lois and she knew what he wanted. So, despite the early start Carmel would have in the morning, Lois said a drink would be just the job. Both Sylvia and Jane too had seen where Paul's interest lay, and so they backed Lois up and Carmel knew the decision had been made. Without being churlish and risk alienating her friends, she would have to go along with it. However, she thought firmly, there was no way that she would drink anything even mildly alcoholic and she would be adamant about that.

Paul had one arm linked with Lois and when he extended his other for Carmel, she pretended not to see it, and Sylvia, feeling sorry for the rebuff, took hold of it instead. Jane and Carmel walked behind, Jane shaking her head at Carmel's foolishness.

'Our Paul is really keen on you,' Lois said as she and Carmel made their way to work a couple of days after her initial visit to the Bull Ring.

'I hope you told him that I'm a hopeless case.'

'No,' Lois said. 'But then he wouldn't listen if I did.'

Carmel shrugged. 'He's going to be one disappointed man then, isn't he?'

'Carmel . . .'

'No, Lois, I've told you, but you don't seem to under-stand it,' Carmel said hotly. 'I'm not interested in Paul, or any other man – not now, not ever. Anyway, isn't there some rule about not fraternising with the doctors?'

'Yeah, for all the notice anyone takes of it,' Lois said. 'Some girls come into nursing and their prime objective is to hook a nice eligible and potentially rich doctor.'

'Surely not?'

'No, straight up,' Lois said. 'I really wanted to nurse, but I bet Jane would jack the whole thing in if the right man came along, doctor or otherwise. You heard what she said the other day and it wasn't totally in jest.'

'I was a bit shocked,' Carmel said.

'Why?' Lois said. 'She is eighteen. Lots of girls our age are at least going steady, or else engaged, if not married. She might as well do something useful while she waits for Mr Right to sweep her off her feet.'

'I suppose.'

'I am more committed than that and I know you are, but I want to have some fun as well.'

'I don't mind fun,' Carmel protested. 'I really enjoyed Saturday.'

'Till Paul came,' Lois said. 'You changed totally then.'

'Well, yes, if you like,' Carmel said. 'I enjoyed it till Paul came. He sort of muscled in and took over, like men always do.'

'I didn't see Paul doing that,' Lois said. 'You seem to have a real downer of the whole male race.'

'You have it at last,' Carmel said. 'And you would be doing your cousin a service if you were to tell him that.'

In the end, Lois decided to tell Paul, because she knew that it would be more unkind to allow him to harbour false hopes. She knew, but hadn't told Carmel yet, that soon she would see more of Paul than she might like, because he had been assigned to work at the General Hospital from the autumn.

However, Paul was more upset than Lois had bargained for when she stressed how Carmel felt.

'Look, Paul,' she said, seeing his desolate face, 'I can't believe you can be this upset. Crikey, you've only met the girl once and for such a short time too.'

'None of that matters,' Paul said miserably 'I think about her all the time.'

Lois felt immensely sorry for her cousin, but she knew for his own sake, he had to get over this fixation with Carmel. 'Well, you will have to stop. I have told you how she feels, Paul. This is just silly. You don't even know her.'

'I tried to get to know her,' Paul said. 'God, it was like pulling teeth.'

Lois smiled. 'We have all had a taste of that,' she said. 'Carmel might sometimes make a comment about her family, though she does that rarely, and whatever she says has to be left there, because if you start asking questions, she clams up. We all know her parents' marriage isn't a happy one – in fact it is so miserable it has put her off for life. You must forget her, dear cousin. Good heavens, isn't the world full of pretty girls who would fall madly in love with you if you gave them the slightest encouragement?'

Paul smiled and Lois caught her breath and regretted anew that he was her cousin.

'You have an exaggerated opinion of me, cousin, dear,' Paul said. 'And a biased one, I believe.'

'Take a look in the mirror, Paul,' Lois said. 'Then go out and conquer the world.'

Paul doubted that he would ever forget the girl who seemed ingrained on his heart, but he also knew that Lois was right: to try to put her out of his mind was the only thing to do.

CHAPTER FIVE

The weeks rolled by and turned into months. Carmel finished her first year and when her holidays were due, she went to stay with the sisters at St Chad's Hospital. It was rather a busman's holiday because she helped out on the wards, but she was quite happy about that.

She began her second year with no change in her attitude towards men, and was surprised and a little dismayed when she learned that Paul was working at the hospital with a fair few other student doctors.

'Why didn't you warn me?' she asked Lois.

'There seemed little point,' Lois said with a shrug. 'I knew that you would find out eventually. He likes the situation even less than you do. None of them has had any choice about where they were sent.'

Carmel knew that was true. To give the probationer nurses the maximum exposure to a variety of medical conditions, each one spent a minimum of nine weeks and a maximum of twelve on a different ward. Carmel valued the experience this was giving her and she imagined that it would help the budding doctors to learn in different places too. As the General and Queen's were the only two teaching hospitals in the city, it was inevitable that some medical students should be sent there. She knew she wouldn't be able to avoid seeing Paul, but Lois had assured her that Paul had been told and understood how Carmel felt. She was glad about this for it meant she would be able to treat him in a respectful and professional manner, as she did the other doctors she came into contact with.

'Has anyone else see that gorgeous doctor?' Aileen Roberts said at breakfast one day at the beginning of October.

No one had apparently, so Aileen went on, 'He is wonderful, terrific. He has blond hair and the deepest blue eyes.'

Carmel and her room-mates weren't there, or Lois would have said the man was probably her cousin Paul. Everyone was used to Aileen and her ways, anyway, and liked to tease her.

'I thought you liked them tall, dark and handsome like Dr Durston,' another girl, Maggie, said. 'Weren't you madly in love with him just a few weeks ago?'

'Yeah, and then it was that surgeon – what's his name, Adams – Mr Adams that you said had smouldering eyes that turned you weak at the knees,' Susan, another young probationer, added.

There was a ripple of laughter and then Maggie said, 'You even had a thing going for Jimmy, that cheeky young porter, as I remember.'

'Face it, Aileen,' put in Susan, 'with men you are a

right pushover and you fall in love more often than I have hot dinners.'

'This is different,' Aileen maintained. 'They were just mere mortals, but this man is a god, a true god. You'll know when you see him yourself.'

'Has he a name, this man?' Maggie asked with a wry smile. 'Just in case there is more than one god trailing about the hospital?'

Aileen cast her a withering look. 'Connolly, that's what he's called. Dr P. Connolly.'

'Haven't you found out what the P stands for yet?' Maggie cried. 'God, Aileen, you're slipping.'

'Give me time,' Aileen said. 'I have only just spotted him. It could be Peter.'

'Or Philip or Paul,' Susan said.

'Or Patrick,' said Maggie, and went on mockingly, 'But surely these are such ordinary, mortal names for such a superior being?'

'You wait till you see him,' Aileen said, getting in a huff at all the teasing. 'And when you do, remember that I saw him first and that makes him mine.'

'Haven't you heard the expression that all's fair in love and war?' Maggie asked.

'I don't know about fair in love and war,' said Susan. 'But I do know no one will be fair on us if we don't head on to the wards, and mightily quickly too.'

There was a resigned groan as the girls, realising that Susan was right, got to their feet. The matter of Aileen and the dashing doctor was shelved for the moment.

It soon filtered around the hospital that the Adonis that Aileen had described was Lois's cousin Paul. Aileen was delighted that one of the girls was related to him.

'That's wonderful. Maybe she can put in a word for me,' she said at breakfast one morning.

'Why should she?' said Jane with a laugh.

'Anyway, I'd say a man like that will make up his own mind,' Sylvia said. 'And from what I remember from the night we met him down the Bull Ring that one time, it was Carmel he was showing an interest in.'

'Carmel!'

'Don't sound so surprised,' Sylvia said. 'She's very pretty.'

There was no denying that. Aileen thought it a shame that such beauty should go to waste, for Carmel seemed to have no interest in men. 'I bet she didn't take no notice,' she said.

'No, she didn't.'

'I don't understand her,' Aileen said. 'I don't know why she don't go the whole hog and be a nun if she ain't a bit interested in men. Anyway, it don't matter, she has had her chance and if she don't want Paul, plenty will – like me, for instance.'

'You'll have to get in the queue for that then,' another girl said from further down the table. ''Cos I will hand it to you this time, Aileen, he is very dishy, this Paul Connolly, and I intend to be very nice to Lois.'

In actual fact, probationers had little to do with the doctors anyway, and so it was a couple of days before Carmel confronted Paul face to face.

'Good morning, Dr Connolly,' she said, and saw that he was more shaken than she was, but he took his guide from her.

'Good morning, Nurse Duffy.'

Carmel passed him then, giving him no chance to linger. Paul, watching her go, felt as if his limbs had turned to water. He knew then that he was in love with Carmel Duffy.

Carmel, however, seemed completely content. She still hadn't much money – none of them had – but thanks to the second-hand stall at the Rag Market she had been able to add to her wardrobe a little, and though she enjoyed going out with a crowd of nurses, especially her room-mates, she would never make arrangements to see later any of the boys they might meet. When others did and would go out on dates, Carmel would be quite happy to stay in by herself, or pop over to see the nuns at St Chad's Hospital.

The other student nurses would often shake their heads over Carmel's determinedly single state. As far as they could ascertain, Paul Connolly didn't go out much either, and though he didn't appear to have anyone special in his life, he showed no interest in any of them.

In fact, Paul was more miserable than he could ever remember. He was finding it harder than he had ever thought it would be, seeing Carmel, going about her duties, or laughing and joking with the patients or her friends, but treating him so formally.

However, there was nothing to be gained by mooning over her, he knew, so, coaxed and bullied by his friends, he did start to go out more, though he still took no more notice of the student nurses than he ever had.

That year, Paul volunteered to work over Christmas and so did Carmel. Lois was having that Christmas off and so was Sylvia. Jane was on duty, but courting strong, and

Carmel guessed she wouldn't see much of her outside of their working hours. She told herself she didn't mind this, but for the first time she felt left out and knew she would be glad when the others were back and Christmas over and done with.

She was surprised how good Paul was in the pantomime, put on for the patients on Christmas Eve. She would have imagined a man as handsome and well set up as he appeared, and also training for a serious and respectable career, would not feel happy in such a frivolous production. However, not only did he throw himself into it with great enthusiasm, he seemed to be having as much fun as the audience. She saw with amusement that many of the nurses were gazing at him with more that just admiration in their eyes, and that Paul was either unaware of it, or else giving a very good impression that he was.

He also had a very good tenor singing voice, Carmel discovered, as the staff sang the age-old carols together with the patients. She felt a momentary pang of sympathy for Paul's younger brother. It must be hard to follow this golden boy, who seemed to have it all, without a certain amount of resentment creeping in, she thought, and that in turn would make him less likeable. Look how Lois had first described them: 'dishy Paul and annoying Matthew'.

She slipped out after the concert to attend Midnight Mass, having been given an especially late pass for the purpose, feeling the bone-chilling cold seep into her, even on the short walk to St Chad's, despite the thick coat and scarf she had picked up for a song at the Rag Market.

The Mass had just begun when someone slipped into the pew beside her and, glancing across, she was surprised to see Paul. Carmel felt decidedly uncomfortable all through that Mass, being so close to him and unreasonably resentful that he should spoil her enjoyment of that Christmas service. He seemed unaware of how she felt and he turned and gave her one of his devastating smiles. Even she acknowledged then how truly handsome the man was and saw how the smile made his eyes dance and shine, just as if someone had turned a light on behind them.

That's it, she thought as she tore her eyes away from Paul, this man is dangerous and the less I have to do with him the better.

When Carmel left the church, with the greetings of Happy Christmas from one to another ringing in her ears, she was nearly lifted off her feet by the power of the wind that brought with it icy rain spears, which stung her face.

'Link your arm through mine,' urged Paul, who had suddenly appeared beside her, and as she hesitated he grabbed her arm, tucked it through his and held tight. 'Come on, be sensible,' he said when Carmel tried to pull away. 'This wind could have you over.'

The words had barely left his lips when a sudden gust cannoned into Carmel causing her to stagger and almost fall against Paul. He dropped her arm and instead held her round her shoulders.

'Lean in to me,' he said, giving her a little squeeze.

Carmel was well aware that she shouldn't allow such familiarity with someone she really knew so little of, but it was so very comforting being held that way and she didn't protest any more. She was glad, though, there was no one from the hospital to see them walking snuggled together like a courting couple for the short journey to the door of the nurses' home.

'Merry Christmas, Carmel,' Paul said softly, and he kissed her gently on the cheek and waited until she had gone in the door before making for his own lodgings.

Carmel thought about the evening as she lay in bed, and despite her tiredness, sleep eluded her as she went over everything in her head. She decided that she was glad that she had met up with Paul. She knew he was a kind man and a gentle one, for she had seen the way he was with patients, but she had seen another side to him that night. She had met the Paul with a sense of humour, and who refused to take himself too seriously – and she liked that. No more than that, of course, but if they liked one another, they could perhaps behave more naturally in the hospital if they should meet.

By the evening of the twenty-eighth, Carmel was exhausted. She had worked long hours straight through from Christmas Eve, and she was heartily glad she had the following day off. She met Paul in the dining hall and they went in together and then sat at the same table, though Carmel did say, 'I hope you are not expecting sparkling conversation. I'm really no fit company for anyone tonight in fact, it is hard enough to just string a few words together.'

Paul smiled. 'If you did manage to deliver a marvellous oration, I know for a fact I would be too tired to appreciate it.'

Carmel knew that Paul had been working as hard

and just as long hours as she, and she said, 'Are you off tomorrow too?'

Paul nodded. 'From ten o'clock I am. Just pray that nothing serious happens before then that might mean me stopping later, for I fear they would have to prop my eyes open with matchsticks.'

'Poor you,' Carmel said. 'I don't think I could work a minute longer. I will be making for my bed as soon as I possibly can, and stay in it most of tomorrow too, if I get my way.'

'Surely not,' Paul said. 'Resting is for old bones.'

'Right,' Carmel said nodding sagely. 'Of course, how silly of me. I will be up with the lark and run the marathon instead.'

'Do you know, Miss Duffy, that sarcasm is the lowest form of wit?'

'And the highest form of intellect, so I'm told,' Carmel retorted.

Paul burst out laughing. '*Touché*, as the French would say.' Then he went on, 'I was actually thinking of leaving the marathon until next week and taking in a pantomime tomorrow. *Aladdin* is on at the Alex.'

'A pantomime!' Carmel breathed, because she'd never seen a pantomime, though many of the other probationers had and had described them to her. Her chances of seeing one with her friends were less now than the previous year, for her three room-mates were dating fairly seriously so the girls' nights out had been severely curtailed.

Lois had told Paul this. Now he said, 'Point is, a pantomime will be no fun on my own.' He raised his eyes. 'I don't suppose that you . . .?'

84

'No, Paul.'

'Why not? Have you already seen it?' he asked, knowing that she hadn't.

'I have never seen a pantomime in the whole of my life.'

'Then why?'

'I don't think that it would be sensible.'

Paul stared at Carmel for a minute or two and then said, 'Can you tell me what is so unsensible about two friends, both at loose ends, going to the Alex together to see a pantomime?'

'Two friends?'

'Yes, friends,' Paul said. 'We're sure as God aren't enemies, are we? Unless I am missing something here, that is.'

'No, of course not. It's just . . . I don't know. I mean, what if people sort of misconstrue the whole thing?'

'What if they do?' Paul said. 'Do you give a tuppenny damn for what people might think?'

'Not usually,' Carmel admitted. 'But, honest to God, Paul, you wouldn't believe the nurses' home. It's a hotbed of rumour and speculation.'

'So you're passing up on something you want to do in case people tease you about it,' Paul said. 'I honestly didn't think you were so feeble.'

'I'm not feeble!' Carmel cried. 'Don't you dare call me feeble!'

'Prove that you are not then,' Paul taunted.

'Right, I'll show you,' Carmel said.

'So you'll come with me?'

'Yes. Yes, I will.'

Despite his weariness, Paul was in a jubilant mood

as he returned to the ward, though he knew he would have to treat Carmel as the friend he had claimed to be and not the lover he hoped to become.

The night was a magical one. Paul called for Carmel in the afternoon and, though the day was bleak and raw, with all the promise of snow from the leaden skies, they wandered around the shops first, all preparing for the January sales, the streets outside still festooned with Christmas lights.

Before the pantomime, they went for a meal at Lyons Corner House and then on to the Alex. The pantomime was every bit as good as Carmel had hoped. She loved the glitz and glamour and sheer splendour of it all. She loved the audience participation too, and she booed, hissed and cheered with the best of them, laughed herself silly at the jokes and clapped until her hands were sore.

Paul would have taken Carmel for a drink after the show, but she said she wasn't keen on pubs and, anyway, it was late enough. Paul didn't argue and as they walked back he said, 'Did you enjoy it?'

'Oh, Paul,' Carmel said, 'I can't tell you how much. I have had such a wonderful time. I feel as if I'm still in it, you know? As if I could dance madly along this road now.'

Paul laughed. 'Shall I catch up your hand and we'll cavort along together?'

She gave him a push. 'You'll do no such thing. They'll think the two of us crazy.'

'I thought we weren't going to care what people thought.'

'Maybe not,' Carmel said, 'but I'd care very much if I was encased in a straitjacket.'

'So if I promise to behave, could we, maybe, do this again?'

'Yes,' Carmel said. 'I'd like that, but don't forget my prelims are looming and I will have to get my head down to do some revision.'

Still, Paul was amazed at the progress he had made in one evening.

Carmel was right about one thing: nothing could be kept quiet in the nurses' home. Though her room-mates knew she had gone out with Paul she had told no one else, but still they had been spotted. Aileen stopped Carmel and Lois when they came off duty the night after the pantomime.

'Are you going out with Paul Connolly, Duffy?' she demanded angrily.

Carmel looked at Aileen's angry face and she was irritated by the way the girl had spoken to her. 'I don't know what it has got to do with you, but, no, I am not "going out", – not in that sense. We are just friends.'

Aileen gave a sniff of derision. 'Don't give me that,' she snapped. 'Do you think I was born yesterday? The two of you were seen all very pally walking the town.'

Later, up in their room, Lois said, 'Is anything going on with you and Paul?'

'No,' Carmel said. 'We're just friends, like I told you.'

'Hmm,' Lois said. 'Don't play fast and loose with Paul's feelings, will you? He is really gone on you.'

'He might have been once,' Carmel said, 'but, he's over that now and knows full well where he stands.'

But Lois remembered that, less than half an hour before, she had seen Paul gazing at Carmel as she walked down the ward. Carmel had been unaware of his scrutiny and for a few moments Lois saw the naked love printed across Paul's face. Then he seemed to remember where he was and the moment passed, but now Lois knew, whatever Carmel thought, that he wanted to be more than a friend and she just hoped he wasn't heading straight for heartache.

However, though they went out together again to see *Cavalcade* in mid-January, Carmel wasn't able to see much of Paul at all after that, for the prelims, or mid-term exams, were early in February and any spare time was given over for revision, because if she failed she would be unable to continue nursing.

Carmel and Lois received news that they had passed their prelims on Carmel's birthday and were given different caps to denote their new status just two days before starting their annual three-month block of night duty.

As before, Carmel felt as if her life was put on hold because she was so constantly tired. She saw Paul rarely, usually in the company of others and never for very long. Paul knew the stresses and strains of working long and unsociable hours and could quite appreciate Carmel's exhaustion.

Not everyone was as understanding. Lois's boyfriend finished with her before the stint was over in mid-June and Lois was pretty miserable about it. Carmel suggested they go to the cinema together to see *King Kong*, which some of the others had been raving about. It was a long time since Lois and Carmel had been out together and at first, when Paul turned up with his friend and fellow medical student, Chris, Carmel was quite annoyed, but they could hardly let the two men sit on their own.

Carmel was soon glad of Paul's solid presence beside her because the film was more than just scary, and when his arm encircled her shaking form, she was too frightened to make any sort of protest. Anyway, she saw that Chris was comforting Lois the same way. Chris wanted to go for a drink afterwards, but Carmel again refused. Lois saw that Paul didn't mind and what he wanted was to get Carmel on his own and so they parted at the pub, and Paul and Carmel took off into the night.

It was balmy and still quite warm, and as they walked Carmel suddenly said, 'Why did you go in to be a doctor in the first place, Paul? You told me once that it was because you were interested in people.'

'Yes, that was it really,' Paul said. 'I wanted to make things better for them. I don't remember when I first wanted to be a doctor. It didn't come in a blinding flash or anything like that. It was as if it had sort of always been there. Mind you, it might have been harder to convince my parents – my mother, anyway – if I didn't have a younger brother to take over the business.'

'That's Matthew, isn't it?'

'Yes. How did you know?'

'Lois told me,' Carmel said. 'She told me lots about you, as a matter of fact. Don't look like that either; I didn't ask her. She told me not long after I met her and ages before I met you for the first time. She said you studied at the Sorbonne in France for a couple of years.'

'Yes I did. I enjoyed my time there,' Paul said. 'Matthew is there now, studying engineering.'

'Can you speak fluent French?'

'Pretty much. Did you take French at school?'

Carmel suppressed a smile at the thought of French introduced at the little county school in Letterkenny. It was as likely as someone having two heads or taking a trip to Mars, but she answered seriously enough. 'No, Paul. French wasn't offered in my school.'

Paul seemed surprised. 'Oh,' he said, 'I thought it was pretty well standard now, but there you are. Anyway, when Matthew gets back, he will join the old man at the factory. Without him, I might not be on my way to being Dr Connolly, or not at least without some argument and unpleasantness.'

'I nearly didn't get here either,' Carmel said.

'Was there some opposition from your parents too?' Paul asked, and then without waiting for a reply went on, 'Your father, I bet. Lots of fathers object to their daughters working. Hell of an old-fashioned idea today, I think. Was that it?'

Carmel wondered what Paul would say if she was to answer, 'No, Paul, not quite. My father had me out grafting for his beer money since I was fourteen years old and the opposition he felt when I attempted to escape his clutches led to him beating me so severely I still have the marks of his belt on my back.' But she wouldn't say that, couldn't say it. Instead she said, 'Something like that.'

She knew that Paul moved in circles far different from her own. His family owned a factory, for heaven's sake. Paul and his brother had probably gone to private school, places where the teaching of languages was standard, and they could both swan off to France without causing any sort of financial constraint. He lived in the sort of world where many daughters did stay at home until they were married, where it wasn't considered quite the done thing to go out to work, but did it matter that friends came from different backgrounds?

However, Paul wanted more than friendship. He knew he was risking the relationship they had, speaking from his heart, and yet he felt he had to tell Carmel how he felt because it was chewing him up inside.

He slid his arm tentatively round her shoulders. Usually he never touched her, but what she had allowed him to do in the cinema had heartened him and he was filled with hope when she didn't throw his arm off.

In fact Carmel thought she should, for she remembered Lois's word about playing fast and loose with Paul's feelings, but she didn't want to. It felt just so right resting there.

Paul said 'If friendship is all you can offer me, I will take it and welcome, for I value that highly, but you should know that I love you with all my heart and soul. I have done since the moment I saw you in the Bull Ring and I imagine I will go to my grave loving you. Whether you return that love or not, I have to tell you how I feel.'

Carmel didn't reply straight away. Then she chose her words with care. 'This has come as a bit of a shock,' she said. 'I mean, I knew how you felt about me once. I suppose I thought you'd got over it, come to your senses.' She stopped, gave a sigh and then said, 'I don't know how I feel about you now and that is the honest truth.

What I will say is that I have a higher regard for you than any other man I have ever met.'

'Will you think about what I have said?'

'Of course, but what if I cannot return your feelings?'

'Then we will go on as before.'

'Won't that be hard for you?'

'It's hard for me now.'

'Maybe,' Carmel said, 'it would be better for you to cool our friendship, give you time to meet someone else who could love you the same way you say you love me now.' She realised as soon as the words were out of her mouth how upset she would be if he did that, but for his happiness she would bear it.

Paul suddenly caught her hand and swung her round to face him. 'It would break my heart if I were never to see you again,' he said earnestly. 'That is the honest truth.'

They had reached the door of the nurses' home, and Paul leaned over and kissed Carmel on the cheek. 'Sweet dreams, Carmel,' he whispered softly.

She was smiling as she closed the door behind her.

The room was quiet and in darkness, Jane and Sylvia asleep, Lois not in yet, and Carmel was glad of it. She had to sort out her feelings before she would be able to share them and she was soon in bed and reliving the time she had spent with Paul again and again.

She eventually fell into a deep sleep, so deep she didn't hear Lois come in. She dreamed that she was back in Ireland with her drunken father roaring at her mother and lashing at her and any who tried to go to her aid. When she felt the belt cut across her back, she was jerked awake with a yelp of terror. She lay back down and tried to still the panic. It was just a dream, she told herself, that was all. This here and now was reality.

Eventually, her breathing got easier and she was ready to drop off again, when suddenly her eyes shot open as she suddenly realised that she owed it to Paul to tell him all about her background. She shouldn't have secrets about where she came from, what her beginnings were, though she had never wanted to bring that sordidness and brutality into her life here. Ah, dear Christ, she thought, when Paul knew the type of home she came from, it would wipe the love from his eyes all right.

Should she break off any friendship they shared before they got in any deeper? But then she remembered him saying that his heart would be broken if she did that, and the bleak look in his eyes when he said it. Could she inflict that hurt on someone she cared for?

The dilemma she found herself in drove sleep well away and when it was eventually time to rise she felt like a bit of chewed string. She hoped that Lois wasn't going to ask questions about Paul, but fortunately she was more interested in talking about her and Chris, and Carmel was grateful.

As soon as her shift was over and she had eaten a scratch meal, she set off for the church, knowing the priest would be there to hear confession in the evening. She wanted so badly to pour her feelings out to someone.

When Father Donahue saw Carmel enter the church, and the dejected stance of her, he rushed forward and led her to one of the pews. 'Carmel, my dear child, what is all this? Are you in trouble of some kind?' He hoped, even as he spoke the words, that she wasn't in *that* kind of trouble.

Carmel looked at the priest, her eyes glistening with tears and said. 'It's trouble of my own making, Father, for I think I must tell Paul our friendship is over.'

'And why is this, my dear?' the priest asked gently, sitting down beside her.

'It's because of something from my past. Something no one can help me with.'

'I see,' the priest said. 'And this thing – was it something you did, something you could confess, get forgiveness for and put behind you?'

'It wasn't anything I did, Father.'

'But you are not responsible for the sins of others.'

'I know that deep down, Father,' Carmel said. 'It's just . . . I can't expect Paul to . . . He's going to be a doctor, Father.'

Father Donahue had seen Carmel in the church a few times with Paul and had been delighted that she had found herself a good Catholic boy. Carmel's duties prevented her from doing more than attending Mass on Sunday and Holy Days and she had been unable to go to any social events where she might meet other Catholic young people.

When he expressed this regret not long after Carmel made herself known to him, she had told him not to worry; that she didn't intend marrying anyone. He had hidden his smile, though he did say she was young to make such a momentous decision. He couldn't help thinking, however, that a doctor was a good catch for this girl, whom the nuns had told him came from one of the most desperate families in Letterkenny.

Suddenly the priest knew what Carmel was talking about because shame and degradation were mirrored in her eyes and he said gently, 'Carmel, I know the sort of home you come from and the sort or rearing you had.'

Carmel's head shot up and she looked at him in sudden alarm.

He went on in the same soothing voice, 'The nuns told me. They thought I should know.'

'Oh, Father,' Carmel said, and the tears began trickling down her face. She covered her face with her hands and moaned.

The priest took hold of those hands and pulled them from her face as he said, 'Come, come now, Carmel. Don't distress yourself like this. There is no need. Have I ever treated you differently because I had this knowledge?'

Carmel made an effort to control herself. 'No, Father, you haven't,' she said. 'In fact you have always been kindness itself to me. But that isn't the same everywhere. In Letterkenny, for example, there were many there who looked down on us and I can't expect Paul to want even friendship from the likes of me.'

'Are you ashamed of your family, Carmel?'

'Aye, Father,' Carmel said. 'And ashamed of being ashamed.'

'Then be ashamed no more,' the priest said. 'Pity them instead. Take responsibility just for yourself. Seek out your young man and tell him about your background and see what he says.'

'I couldn't, Father,' Carmel said. 'I couldn't bear it if he despised me.'

The priest gave Carmel's hands a small shake and looked deep into her eyes. 'He will never despise you. The love he has for you shines bright in his eyes and that will not be dimmed when he hears how you were reared. Carmel, you owe it to him to tell him.'

'You really think so?'

'I know so. And you speak of friendship – is that all you really want from Paul?'

'Yes, Father,' Carmel said. 'As I said, I never intend to marry.'

'And how does Paul feel?'

'He admitted last night that he loves me, Father.'

'And you can't feel the same?'

Carmel shook her head and the priest said, 'I know that I am a fine one to talk about love. But sometimes you have to open your heart and see what God wants for you in the future. I had to open my own so I could hear him calling me to the priesthood. Maybe you are approaching this with your head only, giving reasons why it isn't sensible to become involved with someone, when really a person's heart is often a better indicator of what will make them happiest and bring the greatest fulfilment in their lives.'

'So you think I should keep seeing Paul?'

'Not if you continue to feel only friendship,' the priest said 'That way only pain and anguish wait for him and, knowing you, even as well as I do, you will feel guilty for the hurt inflicted. However, the stumbling block in all this is your background and your home in Letterkenny. You must tell Paul. Give the man a chance and then see if it makes a difference to the way you feel.'

'All right, then,' Carmel said with a sigh. 'I will be guided by you, but it will be the hardest thing I will ever do.'

CHAPTER SIX

Over the next few days Carmel didn't see Paul to speak to. Any time they had off never fell together and, anyway, he was in the throes of studying for his finals, as Chris was. So Carmel and Lois were thrown together quite a lot, for Jane and Sylvia were courting strongly. Carmel had admitted to Lois what had happened on the walk home after the pictures, and some of what the priest had said, omitting all mention of her background.

'So how d'you know you don't actually love Paul, then?' Lois asked.

Carmel shrugged. 'How would I know? How does anyone know?'

'Well, do you think about him a lot?'

'It used to be just now and then,' Carmel said. 'But he's rarely out of my thoughts at the moment.'

'And can you imagine life without him, if he wasn't here, or if he got on with someone else?'

Carmel had to think about that and eventually she said, 'Yes, when I suggested Paul see other people, as I couldn't feel for him the way he wanted me to, it gave me quite a pang to think of Paul with another girl, and that quite surprised me. Yes, I would miss him if he was no longer around, if he wasn't an important part of my life. Oh God!'

'You have answered your own question,' Lois said, and hugged her in delight. 'You are in love with Paul and I know he is besotted with you. I tell you, Carmel, if I can't have the man myself, there is no one I'd rather he take up with than you. You'll still have to be careful, though, for if Matron gets one sniff of romance between a junior doctor and one of her probationers they'll likely be "wigs on the green", as my Uncle Jeff is fond of saying.'

But, Carmel couldn't think about Matron or anyone else. All she could take on board was love for Paul awakening in her and the joy and wonder of it. The thing spoken about in literature and poems, and sung about in ballads and laments down through the centuries, and the one thing she thought she would never experience because she wasn't going to allow herself to. Oh, how she had underestimated the power of that emotion, she realised. Then she remembered that she still had to tell Paul all about herself and her family and she still shrank from doing that.

She decided to shelve everything till after her holiday, which despite the pleading of her mother for her to go home, she was spending again at the convent on the Hagley Road.

'What about Paul?' Lois asked.

'What about him?' Carmel said. 'When his exams are over he can come and see me. I have my own room there and far more chance of privacy than here in the nurses' home. I haven't even had a chance of telling him my feelings have changed so drastically and I will need privacy then.'

Lois could see the sense of that and so could Paul when she told him of her plans. But really all his energies were centred on his finals.

At last, by early July, the dreaded exams were over and Carmel and Paul were making up a foursome with Chris and Lois the following night to celebrate that fact. Carmel was feeling very happy that evening as she was returning from benediction. It was just turning dusk and she was glad that she would be back in the hospital before the dark had really set in, when she heard a distinct groan coming from an alleyway to her right.

She stopped, her senses alerted, and listened as she peered into the gloom of the entry. The low moan came again. Tentatively, Carmel went towards the black hole. Attacks on individuals in the city centre had been getting frequent of late and had made everyone nervous. Carmel did wonder if this was some sort of trick to lure her into an unlit place. Her senses were on high alert as she moved cautiously, feeling the walls with her shaking fingers, expecting any moment to feel hands grabbing at her, pulling her further in.

Scared though she was, she knew even if she hadn't trained as a nurse, she couldn't walk past a person groaning in pain as if it was no business of hers.

Anyway, she told herself wryly, if anyone was to attack me in the hope of rich pickings, they would be on a losing wicket because I haven't a penny piece on me.

All thoughts of it all being some sort of trick fled a

few moments later, however, when Carmel's shuffling feet came in contact with something on the ground. She could see virtually nothing, just a vague mound, and she was suddenly so scared the hairs on the back of her neck rose. She kneeled and put her hands out hesitantly and felt clothing, like a jacket. She wished to God she had some sort of light for she knew there was a person lying there too injured to move. More confidently now, she ran her hands expertly over the prone and twisted form, checking for any kind of injury. She could find nothing obvious until she came to the person's head, where her fingers located a gaping sticky wound with blood still seeping from it. Gently, she laid two fingers against the neck and felt the pulse. She pursed her lips at the irregularity of it.

She knew the man needed help and fast, and yet she hesitated to leave him. Maybe there was someone still in the church? She ran to the edge of the entry and was greatly relieved to see Father Donahue in the church doorway. 'Oh, Father,' she cried.

'What is it, my dear?' the priest said, hurrying towards Carmel, taking in her agitated state first and then seeing her fingers covered in blood. 'What has happened?'

'There is an injured man in the entry, Father,' Carmel said pointing. 'At least from his clothes and haircut, I take it he is a man. I heard him groaning, that's what alerted me, but now he seems to have lapsed into unconsciousness. He is bleeding profusely from a head wound and his pulse rate is erratic. He needs treatment, and as quickly as possible, but I would hate to leave him.'

'I will alert them at the hospital, never fear,' the priest said. 'But shouldn't we try to bring the poor unfortunate person more into the light?'

'We should not move him, Father,' Carmel said. 'Tell them to bring torches, flashlights, anything, but hurry, Father. I will stay with him till someone comes.'

It was easier this time to go into the entry. When she got to the man, she felt the floor around him and the pool of blood, and she knew she had to stanch the wound. Glad there was none to see her, she pulled her dress and underslip over her head and ripped the slip into strips to pack and bind the wound before replacing her dress.

When the doctors came in with the stretcher and flashlights they found Carmel kneeling in the puddle of blood herself, as she had lifted the man's head slightly on to her knees so that she could stanch the flow more effectively.

'Good work, Nurse Duffy,' one of the senior doctors said to her. 'Now if you let us in we will see what is the matter with the poor fellow.'

'Certainly, Doctor,' Carmel said, easing the man's head from her so that she could get up. One of the doctors played the flashlight on to the injured man's face and when Carmel saw who it was, she staggered and would have fallen if the doctor hadn't caught her arm.

'You've stiffened up sitting there so long,' he said, not understanding.

But Carmel saw that the man whose head she had cradled in her lap was none other than Paul Connolly, whose face had been battered so badly he looked more dead than alive.

'Christ Almighty,' she heard the doctor exclaim behind her. 'It's young Connolly.'

There were a thousand questions burning in her

brain. What was Paul doing there? What had happened him? How badly hurt was he?

'It's Paul,' she told the priest, still waiting at the entrance with the orderlies who had brought the stretcher. 'I am going to go down to the hospital with them. I need to see if he's going to be all right.'

The priest saw Carmel's bleak eyes filled with worry and he said, 'I'll come with you.' Carmel just nodded and knew she would be glad of the man by her side.

'They'll not likely be able to tell you anything for some time,' one of the orderlies said. 'And you really need to get cleaned up.'

Carmel looked down at herself. Blood covered her dress from the waist, though there were also some splashes on the bodice, and her legs and hands were coated with it. But none of this mattered. The only thing that did was that the man she had just realised she loved above all others was desperately ill. She said, 'I will wash my hands but the rest can wait. Knowing that Dr Connolly is going to be all right is the only thing that counts.'

Many saw the state of Carmel as she went into the hospital that evening flanked by the priest. Then the young doctor was carried in on a stretcher and everyone was agog with curiosity.

Father Donahue sought out the staff nurse on duty and informed her of events. 'Carmel tells me Dr Connolly has a cousin here in the hospital,' he went on to say, 'a probationer called Lois Baker.'

'Yes, I was aware of that,' the staff nurse said. 'I will see that she is informed, as well as Dr Connolly's parents.'

Minutes later, Lois scurried down the corridor. She

hadn't been told of Carmel's involvement and when she saw her sitting there beside the priest, she was surprised, but as she drew closer and saw the bedraggled and blood-stained state of her, she became alarmed.

'What is it? What's happened to you?' she cried.

'Nothing,' Carmel told her. 'This isn't my blood, it's Paul's.'

'Paul's?'

'What have you been told?'

'That Paul has had some kind of accident.'

Carmel hesitated and then said, 'He has a head injury that was bleeding quite badly. I don't know if he was injured anywhere else, it was too dark to see.'

'Why? Where was this?'

'I found him in an entry off Whittall Street, not far from St Chad's,' Carmel said. 'I think he was attacked.'

'Is he badly hurt?' Lois asked in a voice so low it was almost a whisper.

'I don't know,' Carmel said sorrowfully. 'That is why I am waiting – to find out.'

She was suddenly overcome by the enormity of it all and the self-control she had kept a tight rein on began to dissolve. Her voice broke as she turned anguished eyes to Lois and cried. 'Oh, Lois, what am I to do? I couldn't bear to lose Paul now.'

'Hush,' Lois said, holding her friend's shuddering shoulders as she wept. 'I'm sure he will be all right.' But she was aware she was only hoping.

'It's the not knowing anything that gets to you in the end,' Father Donahue said.

'Yes,' said Lois. 'No one seems to understand what loved ones go through, sitting in corridors like this, not knowing anything hour after hour. I fully understand that the doctors hate being harassed when they are busy with a patient, but someone could come out now and again and tell you something. You will find that when my uncle comes he will not be content to wait around. If there is no one to tell him anything when he arrives he will go and find out for himself.'

Lois was absolutely right. Paul's father was a big man with quite a ruddy complexion. His hair was almost black, as was the moustache he sported above his wide and generous mouth, but it was his wife that Paul had got his looks from. Emma was still a very beautiful woman, with creamy skin, a rosebud mouth, and dark blonde hair.

Lois introduced Carmel and the priest to Paul's parents. Carmel saw that though Emma's blue eyes and Jeff's dark, rather brooding ones, were filled with concern, Emma was also alarmed at the state of Carmel. This didn't lessen when Lois explained that it had been Carmel that had found Paul injured in the entry and that was why she was covered with blood. Carmel was heartily glad she had recovered her composure a little and stopped crying, though she could do little about her puffy eyes, for she had the impression that appearance meant everything to Paul's mother.

'And how is Paul now?' Jeff demanded.

Lois shook her head. 'We've heard nothing since we arrived.'

'Well,' said Jeff, 'I'll not stand for that. I'll find someone to tell us something, or my name isn't Jeffrey Connolly. Come on, Emma, we deserve to be told what's going on.'

'Told you what he would do,' Lois said as they watched Jeff authoritatively push open the door they had been sitting outside and march through it with Emma on his arm.

'I'm glad he has,' Carmel said. 'It's awful just sitting here.'

'Don't I know it?' said Lois, morosely.

Jeff was back in a relatively short space of time to tell them that Paul had been severely beaten.

'A right bloody mess he is,' he said angrily. 'Beg your pardon, Father, but it's the thought of what some madman has done to my boy.'

'I fully understand,' the priest said. 'Was it theft?'

'Yeah, so they say. Everything was lifted from him,' Jeff said. 'They say he probably put up some sort of resistance and that was why the attack was so severe but, God Almighty, Father, you should see him. He has quite a few broken ribs and his body and face are a mass of bruises, but, of course, it's the head wound and him still being unconscious that's worrying them. They are preparing him now to go down for X-ray. I just popped out to tell you, like. Oh,' he said to Carmel, 'the coppers have been informed, so they might pay you a visit, as you found him.'

'I can hardly help them,' Carmel said. 'I mean, I saw nothing.'

'Well, they will probably come and question you anyway,' Jeff said. 'You know what the police are like. I'm going back inside now, because I want to be there when the X-ray results come back.'

'And I am going to phone Daddy,' Lois said, and Jeff nodded his approval.

When the door had closed behind Paul's father, Carmel asked incredulously. 'Have you a phone right inside the house?'

'Yes,' Lois said. 'Lucky, aren't we? It was put in when I began training, for Mother, you know, but it's handy now.'

When Lois had gone, Carmel turned to the priest. 'I think I'll leave now,' she said. 'I know at least that Paul isn't dead and no one is likely to know any more for some time. Anyway, this is a family time. If the police want to see me I would like to get out of these clothes and have a bit of a wash first.'

'I don't blame you,' the priest said. 'I'll wait on a wee while longer.'

'All right, Father. Good night then.'

Carmel had only just washed and changed into clean clothes when Sister Magee knocked on the door to tell her there was a policeman downstairs to talk to her and that she had made her office available.

Carmel thanked her and ran down the stairs. The policeman had been seated, but he rose as she came in. 'I honestly don't know what I can tell you,' she said, taking a seat the policeman indicated. 'I mean, I am not being awkward or anything, but I had just come from the church and I neither saw nor heard anything till that first groan.'

'Just tell us everything in your own words,' the man said, 'and we'll go from there.'

Carmel told him all she remembered. Sometimes the policeman stopped her to go over a point, but still, she was done in only a few minutes. 'That's about it. I don't know whether that helps or not,' Carmel said.

'You never know in a case like this with no witnesses,' the policeman said.

'One thing I did think odd,' Carmel said. 'Paul was in an entry in a side street. Haven't the other recent attacks being in the city centre and the victim just left there?'

'We don't think Dr Connolly was attacked in Whittall Street at all,' the policeman told her. 'We won't be sure of where he was attacked till first light and we think he put up one hell of a fight. The doctors have verified this. Possibly because he retaliated, his attacker or attackers really laid into him. Probably thought they had done him in, didn't want him found too soon and dragged him to the entry. We've been up and seen the scuff marks and spots of blood on the pavement leading away from the city centre. You saved that young chap's life tonight.'

Carmel flushed in embarrassment. 'Oh, surely . . .'

'Straight up, the doctor told us himself,' the policeman said. 'He said the young man had lost a lot of blood and if you hadn't heard him and used your expertise to stop the bleeding, he wouldn't be here now. So, you can feel right proud of yourself. I bet that Paul Connolly will be grateful when he hears about it.'

There was a sense of unreality about the next couple of days as the news of the heroism of Carmel flew round the hospital. Carmel thought the whole thing silly. It was what anyone would have done, she said; it was nothing special.

Each day she asked after Paul but as she couldn't claim any special relationship with him she was only told that he was 'satisfactory' or 'as well as could be expected'. Lois learned little more and Carmel cancelled her holiday, not wishing to be far from the hospital while Paul lay critically ill. She knew that his condition would remain critical until he regained consciousness. This happened four days later. It was Lois who told her and she also said the first indications were that there was no brain damage.

'He still has to be careful, of course, because he has been well bashed about,' Lois went on. 'And then whatever he was hit with fractured his skull, but he is now off the official danger list, though it will be weeks yet, they say, before he will be completely recovered. Anyway, because there is no brain damage, and providing he continues to improve, he is allowed visitors from tomorrow. Paul is asking to see you and, I'll tell you, if it had been anyone but you I would have been as jealous as hell.'

Carmel had the urge to grasp Lois by the waist and dance a jig around the room, but she contented herself with a hug. 'Oh God! That is the best news I have heard in ages.'

When Carmel did see Paul the following evening she was shocked, but managed to bite back the gasp of dismay. He was lying flat on his back with foam pads supporting his head, immobilising it. Almost a week after the attack, the bruising was well out on his face, which was a mass of colours from mauve to green, his nose looked as if it had been broken and his bottom lip had been split open and was stitched but swollen to twice its normal size. He also had a bandage swathing his head and smudged blackness was around and underneath both eyes, but the eyes themselves, as soon as he realised she was in the room, lit up with delight.

Carmel saw the pain still reflected in those eyes and felt immense pity for Paul and how he had suffered and was still suffering, but she knew he'd hate to guess her thoughts and so instead she said, 'Hello, Paul. What did the other fellow look like?'

She was relieved to hear the chuckle she loved so much as he answered, 'Worse, death's door, I believe, and thank God for you. Everyone else is pussyfooting around me, treating me like a bloody invalid.'

Carmel thought this was not the time or place, nor did she have the right to say what she would like to do this moment, which was to wrap him in cotton wool herself and not let any harm come to him ever again. Seeing him lying there so vulnerable was doing funny things to her innards.

'Come on up and sit on the bed where I can look at you.'

'Dr Connolly,' Carmel said in mock severity, 'you know that sitting on the bed is expressly forbidden.'

'Yeah,' Paul said. 'And you know what? Since I have been on the other end, so to speak, I have come to realise that we have stupid rules that don't make any sense. How can I tell you how grateful I am to you for saving my life so that you can see in my eyes that I mean every word from the bottom of my heart if you don't sit on the bed?'

Carmel waved her hand dismissively, but Paul caught hold of it and held it tight. 'Don't say it was nothing, please,' he said. 'The doctors gave it to me straight. If you hadn't found me, I wouldn't be here today.'

Carmel was embarrassed by Paul's humbleness and relieved to see his parents approach the bed. She got to her feet and extended her hand to greet them.

'Good evening,' she said. 'We only met the once. You'd hardly remember me. You were rightly concerned about Paul then.'

As she shook Carmel's hand Emma noticed the easy way the girl used her son's Christian name and she saw a light shining in her son's eyes that had never been there before.

'Please stay a little longer,' Paul pleaded. 'My parents too would like to thank you.'

'I can only stay a minute or two,' Carmel said. 'You know there are only two allowed at the bedside and if Matron was to see me breaking yet another hospital rule, she really would haul me over the coals.'

Emma knew she had much to thank this girl for because she had saved her son's life, but she hoped Paul's gratitude didn't run to him fancying himself in love with her. She was just a nurse and not the right companion for Paul, even if she was a friend of her niece's. Emma had set her sights for Paul a little higher than that. However, she knew she had to keep these thoughts to herself and so she thanked the girl.

Carmel accepted her thanks graciously, although she had noticed Emma's cold eyes and knew the woman was just going through the motions.

Jeff was as different again. Always naturally effusive and swayed by a pretty face, he was busy pumping Carmel's hand up and down as if he never intended to let it go, while he told her over and over how grateful he was.

'We don't know how to thank you. Indeed, we are all indebted to you,' he went on. 'When I think of how the outcome could have been so different . . . Well, it doesn't bear thinking about. If it hadn't been for your intervention and with you knowing what to do as well . . . Lois has done nothing but sing your praises. You really are a remarkable and very brave young lady. And don't you try and pass it off as if it was nothing,' he said, wagging his finger at her in mock severity. 'You were brave. Those doctors told me how it was – the dark entry you ventured into when you heard Paul groan, when many would have passed by, just kept on walking and told themselves it was none of their business. But you are made of sterner stuff. As I say, without you, this son of mine might not be lying in a hospital bed today, getting the best of treatment and being waited on hand and foot, and let me tell you—'

'Dad,' Paul interjected, 'you have told enough. You haven't let Carmel get a word in edgeways and you have embarrassed the life out of her, so that her face is the colour of beetroot at the moment. Leave her alone now. I think she has established just how grateful you are.'

Jeff took his son's rebuke and said sheepishly, 'I do get carried away. Sorry, lass.'

The apology made Carmel feel worse. 'Please don't apologise,' she said. 'I do understand how you feel, but truly, anyone would have done what I did and I'm just thankful that Paul has made such a remarkable recovery. And now I must leave you, because out of the corner of my eye, I can see Matron making her way towards me with all guns blazing.'

Paul knew she would get into trouble if she lingered further and so instead he said, 'Will you come again?' And when she hesitated he went on, 'Please? Come tomorrow.'

'All right then,' Carmel said. 'I am on days this week. I'll come tomorrow evening. Now I really must dash. Lovely to meet you again,' she said to Paul's parents before beating a hasty retreat.

'That wasn't so hard, was it?' Lois said, when Carmel got back to their room.

'I don't suppose so. Now everyone has got their thanks out of the way, maybe I can have a normal sort of visit next time.'

'And mop his fevered brow, like?'

'Do you know you are just about the most aggravating person to know?' Carmel said. She lobbed a pillow at Lois's head and the two collapsed in giggles.

CHAPTER SEVEN

Carmel wasn't the only one to visit Paul – in fact, he often had a plethora of visitors. His friends went usually in the morning, the rules relaxed somewhat with Paul being a doctor. His parents also went frequently and Paul told Carmel one evening that even his brother had made a flying visit from Paris. Lois wanted to see Paul too, of course, and her parents, and yet if he was asked, Paul would have requested they all stay home for it was Carmel's visits he longed for. But of course he never said this.

Carmel too looked forward to seeing Paul, taking joy in the fact that he was improving slowly. His mouth had been so damaged he had had to have his food puréed at first, and he was ecstatic the day the stitches were removed from his lip and he could start to enjoy normal food again. Other milestones were when they said he no longer needed the drips, and when the foam pads were removed and he was able to move his head from side to side. The bandage encircling his head was removed a little later and Carmel saw where his head had been shaved for the large wound to be stitched, although hair like soft down was already beginning to cover it.

Just days after this, the nurses began propping him up in the bed, for short periods at first, but these would be extended. Paul couldn't help but be excited about that and Carmel understood, knowing how frustrated he often was. She visited him every day and they talked about everything under the sun, but never about anything that mattered, the confines of the public ward, which Paul had now been moved to, making that impossible.

Then one day, when Carmel had been visiting Paul for over five weeks, she found him propped up in the armchair by his bed, with a rug tucked around him. 'I'll try and get a wheelchair for when you come in tomorrow,' he told her excitedly.

Carmel was as pleased as he was, but she commented drily, 'You are very sure of yourself, aren't you? What makes you so certain I will visit tomorrow?'

'Because I command it and you must do what a poor, sickly patient asks.'

'Since when?' Carmel asked with a smile and added sarcastically, 'What hospital did you say you trained at?'

'This one,' Paul said. 'But I'll not be at it much longer. As soon as they discharge me, I am away out of this.'

Carmel felt a stab of disappointment. 'Where will you go?'

'Queen's,' he said.

'Queen's?' Carmel repeated, puzzled for a moment, and then she cried out, 'You have had your exam results?'

Paul's grin nearly split his face in two. 'Yes, and I passed everything so I have accepted the post at Queen's that they offered to me provisionally, dependent on my grades.'

'Oh, Paul!' Spontaneously Carmel threw her arms around him and felt the beat of her heart match his. She melted against him as he held her fast and wished the moment could go on and on.

'Carmel, I—'

'Hush,' Carmel said, putting a finger to his lips. 'Not here and not now.'

She pulled away reluctantly and wondered if her face was as flushed as Paul's was. She knew soon she and Paul would have to talk seriously and this time she wouldn't back out of it or try to dodge the issue.

When Carmel went into the hospital the following evening, it was to see Paul sitting up in a wheelchair with a broad and triumphant grin on his face.

'I had to fight for this,' he said, pointing to the wheel-chair. 'But I won in the end. I thought we might sit in the day room for a change.'

The day room was at the end of the ward and usu-ally virtually deserted as most patients were still unable to leave their beds. Without a word of protest, Carmel took hold of the handles of the wheelchair.

She had never been in the room before and thought it a very unwelcoming place. The bare walls were a dull dirty beige colour, while the paintwork was dark brown, and rigid and uncompromising chairs were grouped before the wireless, or beside one of the tables, which had magazines and papers scattered across it.

The drabness didn't help Carmel's mood or help her form the words she had to say if she and Paul were to move forward, have any sort of future together. She sat down beside him in one of the uncomfortable chairs, aware that her heart was hammering against her ribs and her mouth was so dry she wondered how she would be able to speak at all.

Sensing her nervousness, Paul took up one of her hands, noting that it was clammy with sweat. His heart went out to her. 'Go on, darling,' he urged. 'Nothing on God's earth should cause you this much pain.'

Carmel tried to swallow the lump in her throat threatening to choke her. Her eyes were full of trepidation, 'Oh, Paul,' she breathed.

Paul gave her hand a squeeze and Carmel took a deep breath and slowly and hesitantly she told him of her family. She didn't exaggerate, but nor did she pull any punches.

Paul listened and said not a word. Inside he was raging that such things had happened to the girl he was beginning to realise meant more to him that life itself, but knew that wasn't the way to deal with this problem, which Carmel saw as such an obstacle to her own happiness.

So, when Carmel eventually drew to a close, Paul said, 'Is that it?'

'What do you mean?'

'You know what I mean,' Paul said. 'You have let people who aren't even here dictate to you. Because of your family and primarily because of your father, you were half prepared to say goodbye to me, weren't you? I felt it and that is why I made that declaration that evening. It was done in desperation.'

'But . . . I don't know what you are talking about,' Carmel cried. 'I have told you how it is, how my father—'

'Stop, right there,' Paul commanded. 'You are talking of your father, not you. I am not interested in your father – in fact, after the way he has treated you, I would be hard-pressed to even be civil to the man – but what I think of your father bears no relation to how I think about you. You shouldn't have to ask how that is, but I will tell you anyway.' He looked deep into her eyes as he said, 'I love you, Carmel, with every fibre of my being, and until the end of time, and I need to know how you feel about me.'

Carmel, seeing the passion in Paul's face and hearing it in his voice, knew if she rejected this man that she loved because of the actions of her father, he would have won and she would be miserable every day of her life. She was determined now, as she had never been before, that she wouldn't let that happen. And so she said, 'There are not enough words written to tell you how much I love you, but I'll try. I love you, I love you, I love . . .'

But her words were lost as Paul gave her a sudden tug and she fell against him. When their lips met, the words no longer mattered.

They talked and talked, but now it was as if she was on another plain altogether, a wonderful place where only she and Paul existed. Now that she had at last admitted her deep love for him, she drank in everything: the timbre of his voice, the way he held his head, moved his hands, his beautiful smile that lit up his whole face, and the full and luscious lips she longed to kiss. When Paul lifted one of Carmel's hands, which he still held, and kissed her fingers one by one, the tremors went all through her body.

Paul smiled in satisfaction. Nothing mattered any

more now that Carmel loved him as much as he loved her.

'Carmel, forgive me for not getting down on one knee,' he said, 'but the sentiment is the same. You wondrous, beautiful and desirable girl, will you do me the honour of becoming my wife?'

'Oh, yes, Paul,' Carmel cried. 'Yes, yes, yes. A thousand times yes, but . . .'

Paul knew what was disturbing Carmel. 'When you have finished your training, of course. In the meantime I will get established at Queen's and then I will decide whether I want to carry on there, move somewhere else, or possibly specialise.'

'You wouldn't fancy being a GP somewhere?'

Paul shook his head. 'Not at the moment, certainly. Maybe when I am older and greyer, but for the moment I like hospital work. D'you mind that?'

'Whatever you do is fine by me,' Carmel said. 'And I would go with you to Outer Mongolia, wherever that is, if you wished me to.'

'I don't think there will be a call for you to do that,' Paul said with a grin. 'I was thinking more about another area of Brum.'

'Were you?' Carmel said in mock disappointment. 'What a boring man you are.'

'I'll give you boring, my girl, when I am out of this damn thing and on my two legs again,' Paul said.

'I can hardly wait,' Carmel said, and at the seductiveness in her voice and the light of excitement dancing in her eyes, Paul felt as if his whole body was on fire.

'Oh, Carmel, I do so love you.'

Before Carmel was able to make any sort of reply,

the bell denoting the end of visiting trilled out. Carmel looked at Paul bleakly. Never had time passed so quickly. 'Oh, Paul.'

'I know, my darling,' he said. 'But I won't be in here for ever, never fear. Will you be able to come tomorrow?'

'You just try and keep me away,' Carmel said. 'But for now I'd better take you back on to the ward.'

'One more kiss before you do?' Paul pleaded.

Carmel kneeled on the floor beside the wheelchair and put her arms around Paul, and when their lips met it was as if a fire had been lit in both of them, and Carmel moaned in pleasure.

Paul thought briefly of teasing her mouth open, but decided against it. He knew Carmel would have been untouched by any man and he would have to proceed slowly, or he could frighten her. Anyway, there was no rush. They had a whole lifetime before them.

The news of the engagement of Paul Connolly and Carmel Duffy flew around the hospital and everyone, except perhaps Aileen Roberts and Matron, seemed pleased. Paul was no longer a student, but a qualified doctor and had never been under Matron's jurisdiction anyway, but the situation was different for Carmel. When Matron sent for her, Carmel went with her heart quaking.

'You know that fraternising with the doctors is expressly forbidden,' Matron said. 'And yet you must have disobeyed my instructions because no one gets engaged in five minutes.'

'I'm sorry, Matron,' Carmel said. 'I met Paul through Lois, who is his cousin. We were just friends at first. I didn't intend this to happen at all.'

'Does nursing not matter to you?'

'Of course, Matron,' Carmel said. 'I wouldn't dream of getting married before I qualified. Paul understands this perfectly.'

Catherine Turner was disappointed with Carmel. She had had her marked down as a girl fully committed to her career, and now look. But there was nothing she could do about it. Once married, most husbands wanted their wives at home and most women wanted to care for their man, and it would be one more good nurse lost.

Paul's parents congratulated them both, though Carmel knew that only his father was sincerely pleased. Carmel hoped that in time Paul's mother would accept her, for she certainly didn't want to cause any sort of rift between them. He had made clear that he thought a lot of his parents. Carmel knew he owed them a lot, for they had supported him through medical school, and without their support it would have been a lot more difficult for him to have qualified as a doctor.

Emma Connolly did think it was hard to hold resentment for a girl that might possibly have saved her son's life, and doubtless Paul was grateful to her, but she thought a person could carry gratitude too far. Surely Paul could see that he didn't have to marry the girl.

He had virtually been promised to Melissa Chisholm since birth, and she had all the right connections. Paul and she had had a thing going before medical school and finishing school separated them. Emma had thought that by the time he qualified, Paul would have sown all the wild oats he needed and be ready to settle down with Melissa. It would have happened that way if the nurse Carmel Duffy hadn't happened along when she did, when

Paul was sick and vulnerable. If Paul couldn't see how unsuitable such a marriage was, Emma was certain the girl would when it was pointed out to her.

She had mentioned her concerns to Jeff and really didn't know why she bothered because as usual he couldn't see a problem. 'Paul's happy enough,' he said. 'I can quite see why he's attracted to Carmel, for she looks such a fragile little thing, though to be a nurse she must be very strong. Added to that, she is very easy on the eye, and a friend of our Lois's. What more do you want? And you know if she was none of these things and still Paul's choice, then that would be that.'

'The girl will never fit in,' Emma said through tight lips. 'Surely you can see that?'

'No I can't,' Jeff said. 'Paul is no longer in short trousers, but a man of twenty-five and he must be let live his life without interference. Anyway, I reckon, he could go further and fare worse. Carmel is his choice and that, as far as I am concerned, is that.'

CHAPTER EIGHT

It was the last week of September and Paul was preparing to leave hospital after nearly ten weeks. His parents had planned a big celebration, both to welcome him home and also as a belated congratulations party for his exam successes.

Carmel thought the party might be to announce his engagement too, but Paul explained his mother wanted no one to know yet, not until the ring was bought, and then she would put an announcement in *The Times* and have a proper engagement party. Carmel thought it odd, but decided in the end to go along with the plan. Maybe in the middle classes it was how things were done. How would she know?

She was nervous about the party, and immensely glad Lois and Chris had been asked too. She was certain she would be amongst people from a different social class, and not at all sure whether she would pass muster.

This was exactly how Emma wanted her to feel. She had arranged the most lavish party. Jeff had grumbled at the expense and even Paul had queried the flamboyance.

'And why shouldn't it be a magnificent affair?' Emma asked teasingly. 'Not only is my son soon to be an eminent doctor, but he was also only recently snatched from the jaws of death.'

Paul laughed. 'A little dramatic, Mother,' he said, giving her a hug. 'But that's you, isn't it? Should have been on the stage.'

'What a tease you are, Paul,' Emma said, tapping him playfully on the cheek.

With another smile, Paul went off to find his father, who was the one who would have to pay for his mother's latest foolishness. And that is all he thought it was: getting one over on the neighbours, rubbing their noses in his success and stressing the fact that the Connollys could afford to celebrate in such a way.

That was only a part of Emma's plan. The biggest part was to make Carmel feel uncomfortable – so uncomfortable that she would realise, without a shadow of a doubt, that she would never fit into their world. The guest list had been worked out carefully and Emma had adjusted the original seating plan to her advantage.

Unaware of Emma's deviousness, Carmel worried what she would wear to such an occasion, though clothes were usually not a problem any more because the girls, much of a muchness in size, usually pooled all they had. Lois had a lot more than the others, and more expensive usually, but was always generous at sharing. So Carmel set out that night in a dress borrowed from Lois. It was pure silk of swirled autumn colours, the skirt billowing out from the waist and held out with petticoats that rustled deliciously when she moved. The hem was just below the knee. The court shoes were her own. The dark brown stole, which set the outfit off a treat, was one that Jane had got second-hand at the Rag Market.

Paul's parents lived in a house Four Oaks, Sutton Coldfield. The first Carmel saw of it was two stone lions that sat atop posts supporting wrought-iron gates. That night the gates stood open for arriving guests and the taxi drove down the sweeping gravel drive to pull up with a crunch in front of a house of enormous proportions.

Carmel looked at the three-storeyed dwelling with the beautifully tended flowerbeds either side of the white steps that led to a balustrade that ran around the house front and also to the oaken and studded front door. She felt her insides quiver with nervousness.

'D'you live in something like this?' she asked Lois in an awed whisper.

'Not half as big or impressive,' Lois said. 'Uncle Jeff has real money.'

Carmel could feel her fragile shreds of confidence falling away.

Chris, seeing this and feeling very sorry for her, caught her up with his free arm, his other already entwined with Lois. Then arm in arm with both girls he announced, 'We'll do this in style, as if this is the sort of thing we are used to doing every day of the week.'

Carmel was grateful to him for lightening the atmosphere. She truly liked Chris and thought he and Lois well suited. Then Chris, with a huge smile of encouragement, fairly swept them along, their shoes crunching on the gravel, taking the steps at a run and ringing the bell with no hesitation.

'God, Aunt Emma has surely pushed the boat out for

this,' Lois breathed in Carmel's ear as a man, dressed in a butler's uniform, opened the door and took their outer clothing, to be put in the cloakroom.

Paul came out to meet them. He took Carmel's arm and led her into a huge room, which he called the drawing room, that seemed filled with people with drinks in their hands. Carmel was glad there were soft drinks on offer too and she took one of those while she wandered around happily listening to this one and that talking to Paul and addressing the odd word to her.

Then, she was claimed by Emma, who was pleasantly surprised by Carmel's outfit, though she hadn't revised her opinion of her lowly breeding. Carmel saw, with a little dismay, that almost as soon as she left Paul's side he was surrounded by girls. Emma wasn't surprised, for he had always been a popular boy and he was very hand-some – and now, of course, as a qualified doctor, he would be very eligible indeed.

'They are girls Paul has known for years,' Emma told Carmel, following her gaze as she watched Paul almost being mauled by some of these rapacious girls, and laughing as if it was all one big joke. 'They are part of our set, you see.'

Carmel looked at her. She might as well have added, 'As you will never be,'

Emma went on, 'Most have known Paul since their nursery years and they are members of the tennis club, or yachting club or sometimes both. Do you play tennis, Carmel, or have you any experience of sailing?'

Carmel's eyes narrowed for she realised what Emma was doing and could do or say nothing about it without making an almighty fuss. But she wasn't going to allow her to talk to her in that supercilious way and get away with it.

'You must know, Mrs Connolly, that I would have little experience of either of those pastimes.'

'But you see, my dear, I don't,' Emma said. 'In fact, I don't know the least thing about you and that is quite worrying because we really need to ascertain whether you are the right sort of wife for Paul.'

'The right sort of wife?' Carmel echoed.

'Yes, one that will help him, enhance his career. Believe me, the right wife can make all the difference to a man's prospects.'

They loved each other. Did that count for nothing? 'Isn't it up to Paul who he marries?' she asked Emma. 'Paul and I love each other and—'

'D'you know, there is a great deal of nonsense spoken of love?' Emma said disparagingly. 'Left to myself I would never have married Jeff. I fancied myself in love with a most unsuitable man and really I wasn't all that keen on Jeff at all. It was my father who advised me to make a play for him. The other man could never have provided for me as Jeff has, and we get on well enough together. I never gave the other man a moment's thought, for love, you see, fades and it is a very unstable base to build a marriage on that is to last a lifetime.'

Jeff appeared beside Emma before Carmel could think up a reply. 'Come, my dear, don't monopolise Carmel all evening. I want her to meet Matthew.'

Carmel had never met Paul's brother before and he welcomed her with a bow and then, in a voice dripping with charm, commented on her small stature, her luxuriant hair, her absolute beauty so that soon he had her blushing. He kissed her hand with a flourish, but the hand was held a little too tightly, and the kiss went on too long, and when Carmel tried to pull away she couldn't, or at least not without making a fuss. It made her feel uneasy.

Later she saw him walk across to Paul and, after looking pointedly in her direction, said something to him in French. Paul was annoyed with him and Carmel didn't need to understand French to know his retort was angry. Matthew was not the slightest bit abashed and had a smirk on his face as he shrugged and moved off.

Carmel longed to ask what Matthew had said, but the party was too crowded to do that without being overheard, and Paul too much in demand to slip away. Anyway, she told herself, Paul had dealt with it. It was likely nothing at all, but she couldn't help wishing that the party was over and she was back in her room at the hospital where she felt so at ease and could really be herself.

Things got worse when the gong was struck, alerting everyone that the food was ready to be served.

'We are eating in the supper room,' Paul said, as he crossed to stand at Carmel's side.

'The supper room?' she repeated, never having heard of such a place. Then, when she glimpsed the room they were to eat in, her mouth dropped open in amazement.

The whole room was lit by three shimmering chandeliers overhead, and by flickering candles in shining silver candlesticks set down the whole length of the table, which was laid with a pure white cloth. Navy-blue napkins, folded in the shape of flowers, decorated each plate, and Carmel noted they matched the décor and the carpet.

But the napkins didn't concern Carmel as much as the collection of gleaming cutlery either side of each place or the glittering array of glasses that glinted and sparkled as the light caught them. Carmel thought before she picked anything up she would watch Paul carefully.

As if aware of what she was thinking, Paul gave the arm she had thrust into his a squeeze and whispered, 'Don't be nervous. You'll soon get the hang of it.'

Carmel nodded, though she doubted that. She had hoped that she might have been seated by Lois and Chris, but she was nowhere near them. Paul, as guest of honour, was at the head of the table, his parents and then his brother beside him, which left Carmel around the corner next to an oldish man who introduced himself to her as Colonel Thorndyke.

The food was brought in by young girls dressed in black dresses and white pinafores, while waiters hovered with bottles of wine. If Carmel had hoped that Paul might have been there to reassure and help her, she was to be disappointed, for Emma, on the other side of him, seemed to have important things to say to him most of the time and all Carmel saw was Paul's back.

As the bowls of soup were served, she watched what Colonel Thorndyke did and copied him. He didn't seem to have anything to say to her and she couldn't think of any topic that might interest him and so they ate in an uncomfortable silence.

Obviously, the colonel must have thought this too, for when they began the fish course, he had suddenly leaned towards her and said, 'Do you shoot at all?'

It was the very last thing Carmel would expect anyone to say as the opener to conversation with anyone, and she looked at him in stupefaction and repeated, 'Shoot?'

'Yes,' the colonel affirmed. 'Shoot. Birds, don't you know? Pheasant, partridge, that kind of thing.'

'No, I'm afraid I don't do anything like that.'

'I bet then you ride to hounds?'

Feeling more uncomfortable than ever, Carmel said, 'No, I don't ride at all, actually.'

The man was nonplussed for a moment and then said, 'There might be the chance for a spot of bridge later. You do play bridge, I suppose?'

Carmel's face was as red as a beetroot. In the whole room she doubted she could have sat near anybody who would more completely confirm Emma's words that Paul was out of Carmel's social class, and therefore out of reach, than this old colonel. 'No, I'm afraid not,' she said.

'Hmph,' the colonel grunted, and for a while there was silence. Then he suddenly leaned towards her again and said, 'see that you are not married and that from your accent you are from the Emerald Isle – what industry is your father in?'

For a second, Carmel could feel hysteria rising in her and she had the urge to say to this old duffer that her father was in the industry of being in an almost constant state of drunkenness, with a nice spot of brutality thrown in now and again. Oh, what consternation there would be if she did. She would scupper all chances of ever being on even passable terms with Paul's mother. As for Paul himself, he might say that he wanted to marry Carmel, not her family, but he would probably not wish her father's excesses broadcast in such a way.

And so she turned to the colonel and said, 'I am afraid I am here under false pretences and was only invited because I am a room-mate of Paul's cousin Lois.' She pointed down the table to her friend and went on to explain, 'We are probationary nurses together at the General Hospital.'

'Oh,' the colonel said in surprise and then muttered, 'Noble profession, noble profession.'

Noble he might regard it, but after that he couldn't think of anything else to say, and silence lapsed between them again as the waitresses began to serve the main course.

Carmel was astounded at the amount of food she had eaten already, and from the card by her place name she saw that after the huge main course there was dessert, followed by cheese and biscuits, and then coffee and liqueurs, whatever they were.

The talk around the table had become more animated as people ate their fill and drank the wine copiously. Carmel watched the waiters constantly refilling the glasses. She had refused wine from the first, not sure about it at all, and availed herself instead of the iced water from large glass carafes left for people to help themselves. She noticed many ladies' faces were flushed. The talk got louder and more garrulous and sometimes the voices were slightly slurred.

She felt quite lonely and exposed on that table. Everyone but her seemed to be having a good time – if you went by the raucous laughter, anyway – and everyone seemed to have something to say to someone interested enough to listen to it.

Occasionally, Paul would turn to her. 'All right?' he would ask, and what could she do but plaster a smile on her face and say, 'Fine!'

She felt uncomfortable as she watched the amount of wasted food returning to the kitchens a little later and thought that it was hard to believe that more than half the country was in the grip of deprivation, some of its citizens near starving. She wondered if the people around the table were even aware of this, or if they knew full well and averted their thoughts away from such unpleasantness.

But then, who was she anyway to judge Paul's parents and their way of life? Paul did have a social conscience. He had shown that in many ways, not least in the fact that he was working in a voluntary hospital, instead of slipping comfortably into the seat in industry his father would vacate for him, as his brother intended doing. She told herself to relax. Paul had insisted that he was marrying her and not her family. Couldn't she afford him the same courtesy? No one could help the family they were born into. It wasn't as if anyone had a choice in the matter.

By the time all the courses were over and Carmel was sipping delicately at the small cup of slightly bitter coffee and even more gingerly at the liqueur the waiter had insisted she try, which she found surprisingly pleasant, she was feeling almost uncomfortably full.

Then the waiters were there again, this time filling long tall glasses with something frothy and bubbly.

'Champers,' the colonel said, licking his lips in anticipation. 'Can't beat a bit of bubbly.'

Champagne! Carmel would have covered her glass again, but Emma wouldn't let her. 'We are here for Paul tonight,' she said stiffly as the waiter hovered above her, bottle poised, 'and you have drunk nothing but water.

131

Surely you can manage to drink one glass of champagne to toast his health?'

What could she say to that? She removed her hand and the waiter, with a wink in her direction, filled her glass almost to the brim.

Then Jeff was on his feet. The speech went on and on. They drank numerous toasts to Paul and his many achievements and accomplishments, to his full recovery from the dastardly attack and his success in his examinations, and then they toasted his future. Carmel thought champagne, with its frothiness and the way the bubbles went up her nose, just the nicest thing she had ever tasted and when the waiter filled her glass again she didn't object.

'Shall we rise, ladies?' Paul's mother said suddenly, as Carmel was draining her second glass of champagne. All the woman in the room obediently stood.

Now what was up? Carmel tugged on Paul's jacket urgently and when he turned she saw from his slack mouth and his slightly vacant eyes that he had drunk more than was usual for him and that was before he spoke and she heard the slight slur in his voice.

'It's tradition,' he told Carmel quietly. 'The women leave the men to have brandy, cigars and a manly chat for a little while. I will be along shortly.'

Full of trepidation, Carmel arrived after the others, trying and failing to manoeuvre herself nearer to Lois. When she reached the drawing room, Carmel was forced to sit down next to a buxom woman she hadn't spoken to before, who almost glowered at her.

Lois watched Carmel with concern, for she knew now what her aunt was about and she guessed some of the ladies could give Carmel a hard time too if they had a mind to, especially if they'd had a lot to drink.

Barely had they sat, before Emma said, 'We have a mystery person in our midst,' pointing to Carmel. 'Name of Carmel Duffy here. She's from Ireland. That much we know, but she doesn't seem to like talking of her background at all.'

Carmel's gasp was audible to those near to her, which brought their speculative eyes upon her. In fact, Lois saw many of the women's eyes light up. It was obvious that Emma resented or in some way disliked Carmel and so she was fair game to harass or annoy.

And harass her they did, throwing one question after another at her. She parried many of them – after all, she had had lots of practice – but they ridiculed many of her replies. Lois saw how agitated Carmel was becoming at the constant barrage of questions and in the end Carmel was almost forced to say that her father's ill health made him unfit for work.

'Why did you not tell us this earlier, my dear?' Emma said, her voice dripping with sarcasm. 'It is nothing to be ashamed of, but when you are so secretive, it makes people think perhaps you have something to hide.'

'That's right,' said Melissa in her drawling and slightly supercilious voice. 'Makes one suspicious, you see? Are you sure there isn't some other skeleton lurking in the cupboard that you would like to tell us about?'

Carmel looked at Melissa's malice-ridden eyes and felt like one of the foxes some of these women hunted. Suddenly she seemed to be a source of amusement, and almost all the woman seemed to be laughing at her as an object of scorn and derision.

Lois, watching the scenario with worried eyes, didn't know what she could do to help retrieve the situation, especially when she saw the woman beside Carmel touch her knee and urge, 'Do tell what it is you are hiding, my dear. I love a good gossip.'

'And you are among friends,' said another.

Like hell I am, Carmel thought, and wished she had the courage to tell them all to 'Piss off!'.

That at least would give them something else to focus on. Emma was giving her friends licence to behave this way, urging them on as she said, 'We'll be discreet with anything you tell us, Carmel. You needn't worry on that score.'

Carmel was feeling very hot. Her heart was thudding in her chest and she wondered if she was going to pass out, though she had never done that before.

But then it didn't matter any more, for with a flurry of greetings and gales of laughter, the men joined them. Paul was by Carmel's side and she felt immediately calmer.

Her calmness didn't last long, however. When, a little later, the party returned to the supper room, it was to see it transformed with tables now lining the edge of a space cleared for dancing, and a band setting up on a makeshift stage. Emma had found out that Carmel didn't know how to ballroom dance, so, using the excuse that she was sure Carmel would like to watch proceedings, Emma inveigled her to one side of a table facing the dance floor. She was flanked by two matronly ladies. Paul was on the other side of the table and grouped around him were the other young women. Lois and Chris were on another table altogether.

Paul, pleasantly mellow, seemed unaware of any undercurrent and just sat there smiling benignly at everyone. He was certainly enjoying the attentions from the girls, who seemed determined to make this a night for him to remember.

Not that he sat for long, for he danced with one girl after another, and some of their mothers, and then with his own. Carmel sat and watched it all in hurt-filled misery.

Lois and Carmel could not make a very late night of it because their late passes only allowed them to stay out until eleven, despite the fact they had booked the next day off work. When Carmel had first mentioned this to Paul he had told her he would leave when they did and travel home with her so that they could have some time together, but by the time they were ready to go, Paul was too drunk and having too good a time to remember any promise. She left him without even a kiss, just a desultory wave as she made her way outside to the waiting taxi with Lois and Chris.

Lois knew how upset Carmel was, and little wonder, but it was no good rehashing the evening in the taxi. Chris was nearly as drunk as Paul was anyway, and probably wouldn't see any problem at all, so they would have to wait to talk about this until they got home.

By the time they reached their room, though, the wretchedness and disappointment of that evening seemed burned on Carmel's very soul and she felt very depressed about the whole thing. They intended creeping into the room quietly, certain Jane and Sylvia would be asleep, but found instead they were waiting up for them.

'We couldn't sleep without knowing what it was like,' Jane said. 'Was it terrific?'

Carmel knew the girls were agog with curiosity and she suddenly realised she wanted to talk it over, and preferably with someone who wasn't there, who hadn't already got preconceived ideas. Maybe she had over-reacted.

'What was the house like? Was it a mansion?' Jane asked.

'Yes, near enough, anyway,' Carmel answered.

'Someone took our coats and things as we went in and there were waitresses with white pinafores like those at Lyons Corner House serving the food, and really smart waiters serving drinks,' Lois added. 'I've been to plenty of parties at that house before and they have been nothing like this one. And the guests . . . well some I had never seen before and they were all well-heeled, you know?'

'And I think it was all for a reason,' Carmel said.

'What do you mean?'

'Well, I'll tell you it as it was,' Carmel said, 'and you let me know what you think.' She began to recount the evening, beginning when they had first rolled up in the taxi. She had no trouble doing this because the events of that night had been etched on her brain.

Jane interrupted at the point where Carmel said that Paul's mother didn't think she would make a suitable wife for Paul.

'Did she actually use those words?'

'Yes,' Carmel said. 'She is an out-and-out snob, Paul's mother, and as I haven't come out of the top drawer, I might as well not exist.'

'You're kidding?'

Carmel sighed. 'I wish I was. The bloody woman virtually told me that I wasn't of their class and wouldn't really fit in. I'm sure she doesn't want me in the family. I'd say she already has someone in mind for Paul.'

'I can't believe I'm hearing this,' Sylvia said. 'We don't live in the Dark Ages any more.'

'Maybe someone should mention that fact to her then,' Carmel commented grimly. 'I mean d'you know one of the questions she asked me?'

'I couldn't imagine.'

'If I could play tennis, or had any truck with sailing, and then went on to ask me whether I thought I could make Paul the "right" sort of wife.'

'Bloody cheek! And where was Paul while all this was going on?' Jane asked.

'Well,' said Carmel, 'there were these three girls that his mother took pains to tell me he had known from the year dot. Obviously the "right" sort of girl, only they are no longer in the nursery and they were all over Paul like a rash. And no one knew about the engagement either. Paul's mother engineered that too. She told Paul that it was a little shabby to just turn up and say we were engaged when we hadn't got a ring. She said to leave it a little and make the announcement later. I just thought it might be how it was done in the middle classes, but now I think she planned the whole thing.'

'God, she sounds a vicious cow,' Sylvia said.

'She is,' Carmel said. 'Sorry, Lois, but she is.'

'Don't be sorry,' Lois said. 'I agree with every word, and I was ashamed of her, if you want the truth.'

'It isn't just her, though, is it?' said Jane. 'If my bloke did something like that with some girl, however long he had known them, I would give him such a clout.'

'I know,' Carmel said with a sigh. 'It was incredible really. There were these girls, pawing at him and stroking him and showing him in every way that they were available and his for the asking and he was enjoying every minute of it.'

'What man wouldn't?' Sylvia said.

'He might want to,' Jane put in, 'but he doesn't do it when he is spoken for, not if he knows what is good for him.'

'It made me look really stupid, especially in front of his mother, but I couldn't do anything about it,' Carmel said. 'In that sort of situation you can't act in any sort of normal way. I already felt awkward and out of place and so I could hardly start berating Paul and acting like a fish wife.'

'In defence of Paul,' Lois said, 'though in all honesty it isn't much of a defence, he was very drunk. I mean, I have known Paul for years and I have seldom seen him so bad.'

'Yeah, and I think that was his mother's intention too,' Carmel said. 'She went all out to get him drunk over the meal. It worked too, and he was pretty far gone when all the woman in the room left the men to their port, brandy and cigars.'

'Straight up?' Sylvia said in amazement. 'Do people still do that? I have read about it in books and that, but I never thought that in this day and age it was still done.'

'Well, it was done there all right,' Carmel said. 'I would say with people like the Connollys, tradition is alive and well. Once in that room away from the semi-protection of the men Emma and her cohorts really had a go at me.'

'What d'you mean?'

'They wanted to know all about Carmel, and were ridiculing what she said and everything,' Lois said. 'I honestly didn't know how to divert their attention and then the men came in and it was better for a bit.'

'Until the dancing,' Carmel said.

Lois nodded in agreement and both girls went on to describe how Paul's mother had effectively isolated Carmel from Paul, but made sure he was sitting by the girls she did approve of.

At the end of their account of the awfully humiliating night that Carmel had endured, Jane said to Lois, 'I do think you might have done more to help. After all, you are related.'

As Carmel had spoken, Lois had begun feeling bad that she had left her to flounder on her own so much and so she took the rebuke. 'You're right and I'm sorry. But, in an effort to make amends, Carmel, how about if I was to teach you how to dance properly?'

'How?' Carmel said. Knowing that ballroom dancing was very popular, she had made enquiries when she had first come to Birmingham, but with her shift patterns and the lectures and study, she couldn't fit the lessons in. But it was, she thought, important to learn now. She could do nothing about the tennis or the yachting, but she should surely be able to dance.

'I'll teach you,' Lois said. 'Why I didn't think of it before I will never know. We have a gramophone at home and lots of dance records because I used to practise when I came home from lessons when I was younger. I could bring them and we could have a go in our spare time. What d'you say?'

'I'd say I'd really liked it. I always liked dancing when I was younger – Irish dancing, that was, of course – so I'll do it to please myself, not to please Paul, nor his mother either.'

'That's the spirit, Carmel,' Jane said approvingly.

'We'll all help,' Sylvia said.

'D'you know how to dance too?'

'Course, it's easy,' she said. 'I learned at school. Most girls did. We'll have you dancing the light fantastic in no time.'

'That will be one in the eye for your future mother-in-law,' Jane put in.

'Aye,' Carmel said and added, 'That's if she ever becomes my mother-in-law.'

'Carmel, what are you saying?'

'I'm saying that Paul had better apologise and realise how wrong he was because I won't tolerate being messed about like that ever again.'

'No one would blame you for that,' Sylvia said.

'Bloody parents,' Carmel said. 'Nothing but trouble, in my opinion. I mean, did you know I nearly told Paul it was all over because of mine? Huh, that would have pleased his damned mother.'

'How could your parents cause you to make a decision like that?' Jane said. 'You have been here for over two years.'

'It's all linked to my past,' Carmel said. 'The past that you are curious about, which I will tell you all about now, if you like.'

'Tonight I heard for the first time that your father is too sick to work,' Lois said. 'So, do you want to go on from there?'

140

'Hah, too bloody idle more like,' Carmel said, and added, 'the only sickness my father has is the one in his mind because you have to be sick to like inflicting cruelty like he does.'

The three girls didn't listen to the enfolding tale in silence as Paul had done. They stopped Carmel often to verify or elucidate something. As for Carmel, once she had begun, the words spilled from her mouth in her effort to rid herself of the burden that she had carried around with her for so long.

All the girls were shocked, but also outraged on Carmel's behalf.

'No man has a right to get away with this,' Lois said fiercely.

'Do you think I don't know that?' Carmel said testily. 'What's "right" got to do with anything? I'm ashamed I am even related to the man.'

She went on to tell them how it was for her mother and siblings; had been for her too until she had left. The others were shocked into silence as they listened to the true story of a family locked in a life of poverty and deprivation, made worse by the actions of a selfish brute of a father and could better understand Carmel's attitude to the poor in the Bull Ring.

'Anyway,' Carmel said at the end, 'with my father as an example, I had little time for men and long ago decided marriage was not for me. I didn't account for falling in love.'

'Yeah, that gets most of us in the end,' Lois said. 'But your marriage to Paul would be different altogether, Carmel. I think he would cut off his right arm before he would lay a hand on you.'

'I know that,' Carmel agreed happily. 'I have no worries on that score, but I did have concerns that I wasn't doing right by him, but he said he was marrying me, not my family, and the same goes for his too, I suppose. He isn't to blame for his bloody mother.'

'Why didn't you tell us what you were fretting over?' Lois asked. 'After all, we have become very close.'

'That was part of the reason I didn't,' Carmel said. 'You are the only friends I have ever had and I had never got in the habit of confiding in anyone, telling secrets, and I didn't want you all to look down on me.'

'Why should we?' Jane said.

'Anyway, true friends would never do that,' Lois said firmly.

'I know that now,' Carmel said. 'But I'd had no experience of friendship when I first arrived here.'

'I'm surprised that your father agreed to you coming here to take up nursing or any other damned thing,' Sylvia said. 'He sounds such a selfish brute.'

'He didn't agree,' Carmel cried. 'He nearly killed me.' She described the last beating she had endured at her father's hands and went on, 'And though it was bad, it was my passport to freedom because I confronted the priest and he too was shocked by the level of the violence used. He and Sister Frances fully supported me in the end. And then, once I was on my way here, I knew that I had won,' Carmel said. 'I had pulled myself out of the mire and I wanted to dust off the shame I had always felt about my family, leave it behind in Ireland and start here on equal terms with everyone else, almost as if my past had never happened.'

'I understand how you feel,' Sylvia said. 'But no one can ever do that.'

'I know that, but when you asked me things, I would find all the memories crowding back into my mind and I was scared that if you found out, you would all feel differently about me.'

'I do feel differently about you,' Jane said. 'I feel tremendous admiration for you. If I had to cope with all you did, I doubt that I would be here today. You must be a terrifically strong woman, Carmel, who will be able to cope with all that life might throw at you.'

'Let's hope it isn't all that much,' Sylvia said. 'We are all going to lead charmed lives, surely?'

'Course we are,' Lois said.

Suddenly, tears of gratitude for the friendship of the three girls stung Carmel's eyes.

'You are not crying,' Sylvia said accusingly.

'No,' Carmel said, giving a surreptitious sniff.

'God, but you are one bloody awful liar,' Sylvia said, giving Carmel a push.

Lois handed her a handkerchief she had tucked up her sleeve and Jane said, 'We'd best hit the sack. Sylvia and I are on earlies tomorrow and you will have to be up too if you are meeting lover boy.'

Carmel laughed. 'I'll have plenty of time, I'd say. Judging by the state he was in last night, I don't think he will be going anywhere till almost lunchtime.'

CHAPTER NINE

About the time Lois and Carmel, who had slept late, were tucking into their breakfast, Emma was tapping on her elder son's door. She had a tray with a cup of tea and plate of hot buttered toast on it, together with a couple of aspirins.

'Come on, darling. Rise and shine,' she said as she entered the room.

Paul opened his heavy pain-filled eyes reluctantly. God, he felt rough. His mouth was so dry it hurt to swallow, and he felt as sick as a dog. He knew he couldn't stomach anything to eat, but the tea looked good and he could definitely do with the aspirins, if he could just sit up without throwing up.

His mother put the tray on the bedside table and opened the curtains. Sunshine spilled into the room.

'Ouch,' said Paul. 'I don't think the sun should be allowed to shine so brightly so early in the morning.'

'It's not early in the morning, it's after nine,' Emma said. 'And a beautiful day that you are missing.'

'To me that's early,' Paul said. 'I have a bloody awful

headache and don't feel too hot, to tell you the truth. What's the panic, in any case?'

'The headache is self-induced,' Emma said unsympathetically. 'You did imbibe rather freely yesterday. Never mind, darling – it was your party, after all. A trip to the sea is just the thing for a raging hangover, and days as warm as this don't happen much this late in September.'

'What are you on about?'

'We are spending the day with the Chisholms on their yacht.'

'What?' Paul cried, sitting upright in the bed, and holding his hands to his aching head.

'You heard what I said.'

'I thought I did,' Paul said. 'I thought you said we are spending the day with the Chisholms.'

'That's right. Melissa asked you especially and you said it sounded just the thing.'

'But Carmel and I are choosing the ring today.'

Emma laughed. 'Is that wise, my son, all this haste to get engaged? Are you really ready to settle down? Going by your behaviour at the party I would say maybe you need to play the field a little longer. If fact, if that young nurse has one spark of pride, she'll not want anything more to do with you ever again, never mind getting engaged.'

The events of the party were hazy to Paul, and from the time the meal was finished, some areas were complete and utter blanks. He took a couple of grateful swallows of the hot sweet tea, before asking, almost in a whisper, 'What did I do?'

'What didn't you do?' Emma said, embellishing a little. 'You were kissing and cuddling Melissa and her sister,

Kate, and Penelope Crabtree all night, and in full view of everyone – Carmel too, I might add – and holding them almost indecently close when you danced. It was Melissa you took outside later – that was fortunately after Carmel had left – and both of you came back very dishevelled. I do think, Paul, it was a very shabby way to treat a girl you purport to be fond of.'

'I am more than fond of Carmel, Mother,' Paul said with a hint of exasperation. 'I have told you this before. I love her.'

'Funny way you had of showing it, that's all I can say,' Emma said through tightened lips. 'And kindly do not use that tone with me. I was not the one who behaved so disgracefully.'

Paul was suddenly engulfed with shame for what he had put Carmel through. He had been drunk, very drunk, but that was no excuse for the conduct his mother had described. It was imperative now that he saw Carmel and tried to explain and, most of all, apologise, beg her forgiveness and promise that such a thing would never happen again.

'You put the girl into an almost impossible situation,' Emma told her son irritably. 'All it did was show her how out of place she was. She is not of our set or class and never will be. Can't you see that?'

Paul could hardly believe what his mother had just said. He finished the tea and replaced it on the tray before saying, 'You, Mother, are a snob and living in the last century. It is not all this class-conscious and knowing-your-place stuff at the hospital, Mother. There it is totally different.'

'It is not snobbish to know where you stand in the social

order,' Emma protested. 'And you mock people knowing their place, but let me tell you, it oils the wheels that civilisation runs on. Not everyone can be a boss. Don't bite the hand that feeds you, Paul,' she chided. 'If we hadn't had the means to finance you, you would be no doctor, so don't go all high and mighty on me now. You have a duty to us, your parents, and the class you were born into to take your proper place in society once you have finished this compulsory year at the hospital.'

'I am grateful for your help and support,' Paul said. Then added, 'I wasn't aware it came with conditions.'

'Don't be like this, Paul,' Emma said. 'It's just when all this socialist claptrap is over and you go into private practice, when you take a wife, she will need to have the right sort of breeding and gentility to help further your career.'

'Someone like Melissa, in fact, who wouldn't go along with the socialist claptrap at all?'

Emma missed the sarcasm in Paul's voice and the sardonic glint in his eye. 'Exactly like Melissa,' she said, 'Now, your father has been making an few enquiries and he says—'

'Mother,' Paul said in slight amazement, 'you do not know me at all. There is no way on God's earth I want either to marry Melissa or to have a private practice.'

'Don't be so foolish, Paul. Of course you do.'

'No, Mother, I do not,' Paul said. 'Anyway, if you will excuse me I need to dress. I have a date with a beautiful girl who I know will be waiting for me.'

'But what about the Chisholms?' Emma cried. 'Melissa will be so disappointed.'

'Haven't you listened to a word I've said?' Paul cried,

exasperated. 'I can't go. You must see that. I have a prior engagement,' he added with a slight smile.

'You can't do this,' Emma cried. 'You can't shame me in this way. At the party you agreed. You said it was a grand idea.'

'Then you must apologise on my behalf,' Paul said. 'But you know as well as I that the arrangements I made with Melissa and her parents, I wasn't really capable of making. Take Matthew to make up the numbers.'

'Matthew is dead to the world,' Emma said. 'And likely to remain so for many hours. Anyway, they don't want Matthew. It is you Melissa is sweet on.'

'That is the very thing I don't want to encourage,' Paul said. 'You said I am not ready to settle down, Mother, but I am; with the right girl I am more than ready and that girl is Carmel. So, if that is all, Mother, I really have got to get dressed.'

Emma gave Paul a baleful look as she swept angrily from the room.

Paul did feel guilty about upsetting his mother, but not half as guilty as he would have done if he had let Carmel down. Despite the claim that he was not up to rushing, he leaped from the bed as soon as the door closed and dressed as quickly as he could, ignoring his thumping head and churning stomach, desperate to be out of the house and on his way to meet Carmel.

After Carmel had eaten breakfast, she returned to the room with Lois and changed into the outfit she had specially chosen for the day she would spend with Paul. The dress was pale green and had a matching jacket. She had bought it in the second-hand stall in the market and although it had been cheap enough, with the vagaries of the British climate, she had thought at the time that she mighty get little wear out of it. But it was made for a day such as this. The September sun shone down from a sky of Wedgwood blue and the only clouds were light and fluffy.

'It sets your hair off beautifully,' Lois said enviously. 'You lucky thing. All you need do is brush it and it falls into natural curls and looks terrific. You just need a wee bit of powder . . .'

'Oh, I don't know Lois,' Carmel said, for she wasn't at all sure about using cosmetics.

'Do you want to meet Paul with a shiny nose?'

'Oh God!' cried Carmel, her hands flying to her face. 'Have I a shiny nose?'

'No,' said Lois with a smile, 'but are you prepared to run the risk of getting one? Come on now, trust Auntie Lois.'

A few minutes later in the washroom, with powder dusted across her face, rouge on her cheeks, brown shadow on the lids of her eyes and her lips scarlet, Carmel gazed at her reflection in the mirror.

'I don't look fast, do I?' she asked worriedly.

'No,' Lois stated. 'Why should you? How can you think that just because you are wearing cosmetics to enhance your natural beauty? It isn't a sin, Carmel. You're not in some little town in Ireland now either, but in Birmingham where people think it is all right to get dressed up, made up and off out to have a good time.'

Carmel was still biting her bottom lip in uncertainty and Lois caught hold of her hands. 'Listen to me,' she said. 'You are a truly beautiful girl and out in the street there will be few to even come close to you. You will dazzle the eyes from Paul when he sees you. Now will you stop fretting? This lesser mortal, namely me, needs to get herself ready for her own day out with her own man and, God knows, I will have to work harder than you for less effect. So, I would be obliged if you would stop worrying and sling your hook while I start on myself.'

Carmel left Lois alone, but she was at a loose end. She felt overdressed for the common room and yet her nerves were jumping about too much for her to settle to read. The room too was rather stuffy and she wished she could go outside and wait for Paul, but she was certain sure that Lois would frown on that idea and say it made her look forward and quite desperate.

The fact was, she *was* desperate. After that awful party, she needed to see that Paul had not changed, that he loved her still and as soon as she saw him she would know.

Lois had finished her ablutions, dressed in her finery and gone out to meet Chris before eventually Sister Magee knocked on the door and said that Dr Connolly was waiting for Carmel downstairs. She stopped only to pick up her bag, before flying down to meet him. She took in his slightly bloodshot eyes as she came closer, and guessed he would be suffering a hangover, but she saw also those eyes were full of love for her and she felt her whole body relax.

Paul thought he had never seen anything lovelier than the sight of Carmel that day, descending the stairs at a rate of knots in her beautifully made clothes and smart high-heeled shoes. But better by far was the love light shining in her beautiful eyes, and he felt his heart skip a beat and his stomach tighten. He knew he would love Carmel and only Carmel till the breath left his body, and that a lifetime wouldn't be long enough to show her how much he loved her.

He caught her up in his arms at the bottom of the steps and swung her round. 'I am so sorry I am late,' he said, seeing her face light up with delight and a little relief. 'To my shame I overslept.'

'It's all right,' Carmel assured him. 'We hadn't specified a time.'

'Even so . . .'

Carmel didn't want to discuss it further, discuss anything at all under the watchful eye of the home sister. She could see Sister Magee's lips pursed tight in disapproval and knew that though she would say nothing to Paul – for he was now Dr Connolly, no errant medical student – she could say plenty to Carmel on her return about the proper way to behave.

'You still do want to marry me?' Paul asked, as the two of them made for the city centre, remembering his mother's words that morning.

'What a question!' Carmel said. 'What made you ask it?'

'I thought maybe you had doubts,' Paul said. 'After the party, I mean.'

It was on the tip of Carmel's tongue to say that it was all right now, that she had no problem. However, there were unresolved issues from that party that she had been dreadfully upset about. If she didn't speak of this now, while she had the chance, it could easily fester in her head and cause suspicion to enter and maybe spoil their relationship.

And so she said, 'We do need to talk about what happened at that party, Paul, but not in the street. Let's go to a coffee house and discuss it properly.'

Neither Paul nor Carmel spoke until the coffee was before them, and then Paul reached across and took hold of Carmel's hands.

'I want to apologise for the awful time you had at the party. I can, in all truth, remember little of it, but my mother filled in many of the blanks, and even the bits I can recall I am bitterly ashamed of.'

'I'm glad you feel that way, truly I am,' Carmel said. 'For I have seldom been as miserable as I was last night. To see you with other girls draped all over you and you seeming not to care, lapping it up, rather . . .'

'They are girls I have known for years,' Paul put in defensively.

'I know, your mother told me that,' Carmel said. 'She actually took great pleasure in telling me. The point is, Paul, it really doesn't make a ha'p'orth of difference how long you have known someone; there is a way to behave when you are promised to another and in my opinion you went way, way beyond that. I mean,' she went on, 'how would you feel if a few fellows were to come here from Ireland and I was to sit kissing and cuddling them and tell you that it was all right, that I had known them all my life? Would that be all right with you, Paul?'

Just the thought of another man putting his arms around Carmel made Paul feel sick and he realised how deeply he must have hurt her. 'No, of course it wouldn't, and I quite see that that was very wrong. The girls weren't aware I wasn't available.'

'I know that, but you did, and so you shouldn't have entered into it quite so wholeheartedly,' Carmel said. 'Anyway this whole thing was engineered by your mother.'

'How do you mean?'

'I mean this business of not telling people we were engaged until we got the ring and made the announcement properly,' Carmel said. 'The announcement could have been made at the party, made part of the celebrations. You had been in hospital for weeks. No one would think it strange that we hadn't bought a ring yet, and those girls would know then that you were spoken for. You have done them a disservice too, because you were sending them the wrong messages, especially the tall one with blonde hair.'

'Melissa?'

Carmel shrugged. 'If that is her name, yes, Melissa.'

'She and I were rather a couple before I began medical school,' Paul said.

'Well, she wouldn't be averse to taking up again where you left off,' Carmel said. 'She made that patently obvious.'

Paul knew Carmel spoke the truth. His mother had actually said that she was still sweet on him and she had also said he took her outside and they came back looking dishevelled. He could remember nothing and just hoped he hadn't gone too far with her.

'Paul, what is it?' Carmel said, noticing his preoccupation.

Paul made an effort to pull himself together. Carmel must never know about that. 'Nothing,' he said. 'The point is, Melissa and I were just kids then, and we both agreed we were too young. I was off to med school and she had her higher certificate to do and then was off to finishing school in Switzerland for two years.'

'Well,' Carmel commented drily. 'Melissa is no longer a kid and I would say has been finished off very nicely. Now she is a very beautiful young lady who wants Dr Paul Connolly and nothing would please your mother more.'

Paul didn't deny it. He might have done but for the words he had had with his mother that morning. He nodded his head. 'Melissa probably did want that,' he said. 'And I must take some responsibility for it because I made no effort to put her straight. In fact, I played along with her so that, in all fairness, she could easily think that I was as interested as she was. As for my mother . . . look, Carmel, you may as well know, because I want no secrets between us. Apparently sometime yesterday evening, after you left, I agreed to go sailing today with Melissa and her family. I had no recollection of it and was in no fit state to make any sort of arrangement by then anyway.'

'What happened?'

'Well, I'm here, aren't I?'

'That isn't what I asked.'

'All right,' Paul said with a sigh. 'I had a row with my mother and refused to even think about going sailing with Melissa or anyone else. And you are right: she admitted she would like Melissa or someone like her to be my wife eventually.'

'Did she actually say so?'

'This morning she did,' Paul said. 'She has my whole

future mapped out. She wants me to marry someone like Melissa and then, when I have finished the stint at the Queen's Hospital, she wants me in a private practice.'

'And Melissa would be a more suitable wife for you in that sort of life,' Carmel said. 'She said as much to me. And how do you feel, Paul?'

'Do you need to ask?'

'Yes,' Carmel said. 'Yes, I really think I do, because this isn't just about your mother; it is about you and being responsible for your actions and not making excuses and blaming others.'

'What do you mean?'

'I'll tell you what I mean,' Carmel said. 'You knew that I would be nervous in those surroundings. I never knew you lived in such luxury, with servants and everything.'

'We haven't – well, I mean, not that many servants, only a cook, a daily and a gardener. All the others were hired for the evening.'

'Lois said that too. She was surprised the whole thing was so extravagant. I think your mother planned that to make me feel even more inadequate and I can tell you now, she succeeded.'

Paul looked sheepish. Carmel was no fool and she had just hit the nail on the head.

'And then we went to dinner and things got worse,' Carmel continued. 'I hadn't a clue what cutlery or glass to use and you knew that too. You told me to watch you and then spent almost the entire meal talking to your mother and what I saw most of the time was your back.'

Paul remembered that his mother had seemed to have a lot to talk about with him. If he did turn around to see how Carmel was getting on, his mother would be plucking at his sleeve to bring his attention back to her, and his wine glass, he recalled, was constantly full. He faced the fact that his mother had gone out of her way to scare Carmel off and though he resented her for this, he hated himself more for not even trying to do something about it.

'I can't tell you how bad I feel about all this,' Paul said. 'To be perfectly honest, after the meal much is hazy, but I do remember when the dancing began you were sitting as far away from me as you could be. Was that Mother's doing as well?'

'Of course it was,' Carmel said. 'She was trying her best to split us up.'

'Carmel,' said Paul, 'my mother said this morning that she wouldn't be surprised if you didn't want to see me any more and now I understand why. I behaved disgracefully towards you. I promise here and now that such a thing will never happen again.'

'No, it won't,' Carmel said fiercely. 'Because I won't go to your house again. If ever I have to meet your parents I will meet them on neutral ground somewhere.'

'I don't blame you at all,' Paul said. 'And knowing how my mother feels and what she is capable of, though I had thought I would stay at home for a little while and my mother expects it, I will go into lodgings with Chris. We've talked about it anyway. One thing I do know, I will not stay at home and have my mother nearly pushing me into Melissa's arms at every opportunity.'

'Would she still do that even if we were officially engaged?'

'She might easily if she could convince herself that it

was for my own good,' Paul said grimly. 'Anyway, I am not prepared to risk it. Come on,' he said, standing up and pulling Carmel to her feet, 'let us away to choose the ring so that everyone knows where my heart lies.'

The ring Carmel chose, a larger diamond surrounded by a cluster of smaller ones, was not the dearest in the jeweller's range by any means. Though it did look perfect on Carmel's hand, the man knew many women would have gone for the most expensive, whether suitable or not. He warmed to the young and very handsome couple and he congratulated them heartily and wished them a happy marriage well blessed with children.

Carmel said nothing about this until they were aboard the train that was taking them to the huge park in Sutton Coldfield where they had decided to spend the day. Then she said, 'Paul, you know what the jeweller said about children?'

'Mmm,'

'Well, the thing is, I don't want any.'

'I don't either,' Paul said. 'Not yet, anyway.'

'I mean not ever,' Carmel insisted.

'Oh, darling, ever is a long time,' Paul said.

'I mean it, though, Paul. I have seen enough of children to last me a lifetime and, anyway, I want to nurse.' She bit her lip in consternation and said, 'I just hope I won't be expected to give it up once I am married.'

'Why should you?'

'Well, you know, there are stupid rules and things,' Carmel said. 'And Matron was far from happy when I got engaged.'

'We'll look into it,' Paul promised. 'But it would be

mad to throw out all the nurses they had spent four years training, just because they became hitched. When they start a family it might be different.'

'That is just what I mean. And that might happen to me unless we do something about it, and that is down to you really.'

'You know what you are asking?'

'Of course I know, and that does concern me because it is totally against what the Catholic Church teaches. Does that worry you?'

'Not unduly,' Paul had to admit. 'I mean, what does a celibate priest know about the sins and temptations of the flesh? Don't fret yourself, Carmel. I will see to this and there will be no children until you give the word. Tell you the truth, I can take or leave children. It is you I want to marry, you I love, and we will play this whichever way you want to.'

Was there ever such a man? Carmel asked herself. People so selfless were few and far between, be they man or woman, and she knew that she had found herself a gem in Paul.

When they alighted from the train, Paul first took Carmel for some lunch at the edge of the town, not far from one of the park's many entrances. She was almost too nervous and excited to do the meal justice, but Paul more than made up for it.

'First thing I have been able to stomach today,' he said. 'I don't usually get into a state like I did last night, you know. It isn't normal behaviour.'

'I know that,' Carmel said. 'Don't worry about it now. We have discussed it and needn't ever refer to it again.'

'I don't intend to,' said Paul. 'Except to say that it would have been far better all round to have defied my mother and introduced you as my intended, my fiancée, where you would have taken your rightful place at my side, where you will be from now on, never fear.'

'I don't fear, Paul,' Carmel said reassuringly. 'In fact I fear nothing. The future looks rosy from where I am sitting.'

'Well, let's take a gander through the park and see what it looks like from there,' Paul said. 'Have you ever been?'

Carmel shook her head. 'The others have. Lois said it is massive and there are roads running through it. You can take a car in and most people have to pay.'

'That's right,' Paul said. 'Everyone has to pay unless you live in Sutton Coldfield, as I do, and then you get a pass.'

'I have never heard of paying to get into a park,' Carmel said.

'You will probably have never seen a place like this,' Paul maintained. 'Wait and see.'

Paul was right. Although roads did wind around the park, it was big enough for he and Carmel to be able to find secluded areas. They walked along woodland paths, where the fallen leaves rustled beneath their feet and those still on the trees were painted in wonderous shades of brown and orange. Sometimes, they came to the edge of the woodland and before them there was pasture land. Carmel was surprised to see cows gazing, watching them pass with doe-like eyes. She asked Paul about it.

'The park was given to the people of Sutton Coldfield

by Henry the Eighth,' Paul explained. 'I don't know if you learned about the chap in Ireland.'

Carmel shook her head. She had learned only Irish history at school. She had been born in 1913 and by the time she was ready for school, 'The Troubles', forerunner of the Civil War, was raging through the land and everything Irish was the rule in the schools.

'Well,' Paul went on, 'when, under Catholic law, Henry wasn't allowed to marry his second wife while his first was alive, he divorced the first woman and set up his own religion where divorce was allowed. Kings could do that then. Anyway, one good thing he did do was to give this enormous tract of land to the people of Sutton with permission for certain farmers to graze their cattle on it.'

'It's nice to see them,' Carmel said. 'I always had a soft spot for cows. I like the sound of water too.'

Nowhere in the park was far away from streams and rivulets, chuckling and rippling across their stony beds on their way to feed the five large lakes. When they came upon the first one, Carmel gasped in pleasure.

Paul pulled her down on a grassy incline. 'God, I am melting,' he said, taking off his jacket and pulling off his tie, which he stuffed in his pocket. 'Aren't you?

Carmel giggled. 'I know you're hot,' she said. 'Your face is the colour of a tomato. I'm not bad – my clothes are lighter than yours anyway – but if we are to sit here for a while, I will take off my jacket.'

Paul helped her and then, throwing her jacket to one side, he pushed Carmel back on the grass. 'Oh, Carmel, I love you so much,' he said, his voice husky with desire.

Carmel wriggled beside him with pleasure and

returned his kisses unreservedly. She had wondered if, now they were properly engaged with a ring to seal it, Paul might want to move their fairly chaste courtship up a notch and didn't know how she would react, how she *should* react, if he did that. No one ever talked about that side of things. All her mother had ever told her was, 'Be a good girl and respect yourself, for if you don't no man will respect you.'

So what should a girl do when she is lying on the grass beside a man she loves more than life itself and tingling with desire? And then Carmel stopped trying to analyse it and gave herself up to the pleasure of kissing and caressing Paul.

Paul very much wanted to make love to his wonderful, luscious Carmel. The longing for her was pounding through his veins. He had had quite a few sexual encounters, even with Melissa, who had enjoyed sex quite as much as he had, but he knew with Carmel it would be different and he decided to take his time. He sensed the passion in her and he guessed eventually she would be as eager as he was to consummate their relationship. Until then, he decided, he would have patience, knowing that it would be all the sweeter for the wait.

And so he did nothing to alarm Carmel, and she felt the tension ease in him and began to relax herself. She knew, despite her naïvety in these matters, that though they lay for some time entwined together kissing and embracing, Paul would ask no more than this, although she had no idea what it cost him to put such a brake on his feelings.

Many hours later, after a sumptuous tea, they took the train to New Street Station, walked from there through the balmy streets, and Carmel couldn't remember a time when she had felt so happy. When they reached the door of the nurses' home, Paul drew Carmel into his arms and held her tight as his lips descended on hers and she was transported to paradise.

All too soon it was over and she was the other side of the door. She had a sense of unreality as she sort of floated up to her room.

Inside, though all were agog to see the ring, Lois had news of her own. She too had a ring adorning her left finger because she had become engaged to Chris that day. The two girls hugged each other in shared delight.

CHAPTER TEN

Jeff Connolly was feeling very mellow. They had had a lovely day sailing the coast with the Chisholms. Pity that Melissa had got in a sulk about something or other. In fact, none of the woman had been right, except Melissa's younger sister, Kate, and she had been like the cat with the cream, as if she was pleased about whatever it was troubling her sister. Maybe they had had a row, for whatever it was affected the mother too, and even Emma was a bit scratchy.

When Emma had told him that morning that Paul wouldn't be joining them, Jeff hadn't been surprised. Paul had told him early the previous evening that Carmel had the whole day off and they intending buying the ring.

'Last night he promised to come sailing with us,' she said, tight-lipped.

'Did he?' Jeff asked in surprise. 'If he did, I doubt he would have remembered it. In fact, I have very little knowledge of anything much myself after the meal, especially after we all cut big holes in the brandy bottles. You could have told me I had signed my own death warrant and I still wouldn't have any sort of recall about it. I do remember Paul being in the same state as myself or worse, and a promise from a drunken man is no promise at all. Before the party, when he was stone-cold sober, he told me he was off to buy the ring today to make it official with the wee nurse he is so fond of.'

'That is the problem.'

'What is?' Jeff asked, perplexed.

'Oh! Men!' Emma shrieked, almost beside herself with frustration. 'What on earth is the use of talking to them? They understand nothing of any importance.'

After that, the atmosphere was strained, to say the least, and within minutes of meeting the Chisholms, Jeff realised Charlie Chisholm was having similar trouble with his own womenfolk.

'What's up?' he asked as he and Charlie loaded the car.

Charlie spread his arms and gave a shrug. 'How would I, a mere man, know what goes on in a woman's head?' he asked with a sardonic grin. 'All I know is that if I am not very careful, it will somehow turn out to be my fault. And I will tell you this, Jeff, with this little lot, if you upset one then you upset them all. I keep my head down and my mouth shut, and I am bloody glad that you are coming along today or it would have been damned miserable. I tell you, man, you don't know you are born with sons.'

Jeff had thought so too, but now he looked at one of those sons, standing glowering before him, and wondered what had put him in such a tear. Jeff and Charlie had been drinking most of the day on and off, and when they arrived home, the cook had a marvellous dinner waiting, which just screamed for plenty of wine to wash it down.

He had been glad when Emma declared she was off to bed straight after dinner. He valued time to himself, and he was into his second brandy when Paul came in and demanded to know what he was playing at.

'In what connection?' Jeff asked mildly. 'Why don't you help yourself to a brandy and sit down and we will talk about this?'

Paul did as his father suggested and then said, 'Mother said you had been finding out about a private practice for me.'

'Your mother said that is what you wanted,' Jeff said. 'I was just doing what I was told. I was surprised, knowing your politics and social conscience, but I thought you were examining all the options.'

'And you had no idea that Mother thinks I should marry Melissa or someone like her, who would make a more suitable wife for me?'

'I had no idea at all,' said Jeff grimly. Suddenly he knew that Paul's party, which had been ostentatious enough to make even him feel uncomfortable, would have made Carmel feel really out of place, and that that had been Emma's intention. No wonder the girl had often looked downright miserable. And then eliciting a promise from her drunken son, when she knew he had already made arrangements of his own, was a despicable thing to do.

However, Emma's scheme to throw Melissa in his son's path had gone awry. Charlie Chisholm's wife, Millicent, and his elder daughter had spent the day sulking about it and only Kate, always jealous of Paul's obvious preference for her sister, had been pleased he hadn't turned up after all.

Jeff glanced across at his son and said, 'I'll tell you the right sort of wife to have: one that loves you, heart, body and soul, and one that you love the same way. Love like that will stand against all of life's knocks and I think that the right wife for you is that wee nurse. I would feel less for you if you were to throw her over for Melissa, or anyone else you might have a passing fancy for.'

'I have no passing fancy for anyone and I love Carmel so much it hurts,' Paul confessed. 'Today, as I told you, I have bought her a ring and you can tell Mother she can announce it to anyone she likes, but there is to be no party. It will only be another occasion to belittle and humiliate Carmel. Anyway,' he went on, 'after Mother's behaviour, which I feel is unforgivable, I will be moving out as soon as possible into lodgings with Chris for the time being.'

'I do understand how you feel, son, don't think I don't,' Jeff said. 'But this will cut your mother to the quick. She thought she would have you home for a good few months.'

Paul gave a humourless laugh. 'Huh, course she did, so that she can work on me and see if she can turn me from Carmel and mould me into the kind of doctor son she wants,' Paul said with a trace of bitterness. 'With the wife she has had a hand in choosing. No thanks, Dad. She has cooked her own goose and only has herself to blame. My mind is made up.'

Jeff saw there was nothing more to say. His son was a man and he had made a man's decision. He clapped him on the shoulder. 'Never tell your mother,' he said, 'but I am proud of you and, all things considered, think you are doing the right thing. Your mother won't see it

166

in the same light, but for what it's worth, you have my blessing.'

'It's worth a great deal, Dad,' Paul said, extending his hand to his father. 'Thanks.'

Jeff grasped Paul's hand and the two shook in mutual respect.

Emma was dismayed when Paul told her the next day that he was engaged to Carmel.

'I suggest you hotfoot it over to Melissa and tell her and any other young ladies who might have thought I was available,' Paul told her almost coldly. 'Whatever happened at that party, I am now spoken for, well and truly.'

Emma recovered herself. The man wasn't married yet and couldn't marry for some time, for he had told his father they were waiting until Carmel qualified. Before then Emma would make sure Carmel would be made well aware of her shortcomings as the proposed wife of an up-and-coming doctor at the lavish engagement party she would organise.

Paul, watching his mother's face, could guess her thoughts and before she could give voice to them, he said, 'There will be no engagement party, which will only be an excuse for you to try and humiliate Carmel, as you did on the last occasion that she was in the house.'

'Paul, I—'

'Don't give me innocence and excuses,' Paul said. 'I know you too well, Mother, and now I know what you are capable of I feel I cannot stay on here as we planned. I intend to move out as soon as I can.'

The blood drained from Emma's face. Paul was her

darling, favourite son. 'You . . . you can't do this, Paul,' she pleaded, her hand to her throat.

Paul had usually given in to Emma's wishes in the past. He had always been a compliant boy who hated unpleasantness, but now there was Carmel to consider. Remembering her hurt and slightly reproachful eyes on him as she recounted the events at the party that he knew his mother had engineered much of, he hardened his heart.

'I'm sorry, Mother, but I can,' he said. 'It is best in the long run, because I know how you feel about Carmel and so does she. She has no real desire to come here again and so getting my own place makes a great deal of sense.'

Emma, knowing her elder son's soft centre, tried again. 'Paul, you will break my heart if you leave.'

'And Carmel's if I stay,' Paul said. 'Don't worry, Mother. Your heart is safe. Hearts are not that easy to break.'

'Paul, what has got into you?' Emma pleaded.

'Nothing has "got into me", Mother,' Paul said. 'But my mind is made up.'

Emma saw the lift of his chin and knew she had lost him to Carmel Duffy. Suddenly she was very angry. She'd had Paul's life planned out from when he was a little boy, certain that she would always be able to influence him to her way of thinking.

Her eyes filled with malice and discontent, her mouth set in a sneer and her voice was clipped as she spat out, 'Well then, go. Stay grubbing about in a voluntary hospital all the days of your life and living hand-to-mouth in some slum, which is probably only what Carmel is used to anyway. But if you insist upon this course of action, you'll not get a penny piece from us.'

'I don't want it,' Paul said. 'I am grateful that you sponsored me through medical school, but any financial contributions seem to be given with conditions and I could never meet those.'

Emma watched Paul stride from the room, his back straight and his head held high. Then, as the door closed behind him, just as suddenly as her anger had flared in her it extinguished itself, leaving her with just an unbearable sadness, a feeling that something had been broken, maybe irretrievably, and she sank onto the settee in tears.

Paul never told Carmel of this conversation with his mother, nor of the strained atmosphere in the house. A couple of evenings later, the family had sat around a tense dinner where Emma's words to anyone, if she had to speak at all, dropped from her mouth like chips of ice.

Matthew, now back from the Sorbonne and waiting to start at the factory with his father in a few days' time, said afterwards to Paul, 'What the hell have you done or said to upset Mother? Whatever it is, fix it, for God's sake. She is like a bear with a sore head and Dad is bearing the brunt of it.'

'I know and I do feel sorry for Dad, but there is nothing I can do,' Paul said. 'This is all because I have told Mother that I am moving out instead of staying here, as planned.'

'Well, you knew that wouldn't suit, didn't you?' Matthew said sneeringly. 'Seeing as our dear mama thinks the sun shines out of your arse.'

'Don't be so coarse.'

'Mind you,' Matthew went on, don't blame you wanting your own pad. That ring might choose to be an investment after all. Everyone knows about nurses and about how they can't get enough of it. I bet your Carmel is a right little goer.'

'Look, I told you at the party, mind your own business.'

Matthew just laughed. 'I am only jealous,' he said. 'God, if you were determined to tie yourself down, you could do worse than latch up with Carmel. She is a stunner.'

'Glad you approve,' Paul commented drily. 'You can admire from a distance, but don't you dare lay a hand on her.'

''S all right,' Matthew said. 'She's not that keen on me, I think. Likes the old man, though, and he likes her well enough too, but that, of course, doesn't go down too well with the old mater either.'

It didn't at all. That night Emma accused Jeff of being all for the match and when he said he couldn't see much wrong with the girl and he refused to see Paul to try to 'talk some sense into him', Emma flew into such a rage that he was given the silent treatment and banished to the guest bedroom.

Carmel knew none of this. She had worries of her own and these were down to her work on the wards. She was now in her third year and expected to deal more personally with the patients. She learned among other things, to treat infected wounds using sulphonamide cream spread on rolls of lint. She was also shown how to give intramuscular injections into the thigh, administer a bladder wash out, and chest drainage, and how to insert a Ryles stomach tube.

'It isn't that I don't know how to do all these things,' she complained to Lois. 'I mean, I do it, and right most of the time. But it is remembering it all step by step and explaining it in an exam that I am worried about.'

'I know just what you mean,' Lois said. 'When you are in the throes of anything that you are doing like that, you do it as if it is second nature because you have to. It isn't something you think about or take a study of. And you know what else bothers me? You said you do it right most of the time and so do I. Say we pass our exams and we are let us loose on the wards afterwards, we can't afford to make mistakes because we are dealing with people's lives.'

'I know. Scary, isn't it?'

'Not half,' Lois said fervently. 'And I really wish that we hadn't got to do nights in the new year. I think I need more practice on the wards with wide-awake patients needing treatment.'

'Me too,' Carmel agreed glumly 'And then, of course, we will never have a hope in hell's chance of seeing either Paul or Chris.'

'No change there then,' said Lois, because the scant time the men had off seldom coincided with the girls'. They both said they would be more fed up with this if they hadn't each other for company, for as nice and under-standing as Jane and Sylvia tried to be, they weren't expe-riencing such frustrations on a day-to-day basis as Carmel and Lois. Their boyfriends worked more normal hours and they could nearly always see them in their free time.

Carmel often used free time to practise dance steps. She had thrown herself into ballroom dancing as soon as Lois's father had arrived with the gramophone and stack of records a week or so after the awful party.

'There are five main dances,' Lois had said that first day, as she wound up the gramophone. 'And they are the slow waltz, the viennese waltz, the foxtrot, the tango and the quickstep. There are lots more, of course, as well as the young people's dances my sister, Susan, taught me, like the shimmy, the black bottom and the charleston. They're great fun. We used to dance them in the bedroom on the quiet because Mother, of course, didn't approve, but the ballroom dances will do for now. We will have a go at the slow waltz first because it is the easiest and we won't progress to something else until you feel confident about that. All right?'

Carmel had nodded eagerly and seconds later the haunting music of Strauss filled the air.

Carmel was used to listening to and moving with music and she was also agile and keen to learn, so she proved a natural-born dancer.

She wasn't content, though, with just being able to dance; she wanted to dance well, really well, and she was constantly rolling back the rugs and practising the steps. Lois would help her, taking the man's role, full of admiration for the dedicated way Carmel had approached ballroom dancing. Lois knew when Carmel had the opportunity to show her skill and expertise in front of her future mother-in-law, the woman would be astounded and she hoped she was there to see the look on her Aunt Emma's face.

'Does your mother know about Paul?' Lois said when they were halfway though their night duty in the new year.

'Well she knows that I am seeing him, though just at the moment, not seeing him would be more accurate,' Carmel said.

'You haven't said that you are engaged?'

'No.'

'Why not?'

'No reason really,' Carmel said. 'They would probably wonder at the length of the engagement, because the wedding is going to be over a year away yet. Plenty of time to let them know.'

Lois could read Carmel like a book. She looked at her and said, 'You don't want any of them to come at all, do you?'

'No, if I am honest,' Carmel admitted. 'If they came, I just know that they would show me up, and I know it's not nice, but I am ashamed of them. Anyway, they wouldn't have suitable clothes and they wouldn't be able to raise the fare.'

'Then shouldn't you go over there? Wouldn't your mother at least like to meet the man her eldest daughter is marrying?'

'Time enough,' Carmel said. 'And don't raise your eyes to the ceiling, Lois. You know that Paul has barely time to blow his nose, never mind gallivant over to Ireland. And just how many times have they made arrangements with us, only to break them at the last minute?'

'Too many times,' Lois said grimly. 'And I do hear what you say, but your family will have to know sometime.'

'After I have taken the exams I will concentrate on it,' Camel promised. 'Mammy will want to know how I did anyway. When Paul and Chris have done a full year in September maybe life will settle down more.'

'And maybe pigs might fly,' Lois said.

'They just might,' Carmel agreed, and the two girls laughed together.

Carmel had thought that her twenty-first birthday would pass unnoticed like the previous one, which was annoying because she finished her spell of night duty just beforehand and that meant she had the day of her birthday and the day after off duty. She tried very hard not to feel sorry for herself.

'We have to go out for a drink at least,' Jane said.

Carmel wasn't keen. Pubs weren't her favourite places, but she knew that Jane and Sylvia were trying to be kind and so she agreed to go – to find half the staff at the hospital gathered in the back room of the pub, which Jane and Sylvia had decorated for Carmel's coming of age. She was so overcome with their thought-fulness and kindness that she felt tears sting the back of her eyes and knew she was lucky to have so many good friends.

She didn't let anyone see the tears and threw herself into enjoying the party, knowing this was the way to please them most. She was even inveigled into drinking the odd glass of sweet white wine instead of her more usual orange juice.

She had been at the party more than an hour or so when Paul turned up. Though Carmel noticed the fatigue etched on his grey face and the bags beneath his slightly rheumy eyes, she said nothing, knowing Paul wouldn't want her to. She loved the gold locket he gave her, which she would treasure always, but most of all she was glad to see him. She wanted to feel his arms around her, his lips on hers. Paul was more than willing to oblige and Carmel returned to the nurses' home happier and more content than she had been for a long time.

Then it was heads down to revise for the final exams. There were three components: written, oral and practical. Everyone during this time was very stressed, constantly testing themselves and one another, and convinced they were all going to fail drastically.

On the day of the exam itself, Carmel was given practical tasks that she could do well and efficiently. She could answer all the oral questions without faltering, and when she turned over the written paper, all the things she thought had flown out of her head came back to her.

'I think it went all right,' she told Paul, who arrived that evening with Chris to see how the girls had got on.

'I don't doubt it for a minute,' Paul said. 'And I'm sure that you're going to pass with flying colours. Now that you've got that out of the way, you must write to your parents.'

Immediately the image of her bullying father towering over her cowering mother with his fist balled, a scenario she had witnessed many times, superimposed itself over the memories of the day, yet she said, 'I know.'

'And,' added Paul, 'so must I.'

'You?'

'Yes,' Paul said. 'I must ask your father for your hand in marriage formally and it's no good putting up your hand, or saying he wouldn't be interested,' he went on as Carmel was about to protest. 'It is the correct way to go about things. I would never have your father be able to level at me the criticism that things were done in an underhand way.'

Carmel shook her head. 'You really don't understand how my parents are.'

'Do any of us really understand our own parents, let alone the parents of our boyfriends and girl-friends?' Paul asked. 'But we need to observe tradi-tions and then we will be married and can live in any way we want and see the parents as little or as often as we want to.'

'Paul, it sounds marvellous.'

Paul kissed her and said, 'It will be marvellous. How could it be any other way, with two people who love each other as much as we do? I have some holidays due and you must have too. September would be a good time for me to go over, because most people from the hospital will be back from their holidays by then, but the illnesses of the autumn and winter will not have begun.'

Carmel sent her letter together with one from Paul, introducing himself to the family and asking her par-ents' permission to marry their daughter. Two days later came the reply.

'They want to meet you,' Carmel told him. 'Mammy must have written by return and she says my father won't give his permission unless he meets you, and September suits them fine.'

'Well, as you are over twenty-one we don't really need

their permission, but I can quite see why he wants to see me,' Paul said.

'I can't,' Carmel said. 'Is he going to ask you if you can keep me in the manner I am accustomed to?' she went on drily. 'It would be easy enough – some old slum to live in and surviving on St Vincent de Paul vouchers and fresh air and I'd definitely feel I was back home.'

Paul laughed, though the word 'slum' brought to mind his mother's angry words and his own fruitless searching for a property. He said, 'We might both be living in a slum before we are much older, and glad of it. I think your father's concern is just to see the type of person I am; that I will treat you right.'

'Yeah, like he never did.'

'That's people for you,' Paul said. 'Book a fortnight off and I will do the same and we will spend the first few days at your home. It makes sense to go now too, because I have the funds at the moment. My paternal grandfather left money in a trust fund, for myself and Matthew to be given when either we graduate or reach the age of twenty-five, whichever came first, and so mine, at the moment, is just resting in the bank. When we come back we will have to get down to some serious house hunting.'

Paul had made the odd enquiry about somewhere to live, and so had Chris, for the lease on the lodgings they shared would have to be renewed for a further year or else they had to find somewhere else to live. With marriage planned the following year, it seemed sensible to look around for a house that the men would live in alone for the time being. 'Even if we could move into their lodgings I wouldn't,' Lois said. 'Apart from its nearness to Queen's it has got little to recommend it.'

Carmel knew just what she meant. The house Paul and Chris shared with two other men was worse than seedy.

'Anyway, I don't want to live in Edgbaston,' Lois went on. 'I fancied living closer to my family.'

'Won't the houses in Sutton Coldfield be expensive to rent?'

Lois wrinkled her nose. 'That's what Chris said. But Erdington is right next door and so we are going to concentrate our search there.'

'And we might help you,' Carmel said, 'when we have been to Ireland to see the family.'

First, though, there was the formal presentation that both Chris and Paul attended to see Carmel and Lois and many other friends receive badges from the GNC (General Nursing Council) and their registration numbers, qualifying them as state registered nurses.

It meant all the girls who had got this far would now be junior staff nurses. As Matron said, 'There will be no more exams, no lectures, but you will all have another twelve months on the wards under the direction and guidance of a senior staff nurse. This will enable you to consolidate all you have learned in training before receiving your certificates next year and I trust you will make full use of this coming year.'

Chris and Paul were immensely proud of the girls, knowing how hard they had both worked, and Carmel's head was in the clouds for she knew the dream of being a proper qualified nurse was now in sight. It was what she'd hankered after for years. Now, though, there was an added complication because she also hankered after Paul, longed and yearned to become his wife, and she fervently hoped she hadn't to ditch one of her dreams to achieve the other.

CHAPTER ELEVEN

As they alighted at Letterkenny station, the September sun was sinking and, in its golden light, Carmel saw the speculative looks thrown her way by some of the people on the platform, and even a nudge from one woman to her husband to alert him to the fact that Carmel Duffy was back.

Paul felt the trembling of her whole body against him and he was filled with compassion for her. 'Chin up,' he whispered. 'You're worth ten of these any day.'

Paul's words gave Carmel the courage to lift her head and she inclined it to those they passed in greeting, but didn't try to speak because she wasn't sure that she would be able to. Her heart was thumping in her chest for she couldn't still the panic coursing through her every time she thought of coming face to face with her father, despite Paul's dependable presence beside her.

Carmel knew the landlady of the lodging house that Sister Frances had found for them a little. She had been one of the kinder of the townsfolk and she greeted them both warmly and showed them to the rooms where they could leave their cases. As Carmel expected, the rooms

were very basic, but they were clean and she looked longingly at the comfortable-looking bed, wishing she could
slip into it and sleep away the weariness of the journey.
But her mother would be expecting her.

'We must buy food,' she said, when they were once
more in the street.

Paul nodded. He had expected that really. A family
as poverty-stricken as Carmel said hers was would have
no spare cash to provide for visitors and he intended to
buy plenty. He wanted them all well fed for once in their
lives.

So the grocer, the butcher, the greengrocer and the
baker were all introduced to Paul and all admired the
ring and wished the young couple their very best. As
they walked towards Carmel's home with their laden
bags, the news flew around the town that the eldest Duffy
girl, her that went in for the nursing, was back to see
her mother and sporting a ring that would dazzle the
life out of you to look on it. And would you credit it,
the man she was engaged to was a doctor!

In that small community, the doctor was only one
remove from the priest in the hierarchy, and a tad more
respected than the school teacher, and between these types
of people and the ordinary folk there was a deep chasm
that it was unheard of to cross. For one of the weans of
Dennis Duffy to even speak to a doctor was bad enough,
but to be engaged . . .! It was totally outside their understanding.

'Mind you,' said one women spitefully, 'the man is in
for a rude awakening, I'm thinking, for he hasn't seen the
house yet. Nor has he met the brute of a father. I just
hope Carmel hasn't got her heart set on him. I think this

will be his first and last visit, and when they go back to Birmingham or wherever it was she went, she'll not see him for dust.'

'Aye,' the women said collectively.

And one commented, 'After all, it stands to reason, you can't make a silk purse from a sow's ear. Carmel must see that they are streets apart.'

Carmel was too nervous for small talk and so she walked beside Paul in silence. Then suddenly, as the lane turned a corner, a small boy slithered out of a tree in front of them. He made no move to approach them, however, but ran the other way instead, shouting, 'Mammy, they're here. Our Carmel's come.'

Paul raised quizzical eyebrows and Carmel said, 'That will be my little brother Tom. He has grown and must be nearly eight now, but it was him all right.'

Paul was shocked. Nearly eight! The child was no bigger than one of five years old. His dirty feet were bare and his arms and legs so spindly he resembled one of the destitute children that hung about the barrows in the Bull Ring, begging. He could say none of this to Carmel and he had no time, for a woman came into view, dancing children surrounding her. When she saw Carmel she ran towards her and, ignoring Paul, she threw her arms around her daughter, as tears rained down her cheeks.

'Oh, my darling, darling girl, how I have longed to see you.'

Guilt smote Carmel and she gently unwound her mother's arms from around her neck and held her hands, giving them a little shake as she said, 'Come, Mammy, this isn't the time for tears. This is my fiancé, Paul.'

Paul shook hands with the woman and made the right responses, but his mind was reeling with shock for he was looking at a carbon copy of Carmel, though a faded bedraggled copy.

He wondered if her eyes ever lit up with excitement or joy, as Carmel's often did, or if she had ever laughed at something that amused her. He doubted it somehow, for everything about her was muted and sad.

When Paul had his first sight of the cottage, he was glad that Eve had kept hold of her daughter's hand as if her life depended on it. He brought up the rear, with the cavorting children leaping beside them, and that gave him time to compose his face. The state of the house astounded him, for it was little more than a shack.

But if Paul was horrified by the house, Eve was mortified. For so long she hadn't seen how bad it was; it was just where they eked out an existence. They had never had visitors and so, until this moment, she had never had to look at her house through someone else's eyes. Now that she did she wanted to sink down to the ground and weep with shame.

She was nervous enough of Paul as it was, for she wasn't used to mixing with doctors. She seldom had reason to call one, for they cost money and few would speak to the likes of her anyway. But now this fine, upstanding doctor man was wanting to marry their Carmel.

She knew she had to meet him, but wished he wasn't quite so fine and, more than that, she wished that he hadn't to see the hovel Carmel was reared in.

'Is Daddy in, Mammy?' Carmel asked as they neared the house.

'Why surely, child, and waiting to welcome you like the rest of us.'

Carmel suppressed the exclamation of disbelief and asked instead, 'Is he sober?'

'Of course,' Eve said in a high voice, as if she thought it odd that Carmel had to even ask such a thing. 'He's looking forward to meeting you . . . and . . . and . . . your young man too, of course. Now come away in. You must be worn out and famished with hunger.'

'We have food, Mammy,' Carmel said. 'Lots of it. We stopped at the shops and stocked up.'

Carmel saw her mother's shoulders sag in blessed sheer relief and she knew if they had brought nothing with them, someone would have had to go without in order that they be welcomed properly.

'I'll unpack it and you will see,' she said. 'And then we will prepare a meal fit for a king. Just wait till I take off my coat.' She spun round as she spoke and came face to face with her father.

Immediately, she felt as if she had a leaden weight in her stomach and her mouth was so dry she was having trouble swallowing. She felt like she had as a young child when on more than one occasion she had wet herself with fear. Her father was dressed in greasy trousers and a check shirt that had seen much better days and which strained to fasten across his large and flabby belly. He had the sleeves rolled up and the reddened arms protruding from it matched the red of his thick and bulbous face, with his wide cruel mouth, squashed nose and eyes as cold as ice.

'So,' said the hated guttural voice, 'have you brought your fancy fiancé?'

'Y-Yes, Daddy. He . . . he's b-behind you.' Carmel hated herself for stuttering and betraying her fear, especially when she saw her father was amused by it.

Paul hated hearing it too, and he stepped in front of Dennis. 'I am Carmel's fiancé,' he said, extending his hand. 'My name is Paul Connolly and I am very pleased to meet you.'

Dennis ignored the hand. He looked at it as if it were an object of disgust and then growled out, 'Is she up the duff?'

Carmel gasped in dismay as Paul said, 'I beg your pardon?'

'You heard,' Dennis said contemptuously. 'Simple enough question. I asked you if her belly was full?'

'Daddy,' Carmel cried in desperation and even Eve said, 'Ah, Dennis, give over, do.'

'Shut your mouths, the pair of you,' Dennis commanded and he turned again to Paul. 'Well?'

'I assure you . . .'

'Is she or isn't she?' Dennis said. 'That's all I want to know.'

'No, she is not.'

'Then why the bleeding hell are you marrying her?'

Paul found it hard before this objectionable and belligerent man to talk of love and devotion and so he said instead, 'I care deeply for Carmel and I wish to marry her.'

Dennis shook his head. 'She ain't your sort,' he snarled. 'Look around you. This is where she comes from, what she is deep down. You best go back and find one

185

of your own set if you have a yen to marry at all. People like you don't marry the likes of us.'

Carmel gave a cry of anguish and Paul, seeing her distress, put his arm around her and led her away through the door.

'I can't expect you to put up with this,' Carmel said, as Paul strode across the yard and turned into the lane. 'We were wrong to come. We should have stayed in our little fantasy cocoon and pretended all in the garden was rosy. And now you know where and how I was dragged up. If you want nothing more to do with me, I will understand.'

Paul stopped, turned Carmel round and gave her a little shake. 'Look at me!'

'I hardly dare.'

'Why? Don't tell me it is because of anything that brute of a father did or said?'

'Don't you care?'

'Of course I care,' Paul burst out. 'I care a great deal that he still has the power to terrify the life out of you.'

'But the things he said, the way he was . . . I can't . . .'

Paul held tight to Carmel's hands and looked deep into her eyes. He said, 'Right, let us establish here and now that you were right: your father is a bastard of the first order and a bully as well. No one should ever let a bully win. He is hitting out the only way he knows and trying to drive a wedge between us, which is exactly what my mother tried to do, using different methods. We cannot allow either of them to do that.'

He pulled Carmel into his arms. 'I love you, Carmel,' he said, kissing her tenderly. 'Please believe me. My life is nothing without you. Will you come back with me now and face your father with your head held high? You have no need to fear him any longer. He has no power to touch our lives in any way.'

Carmel knew that Paul was right and she gave a brief nod. They returned to the house, hand in hand, and she noticed her brothers and sisters looking at her with a kind of awe and suddenly wished she could lift them from this place, give them somewhere where they could be carefree children.

At least, she thought, they could have plenty to eat that day and she was pleased to see that while she had been away from the house, her mother had been busy making a meal from the things they had brought.

Though the food was good, there was tension and apprehension in the air. Dennis demanded that they ate in silence. Only he could speak, and this was usually to pull someone to pieces or make fun or yell at the children or Eve. Carmel remembered it well.

Everyone seemed to breathe easier when Dennis went out to the pub as usual. The children began to chatter and laugh, and were very interested in the tales Paul and Carmel told first about life at the hospital. When they got on to the plans they had for their marriage the following summer, the children were spellbound.

Siobhan and Carmel washed up in the scullery while Eve put Pauline and Edward to bed and settled the others at the table to do their homework.

Siobhan said, 'Did you see Mammy's face when you were talking about your wedding? I am sure she would give her right arm to be able to go. I will be sixteen by then and I'm sure I can see to things for a few days.'

'What difference does that make?' Carmel demanded.

'Haven't you learned yet that the Duffys don't make plans or have ideas? There's little point. I mean, think about it, Siobhan. Even if Mammy had the clothes to wear and she could gather up the fare, do you think our father would be agreeable to it? Do you think that he would wave her off with his blessing and a smile of approval decorating his face for once in his life?'

'No,' Siobhan said, with a sigh. 'Bloody shame, though.'

'I agree,' Carmel said, and added with a grin, 'and if Mammy heard you she would wash your mouth out with carbolic.'

And then, suddenly sorry for her sister, she went on, 'Look, Siobhan, I am taking Paul to see Sister Frances tomorrow at lunchtime and I will have a word with her and see if she can think of something. I'm promising nothing, mind, so don't tell Mammy yet. Sister Frances might be a nun, but I don't know how hot she is in the miracle department and I think that is what we need here.'

The following day, Sister Frances considered the problem of Eve seeing her daughter married. When Carmel told her that Siobhan was more than happy to see to things if her mother did this, she nodded her head slowly.

'I think that is a very good idea.'

'But, Sister Frances, my father would never allow it.'

'Well, it would certainly help me if he could be persuaded, for it would not be fitting for a nun to travel alone and I suppose I am invited to this wedding too?'

'Of course, Sister,' Carmel said. 'I'm surprised you even had to ask, but I was also going to ask your sister,

Mrs Mackay, who spoke to you for the job I had in the hospital and got the ball rolling in the first place.'

'And don't you think your mother would feel it, you asking your teacher and a former work colleague and her getting no invite at all?'

'I know, Sister, and yes, she is bound to but I don't see—'

'Unless there is a drastic change between now and the date of your wedding, there is no way my sister, Eileen, will be able to be away from the house overnight,' Sister Frances said. 'She has her mother-in-law living with her now, for her mind is wandering. A neighbour woman looks after her while Eileen is teaching at the school, for the old woman cannot be left, and as things stand at the moment, she would be unable to come to your wedding. That means I would have to travel alone, unless your mother was to come with me.'

'Sister, even if it were remotely possible, Mammy has no suitable clothes,' Carmel said.

'Leave that to me,' Sister Frances told her confidently. 'We have had some really good quality clothes given in for the missions just lately. There is a costume there would be just the thing for your mother. In fact, it would fit few others. Most people are taller and have more flesh on their bones than Eve. I think too she should have a good haircut.'

Carmel gaped at her. Was she mad? Where in the world was her mother to get the money to have her hair done? The Duffys did not go to the hairdresser's as a matter of course.

'Don't look so astounded, Carmel,' the nun said. 'You know Minnie Doherty that owns the hairdresser's in Main

Street?' Well, her son had the whooping cough so bad the doctor had him admitted to the hospital. The child was very ill and many times we thought we might lose him, but in the end we pulled him through it and I think his mother would be only too pleased to do a favour for me. I mean,' she went on with a merry twinkle in her eye, 'it isn't as if I will ever have need of a Marcel wave, is it?'

Paul smiled broadly at the thought, but Carmel was too concerned to find anything amusing. 'Look, Sister,' she said, 'it's all right going on about costumes and hairdos and all, but aren't we talking a lot of tommy rot here? I mean, can you see my father allowing my mother to go anywhere in the first place?'

'It might need a bit of work right enough.'

'A bit of work?' Carmel burst out incredulously. 'I just can't see—'

'We might have to involve Father O'Malley,' Sister Frances mused as if Carmel hadn't spoken. 'You had intended to see him while you were here, I suppose?'

Carmel hadn't thought of making a special journey to see the priest, but she knew he had great influence, even with her father.

'We'll go up together,' Sister Frances said emphatically, 'and put it to the man straight.'

Carmel knew that even with the priest on their side, it still mightn't work. Dealing with her father most of the time was like trying to handle a raging bull. And then, as she had confided to Lois, she didn't know whether she wanted her mother to attend the ceremony at all.

Though she was more tolerant of what her mother had to put up with than when she had been living with it too, she doubted whether better clothes and a haircut would make Eve that different. Surely she would still be the same downtrodden, feeble person, frightened of her own shadow? However, as Carmel couldn't share these thoughts they had to be pushed to the very back of her mind and she gave herself up to enjoying the visit with the nun she had always got on so well with, glad to see that Paul appeared to like her too.

When Paul excused himself after the meal and Sister Frances had a few moments alone with Carmel, she took hold of her hands and her eyes were shining, 'My darling girl, I am so happy for you. Paul is a fine man and I am sure will make you a marvellous husband.'

'Thank you, Sister,' Carmel said. 'I hadn't thought to marry anyone, you know. I thought to remain single all my life, but when I met Paul . . .'

'You wouldn't have been happy single, Carmel,' Sister Frances said. 'You have too large a heart and too loving a nature. One of the nuns once asked me if you would think of taking the veil as that is another route into nursing, but I didn't even bother posing the question to you as I knew the answer. I think I said something like you would make a good nurse, but a very bad nun. Now your path is set and soon you will be a married woman.

The priest found he too liked Paul Connolly, who spoke with just the right respectful tone as he gave an account of himself and his plans for the future. He thought that Carmel had done well for herself in becoming engaged to him, better than she could have hoped, considering her lowly beginnings.

He listened as Sister Frances told him of her invitation to the wedding the following summer, and how she had intended to go with her sister, who now would probably not be able to go. She went on to say Carmel would love to have her mother with her on her wedding day.

'I can quite see that any girl would want that,' Father O'Malley said. 'However, that maybe problematic. You wouldn't think of getting married here?'

'No, Father, not really,' Carmel said. 'I feel at home in Birmingham now and there is the problem of Paul's relations and how to accommodate them all if they were to come here. I wouldn't be able to house all my family either, of course, but if it were only Mammy and Sister Frances, then I am sure they can stay at the convent on the Hagley Road, no distance from me at all.'

'Ah, but who is to see to things if your mother was to go away?' the priest asked.

Carmel had been expecting this. 'All the children will be at school through the day except for Pauline, Father,' she said. 'And by the time I am married, Siobhan will be sixteen and is quite prepared to take time from her job and attend to things. Kathy will help her, for she will be going on for eleven. We are only talking of a few days.'

'It will give Eve such a boost if she is able to do this,' Sister Frances put in, 'and help me too, Father, for it wouldn't be fitting for me to travel alone.'

'I have a feeling Dennis won't see it that way at all.'

'My feelings entirely, Father,' Sister Frances said. 'And that is where you come in. I'm sure you could put it to him in a way that he will find he could accept.'

Father O'Malley wasn't at all sure. Dennis was not known for his measured responses, but it would be the best solution all round, he decided, and Dennis would have to be made to see that.

Dennis did not see it like that at all and the following afternoon Carmel could hear her father roaring well before they reached the house. She sneaked a look at Paul, longing to take up his hand, run from the place and hide till her father's rage be spent.

As if he knew her thoughts, Paul gazing down at her gave her hand a squeeze. 'We probably helped bring about your father's anger this time,' he said. 'We can't let your mother deal with it on her own.'

Carmel knew this, though she entered the cottage with great trepidation. Dennis had his wife pinned against the wall, his face inches from her as he yelled straight into her face.

'Behind my back, that's what I can't get over. Conniving with the clergy to get your own way. Well, I'll not stand it, do you hear? Do you hear that loud and clear, woman? You are my wife, your place is here, and here is where you will stay, wedding or no sodding wedding.'

Carmel's youngest sister, little Pauline, was cowering under the ramshackle table with her hands over her ears, while tears streamed from her eyes. Carmel couldn't blame her and felt a great temptation to do the same. However, she knew that wasn't an option and she eased Pauline out carefully and, sitting down on one of the chairs, held her tight in her arms.

She was scared herself, but also too angry to be cautious as she cried over her father's bristling anger and her mother's loud and gulping sobs, 'I wouldn't be surprised if they could hear you in the town. You ought to be ashamed of yourself. Does it make you feel more of a man to terrify women and weans?'

'Why you . . .' Dennis said, approaching Carmel with his arm raised.

'Steady!' Paul said. 'If you lay one finger on her, I will knock you into the back of next week.'

'You cheeky young bugger! This is my house and I say what goes on.'

'Not when it involves my fiancée you don't,' Paul said. 'And Carmel is right: I would be ashamed if my wife and child were as terrified of me as yours obviously are of you. What sort of a man are you anyway that thinks that frightening people is the way to live your life?'

Dennis nearly exploded. No one had ever spoken to him like that before. Carmel still sat on the chair with the shaking child clasped to her, stroking her dusty curls in an effort to calm her while she trembled for Paul and his temerity at speaking in such a way to her father. The shock of it had totally stopped Eve's tears.

Paul almost wanted Dennis to attempt to hit him. It would have given him the excuse to trounce the man, to punish him for the childhood Carmel had endured and for what he had seen Carmel's mother subjected to.

And yet one part of his mind knew that if he did, life might be harder for them afterwards and he wouldn't be there to try to protect them. And it would certainly scotch any idea that Dennis might allow Carmel's mother to go to the wedding. And so he dropped his aggressive stance and said in an almost conciliatory way, 'Come on, man, this is no way to go on. If you are annoyed or upset, shouldn't it be talked about, rather than you bawling at everyone else?'

Dennis's eyes narrowed. He knew what Paul was up to and he was angry, bloody angry, and what he wanted to do was punch the life out of him. But he was not a complete fool and he knew Paul was well-muscled, young and fit. He was also aware that the man was unafraid of him and those things would make him a formidable adversary.

He stepped away from his wife and faced Paul. Eve scrubbed the tears from her cheeks with the sleeve of her cardigan before crouching and holding out her arms. Pauline pulled away from Carmel and threw herself at her mother, snuggling into her with a sigh of relief.

'Any man would be bloody annoyed,' Dennis growled. 'You know what it's all about?'

'Yes, I do. I know your wife, who is also Carmel's mother, wants to go to her eldest daughter's wedding and the daughter also wants this. Tell me what is so wrong with that?'

'She should be here, that's what wrong with it.'

'We are talking about a few days, that's all,' Paul said. 'God, man, you are not bloody helpless. And won't Siobhan be here? She is completely capable of keeping the place ticking over for a day or two.'

Dennis shook his head. 'It's not right!'

'Tell me what is not right about it,' Paul said in a reasonable manner, 'and I will try and understand it.'

Dennis had never before been asked to explain or justify his actions. He had decided what was to be done and, if anyone differed, his fist or his belt would always convince them it was a safer option by far to do things his way. He had lived his life like this, certainly since he had married Eve after being brought up in a similar way by his own father, and so he said again, 'It's not right.'

'But why isn't it?'

'I don't have to excuse myself to you. I am the head of the house.'

'All right,' Paul said. 'Maybe you are head of the house, but that doesn't mean an absolute ruler. You are not obliged to explain anything to me – you're right there too – but you do have to have some clarification for yourself as to why you make the decisions you do.'

Carmel's eyes met those of her mother after they saw Dennis, an altogether quieter Dennis, shake his head in perplexity.

Paul pressed home his point. 'Don't you see that it takes a big man to give your wife permission to do this? She will be quite safe travelling with Sister Frances and we will be there to meet them at the other end. She will be staying in the convent attached to St Chad's Hospital, which is just a step away from the nursing home where Carmel lives. You need have no fears on that score.'

Dennis didn't know that he had fears like that, or any other sort of fears either. He was just bloody annoyed that the priest had been along to see them that morning and told him about the wedding plans as if it was signed and sealed, that was all. But now, if he was to give his permission – and it was not a foregone conclusion by any means – it might put him in the better books with the priest, whom he had sent scurrying from the house earlier. It didn't do to make an enemy of the priest when your immortal soul was at stake.

'So,' he said to Paul, 'you think I should agree to all this?'

'Yes, yes, I do.'

Dennis let his rheumy, bloodshot eyes light on his wife's face, still full of apprehension and fear, and when he said, 'Well, I just might see the way clear to let you do this,' Eve looked at Paul as if he should be canonised.

Even Carmel was mightily impressed with the way Paul had handled her father. Later, when all the family had been fed and Dennis suggested sinking a few pints with Paul to seal the decision he had made, she said not a word, although she knew her father's idea of sinking a few pints, and she could guess the state Paul would be in afterwards.

After they had gone, she sat before the fire with Siobhan and Michael.

'You wouldn't think to go with them, Michael?' she said. 'You are well old enough to sink a few pints yourself?'

'Did you hear him ask me?' Michael asked sarcastically. 'Don't worry, I wouldn't have gone anyway. The less I see of him, the better I like it. I've seen enough of how the drink has ruined our lives for me not to have a great taste for it at all.'

Carmel knew just what her brother meant.

Michael smiled at her and went on. 'You have a good chap there. I have never seen anyone handle Daddy like Paul did. I couldn't believe it when he announced at the table that he had agreed to let Mammy go to your wedding.'

'Nor me,' Siobhan said. 'I never thought in a million years that Daddy would agree. I mean, what has he agreed to in the past? He says no as a matter of course.'

'Is that why you offered your services?' Carmel asked her sister, with a smile. 'Because you wouldn't be asked to deliver?'

Siobhan gave her a push. 'Course not,' she said. 'I am delighted Mammy is going and will be glad to help.'

'I would like to bundle you up and take you all over with me,' Carmel said.

'What? And your dear devoted father to give you away?'

'No, I want him nowhere near the place,' Carmel said. 'He would never be invited.'

'Who is giving you away?'

Carmel shrugged. 'I don't know yet. I'd really like it to be Michael but—'

'So why can't it be me?'

'Michael!' Carmel cried. 'Are you mad? Daddy would never agree to you going to England too.'

Carmel hadn't lowered her voice and all were suddenly aware that three children, homework forgotten, were staring at the three grouped around the fire.

'England!' Thomas almost squeaked. 'You going to England, Mike?'

'I may be,' Michael said. 'If I do, it will be on the quiet, so don't breathe a word of this to Daddy.'

'Are you kidding?' Damien said. 'None of us speak to Daddy willingly.'

'Or talk about it amongst yourselves so that he can overhear.'

'We won't betray you,' Kathy said. 'If you go I will be glad for you and only wish I could go too.'

'And me,' Damien said. 'Like Carmel said, it would be nice if we could all go, but,' he added bitterly, 'the

Duffys don't do things like that. They haven't the money or the clothes, and live on handouts.'

'You know whose fault that is,' Michael said sharply. 'Don't you be landing that at Mammy's door.'

'I'm not. I am just saying . . .'

'Well, you are saying it to the wrong person.'

'Well, I am not saying it to any other bugger,' Damien said.

Michael crossed the room and cuffed him on the side of the head. 'Less of that sort of language.'

Damien rubbed his head as he remarked ruefully, 'I wouldn't say anything to Daddy, would I? No one would, unless they had a death wish.'

'Stop arguing,' Eve cried, coming in at that moment. 'I heard what you said, Michael. Have you thought it through?'

'Not really,' Michael said. 'I mean, I have only just thought of it, but there really is no reason why I shouldn't be there too. I will obviously have to arrange time from work, but that won't be a problem since I have never had more than a few days off from when I began. I will give Carmel away if she is agreeable.'

'Oh, Michael, I would love it,' Carmel said. 'It would be like the icing on the cake to have you there.'

'Where would he stay?' Eve asked. 'He can hardly bide with us at the convent.'

'Might put a smile on the old nuns' faces if he did,' Siobhan said with a impish grin.

'Siobhan, behave yourself,' Eve chided, but her heart wasn't in the rebuke, as she was trying to control her own features and Michael was laughing too.

'Oh, I will sleep anywhere,' he said. 'Someone's floor

will do me fine. The one who will be on the sharp end of this when Daddy realises I'm gone, however, will be Siobhan. How do you feel about me hightailing it to England?'

Siobhan wanted to say that she had never thought he would do such a thing and that she needed him there, but then she thought of her sister being given away by a stranger and knew she couldn't do that to her. 'Don't worry,' she said. 'For a few days I will manage fine without you. It shouldn't be too much of a problem.'

'There will be one big problem if you three do not get on with your homework,' Eve said to the children around the table, and though there was a collective groan, they did settle down over their books again, cheered no end by Carmel reminding them that when they were finished there was a big bag of sweets for them to share, courtesy of Paul.

The children had seldom seen a sweet, let alone eaten one, and they settled quickly to their work at the thought of such of treat awaiting them.

Carmel had actually been having pangs of conscience about her younger siblings since she came home. Although her mother had told her the things they had done in her weekly letters, Carmel had thought about them seldom, scrubbing them from her earlier life along with her father. And though she knew they would have grown and changed in the three years she had been away, in her mind's eyes she had seen them as the same ages as when she had left. But now Thomas was nearly eight, Kathy ten and Damien fourteen. As for Siobhan, at fifteen she was a young lady on the verge of womanhood, and Michael a fine young man, muscled by the farm work he did and yet still as alarmed by his father as he ever had been.

Much to everyone's surprise, Paul arrived home just after ten o'clock, alone and comparatively sober. 'I never intended stopping out until all hours,' he said in explanation. 'Nor did I intend to drink myself senseless, but I did have a sort of plan.'

'What?' Carmel wanted to know.

'Your father introduced me as his future son-in-law and so I just waited until I gauged your father had drunk enough and then I let it slip that when we married the following summer, your father was more than agreeable for your mother to travel to England to be there on our special day. I made him sound like some sort of magnanimous saint to do this. His friends were surprised, right enough, especially when your father, sensing their approval, I suppose, made out it had been his idea all along. Anyway, they all thought him grand fellow for it, clapped him on the back, bought him one pint after the other. When I left him, he was well away and being regaled as a sort of hero. The point is, because now he has said what he intended to do in front of so many witnesses, he can hardly renege on it.'

Eve let out the breath she hadn't been aware that she was holding in an audible sigh of relief. She looked at Paul as if he was some sort of being from outer space, because she knew as well as everyone else that now she would be allowed to go to Carmel and Paul's wedding. Paul had achieved the almost impossible. She had no words to convey how much this meant to her and how grateful she was to Paul, but he waved away her thanks and just said he was glad to help.

CHAPTER TWELVE

Both Paul and Carmel were very tired by the time the train pulled into New Street Station where Chris and Lois were waiting for them.

Chris was bursting with an idea that he spilled out in the taxi. He had been hunting for a house just as earnestly as Paul and, like Paul, had found any they could afford to rent were in very bad condition and in very run-down areas, and the better ones they couldn't afford yet as very junior doctors.

'The point is, bigger houses aren't that much more expensive in comparison,' Chris said. 'Harder to let, I suppose. So how about if we have a big house, instead of two small ones and share it?'

Carmel was very taken with it. She and Lois were good friends and it wasn't as if they had no experience of living together, so when Paul said, 'What do you think?' she said, 'It sounds a great idea.'

'It would be a solution for now,' Chris said. 'And then after we are married and the girls living there too, they would be company for each other when we are working all hours.'

'All right,' Paul said. 'We'll look for a larger house and see what's what.'

'The point is, we've found one already,' Chris said. 'Number 17 York Road, Erdington. I have got the details and put a holding deposit on it until we all have a chance for a proper look round it.'

'I hope you weren't thinking of tonight,' Paul said. 'The only thing I want to look at and then fall into is my own bed.'

Chris laughed. 'No,' he said. 'Tomorrow is soon enough, but I would like to get it all wrapped up before we start back to work.'

Paul had no argument with that.

York Road was in a prime position, just off Sutton New Road, which had trams running along it to the city centre and the General Hospital, and was just yards from the High Street of Erdington Village. Carmel was impressed by the position before she even saw the house.

Number 17 had three stone steps running up to the solid wooden door, which opened into a long and narrow hall. There were stairs to the left, and to the right were doors to two sizeable rooms.

'See, one each,' Chris said. 'So we can be by ourselves sometimes if we want to be.'

Carmel thought that a good idea because however fond you were of someone, you probably didn't want to live in their pocket. They followed Chris down the passage. He suddenly came to a stop and they saw a small door to their left-hand side.

'That's probably the entrance to the cellar,' Chris

said. 'The agent did say the house had one. And I came armed with a torch, just in case.'

Paul opened the door and peered into the darkness.

'I'm not going into that nasty, smelly place,' Lois declared. 'It's probably jammed full of spiders.' Carmel agreed with her and the girls stayed in the hall and waited for Chris and Paul, who went exploring the depths.

'It was a coal house once,' Paul said when he emerged, covered with dust and sneezing his head off.

'There is not a trace of coal there now, though,' Chris said, in the same condition as Paul. 'It's just full of junk.'

'The coal is probably kept in the coal bunker in the back garden, which Lois and I spotted when we were having a shufty of the outside,' Chris said. 'I'll show you.'

There was another sizeable room at the end of the passage, but this one led on to the kitchen, scullery and the door to the back garden. The garden had been very neglected, and Paul said that if they took this place that was one of the things they had to attend to first.

'I'll say,' Chris agreed. 'The coal man would have trouble even finding the bunker, with the grass so long. Still, I'd say a couple of scythes will make short work of it. And that gate at the side leads to the entry this house shares with the neighbours, and then on to the street.'

They trooped back into the house and up the stairs, delighted to find the house had four bedrooms and an inside bathroom and toilet.

'Now isn't that the height of luxury?' Chris said.

Carmel agreed it was and Lois said, 'Every small terrace house we looked at had an outside toilet down the yard, next to the coal house, and no bath at all.'

'Fancy,' said Carmel with a smile, remembering the even more primitive conditions in her own home. She said as much to Lois and commented, 'I must be getting soft.'

Lois gave a toss of her head and said, 'You just want better standards now, that's all, and so do I.'

Carmel looked at her friend. Although she had never been to Lois's house, she could imagine that it was fairly luxurious and though for her to be renting a house like this was terrific, she knew Lois might feel differently about it – not that she had ever been the slightest bit snobbish about having more money than the rest or anything like that.

However, when she asked Lois if she didn't perhaps want something a bit better, she shook her head. 'Chris couldn't afford much better than this yet and we really do want to stand on our own two feet as far as possible.'

However, while the house was very handy for the girls to reach their hospital, it wouldn't be that easy for Paul and Chris at the Queen's, but as Chris said, they would hardly be able to use public transport at all anyway because of the unsociable hours that junior doctors were expected to work.

'So what will you do?' Lois asked.

'Well, a car is out of the question,' Chris said. 'But we have been talking to the others and many are buying motorbikes.'

'A motorbike,' Carmel cried. 'Wouldn't you be scared?'

'What's there to be scared of?' Lois said. 'As Chris said, if you can ride a push bike, you can ride a motorbike.'

'But they are very powerful, and with all the traffic on the roads I would be petrified.'

'Well, I can't think of a better solution,' Paul said. 'We will have to look around and check out the prices.'

'And quick,' Chris said.

It was quick. The very next day Chris and Paul found a small garage in Deritend down way past the Bull Ring, which did second-hand motorbikes. Soon they were the proud owners of two Triumph Royal Enfield bikes that were just a few years old and in very good condition. They already had panniers fitted and a pillion seat, though Carmel thought she might be too scared ever to ride on the back.

Paul understood her reticence and he said, 'I'll not force you to go on it if you really don't want to, but it is our transport problem solved.'

Jane and Sylvia were green with envy when the other two told them what their plans were. Carmel could understand how they felt, for she knew many young people had to start in poky rooms or, heaven forbid, with parents. She tried to imagine what it would be like for her, living with Paul's parents. God, it would be a fate worse than death and didn't really bear dwelling on.

As for the two powerful and noisy machines that Paul and Chris were the very satisfied owners of, although they still frightened her a little, Carmel couldn't help being a little awed by them. The news, of course, flew around the hospital and she couldn't help the little thrill of pride she felt when Paul and Chris both pulled up their motorbikes in the hospital car park the following day and were surrounded by a gaggle of interested nurses.

No one could believe that Carmel was too nervous even to sit astride Paul's machine, while Lois straddled Chris's with ease and claimed that she couldn't wait to go for a ride.

'Do you really feel like that?' Carmel asked Lois, 'because I think it is all eyewash. I know you too well and I think you are just saying it for effect,'

'All right,' Lois admitted. 'I am a bit apprehensive, but I am not saying it for effect, but to please Chris. He would like me to feel as excited about that blooming motorbike as he is and he would be disappointed if I wasn't. I know that, so to please him I say what he wants to hear.'

'Paul isn't like that,' Carmel told her. 'He says—'

'I don't care what he says,' Lois said, cutting across her. 'Look at his eyes if you want to know what he thinks. That motorbike is his pride and joy. Obviously he wants you to feel the same way. Chris wants to take me out for a spin on Sunday. What will you and Paul do then, and how do you think Paul will feel?'

The two other girls thought the same way as Lois. Jane said, 'If you don't want to go out with dishy Paul on that fabulous machine then move over, I will.'

'I think,' commented Sylvia wryly, 'you would have to join the queue, but Jane is right in a way because you do have to put yourself out when you love someone. It tells you this in all the women's books – you know, the tips they print on keeping a man happy. They all tell you to take an interest in his hobbies.'

'Are you saying regardless of how I feel I should force myself to go on that dreaded thing?' Carmel demanded.

'In a nutshell, that is exactly what we are saying,' Lois said. 'If I can do it, then so can you.'

The result of this was that when Carmel saw Paul that evening, she told him that if he wanted she would go out on the bike on Sunday, the day before their holidays were over. She was rewarded by a smile that lit up all of Paul's face. Then he lifted her in the air and told her that she was the greatest girl in the world, and she knew then her decision had been a wise one.

He had told her to wrap up well and put a scarf around her head that she could tie securely.

'Are you sure about this?' he said as she attempted to mount the machine behind him. 'I always said I would never force you.'

Carmel hoped Paul couldn't feel the shaking of her limbs as she settled herself behind him and grasped him tight around the waist and she fought to keep the tremor out of her voice as she said, 'But you haven't forced me. This was totally my decision.'

Afterwards, Carmel wasn't sure when, despite the cold and the quite bumpy ride, she gave herself up to the exhilaration of the whole thing. Cuddled as she was against Paul, she felt the excitement running through him and that fuelled her own so that she wanted to shout with the joy of it. They left the town far, far behind and set out for the countryside, zooming down lanes, roaring past farms and sleepy villages and that first day they finally came to rest at the edge of a village called Kingsbury.

Paul was glad to get Carmel to himself at last. 'It seems like ages that I have been sharing you with others, or else on show, like we were in Letterkenny, and not able to be really natural. Soon I will probably have scant time off. Let's enjoy being together for one day at least.'

Carmel too had longed for time with Paul. They wandered through the village hand in hand and then out on the nearby canal and had lunch at a little pub fronting the water. They watched the shaggy-footed Shire horses pull the brightly painted barges along while the sun-bronzed and barefoot children leaped agilely along the barge or on to the bank as confidently and effortlessly as monkeys. After lunch, they turned away from the canal and wandered the lanes hand in hand, and talked about all manner of things. They came to a sunny glade and Paul spread his jacket over the fallen leaves littering the ground so that they could sit in the shade of the oak tree, and when he lay down and pulled Carmel down beside him, she didn't protest.

His initial kisses left her dizzy and aching for more, and when they grew more urgent, she responded eagerly. She groaned with longing when Paul ran his hands all over her body and wriggled in anticipation. Paul was aching with desire when he gently teased her mouth open for the first time, and when his tongue shot into Carmel's mouth, she felt as if an explosion had happened inside her. Her tongue responded to his and she was totally unable to stop Paul's hands slipping beneath her clothes, nor his fumbling fingers snapping her brassiere undone. She felt his hands on her bare breasts and she moaned in ecstasy.

Paul pushed up Carmel's clothes and put his mouth

around one of her nipples, sucking and teasing and Carmel thought she would drown in pleasure. Feelings new and exciting and more intense than she had ever felt before were coursing through her body and she knew she wouldn't even try to stop Paul because she wanted him to go on and on.

Paul knew that too. He felt her submission in every vestige of her being. He knew that any warning words her mother, or maybe Sister Frances, might have given her would have fled from her mind in this first overpowering introduction to her sexuality. Nothing else mattered to her at that moment, and he knew he could not debase and defile the love he had for this girl by taking something that she was too vulnerable and naïve to refuse him.

Carmel had no idea what it cost him to roll away from her. She gave a cry of dismay. 'Don't stop, for God's sake.'

'I must, before I forget myself altogether.'

'Then forget yourself,' Carmel cried. 'I don't mind. I am ready.'

'I'm not,' Paul said, pulling way again with difficulty. 'You honestly don't know what you're saying. Cover yourself up, for Christ's sake, before I leap on you again – and don't say I am quite welcome to,' he went on, seeing Carmel was about to protest.

Carmel was tingling with sexual awareness, but Paul had already withdrawn from her. She tidied herself as best she could and when Paul got up and pulled her to her feet, she went without protest.

After a few weeks, life got into something of a pattern. Paul and Chris continued to work the punishing hours of the first year, and Carmel worried at the spartan way they were living at the house, but they told her not to worry.

'But how do you cook anything?' she asked.

'We don't,' Chris told her cheerfully. 'We eat mainly in the hospital canteen.'

'Or we live on fish and chips, or bread and jam,' Paul put in. 'To be honest, after we have done a shift we are usually too tired to think about cooking anything.'

Carmel knew that it was right about the tiredness. Both men were often white with exhaustion. And yet when they had any free time they would do their level best to see the girls, although often they didn't have time off together. Paul would sometimes pick Carmel up on the bike on his way home and then they would maybe see a picture at the Palace picture house on Erdington's High Street. The cinema had a dance hall above it, but Carmel didn't suggest going there, because she had never told Paul about the dancing lessons and warned Lois to keep it from Chris as well.

Lois shrugged. 'All right,' she said, 'but why all the secrecy? To be honest, you are a born dancer. I suppose it was all those years at the reels, jigs and hornpipes. Anyway, you know as much as I can teach you now and you can give Paul a run for his money, so why not tell him?'

'I will, the same time I break the news to his sainted mother at that fancy hotel they are taking us to on New Year's Eve,' Carmel said. 'I would like to see her face when I take to the floor with Paul.'

From the corner, Jane chortled. 'And so would I.'

'Maybe we'll all come and have a peep at the old buzzard and see how she is taking it?' Sylvia said.

'You dare,' Carmel said, though she was smiling, 'Anyway, aren't you both working?'

'Yeah, worse luck.'

'Well, I am working all through Christmas and so is Paul,' Carmel said. She couldn't wait to get the Christmas festivities out of the way and move on into the year when she would become Paul's wife. On more that one occasion that autumn, Carmel had come perilously near to losing her virginity and each time they had pulled back just in time, but it had got harder. She was eager for the day when they wouldn't have to do that and she could give herself totally to Paul.

Paul seldom mentioned relations with his parents to Carmel, but things between he and his mother were still strained. His father was more amenable and accepting of the situation, certainly when he and Paul were alone, but he had seldom stood against his wife where the boys were concerned for he liked a peaceful life.

'We hardly ever see you these days,' Emma had complained to Paul in mid-November. It was true: Paul saw his parents only in his rare free time when Carmel was on duty. This is what he told his mother and he saw her lips purse in annoyance.

'No need to look like that,' he said sharply. 'Carmel is my fiancée and it is obvious that I would spend as much time with her as possible.'

'Well, surely you will have time off at Christmas?'

'Actually, no, Mother,' Paul said. 'It is thoughtless, I know, but you see, people still get sick at Christmas and I have to work, and so does Carmel.'

'All over the festive season?' Emma asked plaintively.

'I am afraid so.'

'What about the New Year?' Emma said. 'Surely if you are giving up the whole of Christmas they won't expect you to work over the New Year as well?'

'I . . . we haven't been given the roster list for the New Year yet.'

Jeff, watching his son, knew he was lying and later, after a strained meal, when Paul was taking his leave, he went outside with him. Paul threw his leg expertly over the machine his mother hated to think of him riding, much as he tried to point out the practicalities to her.

Jeff said, 'It would mean a lot to your mother if we got to see you over the New Year.'

'I know, Dad, but—'

'Don't tell me about the roster, son, because I know that isn't the truth.'

Paul smiled ruefully. 'How well you know me,' he said. 'The point is, Dad, Mother hates Carmel and you know as well as I do how vindictive she can be when she wants. I don't want to subject Carmel to that. She doesn't want to come here and I don't blame her.'

'I'm not talking of here,' Jeff said. 'The golf club are having their annual bash – dinner and dance, you know – at the Westbury Hotel in town and your mother would love to see you there. Matthew is going too and it would be nice for us all to be together for once.'

'All right,' Paul said. 'All I am agreeing with, mind, is to talk it over with Carmel. I will be guided by her.'

When Paul told Carmel and asked her if she wanted to go, she knew this was her chance to show Paul and, more importantly, his mother how well she could dance

214

in advance of the wedding so she told Paul she would love it.

'It's a dinner dance,' Paul explained, thinking maybe she hadn't understood.

'I know.'

'I mean, you won't feel awkward?'

'No, not at all.'

'You sure?'

'Quite sure,' Carmel said firmly. 'Tell your parents I am looking forward to seeing them there.'

The girls really went to town getting Carmel ready for that most important dance, pooling resources to make her look, as Jane put it, 'the business'.

Lois was as generous as ever, but she was careful to loan Carmel nothing that her aunt might have seen her wearing. She knew, however, that Emma hadn't seen the midnight-blue velvet ball gown, which was floor length and had flowing sleeves. When Carmel pulled it over her head and stood before the mirror she couldn't believe the image looking back at her.

'Bloody hell!' Jane exclaimed. 'Will you just look at yourself? Don't you just look a million dollars?'

'God, you will knock them dead tomorrow,' said Sylvia in agreement. 'And you flush crimson every time someone gives you any sort of compliment. There will be plenty of those thrown your way, I would have thought, and each blush makes you even more attractive. Paul won't be able to keep his hands to himself, I should think.'

'Don't be silly,' Carmel said, and she spun around in front of the mirror, feeling the dress swirl about her legs before saying, 'Why wouldn't I blush, listening to the rubbish the pair of you give out? It isn't me, it is the dress and that really is gorgeous. Are you sure about this, Lois?'

'Of course I am. Daddy bought me this for the pre-Christmas dance at his firm, when I sort of stand in for my mother, and I know for a fact that none of Paul's family have seen this dress on me.'

'It needs something else,' Jane said with a slight frown. 'Oh, wait!' she cried after a moment's thought. 'I have just the thing.' She rummaged in her drawer and found a pair of long white gloves.

'Where on earth did you get those?' Lois said with surprise.

'Where d'you think?' Jane said. 'Where we buy every-thing – the Rag Market.'

'But why?' Sylvia asked, perplexed.

Jane shrugged. 'They were cheap enough and, don't laugh, but I thought they might come in if I was to net me a toff, like we always reckoned we would. Remember?'

'I remember,' Sylva commented wryly, 'like I remember the only one among us who didn't want to do that is the one who has done it.'

'Oh, not that old chestnut again?' Carmel said. 'And, anyway, Paul isn't a toff.'

'His parents are,' Jane said. 'From the way you and Lois described it, there is real money there.'

'There is,' Carmel admitted. 'But that's hardly his fault.'

'We're not saying it's anyone's fault,' Sylvia said. 'All Jane meant is that after Paul's parents' day, all that lovely lolly will, I should imagine, be divided between him and his brother.'

'Maybe not,' Lois said. 'Maybe Paul's share will be donated to the local cats' home because he had the audacity to marry Carmel. Anyway, my aunt and uncle look remarkably healthy to me and are likely to go on for years yet, and this is contributing nothing to Carmel's outfit.' She turned to Carmel and asked, 'Have you something for your neck?'

Camel nodded. 'The rope of pearls and pearl earrings Paul gave me for Christmas.'

'Perfect!' Lois declared. 'They will look lovely against the blue. Now what about a handbag and shoes . . .?'

Carmel usually didn't have a high opinion of how she looked, but as she descended the stairs the following evening, after Sister Magee announced that Dr Connolly was waiting for her, she didn't need to see the open-mouthed appreciation of Paul to know she looked good. The only thing she felt uncomfortable about was the long white gloves. Never in her life had she worn gloves indoors, but Lois assured it they were 'the icing on the cake' and what many people would be wearing at such a prestigious do.

She decided to see what Paul's opinion was. If he said he didn't like them or that they looked out of place, then she would take them back to the room. But for a while Paul didn't say anything at all, just stared at her until she cried, 'Say something, for goodness' sake? How do I look?'

'Breathtakingly beautiful,' Paul said. 'Lovely. Tremendous. There aren't the words . . .'

'Stop all that blathering nonsense,' Carmel commanded, though she was smiling, her eyes sparkling. 'I'll do then?'

'Oh, my darling girl,' Paul cried, catching her by the waist and swinging her around, 'you'll more than do.'

'Even my gloves?'

'Your gloves?' Paul repeated, surprised.

'They don't look stupid or anything?'

'Of course not,' Paul said. 'Why should they? They make you look sophisticated, if you must know – older, no, not older, more sure of yourself.'

'They must have tremendous power, those gloves, if they make me look like that,' Carmel said. 'For I am not a bit sophisticated and the only thing I am sure of is that I will probably make an utter fool of myself tonight.'

Paul laughed. 'Of course you won't, you little goose. Don't worry, it will be nothing like last time. I will not leave your side all night.'

'Oh, that will delight your mother and all the other female admirers you seem to have.'

'They can go to hell, the whole lot of them,' Paul said with determination. 'You are the most important person in the world for me, Carmel, and the sooner that is realised, the better it will be for everyone. And now, madam,' he said in a bantering tone as he took her arm, 'your carriage awaits.'

'Then lead on, sir,' Carmel said, matching his mood, and Paul led her to the waiting taxi.

It was no distance to the Westbury Hotel, but Carmel thought anywhere could seem a distance when the ground crackled with frost, the icy wind would chill a

218

body in minutes and she was dressed in an evening gown and high-heeled shoes. She was glad that Paul had insisted on coming for her in a taxi.

CHAPTER THIRTEEN

Paul felt so proud as he escorted Carmel into the foyer of the hotel for that New Year's Eve ball. There had been a babble of noise for there were a lot of people gathered there, but many of the men grew silent at the entrance of Carmel on Paul's arm, and Paul saw the envy in their eyes.

Carmel was unaware of the men's interest in her and instead noticed the wistful glances many girls were throwing at Paul and the looks of jealousy and sometimes sheer dislike when their eyes slid to Carmel.

Jeff came forward smiling, arms outstretched, a look of appreciation on his face, and in his eyes a genuine smile of welcome. He shook hands with Paul and then took Carmel in his arms and kissed her on both cheeks. 'My word, my dear,' he said. 'How wonderful you are looking tonight. You have gladdened many a man's heart and lightened a room just by entering it.'

Carmel's cheeks lightly flushed with embarrassment at his words, making her even more entrancing. Matthew was standing behind his father, waiting his turn to greet her, and yet Carmel went into his arms reluctantly. She didn't know why it was that she could submit to Jeff's embrace so readily and yet feel herself stiffen when Matthew touched her. She always felt uneasy being near him.

When she caught sight of Emma, however, Carmel saw that her whole face was filled with malevolence and there was such loathing in the eyes she had fastened on Carmel so fixedly that she was quite shaken. And then Emma came closer and put out her hand as she said in flat, insincere tones, 'I'm glad you could join us.'

Carmel knew she was not glad at all and any who had watched that exchange and the formal handshake knew that, while the men in the family approved of Paul's choice, his mother certainly did not. Most would also know who wore the trousers with regards to family matters.

'Look for high jinks, at the very least,' one woman said to her companion as the party was being led into the dining room.

The other woman laughed. 'Oh, yes,' she agreed. 'I wouldn't be totally surprised, though, if the whole thing isn't called off eventually, despite that ring Paul's pretty young fiancée is sporting.'

'Many a slip, so they say.'

'Indeed, indeed . . .'

Paul and Carmel, though they hadn't heard what the women said, knew they would be the subject of some speculation. They had even discussed it. 'It will be a seven-day wonder or whatever the phrase is,' Paul had told Carmel. 'It will be like a baptism of fire, something we have to go through.'

'I know.'

'I really can't understand why people are so interested in one another's lives,' Paul continued. 'I think that they must have too much time on their hands.'

'I think that too,' Carmel said. 'And don't worry, Paul, with you by my side I can tackle anything.'

That wasn't exactly true, and Carmel felt so nervous her stomach was churning as she took her place at the table, grateful that Emma hadn't had a hand in the planning and so she was sitting by Paul. The meal was just as lavish as the one Carmel had endured with Paul's family, and the array of cutlery and glasses just as confusing. This time, though, Paul was very attentive, showing her what to use so unobtrusively that she began to relax, even though she caught sight of Matthew's leering and slightly mocking eyes on her. She was able to ignore him enough to make polite conversation with the man to her other side, who seemed to like talking to her a great deal and who a little later described her to his friends as 'a damned fine filly'.

Carmel didn't hear him and probably would have found it amusing if she had. Unfortunately for the man, his wife did overhear and didn't find it the slightest bit amusing.

The diners had reached the coffee stage when they were informed that the band was setting up in the ballroom, if any wanted to make their way there. Carmel caught the look of malice flitting across Emma's face as she got to her feet. And so, when she reached the ballroom on Paul's arm to hear 'The Blue Danube' playing, knowing Emma was just behind her, it gave her immense satisfaction to say, 'I love this. Shall we dance?'

Paul stopped, stared at her and repeated, 'Dance?'

Carmel laughed at the incredulous look on his face. 'Yes,' she said. 'Dance. You know the kind of thing – you sort of move your feet across the floor to the music.'

'But you can't dance.'

'Can't I?' Carmel asked, almost coquettishly. 'Try me.'

Paul, wondering if Carmel was about to make a fool of herself, if she had perhaps drunk deeper of the wine than was sensible, took her in his arms almost gingerly. He soon found that she was a dancer almost in a class of her own and he began to relax and enjoy himself.

As they swept seemingly effortlessly across the room, Carmel feather-light in his arms, Paul asked, 'How did you learn to dance like this?'

'The normal way,' Carmel said. 'I took lessons.'

Paul shook his head. 'I know that isn't true. With the hours and shifts you work it would be impossible to go to a dancing class. You even said as much to me.'

'Ah, but I didn't say I went to a dancing class,' Carmel said with a smile. 'And I didn't, of course. Lois taught me. The others helped, but it was mainly Lois.'

'And you kept it quiet. You little minx.'

'I wanted to surprise you,' Carmel said. That wasn't strictly speaking true, of course. What she had really wanted was to astonish and possibly disturb Paul's mother, and from the stricken look on Emma's face she had succeeded. That gave Carmel a feeling of elation and she stored it all away to tell the girls later.

After that, it should have been marvellous, and at first it was just that. Paul did do a few duty dances with others but Carmel wasn't left sitting alone at those times. She was claimed by many, mostly far worse dancers than Paul and she had her feet trodden on more than once. Jeff, on the other hand, was surprisingly light on his feet and a good and amusing partner as well. She had just finished dancing with Jeff for the second time when she was approached by Matthew and asked for the next dance in front of both of his parents.

Carmel didn't know how she could refuse, what excuse she could give, though she saw that Matthew was far from sober and she went into his arms with grave misgivings. She found that he too was a good dancer, despite his inebriated state. She was coping with his nearness, which had previously made her so uncomfortable, when suddenly she felt his hands trailing down her back and across her buttocks.

'Stop it,' she hissed in his ear.

'Stop what?' Matthew hissed back. 'Showing a lovely girl how I appreciate her body?'

'Stop this. You have no right to talk to me or touch me in this way.'

'Even though you are enjoying it?' Matthew said, holding her even tighter.

'I am not enjoying it,' she said through gritted teeth. And she wasn't, but she was trapped, especially when she saw Emma's narrowed eyes fixed on the two of them. How could she stamp on Matthews's toes or pull herself out of his arms and tell him what she really thought of him here, in this sort of place?

Anyway, she knew he was the type of man who would blame it all on her, say she was asking for, lapping it up. Even if Paul believed her, it would bring about an impossible situation between him and his brother. Though Paul never spoke of it, Carmel knew she had already caused enough consternation in that family.

So she contented herself with steering Matthew to the opposite side of the dance floor to where his family sat and told herself to put up with it, until the dance was over. When the strains of it eventually drew to a halt, she sighed in thankfulness as she pulled herself away. Before she had reached her seat, Paul came out to claim her on the floor and she went into his arms gratefully.

She said nothing about the way Matthew had danced with her, but resolved to keep out of his way for the rest of the night. She doubted that he would be in any fit state to dance for much longer anyway, for out of the corner of her eye, she saw him watch them morosely for a few minutes and then return to the bar.

She resolved to put Matthew out of her mind and gave herself up to the enjoyment of the dance. Eventually, she was exhausted and hot. Paul steered her to the tables by the terrace, while he fetched her a drink. Sometime earlier, the door had been left ajar and the curtain drawn back to let some air into the room. Paul and Carmel sat and looked out at the stars twinkling in that sharp and clear night, and Carmel thought she had never felt as happy as she was at that moment.

Suddenly the band began playing, 'Let's Face the Music and Dance' for the quickstep. Carmel, who loved the tempo of the dance, was just deciding to get to her feet again when they were approached by a buxom and matronly woman, who had obviously known Paul from infancy and fawned a little over him. She was also interested in Carmel and sat at the table with her while Paul fetched them all more drinks.

When, a little later, the mood changed and the band began playing 'Rhapsody in Blue', a slow waltz, the older lady said to Carmel, 'Would you loan your husband for a little while, my dear? My old duffer of a husband only uses these occasions to get blotto and is in no fit state now to get to his feet. On the other hand, I love to dance, though I believe the tango and quickstep are beyond me now.'

Carmel had no objection. In fact she was quite glad because the unaccustomed drinks had made her quite dizzy. As she watched them take the floor, she slipped out on to the terrace, hoping the night air would clear her head. In the light seeping across from the ballroom she could see the balustrade at the end and, knowing she would see more stars the darker it was, decided to make for there, but had only gone a few paces when she smelled cigarette smoke.

She thought perhaps a courting couple had come out on the terrace for some privacy and was backing into the room again when she felt her hand suddenly grabbed. She gave a little yelp and then she was swung round to face her assailant.

'Matthew,' she cried in alarm.

A very drunk Matthew ground out the cigarette he had been smoking beneath his foot and encircled his arms around Carmel almost in one movement, saying as he did so, 'What's your little game, eh? So prissy on the dance floor and then slipping out to meet me here?'

'I didn't know you were here. I came out for air.'

'Don't give me that,' Matthew said. 'I had to pass right by your table to reach the door.'

Carmel knew he must have done and yet she hadn't noticed him.

As she started protesting again, he went on, 'I always knew that a nurse would be a little goer. It's a well-known fact, and it is always a good idea for brothers to share things.' Then his lips were on hers, and his teeth were grinding against hers as he forced her mouth open. She felt his other hand on her breast and for a moment she was frozen in panic. Then white-hot anger surged through her and she fought like a wild cat, raking Matthew's face with her nails while she struggle to release her lips, and stamping on his toes. Then, finding this was not dislodging him at all, and feeling him rolling one of her nipples between his fingers, she powered her knee into his groin. He let her go with a cry as he fell to his knees and Carmel looked down at him coldly.

'Do you know something, Matthew Connolly?' she said. 'You are not fit to fasten your brother's shoes. You are nothing to me and never will be. You try anything like this again and I will tell your brother. Let's see what sort of a man you are then.'

She didn't wait for Matthew to reply, but after adjusting her clothes she returned to the room to find the dance over and Paul taking the older lady back to her table.

'Oh, darling,' he said, catching sight of her. 'You really are flushed. Are you feeling all right?'

Carmel felt far from all right. Her insides were jumping all over the place. She felt defiled and dirty and her lips were bruised, but she smiled at the concerned face of her beloved Paul and said, 'Never better, my darling, and longing to dance with you.'

After that she danced every dance with Paul, and was with him as they danced the last waltz and shared the

227

last kiss of the old year, then another to welcome in 1935. But for her the evening was tainted and spoiled, and although she knew she would regale the girls with the glitz and splendour of it all later, and her satisfaction about getting one over on Emma, she knew she wouldn't mention any encounters she'd had with Paul's brother.

Jeff had spent the night in the guest room. The reason was that when he had eventually got to bed that night, tired, replete and not entirely sober, he had been treated to a tirade from Emma about Carmel, and for the life of him he couldn't see what the girl had done that had caused such vitriolic abuse.

Years of marriage had taught Jeff it was far more sensible to keep quiet and let Emma have her say. That way his path was an easier one to tread. However, alcohol and common sense seldom go hand in hand, and so he tried to say a few words in the girl's defence. It was a mistake and he realised it as soon as the words were out of his mouth.

The tantrum that his intervention brought on was frightening in its intensity and when he retreated to the guest room, the words Emma flung after him would have shocked a fishwife.

He spent a fitful night, and when he woke the next morning he lay in bed and surveyed the state of his marriage. He didn't like what he forced himself to see. When he had first got to know Emma, she had been a devastatingly beautiful but spoiled young lady. Little had been denied her in her life from her doting parents, and she had wanted Jeff and had gone all out to get him. He'd been unable to believe his luck. Her parents had been all for the match too. Jeff was heir to the engineering works that his father owned and they thought he would be able keep their daughter in the manner to which she'd like to become accustomed.

However, Jeff's father was a drinker and a gambler, and had gambled with the firm's assets, a fact that Jeff hadn't been aware of straight away, so that by the time he had married Emma the receivers were panting at the door.

Neither Emma nor her parents ever knew how bad things were and how hard Jeff had toiled, not only to save the firm but to turn it round. It had worked, but it had taken its toll on him. Jeff had adored Emma as much as her parents had, and had given in to anything she wanted, both because he wanted to please her and because he was often too bone weary, with the crippling hours he was having to work, to argue with her.

She had never been terrific in bed, but Jeff had thought all woman of that social standing were probably the same, and sometimes she could be persuaded. When Paul was born, she was ecstatic. She engaged a nurse to care for and feed the child, but in her way she more than loved him; she worshipped and adored him.

Jeff could have felt jealous of the child, in fact he realised now that he *had* been jealous of him, for Emma had no love or thought for her husband after that. At any rate, Jeff had to redouble his efforts in the still shaky firm now that he had a son to provide for too, and as he was leaving the house before dawn and was never home before ten each evening, he seldom saw Paul for the first few years of his life and when he did see him, he was only too grateful that he hadn't to do that much with him.

Matthew had been born when Paul was four and Jeff saw that the baby only had the scrapings of affection from Emma, which made the child surly, whining and demanding, and so less likeable. When Jeff did try to get to know both boys in the rare free time he had, Emma made it quite plain their rearing was up to her, together with her parents and the servants she had engaged to help her. Jeff's job as a father, it appeared, was in the implanting of the seed and providing the money for them all to live comfortably.

Not a full year after Matthew's birth, Jeff came home one day to find that Emma had arranged for their double bed to be disposed of and single beds installed instead. Emma said that a double bed could cause all sorts of unpleasantness starting and single beds were better altogether, for they had two sons now and didn't have to deal with all that messy business ever again.

Even then, Jeff settled for a sexless and loveless marriage and said nothing. Now he wondered why he had. He was not a weak man generally, and was known as a hard knock in business – a man to be reckoned with, not one to stand any sort of nonsense. Yet he had always given in to Emma. This meant he had backed away from fatherhood. His life centred around the factory and his club. He seldom saw his sons and certainly didn't know the remotest thing about them.

Now he realised what a disservice he had done the growing boys in taking this, the coward's way out. He hadn't even known about Paul's love of medicine, his dreams of being a doctor. He had assumed as the eldest son Paul would inherit and run the engineering works, and it had been a shock to find out the boy had other plans. Jeff had had to do an about turn in his dreams, and at first he'd been disappointed and surprised.

Emma had a great deal of influence with Paul and had always been able to turn him to her way of thinking, but this time she had come up against a brick wall. Paul told her he wanted to be a doctor, he had always wanted to be a doctor and wouldn't be happy doing anything else. In desperation, she had drafted in Jeff to 'talk sense into the lad'. However, when Jeff had spoken to Paul, he had been impressed by the boy's commitment and supported him, once he realised he was serious and had nurtured this idea for years. And now he had done it: he was Dr Connolly, soon to be a married man.

Suddenly Jeff decided to go to take a look at the house Paul seemed so proud of. He got to his feet cautiously, trying to ignore the pounding in his head and queasy stomach. He bitterly regretted he hadn't made this stand sooner.

He knew that Paul would be at home that day because he had said he had the next day off duty, and Jeff knew where the house was for Paul had told his parents the first time he had roared up on the motorcycle he had acquired.

'Come and see the house,' he'd urged. 'See what you think.'

Emma's nose had lifted in the air. 'If you think for one moment that your father and I are going visiting some slum that you have the ridiculous notion of living in, then you can think again,' she'd said.

Emma had nearly always answered for Jeff too, and that day it had irritated him, but before he had had chance to give voice to this, Paul had retorted angrily, 'It's no slum. If you were to come and see for yourself . . .'

'It is all a matter of degree,' Emma said, waving her hand dismissively. 'And why,' she demanded glancing out of the window, 'did you buy that ridiculous machine that your brother is now examining with such interest?'

'I've already told you this,' Paul said, deciding to leave the matter of the house to one side. 'I needed wheels. I work such awkward hours I couldn't use public transport.'

'I see that,' Emma said. 'But why didn't you buy a car?'

'Because I can't afford one.'

'Don't be silly, Paul. Your father would have bought you a car.'

'Then it would have been Dad's car, not mine. And probably bought with conditions.'

'I don't know what you mean.'

'Oh, I think you do.'

'Look, Paul,' Emma had said. 'That motorbike is totally unsuitable. For one thing it is a death trap, and for another it is not the mode of transport for this type of area. I mean, what would the neighbours think?'

'Bugger the neighbours! Who cares what they think?'

'I do. I care a great deal.'

'So, I can't come and see you if I come on the bike, is that what you are saying?' Paul had asked with a voice like steel.

Jeff had held his breath, knowing that if Emma was to say that was what she meant, Paul would leave and God alone knew when they would see him again.

Fortunately, Emma had recognised that fact herself. 'No,' she'd said. 'You have me all wrong-footed.' She'd

232

crossed the room and laid her hand on Paul's arm. 'I'll not have one minute's rest while you are on that thing. You'll drive me into an early grave. As for the neighbours . . . well, they will think there has been some sort of altercation between you and your father when he didn't buy you a little run-around when you graduated.'

'Perhaps the neighbours will think I am standing on my own feet and some might even think it about time,' Paul had replied. 'Isn't that sort of attribute valued any more? As for an altercation with Dad, that would be fairly difficult to do. He seldom takes any part in these discussions, do you, Dad?'

It had hurt – not the words but the look he'd cast his father, which was one of almost pity, as if he wasn't a real person with opinions of his own.

Jeff knew that he deserved little better, but that day, the morning of 1 January 1935, he decided he was going to change. Only minutes later, he was turning his car towards Erdington.

Paul spotted his father outside the house and thought something had happened. Surely only some disaster would have brought him to his door. He dressed hurriedly, flew down the stairs and flung it open.

'What is it?' he cried.

'What?'

Paul's teeth were chattering, both with the cold and the expectation of bad news. 'Come in, for God's sake, and tell me what has happened.' He drew his father inside. 'It's proper brass-monkey weather out there and we'd best go into the breakfast room. We have a paraffin stove there.'

Jeff stood gazing around the quite large room Paul

led him into. The hall had had patterned tiles, but here lino had been laid once, and it was pitted and ripped. Set upon it were a rickety wooden table and four chairs nearly as bad. There was also a kitchen cabinet that had seen better days, filled with an assortment of odd crockery and cutlery, and a battered kettle, which Paul lost no time in filling and placing on top of the paraffin stove that held pride of place in the middle of the room.

'Sit down,' Paul said. 'I will make us some tea.'

Jeff sat down at the table on one of the rickety chairs and said, 'Nothing has happened. That is, nothing bad. It's just . . . Paul, can we talk?'

Paul could hardly believe his ears. As he bustled, setting out cups and saucers, he thought of the years of when he was growing up when he would have given his eyeteeth for his father to say, 'Paul, can we talk?' If ever he had asked his advice when he was a lad, his father would always ask what his mother thought and his mother's decision was always the one he would uphold, even when Paul sensed that he didn't agree with it.

Other boys at school would tell him of going to cricket, or football matches, or fishing with their fathers. How he had envied them. However, when he asked his father if they could do any of these things together, he would shake his head sadly. 'Your mother would never stand it, son.'

'Why not?'

'Well, be a bit mean, leaving her on her own, don't you think? Best say nothing about it.'

And now this father, whom he barely knew, had turned up unannounced at the house he said he would never visit – or at least his mother had said that, and he hadn't contradicted her – and claimed he wanted to talk. It didn't make sense.

The silence in the room stretched out and Paul, busy with his thoughts, was unaware of it. And Jeff watched him apprehensively and wondered what he was thinking. Suddenly the kettle came to the boil, the shrill whistle sliced through the silence and Paul lifted it up and started to fill up the teapot.

'The milk will have to be condensed,' he said. 'We never bother buying fresh. It doesn't keep.'

'That's all right,' Jeff said. 'I'll take it as it comes.'

'Can I get you something to eat?' Paul said, handing his father a cup. 'I mean, I haven't much in, but I could probably do a jam sandwich or something.'

'Nothing,' Jeff said. 'Tell the truth, I'm feeling a little delicate this morning.'

Paul grinned, 'Yeah, I'm a bit hungover myself,' he admitted. 'But I could sell my granny for a cup of tea.'

Jeff gave a small laugh. 'I know just what you mean.'

And then, because he knew whatever this visit was all about, there was nothing to be gained by going all around the Wrekin, he sat down opposite his father and said, 'Go on then. You said you wanted to talk.'

'Yes,' Jeff said. 'And the first thing I want to do is apologise for being such a poor dad for you, and Matthew too, of course, but it is you I am concerned about now.'

It was the very last thing that Paul had expected. He said, 'You weren't a poor dad.'

'Nice of you to say so, Paul,' Jeff said. 'But I let you down badly sometimes.'

'Come on, Dad,' Paul said. 'This is life. Maybe it isn't

235

a good thing to have everything you want.'

'Like your mother does, you mean?' Jeff said. 'And you're right, of course. I never argued with your mother and while it is a good thing in one way to present a united front before children, rules and decisions should be discussed first, maybe compromises made. I found myself agreeing with things that went totally against the grain for the sake of peace and quiet. And I am not blaming your mother here, but myself for being weak enough to just let her get her own way, even when I knew it wasn't what I wanted and often wasn't what you boys wanted either.'

'Look, Dad, isn't this like so much water under the bridge now?'

'Yes, of course it is,' Jeff said. 'No one has a chance to reclaim years or have another go at getting it right.'

'And I haven't grown up too bad, so you must have done something right.'

'You are a fine boy – man now, of course, a boy no longer – and I think you grew up well despite your mother and me,' Jeff said. 'I am proud of you and your decision to work in the hospital rather than to set up in some private practice somewhere. I am even proud of the way you managed to procure this house and settle the problems of affordable transport on your own, but I bet you that there's not much graduation money left.'

'Well, no,' Paul had to admit. 'Most of the graduation money went on the bike. They were reluctant to let me have terms under the hire purchase scheme as I hadn't a guarantor. And I hadn't been working long.'

That brought Jeff up sharp. 'You didn't think to ask me?'

'No,' Paul said, then added more truthfully, 'Well, yes, I did, but I thought you wouldn't approve, or Mother wouldn't anyway, which was always one and the same thing.'

Jeff smarted under the words said in such a matter-of-fact way.

'Then there was the trip to Ireland to see Carmel's parents,' Paul went on. 'They are as poor as the proverbial church mice, by the way, and the father a bully of the first order.'

'Are they invited to the wedding?'

'Just the mother. Oh, and a nun called Sister Frances that Carmel worked with in Letterkenny Hospital.'

'A nun on the guest list, eh?' said Jeff with a quizzical raise of the eyebrows. 'Better be on our best behaviour then.'

'I should think that goes without saying at my wedding,' said Paul with mock severity. 'There is to be none of that dancing naked on the tables you know?'

'Ah, Paul, what a spoilsport you are,' Jeff said, then added with a twinkle in his eyes, 'It might even be worth doing it for the look in your mother's eyes. Can you just imagine it?'

'There is no imagining to it,' Paul said with a chuckle, 'for there would be no expression in them. If you did something half as bad, Mother would be lying stone dead of shame on the floor.'

'D'you know, Paul, I think you are right there,' Jeff said, draining his cup and getting to his feet. 'Now, how about showing me around this place?'

'No problem,' Paul said. 'You can even see all of it because Chris stayed with Lois's parents last night. Mind you, I am not apologising for the state his room might be in, nor mine either.'

'Point taken,' Jeff said. 'Lead the way.'

The paraffin stove took the barest chill off the air in the breakfast room, but the rest of the house was like an ice-box and their breath escaped in visible whispery strands. Jeff was glad he had not removed his coat and noted that even Paul took a jacket from his room as they passed. But though the whole house was as cold as ice and the furnishing less than basic, Jeff saw that they had a acquired a solid house that, with a little time spent on it, would make a lovely home for the two couples. 'You have a grand place,' he said to Paul as they returned thankfully to the breakfast room. 'What is the rent?'

'Sixteen and six,' Paul said. 'And then we had to pay three months' rent in advance and fifty pounds' indemnity in case we break or damage anything.'

'So with your graduation money virtually all used up, how are you going to furnish the place?' Jeff asked. As he saw Paul stiffen he said sharply, 'There is no need to bristle and get on your high horse. Pride and a stiff neck is all very well when you are on your own, but now you have Carmel to consider. You can't expect her to live in these conditions, nor Lois either.'

'Both girls understand. We'll save and do one room at a time.'

'Paul, James intends to furnish Lois's part of the house as a wedding present,' Jeff said. 'He came to see the house and that's what he decided. Told me himself only yesterday.'

'Chris didn't say,' Paul said

'Chris doesn't know, Lois neither,' Jeff said. 'James

intends it as a surprise and I would like to do the same for you and Carmel. James can get it all at cost from Lewis's and, as he said to me, the more he orders, the cheaper it is. Think about it, Paul. You can't expect Carmel to struggle along with rubbish, when beside her Lois has everything new and modern.'

Paul sighed. He knew he could not ask that of any woman. 'All right,' he said. 'It's just that you have already spent so much on me, funding me through university, and I was grateful until I realised by accepting sponsorship I was giving Mother a stake in my life. I swore then that I would accept nothing else.'

'Right,' Jeff said. 'Now listen. First of all, this is me you are talking to, not your mother, and the new me. It is perfectly normal for a parent to give their marrying children a wedding present if they can possibly afford to and this will be mine to you. Your mother will have no part in it and therefore no say. And there will be no strings, no conditions. All I ask is that when you marry, you work to keep the spark alive between you, for when it goes out, it is almost impossible to rekindle.'

Paul felt immeasurable sadness when he saw his father's stark eyes. He felt as if he had been given a glimpse of the bleakness of his life. And he felt a lump rise in his throat as he took his hand firmly and shook it.

CHAPTER FOURTEEN

There is not a woman living who would not be ecstatic on being given a free hand to choose the furniture and fittings for her new home, knowing someone else would pick up the bill at the end of it, and Carmel was no different from anyone else. What was even better was that it was so unexpected. In Camel's world, people didn't do things like that.

Paul watched her face as she sat opposite him in a coffee shop one lunchtime, and he knew he had made the right decision in accepting his father's offer. How could he have faced her and told her what his father had proposed and said he had rejected it *carte blanche*, without even consulting her?

He knew that, even worse, she wouldn't say a word in condemnation. The disappointment would be in the dullness of her eyes, the lack of expression in her face and the general slump of her body, and he would have felt the worst heel in Christendom.

'What about Lois?' Carmel said suddenly. 'Won't she feel it awfully? Maybe we can share some of the things.'

'There is no need,' Paul said. 'Uncle James is doing

the same thing for Lois and Chris. That is the good of it. With her father manager of a huge department in Lewis's, he can get us top-quality goods at a fraction of the cost. You and Lois can pore over the catalogue or wander around the store and make your choices to your heart's content, once Lois is told. At the moment it is all hush-hush. Uncle James wants to surprise her. My father wouldn't take that risk, because he wasn't sure that I would accept it.'

'Oh, I'm so glad you did,' Carmel said.

'What would you do if I had said no?' Chris said with a smile. 'Get angry with me? Rant and rail and call me stupid?'

'I can't think of any occasion when I would be angry with you,' Carmel replied simply. 'As for being stupid . . . when someone does something unexpected, there is always a reason. Maybe I would like to find out that reason, not to change your mind, but perhaps to try and understand.'

'D'you know, Carmel, you are a very special lady?'

Carmel gave an impish grin and said, 'Oh, you're not so bad yourself.'

Paul laughed at her. 'You just wait. If we weren't sitting in a very refined coffee shop finishing a substantially good lunch, I would show you what's what, my girl.'

A delicious tremor ran all through Carmel at Paul's words and the expression in his eyes.

'I can barely wait,' she said, springing to her feet and tugging at his arm. 'Come on. Let's go. We are wasting the daylight and we have little enough of it.'

*   *   *

Paul found keeping the secret from James far less irksome than Carmel did. For a start, although he and Chris shared a house, they seldom met up and if they did, they were too tired or too rushed to talk much. The scant time they had free, they usually spent with their fiancées.

With Carmel and Lois it was different. They were often on similar shifts, on the wards together, in the canteen together. They sometimes went to the theatre or cinema for a treat and they talked about everything under the sun. Now, for the first time, there were vast unchartered waters that Carmel couldn't even dip her big toe in. But because the girls talked and confided in one another, it was Carmel who told Paul one day, at the end of January, that Lois and Chris were going looking at beds on his next day off.

'Trust him to think of double beds first, the dirty old roué,' Paul said with a smile.

Carmel smiled too and snuggled into the crook of Paul's arm. Outside, snow was being blown into drifts by the wind that howled and gusted against the house, but inside all was cosy and warm where a bright fire crackled in the grate. One of the first things Jeff had done, after having his offer accepted, was to arrange for the chimneys to be swept and a few hundredweight of coal to be delivered into the coal bunker. He also filled the shed with bundles of sticks and told Paul to light a fire if he was asking Carmel to the house and not to have her shivering in the breakfast room, and Carmel was very glad that Paul had done as he was told.

'The point is, though,' she said, 'what if they go and buy a bed? Don't you think this secrecy thing has gone on long enough?'

'I do. It has,' Paul agreed. 'And first thing tomorrow I will phone my father from the hospital and tell him. Now that is out of the way, come here and tell me that I am the most wonderful, terrific lover you have ever had.'

'I haven't had that many to compare you with,' Carmel said with a smile and then added, 'What I do know about you is that you are the most conceited, big-headed—' She could say no more, for her mouth was covered by Paul's. As the kiss grew in passion and intensity, Paul couldn't help wishing that he had a double bed upstairs, or anything more comfortable than his rickety old camp bed.

Paul wasn't so consumed by lust though, that he forgot what Carmel had said. The following day, as soon as he had a minute, he found a phone.

'I was only talking of this to James the other day when we met up,' Jeff said. 'I mean, surprises are all very well, but if you are not careful they can turn into shocks – and unpleasant ones, at that. Thanks for telling me. I'll get on to him.'

Two days later, Carmel was getting ready for bed when Lois, who had been over to see her parents, came in. Carmel looked at her glowing face and said with a wide grin, 'I presume that you have spoken to your father.'

'Yes,' Lois almost squealed. 'It's wonderful terrific news and I can't believe you knew and said nothing.'

'It was awful,' Carmel said, 'but I had made a promise. It will be even better now you know.' The two girls threw their arms around each other and danced a jig around the room. Jane and Sylvia, who came in just moments later, were amazed at their good fortune and could quite understand their excitement.

News of it flew around the hospital and most of their colleagues were full of admiration, though some of that was grudging. Then the following week, Lois and Carmel took Jane and Sylvia along to the house to see it for themselves and they were delighted for their friends. 'You can understand some people being a bit resentful, can't you?' Carmel said. 'I mean, we already had so much, with the house and all.'

'That's hardly your fault,' Sylvia said. 'And don't you think if the same chances had come their way they wouldn't have grasped them with both hands? I know I would have done, and anyone who says differently is a liar.'

'That's right,' Jane said in agreement. 'You just enjoy it and don't you bother about anyone else.'

Carmel was so glad that Sylvia and Jane felt that way. Their opinion mattered a lot to her.

When, shortly after this, Carmel and Paul began to make arrangements for their wedding, Carmel was surprised that Paul wasn't to be Chris's best man as she had almost assumed he would be.

'But why not?' she asked.

'Because I am a Catholic.'

'What's that got to do with anything?'

'We can't take part in a service of any other Church,' Paul said. 'Didn't you know that?'

'No,' Carmel said, 'but then it would never have come up, would it? I mean, until I came here I seldom even met anyone who wasn't a Catholic. But what is the reason for a ban like that? Do they think we'll become

244

corrupted by other Churches' services or what?'

Paul laughed. 'I don't know why. I have never asked. That is just the way it is.'

Carmel thought it stupid, but knew that she could do nothing to change it, and together with Chris and Lois they began to lay out their wedding plans. Carmel and Lois's time as junior staff nurses would end on Friday, 19 July and the ceremony when they would receive their certificates and any medals they might be awarded was the following week, on 26 July. In view of this, and because Paul and Carmel were having no honeymoon, it was decided that their wedding would be first, on 3 August, and Lois and Chris's would be the following week as they were having a few days away in Blackpool afterwards.

Carmel and Paul's marriage was being conducted at the Abbey, though Father Donahue from St Chad's was officiating and, their fairly modest reception was to be in the upper room of the Cross Keys public house, just a few yards down the road, as it was all they could afford. After the gift of the furniture, Paul refused to take another penny piece and Carmel was glad, for anything more salubrious would have completely overawed her mother and probably would have spoiled the day for her.

The following day, Paul went up to tell his parents of the arrangements. Emma wasn't a bit impressed. She bitterly resented the fact that her niece was to be married in the imposing Holy Trinity Church in Sutton Coldfield and then the guests were to be taken in chauffeur-driven cars to the Royal Hotel, the oldest and most expensive in the town, for James had pulled out all the stops for his younger daughter. Paul could have had that and more, and then she would have been able to hold up her head with pride, despite the doubtful pedigree of his bride.

Paul had laughed when she had suggested it – not particularly unkindly, but still it had offended her and more especially when he went on to say with a smile, 'We can't afford that kind of wedding, Mother. As I told you, we are to be married in the Abbey just this side of Erdington Village and then just down the road is the Cross Keys pub. They let their upper room out for weddings and functions like that. We have both been to see it and it is perfect, and because it is so close it will save on the hiring of cars.'

'What rubbish you talk sometimes, Paul,' Emma said through tight lips. 'This hole-in-the-corner wedding is not suitable for someone of your standing. I was thinking of something much more lavish.'

'No, Mother.'

'Paul, see sense,' Emma pleaded. 'What is the matter with you? You don't need to worry about cost. Your father and I would pay for it. Traditionally, of course, it is the girl's parents who pay for the wedding, but your father tells me the Duffys are far too poor to be able to do that so we will—'

'No, Mother,' Paul said again. 'For one thing, you have paid too much out on me already, and for another thing, that isn't the type of wedding that either of us wants.'

'You haven't just to consider yourselves in this circumstance.'

'Sorry, Mother,' Paul said. 'It is the one time in our lives when we *can* please ourselves, surely?'

246

'And expect us to go on foot from the Abbey to some odious little public house?'

'It is no distance at all, Mother,' Paul said. 'And the room is very nice. If you would just go and look—'

'I have no intention of going to look,' Emma snapped. 'You are doing this to shame me . . . shame us all.'

'Not at all. I'm doing this because we want just a simple wedding.'

'Well, then,' Emma snapped, 'if you will not see sense in this matter and will consider no point of view but your own, then you needn't think your father and I will attend. What will your fine friends think of that?'

Before Paul was able to reply Jeff said calmly, 'When I need you to make decisions for me, my dear, then I will tell you. If you feel you cannot go to Paul's wedding, then of course you must stay away, but I wouldn't miss it for the world.'

In one way, Paul was glad of his father's support, but he caught sight of his mother's face as she swept from the room indignantly and felt suddenly sorry for her.

Jeff misinterpreted the look on Paul's face and said, 'Don't worry, son. She'll come round when she has time to think about it.'

Paul didn't bother contradicting his father, but he knew that his mother's mind was made up.

'She won't come to the wedding because we are having the reception in some place she described as an "odious little public house",' he told Carmel.

'Surely it is just a bit of a pique she is in,' Carmel said. 'Disappointment, maybe, but she'll get over it. She wouldn't boycott her own son's wedding.'

Paul said nothing, but he knew his mother was more

than capable of carrying out that threat unless he was to apologise and promise to do things her way, and he had no intention of doing that.

Once the wedding plans were made, the girls set to with a will, choosing the furniture and floor coverings to grace their home. Carmel could scarcely believe that she actually owned such beautiful things.

They also toured the Bull Ring for things for their bottom drawer and for the slinky underwear they wanted for their wedding night, which, they both admitted, they were looking forward to with great relish. They discussed what sex would be like and Lois knew a little bit more than Carmel, for she had quizzed her sister, Sue, but still both were a little bit afraid although Lois did say, 'It might not be so bad in the end. I mean,' she went on, 'when we are kissing and everything, you want them to go on and on, don't you?'

'Oh, not half,' Carmel said with feeling.

'Well, our Sue says it's a bit like that, but the point is you *can* go on and on once you are married.'

'Doesn't it hurt?'

'She says only at first and not that much if they are properly gentle and that.'

'Let's hope they are then,' Carmel said. 'I'll tell you what, though, whether it hurts or not, I can hardly wait.'

'Me neither,' Lois agreed. 'In fact, in some ways it's a good job that we don't see much of our chaps, all told. We might well have pre-empted those marriage vows a time or two.'

And Carmel knew exactly what her friend meant.

* * *

The days began to get a tad warmer, and as April drew to a close the talk was all about celebrating the silver jubilee of George V in early May. As an Irish girl, totally unconcerned with the British monarchy, Carmel was perplexed at the patriotic attitude of so many people, just because some old bearded man had sat on the same throne for twenty-five years.

She kept her views to herself, however, when she realised how much in the minority she was. Even the hospitals were celebrating, and the General was no exception. The wards were decorated with streamers of red, white and blue, and Union Jacks, and special food was ordered for the day. A party atmosphere prevailed and the rules for everyone were relaxed. Carmel thought it extremely worrying to see Matron smiling benignly at everyone as she toured the wards. Usually, when anyone saw Matron smiling, they knew some poor soul was going to catch it, but not that day.

As many patients as possible were taken in wheelchairs, or even in their beds to the concert held that evening. They were entertained by comedy acts, enthralled by the sleight of hand of the conjurer, and they thoroughly enjoyed the singsong to round off the whole thing. At first they sang many of the traditional and patriotic songs of the day like, 'There'll Always be an England'. Then they moved on to songs from the Great War, like 'Goodbye Dolly Gray' and 'It's a Long Way to Tipperary'. These then gave way to music-hall songs, such as 'Daisy, Daisy'.

Those patients who were well enough sang with gusto and waved the Union Jack flags they had been given with great enthusiasm. Even Carmel was affected by the zealous pride she saw shining in many of the patients' eyes and knew that, for some, the day had been better than medicine.

Some kind benefactor had donated coronation mugs for each child in the hospital and a coronation crown for each adult, and the patients were really overwhelmed by such generosity. Carmel sincerely hoped the patients might be able to hold on to their treasures and they wouldn't soon be gracing the window of a pawnbroker's. However, she did recognise when it was a case of food on the table, or rent to pay to prevent a family being thrown out on the street, a crown or a mug wasn't much use to anyone. For now, though, at least they had the pleasure of owning the gifts.

The Queen's Hospital had run similar activities. When Carmel saw Paul that night they spoke of it.

'It certainly gave them all a boost,' Paul said. 'If we had a celebration like that once a week, I reckon they would need to stay in hospital less.'

'Don't be daft,' Carmel said with a laugh. 'If we had a celebration like that every week, people would be fighting to get in.'

'Yeah,' Paul agreed ruefully.

'I don't see what the fuss was all about anyway,' Carmel admitted. 'The *Evening Mail* and the *Despatch* carried pictures of the street parties taking place all over the city. What difference will it make to the average man on the street who is on the throne or how long he has been there? I mean, isn't the king or queen just a figurehead?'

'Yes and no,' Paul said. 'You are right, though, that to Joe Bloggs this matters not a jot, but I think it is a national pride thing. Not every country these days has a royal family and it is something we can feel proud about. Let's face it, Carmel, there is little else for the country these days. I mean, we fought a war with Germany and won, and then when the men were demobbed there was nothing awaiting them but the dole and poverty.'

'I know,' Carmel said. 'I suppose this sort of thing raises their spirits even just for a short while.'

'Yes, that's it,' Paul said. 'It shows the rest of the world, and I suppose Germany in particular, that we have something we can be proud of.'

'People say the chancellor Germany has, that Hitler chap, is turning Germany round.'

'So I believe,' Paul said grimly. 'But I would like to know at what cost. There are lots of strange tales coming out of that place that I don't like the sound of at all. And as for the next Olympic Games to be set in Berlin, it's just madness. Still,' he said, kissing Carmel lightly on the lips, 'are we going to stand here all night discussing politics, or are we going to go out and enjoy ourselves?'

'Ah, Paul, what do you think?'

'Come on then,' said Paul, catching up Carmel's hand. 'Let's see what Birmingham has in store for us this evening.'

Lois and Carmel had to have an interview with the manager of the trust fund that ran the hospital, Mr Murdoch, the senior doctor, Dr Humphries, and Matron to see whether it would be acceptable for them to continue in nursing after they were married. There was no policy in place about this now they were fully trained, and while

251

Mr Murdoch and Dr Humphries had no problem with the girls continuing, if that was what they wished to do, the final decision had to be left to Matron Turner.

The two girls knew this full well, and they also knew that the matron had re-examined their experience charts, gone over their examination grades and requested reports on them from the nurses they had worked with.

'Don't you worry your little head over that,' Nurse Chambers had told Carmel. 'I have given you such a glowing reference, you would hardly recognise yourself. I even went on to say that it would be a great loss if you were forced to leave.'

Matron had been impressed with that, and Lois's testimonials were nearly as good. The matron deplored the policy of training nurses to the acceptable standard, only for them to get married and leave as soon as they were qualified. She couldn't see why more girls could make nursing their life, as she had.

In the dark recess of her mind, she remembered Len Bishop, whom she was engaged to in 1914, just before war was declared. 'Over before Christmas, Cathy,' he had declared as he boarded the train full of troops. He had leaned out of the window and kissed the tears from the young girl's eyes. 'Don't you cry,' he'd admonished, but gently. 'I'll be back before you know it, and we'll talk to your father about getting married. What do you say?'

Yes, yes, yes, was what the young Cathy Turner said, for she loved Len Bishop with all her heart. She was twenty-three, more than ready to marry, and had been a qualified nurse for two years. However, she had passed her twenty-fourth birthday six months later when Len's distraught and anguished mother had brought around the telegram and pushed it into her trembling hands.

Catherine cried as if she would never stop. She refused to eat, became ill and didn't care. She had wanted to die, to be with Len, and the doctor her worried parents brought in had little sympathy with her.

'The man had to do his duty – surely you knew that – and now you must do yours.'

'Mine?' Catherine had asked, confused.

'Yes, yours,' the doctor snapped. 'You have a duty to yourself to rise above this, and to your parents, who are worried to death about you, and to that noble profession you broke your neck to enter. All this wallowing in grief is no good for anyone, so get up from this bed and do something useful with your life.'

CatherineTurner had got up. She knew that she would never marry and that she would strive to rise in nursing, for it was all she had left. That had happened twenty years before, in 1915, and she seldom allowed herself to think about it now, but looking at the two girls before her brought it all back. Nothing would spoil their young dream. Her Len and countless more had died in the war to end all wars, and even all this business with Germany couldn't amount to anything much, so these girls would be able to have their cake and eat it on her say-so.

'Well, Matron,' Dr Humphries said, with a little cough, and the matron realised the silence had stretched out between them as she had reminisced.

'Oh, yes. Sorry, Doctor.'

'What sort of nurses then are these two?' the doctor asked her. 'Diligent? Hard-working?'

'They are indeed,' the matron said. 'In fact, I have no problem at all with their work. But, Nurse Duffy,

Nurse Baker, how do you intend to look after your husbands effectively if you are nursing too?'

'Well, you see, Matron,' Carmel said, 'our prospective husbands are junior doctors anyway and so understand – perhaps better than most – the pressures we will be under and the hours we will have to work. They both work odd hours too and have no objections to us continuing.'

'Hmm,' the doctor mused. 'Those men are Paul Connolly and Christopher Fellows, and both doing sterling and necessary work at Queen's, but the girl is right: the men's hours will be anything but regular.'

'And what about when the babies start arriving?' the matron asked.

'We don't intend to have children for some time yet,' Lois said. 'Both of us want to make our mark in nursing first.'

'You feel the same, Nurse Duffy?' the matron asked.

'Yes, Matron.'

'I thought you were a Catholic?'

'I am, Matron.'

'Hmm.'

Carmel was sure that the matron would have said far more, but before she was able to, the doctor said with a smile, 'In my experience babies often appear in their own time, whatever their parents have decided. However, we can cross that bridge when we come to it. I have no objection to your continuing here after your marriage and if Matron feels the same, then I don't see any reason why you shouldn't.'

Outside the room, the two girls hugged each other in delight. Carmel knew that, much as she loved Paul and longed to be married to him, nursing too was very important to her. She would have missed it terribly if she had been forced to leave.

CHAPTER FIFTEEN

When Eve stepped on the platform of New Street Station in Birmingham, on Thursday evening, two days before Carmel's wedding, she could hardly credit that she was there at last. When the people of Letterkenny heard that Eve Duffy, no less, was away to England to see her daughter married, alone except for a nursing sister, and that her truculent bully of a husband had given her permission for this, they had been astounded. Many remembered the fine young man on Carmel's arm from the previous autumn and most women at least could understand Eve wanting to be there on her eldest daughter's big day and felt sympathetic towards her.

As many said, 'The poor woman often doesn't have the money to bless herself with, but that is hardly her fault and God knows she does her best.' Women who had barely bid Eve the time of day after Mass, now shook her by the hand and wished her Godspeed. Some of the men too began to look at Dennis in a new light and said they were surprised at his decision, for all it was the right one as every girl wants her mother near on her wedding day.

Dennis, however, had just a hazy recall of that evening in the pub when he had made the declaration that he was allowing Eve to travel to England and, sure he had been tricked into it, he began to feel resentful. Usually Eve bore the brunt of his bad humour, but Sister Frances had guessed how Dennis might react and when she saw the stiff way Eve was holding herself four days before they were to leave, she brought her and Pauline to bide at the convent with the full approval of Siobhan.

A drunken Dennis, when he discovered Eve gone, and guessing where she had made for, had hightailed it down to the convent, roaring and carrying on until some of the townsfolk were alarmed enough to send for the guard. He told Dennis if he didn't want to find himself behind bars he should head for home quickly, and escorted him to his own door to make sure he went.

Eve was glad of the respite and overwhelmed by the nun's kindness and generosity when she had seen the clothes that Sister Frances had put by for her. She was also filled with relief that she wouldn't let Carmel down, and pleasure that for once in her life she would wear something that didn't look like a wash-rag. The trip to the hairdresser's had been her first and she had been amazed at the difference a good cut and set made, so that she could barely recognise the woman staring back at her in the mirror.

Michael, who was travelling to Birmingham with his mother and had paid the fares for the both of them, was stunned too when he called down to see her the day before they were due to travel. He knew that, in a different life, married to a different man, his mother would have blossomed and that she still was a very attractive woman.

'You look wonderful,' he said sincerely, kissing her on the cheek. 'Beautiful, in fact.'

'Don't be codding on, Michael.'

'I'm not,' Michael declared. 'Wait till our Carmel sees you and the competition she has. God, you'll outshine the bride, so you will.'

Carmel, of course, had endorsed this, for she saw a different woman standing before her. It wasn't just the smart coat, shoes and hairstyle – it was far more than that. She realised that it was an absence of fear that caused Eve's eyes, so like Carmel's own, to shine in her head at the delight of it all.

'Mammy,' she cried, 'you look just terrific! A million dollars, so you do!' She embraced her mother and knew she would be proud to have her there by her side at the wedding. Then she led her mother and brother to the waiting taxi. Michael was dropped off at the house to be looked after by Paul and Chris, who were getting ready for the stag night, and then the taxi headed back into town, for Carmel was also staying with Sister Frances and her mother at the convent until her wedding day.

Eve Duffy, in a costume of pale lilac with a toque hat of a slightly darker hue, and looking every inch the mother of the bride, helping Carmel dress for the most important day of her life so far.

'I can't tell you how happy I am for you, pet,' Eve said, 'for you are marrying for love. I see it shining from every part of you.' She kissed Carmel and continued,

'Go on, my darling daughter, love your man with all your heart and soul, and you will be able to conquer the world.'

'Ah, Mammy, I love you,' Carmel said brokenly. 'I'm so glad you came over for the wedding and I hope heartily that you do not suffer for it.'

'Don't worry about me,' Eve said airily. 'Sure, aren't I just grand? Concentrate on your own day today. And for goodness' sake wipe your eyes before Sister Frances is on top of us and giving out at me for upsetting you.'

Less than fifteen minutes later, Carmel stood at the doorway of the church, with her brother, who looked as smart as paint himself and as proud as punch to be the one to lead his sister down the aisle.

'All right?' Michael asked.

'More than all right. Much more,' Carmel said fervently.

'So if you are ready . . .' Michael said. He proffered his arm and, with a little sigh of contentment, Carmel slipped hers inside his.

As they appeared in the door of the porch, Father Donahue gave the nod to the organist, the strains of the Wedding March filled the church and people got to their feet. Carmel recognised many and she was aware of some dabbing at their eyes, but her own were firmly fixed on Paul, who had left the front pew with Matthew beside him and now stood in front of the altar, leaving Jeff in the pew alone.

So, she thought, Paul's mother hasn't turned up.

She felt angry that the woman should snub her own son in that way. What was wrong with her? She wasn't normal. However, Carmel couldn't help a feeling of relief that Emma would not be there to sneer at her or possibly using her vindictive, intimidating tactics on her mother, which could destroy her in seconds. But still, Emma was Paul's mother and surely he was upset, if not devastated, by what she had done.

Carmel was nearly at the altar. She handed her bouquet to her weeping mother and relinquished Michael's arm. Paul sneaked a look at her and she saw the deep, abiding love reflected in his dark blue eyes and she moved closer to him as the Nuptial Mass began.

Afterwards, they greeted everyone. There were a great many nurses, including, surprisingly, Aileen Roberts and her cronies, the last ones Carmel would have expected to attend, but Aileen could have told her that with Paul lost to her, she had her sights on a gorgeous new doctor, just started, that, now she was a qualified nurse, she was hoping to get to know a whole lot better. In fact she thought Carmel's brother was quite a dish as well. It was a pity really that he was so young.

There was also the gaggle of girls that had surrounded Paul at the first and last party Carmel had attended in Paul's home. Now that she was his wife and on his arm as a right, she had to be acknowledged too by these young women, and in this way she was greeted by them all, including Melissa, her younger sister and her father, Charlie.

There was no sign of the mother and all of a sudden it was all crystal clear to Carmel. The younger set, whether they'd hankered after Paul or not, thought he had a perfect right to marry anyone he chose and came along to the wedding to show him that. The Chisholms, however, were personal friends of the Connollys, and while Charlie had come, probably to show solidarity with Jeff for making the stand, his wife, who quite possibly had plans of her own concerning Melissa and Paul, had sided with Emma and chosen to stay behind.

No one mentioned the absence of Emma, that's what was so weird – as if it was quite normal for a mother not to go to her own son's wedding. When Carmel tried to say something to Jeff, as he gave her a kiss and welcomed her to the family, he just said, 'Emma is one on her own, my dear, and will probably live long enough to regret her behaviour this day, but you are not to let it spoil yours.'

And that was that.

There was no chance to have a quiet word with Paul, who had come to take her arm to lead the guests down to the Cross Keys, the Catholics glad to go, for they had all taken communion and so hadn't been able to eat anything. Now they were more than ready for the food.

The meal was far more than just adequate, and the speech Matthew gave surprisingly witty, though it centred, of course, on the theme of another good man down, which was only to be expected. This was followed by a few words from Paul and then it was time to cut the cake, which had been supplied by the pub. Then everyone left the table so that the room could be cleared for dancing.

Looking back on that day later, Carmel remembered how her mother seemed to charm people so easily and Carmel saw that what she had dismissed as feebleness was in fact innate gentleness and goodness. Eve had asked at the first opportunity where Paul's mother was and she could scarcely believe that Emma had chosen not to go to the wedding she herself had risked all to attend. Sister Frances, who was beside her, could easily guess at what Eve was thinking, for she was shocked and surprised herself.

Jane and Sylvia also wanted to catch a glimpse of the old battle-axe, who had been so horrible and supercilious with Carmel, but they too were to be disappointed, though Carmel said they had the chance of seeing her at Lois's do the following week. Emma would probably decide it was up-market enough for her to deign to attend.

'I can't understand Aunt Emma,' Lois said. 'I mean, she thinks the sun shines out of Paul.'

'Well, that's why, isn't it?' Sylvia said. 'Doesn't want anyone else to have him.'

'Oh, there are some she wouldn't have minded so much,' Carmel said, indicating Melissa standing beside her father and sister on the other side of the room.

Jane and Sylvia took a good look at the girl and then Jane remarked, 'She's all right, I suppose. Pretty enough, or would be if she didn't have such a pout on her, but she doesn't hold a candle to you.'

Carmel smiled. 'Give over, you.'

Suddenly Lois, who had seen her father detach himself from Sister Frances, to whom he had been talking, said, 'Come and talk to Daddy. He's free now.'

Carmel had met James Baker many times before when he had called to collect Lois and, of course, she had seen him over the business of the furniture, but she hadn't actually met him to talk to and she found him to be a charming man. He kissed her cheek and told her how lovely she looked and how much he had enjoyed the wedding, and hoped the one he had planned for the following week would be half as good.

However, it was plain the man loved his daughter so very, very much. Carmel thought she would have given her eye teeth for her father to look at her like that just the once.

She suddenly needed Paul, needed his presence beside her and his arm around her, and she turned away to look for him and came face to face with Matthew, whom she had seen nothing of since the business at the party on New Year's Eve, which she had told no one about, and her insides began jumping in nervousness as he said, 'Have I done anything to upset or offend you?'

'I shouldn't think you need to ask that,' Carmel said, her voice clipped. 'After that business the last time we met.'

'I was drunk for God's sake,' Matthew said. 'Are you going to hold that against me always? I mean you haven't really spoken to me at all today.'

'Can you wonder at it?' Carmel snapped. 'Maybe I am choosy who I speak to. Anyway,' she continued with a dismissive wave of her hand, 'I have been busy. There were other guests to see to.'

'What if I said that I learnt my lesson?' Matthew said. 'I'm sure that Paul would like it if we could become more friendly. 'We have always been close Paul and I.'

Carmel didn't know how close the brothers really were, but though Paul could get irritated with Matthew, he had told Carmel often that he had always felt sorry for the fact that his mother had never had any time for him. She also knew that from that day, like it or not, Matthew was part of her family and that being so, she knew there would have to be occasions when they would have to meet. Maybe today was as good as any to put that drunken assault behind her. 'All right' she said to Matthew with a shrug, 'What do you want me to say?

'I don't want you to say anything. I just want you to prove you like me a little by dancing with me.'

It was the last thing Carmel expected Matthew to say after the previous time and she was taken aback. 'Oh, but I was looking for Paul,' she said.

'You will have a lifetime with Paul,' Matthew said. 'You don't mind, do you, brov?' he said as Paul came forward to lead his wife on to the floor to start the dancing.

Paul did mind. In fact, he minded very much. It was his place and his right to lead the dancing, but then he remembered the scraps of attention Matthew had survived on and he had also heard his brother's last comment and knew he was right. He had a lifetime with Carmel and so he gave a shrug and said, 'If you like, but don't keep her away too long.'

It was unfortunate that it was a waltz, giving Matthew the excuse to hold Carmel so tight against him that even through her dress and petticoats she could feel every bit of him and when she felt the hardness of him she knew she had been right to be nervous of this man.

'Have you noticed our dear mama's absence?' he said into her ear.

'Of course,' Carmel snapped, sharper than she intended. 'I am not blind.'

Matthew chuckled. 'I expected Paul to be more cut up than he is. They were so close, him and Mother, I used to wonder if the umbilical chord had been properly severed, but you have hacked through it successfully.'

'I had no wish to alienate Paul from his mother.'

'Well, you have done it, whatever you intended,' Matthew said flatly. 'That's why dear Mama hates your guts. You are in good company, for she doesn't much care for me either.'

'I don't want to carry on with this conversation,' Carmel said stiffly. 'And can you please get your hands off my bottom?'

'Don't tell me you don't enjoy it?' Matthew said, moving his hands in a caressing movement. 'I bet Paul has done this any number of times and reduced you to jelly.'

Carmel had the urge to stamp on Matthew's toes hard or to swing out of his arms, though he held her so tight she doubted she could do that without making a scene. Then she risked breaking up any relationship Paul and Matthew had and she would hate to do that, especially as she had already successfully alienated him from his mother. Anyway, she knew, human nature being what it was, if she instigated a scene now, it was all anyone would remember of the day and Melissa and her ilk would lose no time is telling Emma just how awful the wedding had been.

So, though she cringed with embarrassment, she bore Matthew's hands pawing at her and willed it to be over quickly. Matthew would have held on to Carmel at the end of the dance but she was having none of it and she swung away from him.

Jane and Sylvia caught up with her before she reached Paul. 'I should watch that brother of Paul's, if I were you,' Jane said. 'He looks a nasty piece of work.'

'He is,' Carmel said with feeling. 'He gives me the willies, to tell you the truth.'

'He had his hands all over you,' Sylvia said.

'Let's hope Paul didn't see that,' Carmel commented grimly.

However, Paul had been talking to his father at the bar and had noticed nothing amiss. He smiled as he saw Carmel approach and went to meet her. Holding her arm, he led her on to the floor. Carmel took care to keep well away from Matthew after that.

Many hours later, when Paul carried Carmel over the threshold of 17 York Road there was no one to see him do it. Eve and Sister Frances had returned to the convent and Michael and Chris were lodging at Lois's house to give Paul and Carmel some time on their own as they weren't going away anywhere.

Paul set Carmel down in the hallway of her new home, slammed the door shut with his foot and said, 'Come on. Let's go to bed.'

'At this time of day?' Carmel protested.

'I need the time to show you just how much I love you,' Paul said. He waved an admonishing finger at Carmel, though he had a large grin on his face as he went on, 'And another thing, you promised only a short while ago to obey me, and here you are arguing already.'

Catching Paul's mood, Carmel touched her forelock 'Yes, sir, no, sir, three bags full, sir.'

'You cheeky monkey! Wait till I catch up with you,' Paul cried.

With a shriek, Carmel was up the stairs with Paul pounding after her. He caught up with her at the threshold of their bedroom door and the two staggered across the floor to collapse on the bed, helpless with laughter.

The laughter abated as Paul gently held Carmel's face in his hands, looked deeply into her eyes and said, 'There are not enough words to tell you how much I love you. I would lay down my life for you and consider it an honour. And now I want to show you how much I love you.'

'Oh, yes, Paul, yes,' Carmel cried as her insides tinglied with anticipation.

They undressed hurriedly, leaving their clothes in crumpled heaps on the floor, such was their urgency and their need for one another, and then slipped naked between the sheets. Carmel thought wryly of the slinky nightdress that she had bought in preparation for this night, which was still folded in the chest of drawers, and then Paul's lips were upon hers. She thought for one fleeting minute of Lois's sister, Sue, and hoped that Paul would be gentle with her, and then she gave herself up to the pleasure of it.

Paul was fully aroused, but knew Carmel was nowhere near ready yet, and he had no wish to frighten her, or hurt her more than he had to. So he gave himself up to bringing pleasure to her. Carmel was giving little gasps of delight as Paul eased her mouth open and began shooting his tongue in and out while he fondled her breasts. When his lips fastened on her nipples and his hands began to slide between her legs, she arched her back and moaned in desire and told Paul, 'Hurry, for God's sake.'

However, Paul had no intention of hurrying for anyone's sake and he went on fondling, caressing and kissing her until there was not much of Carmel's body that he hadn't explored and she was in an agony of desire and felt as if she would die if he didn't enter her as she was begging him to.

When he did, her first sigh was almost of relief and then she felt the stab of pain and cried out against it, but in a second it was over and the rapturous feeling filled her body as she moved in rhythm with Paul until she felt she had reached the pinnacle of joy and she cried out again and again so that Paul knew he had pleased his young wife, and he smiled.

Each time Carmel and Paul made love was better than the one before, as they each learned how to please the other. Sometime that night they had crept downstairs for tea and toast, which they had taken to bed. They couldn't seem to get enough of each other and Carmel did wonder at one point if you could die from sheer happiness. However, eventually they were both spent and, entwined together, they fell into a deep sleep.

Shafts of sunshine through the gap in the curtains, which Carmel had pulled hurriedly closed the evening before, woke her and looking at the clock she saw it was almost eight. Despite the tea and toast hours before, her stomach growled with emptiness, but she couldn't eat until after the nine o'clock Mass, when she would take communion. After that, she had arranged to take her mother and Sister Frances to see the city centre while Paul took Michael for a spin on the bike.

'Why take them into Birmingham on a Sunday?' Paul had asked when Carmel had told him what she proposed. 'The shops will be shut.'

'That's exactly why,' Carmel said. 'Neither Mammy nor Sister Frances has money to spend and you don't see so much with the streets thronged with people. Admittedly the Bull Ring won't be the same, but they will get the essence of the rest of the place.'

However, if she didn't get a move on, she told herself, nothing would be achieved, and she leaned over the bed and kissed Paul awake.

Carmel had been introduced to Father Robertson, one of the priests from the Abbey, the day before. Father Donahue from St Chad's had said the Mass and married Carmel and Paul, and Father Robertson had assisted him. He was plump both in face and body, and his brown-grey eyes would miss little, Carmel imagined. He had a bald head except for a little fringe of grey decorating the edge of it.

Carmel didn't much care for him as a person and guessed that Father Donahue was a kinder, friendlier priest altogether, but the Abbey would be their parish from now on and she thought that Father Robertson was probably all right as a priest.

That morning he greeted Carmel and Paul as though he had known them for years.

'Thank God he didn't ask us if we'd had a good night's sleep,' Paul whispered to Carmel as they hurried home. 'I wouldn't have been able to keep my carnal thoughts from showing in my eyes.'

'Sex-mad, that's your trouble.'

'No, darling, Carmel-mad,' Paul said huskily. 'It is you driving me wild. What say we forgo breakfast for a bit?'

Suddenly the hunger dropped from Carmel as if it had never been. As soon as they were in the door she led the way upstairs.

Eve saw straight away that whatever happened in the marriage bed had pleased her daughter and she was relieved. She knew the nicest man in the world can turn into a sex-crazed monster in the bed, concerned only with satisfying his own desires, and she was glad it was not that way for her daughter.

Though Letterkenny was no little village, Eve and Sister Frances were stunned by the size of Birmingham and dazzled by the array and variety of shops. They wandered through one street after the other in open-mouthed amazement. Carmel took them to the Bull Ring and they stood and looked around the empty cobbled streets, beside the statue of Nelson, St Martin-in-the-Fields church in front of them.

Carmel tried to explain the busy bustling thoroughfare the Bull Ring was six days a week, when the barrow boys lined the streets in front of the shops, flower sellers were grouped around the statue of Nelson and touts sold things from suitcases with someone keeping a watch for the police. She knew it was hard for the women to imagine and harder still when she started to tell them about the entertainment to be had there on a Saturday night as she led the way up New Street to the Town Hall.

They were impressed by the Town Hall, as she had known they would be, and the Council House. Then Carmel led the way down Colmore Row, past the Grand Hotel, opposite St Philip's, with the flowerbeds a blaze of colour, and up Bath Row so that they could see St

Chad's, for they had attended Mass that morning in the chapel in the convent. Then they went down Whittall Street so that they could see the entrance to the nurses' home where Carmel had lived for four years, before emerging into Steelhouse Lane where they would catch the tram home.

They returned home to a meal that Paul had cooked, and Eve, married to a man who didn't know how to boil a kettle, was further amazed – and even more so when it turned out to be so delicious. Michael was thrilled with his first trip on a motorbike, which he said was wizard.

'We went to Sutton Park,' Paul said, smiling at Michael's enthusiasm. 'We'll all go tomorrow, if you like. You have a few days left before you go back and we intend for you to make the most of them.'

Later, as Eve was shown around the house, she remembered the word her son had used, 'wizard', and could have said it herself. The whole house was truly wonderful, magnificent, and Eve, who hadn't an envious bone in her whole body, was just filled with thankfulness that her daughter had effectively fallen on her feet.

Sister Frances, feeling that Carmel needed time with her family, said she would bide at the convent and did not accompany them when, over the next two days, Carmel and Paul took her mother and Michael first to Sutton Park on the train and the following day to the other side of the city to Cannon Hill Park and the Botanical Gardens. Then they went further on the tram to the Lickey Hills. A fine time was had by all and Carmel knew she would miss her mother and brother when they returned home.

Before he left, Michael confided to Carmel that he was glad to get out of Lois's house, where her mother held sway and people danced all day to her tune and her word was law.

'Honest to God, she reminded me of our dad,' he said. 'She might not go around thumping people, though I think she's not averse to the odd slap, but she'd rip a body to bits with her tongue. I tell you, Carmel, it's a shame to waste two houses between the pair of them.'

'Poor Lois!'

'It is "Poor Lois" all right,' Michael said with feeling, 'and the sooner she is married and out of it, the better.'

CHAPTER SIXTEEN

The following Saturday, Carmel and Paul took the tram to Sutton Coldfield to the Royal Hotel to attend Chris and Lois's reception. It was a very upmarket place and Carmel was awed by the liveried footman, or butler, or whatever he was, who welcomed them at the door, took their outdoor things and directed them to the room where the function was being held.

Looking across the foyer, Carmel could see Chris and Lois in the doorway, greeting guests, most of whom had followed them down from the church. The newlyweds were particularly delighted to see Paul and Carmel, who hadn't been allowed to attend the service.

'Lois, you look truly radiant and very beautiful,' Carmel cried. She did, and her dress too was gorgeous. Chris was also smart in a pinstriped suit. However, it wasn't the clothes that made the difference, but the happiness almost oozing out of the couple. They were at one and in love. Carmel hugged them both in delight and declared truthfully she couldn't have been happier. Paul took Lois in his arms as well and shook Chris's hand warmly.

'Glad to be able to congratulate you at last,' he said. 'Bit of a nuisance, the church not allowing Catholics to attend the ceremony, but that's religion for you.'

'Most religions are like that about something or other,' Chris said. 'Give me the agnostic viewpoint any day.' Then, seeing that Lois was engaged in talking to Carmel, went on quietly, 'Left to myself I would have slipped away and married Lois in the registry office and then had dinner with a few chosen friends in a nearby pub. It's the marrying that counts. Course, I didn't bother saying that because I knew it would go down so very badly, but all this is a bit over the top for me.'

'Never mind, mate,' Paul said, punching his friend on the arm. 'Grin and bear it, eh? It is only the one day and her father, at any rate, is as pleased as punch.'

'Oh, he's like a dog with two tails,' Chris said. 'He is all right, James. I have a lot of time for him, but the old harridan of a mother . . . well, I don't know what you'd have to do to please her.'

Paul's eyes followed Chris's to the disgruntled old woman sitting at a table across the room, her whole body showing her dissatisfaction, watching the proceedings with malevolent eyes. 'Don't even try to make up with her,' he advised. 'Whatever you do will not be good enough. Now we had better move off because you have a backlog of guests to see. I'll catch you later.'

Paul, with Carmel on his arm, moved further into the room, each of them accepting a glass of sherry from a silver tray as they went. Paul was immediately hailed by someone from the hospital and as he stopped to speak to them, Carmel made her way to Sylvia and Jane, glad to see familiar faces in the midst of such opulence.

They obviously thought the same because Jane's first comment was, 'A bit posh, this.'

'Bit different from my spartan effort last week.'

'I really enjoyed your wedding,' Jane declared. 'We both did. Didn't we Sylv?'

'Not half,' Sylvia agreed. 'I had a really good time at yours and could definitely relax more. And while this is all right, when my time comes . . . well, my parents won't have the money for anything like this.'

'Well, what did mine have?' Carmel said. 'Not a brass halfpenny. We, or rather Paul, paid for it himself.'

'And very good it was too,' Sylvia said. 'And how is married life?'

'Terrific, thanks,' Carmel said, and laughed at the speculative look that passed between her two friends. 'You are getting no more information than that. Let's just say in all areas it is more than just satisfactory. And what did you mean by "when my time comes", Sylvia? Should we be expecting an imminent announcement?'

'Hardly,' Sylvia said. 'Don't you think that if I had anyone special in my life, he would be here by my side? You couldn't see my man for dust when I casually mentioned getting engaged.'

'Mine too,' Jane said gloomily. 'I mean, what is a girl to do? If we are not careful, the two of us will be left on the shelf.'

Carmel laughed. 'Don't be daft,' she said. 'You are only twenty-two. It's a bit much to be thinking of you as old maids yet a while. But then,' she went on, 'just think who will be so proud of you if you are.'

'Who?' said both girls, puzzled.

'The matron,' Carmel said with an explosion of

laughter. 'She actually said to me just before I was leaving that she couldn't understand this passion to get married and that nursing could be a very fulfilling life.'

'Well, that makes me feel a whole lot better, I don't think,' Sylvia said. 'What about you, Jane?'

'I feel the same,' Jane said. 'And though I enjoy nursing, if I was just to have that in my life, I would think there was something missing.'

'Yeah, like sex?' Sylvia put in.

'If you like,' Jane said. 'And nothing wrong with that either. Makes the world go round, don't it?'

'It certainly does,' Carmel said. 'We would be in a bad way without it. None of us would be here, for a start.'

'Yeah, think of that loss to mankind.'

'It would be a blow the world would never recover from, I'm sure,' Carmel said with a grin. 'And added to that, sex is very pleasurable.'

'Oh, yes? Tell us more.'

'Not likely,' Carmel said, laying her empty sherry glass on the table. 'And just now I am going to do my good deed for the day and say hello to Lois's mother.'

'Oh, God! Lion's den or what?'

'Definitely,' Carmel said. 'But it would look mighty odd if I didn't.'

She didn't relish the prospect and knew just by looking at the old, miserable woman that she was the sort to target the weak and vulnerable and go in for the kill. Carmel straightened her back unconsciously before crossing the room.

She saw that Marjory Baker's mouth looked like a scarlet slash of disapproval in a face so wrinkled in dis-

276

content that the face powder lay in the folds of the skin. She reeked of lavender. She regarded Carmel's approach with blue eyes that were as cold as ice and glittering with malice, and when Carmel sat down in the seat next to her and, holding her hand out, said pleasantly, 'Hello, Mrs Baker,' the older woman smiled like a cat might, just before it kills a mouse.

Marjory ignored the hand of friendship completely. 'You are our Lois's friend?' she growled. 'James pointed you out to me.'

'Yes,' Carmel said, still pleasant and still extending her hand. 'How do you do?'

The woman looked at the hand as if it was a snake and her lip curled in contempt as she said, 'Another who couldn't wait to be married. Not long out of the school room and now married.'

Carmel sighed and, giving up the idea of shaking hands with this woman, gave a grim laugh before she said, 'It's a long time since I was in the school room. I have been working since I was fourteen, trained as a nurse at eighteen and now I am twenty-two, an adult, and old enough to decide when I want to get married.'

'Oh, a hoity-toity miss?'

'Not at all,' Carmel began, and then stopped for she suddenly saw Emma Connolly enter the room and head straight for her. She felt her insides quiver with nervousness.

She needn't have worried, as Emma totally ignored her. 'Marjory, my dear. How are you now?'

Marjory's eyes narrowed. So, that's the game, she thought. Emma isn't happy with Paul's choice. 'I'm not so bad,' she said. 'But would be better if I wasn't sitting next to this young woman who seems to think she knows better than her elders.'

It was as if Marjory had not mentioned Carmel at all. Never by the slightest twitch did Emma acknowledge her presence and instead said to Marjory, 'I am glad to see you looking so well.'

Carmel got up. There seemed no point in staying to be ignored and she hadn't gone more than a few paces when Jeff grasped her hand.

'My dear, can I apologise for my wife's arrant bad manners?'

'There's no need. It isn't your fault.'

'There is every need,' said James, coming to join them. 'I can hardly believe Emma is my sister, and my wife is little better.'

'You're not the only one being given the silent treatment either,' said Jeff. 'Emma cut Paul dead when she came face to face with him in the hallway just a few minutes ago.'

That did shake Carmel. She didn't think Emma would ever do that to Paul. Paul obviously didn't think so either, for when she caught sight of him just a minute or so later he was white-faced and carried their coats over his arm. 'We're leaving,' he said.

'Oh, but—'

'Look, love,' Paul said, 'at the very least there will be a terrible atmosphere if we stay, and at worst I will end up telling my mother exactly what I think of her. We can't spoil Lois and Chris's day like that. I have explained it to them and they understand.'

'I wouldn't let anyone push me out,' Jane said fiercely as Paul went to have a few words with his father. 'I mean,

I agree, your mother-in-law is a cow of the first order, but she would leave before I would.'

'Hear, hear,' Sylvia agreed.

Carmel shook her head. 'No,' she said, 'Paul is right: we can't risk spoiling the day for Chris and Lois.' She hugged both her friends and said, 'You know where we live and I expect to see you there before too long. And now that I am an old married woman, I want all prospective boyfriends paraded in front of me, so I can give my expert opinion on their suitability. We will have the pair of you married off in no time, you'll see.'

'We'll bear it in mind,' Sylvia said with a laugh as Paul came to claim Carmel.

Things might have been explained to Lois, but she was still mortified with shame and she had tears streaming down her face as she hugged her friend when they met in the little lobby by the front door of the hotel.

'Don't cry,' Carmel urged. 'Please don't. It is terrible to cry on your wedding day.'

'But I wanted you here, you of all people.'

'Listen, Lois, our Church prevented me from attending the actual wedding. This is just the party afterwards.'

'Yes, but—'

'So, how about us arranging a house-warming when you come back from your few days' honeymoon and invite just the people we want to invite?'

'I'm all for that,' Chris said. 'Damned shame, though, about all this unpleasantness.'

'That's all right,' Carmel said. 'We are stuck with our relatives. Thank God we can choose our friends.'

'You said it,' Paul said. He glanced back into the room. 'You had better get back to your guests.'

'Put some powder under your eyes first to hide the puffiness,' Carmel suggested, and Paul and Carmel slipped away as Lois was trying to repair the damage to her face.

However, despite the assurances Carmel had given to Lois, she felt slightly despondent as they wandered down Mill Street hand in hand. She tried to hide this from Paul, knowing he would start blaming himself, and yet she knew he had made the right decision to leave the reception. Paul, though, did know how Carmel was feeling, for he was disappointed himself and when he pulled her into his arms and said, 'What d'you say to a slap-up meal for the pair of us, somewhere posh to suit the finery we have on, as we are not going to get a sniff of the wedding breakfast?' Carmel had to feign more enthusiasm than she felt.

By the time Lois and Chris were back from their few days' honeymoon in Blackpool, Carmel had come to terms with the way she had been slighted at their wedding reception and told Lois, who was still fretting, not to worry about it.

'For a start,' she said. 'Paul's mother is crackers. I mean, he told me he didn't expect his mother to go to our wedding because she had said basically she didn't think it posh enough. But any normal person, even if they had been daft enough to think that months before, would surely to God had got over it by the day of the wedding. Mind you, judging by the way she was at yours, I can only be glad she didn't make it. We left to prevent

280

a scene that would have spoiled your day. She is not used to being thwarted, that's her trouble.'

Lois nodded. 'You're right. We used to go for a visit and Uncle Jeff would spend the whole time running around after her and sort of deferring to her in everything and agreeing with her all the time. I hated to see him like that, to tell you the truth. I mean, he wasn't at all like that about other things.'

Carmel said, 'It probably got to be a sort of habit so that he didn't think about it; it was just something he had always done. It spread to the children as well – Paul, anyway, because he was always being warned, as he was growing up, not to upset his mother. That gets kind of ingrained in a person like the fear we all had for my father. Even to think of him now ties my stomach in knots.'

'Yes, and we were encouraged to think of our mother as delicate,' Lois said. 'D'you know, we're not well blest with our parents, are we? Perhaps my mother, your father and your mother-in-law should get together sometime and compare notes.'

'Yeah,' Carmel agreed with a smile. 'I have a better idea. Let's leave them on a deserted island somewhere and they can bully or roar at one another to their hearts' content.'

'Oh, if only we could,' Lois replied with feeling, then went on, 'Uncle Jeff was furious with Aunt Emma after you had gone. I have never seen him so angry and it was worse because he had to sort of control it, you know. Anyway, as soon as the meal was over he fetched Aunt Emma's coat and hauled her off home. I bet he really let rip then.'

281

'Oh, to be a fly on the wall.'

'I'll say. I'd be rubbing my hands with glee to see that woman get her comeuppance, for all she is my aunt.'

'Oh, let's draw a line under the bloody woman,' Carmel said. 'I am fed up talking about her. Let's plan the party instead – a much nicer subject to discuss altogether – and I think one of the first things to do is introduce ourselves to the neighbours. I haven't seen them except to nod to, taking things to the bin or hanging out a bit of washing, because I thought I would leave formal introductions until you arrived. They are an oldish couple and as tomorrow is Saturday we might get both of them in if we go round in the afternoon. I'd hate to get off on the wrong foot and let the first time we meet them be when they come round to complain about the noise of the house-warming.'

Lois could see the sense of that. The next afternoon, the two girls knocked at the house next door and met George and Ruby Hancock. The couple had been intrigued by the set-up next door to them and were delighted to discover two young married couples would be living there, all with respectable jobs and the girls, at least, with impeccable manners.

'We've been here all our married lives,' Ruby said. 'Brought a family up, only now they are grown and scattered. The house is too big for us now. Me and George rattle around in it and we keep saying we should move to somewhere smaller, and we probably should but . . . well, the house is full of memories. Anyroad, we know the area here and it's that convenient for everything, as you will find out before you've been here very long.'

'I'm sure we will,' Carmel said. 'I am impressed

already with the amount of shops just a stone's throw away. But the point is, we wanted to give a house-warming party and—'

'Don't you worry about making a bit of noise,' Ruby said. 'Young people have to enjoy themselves, we know that.'

'You're more than welcome to join us.'

'Well, it's not really our thing, but we may look in.'

They did look in, for as Ruby said to her husband later, 'I mean, when you think of rented houses like this, we could have all sorts of riff-raff living next door instead of those two lovely girls. I would like the opportunity to meet their husbands too.'

'Well, I don't mind showing my face,' George said with a sneaky smile at his wife. 'They'll likely have some good beer in and a chance of a bit of decent food for once in my life.'

'Any more comments like that, my lad, and you will be in no fit state to go there or anywhere else,' Ruby commented grimly, and George burst into gales of laughter at the outraged look on his wife's face.

The Hancocks fitted in remarkably well. They obviously liked young people, and they confessed they were never happier than when their grown children converged on the house, filling it again with noise and bustle.

All in all, the house-warming party was a terrific success. Many of Carmel and Lois's fellow nurses came, and Paul and Chris had invited some junior doctors and medical students too. Lois was particularly pleased to see Sylvia and Jane. They, of course, wanted to talk about Lois's wedding and what had happened at it. They both said they'd never seen such a display of bad manners and it was hard to believe that such nice people as Paul and Lois had grown up so normal. Carmel could do nothing other than agree with them.

Carmel had been impressed and relieved to find out that Lois could cook well.

'I learned fast when I was looking after my mother,' she said. 'Nothing fuelled her rage more than singed meat, inadequately drained cabbage or lumpy gravy.' She smiled and went on, 'The odd slap is a great incentive to getting it right.'

'You had better mete it out to me then,' Carmel said with a grin. 'There was never much in the way of food to cook in the house I was reared in and, of course, then I had all my meals at the nurses' home, as you did, so I have no idea how to go about it.'

'Oh, you will soon pick it up. The basic things are just common sense, really, and even the other stuff – well, anyone can follow a recipe,' Lois said. 'I bet you will be a dab hand at it in no time at all.'

However, the good food did help the party go with a swing and afterwards there was dancing, the music emanating from Lois's gramophone records, and everyone talked of the party for days afterwards.

The months slid by, the two young couples adjusting to married life and the crazy hours they all seemed to be working, and looking forward to the festive season and a chance of a little time together. Carmel had never had Christmas off since she had begun at the hospital but this time she had put in for it and so had Paul, feeling they would like to spend their first Christmas as a married couple together rather than in two separate hospitals. Lois and Chris felt the same and the four of them were delighted that their applications were successful.

In the very early hours of Christmas Day, as Carmel and Paul left the Abbey after Midnight Mass, it was so bone-chillingly cold Carmel thought she could smell it. She also felt and heard the frost crackle beneath her feet as, hand in hand with Paul, she scurried home and, despite the arctic chill, with, the beautiful Latin words of the Mass and the familiar carols still running around her head, she felt at peace with the world.

The house was chilly too: the fires banked up for safety lent little heat to either the breakfast room or their own lounge, and Carmel was glad she had had the foresight to put the hot-water bottles in the beds before they had left the house.

'Go on up,' Paul said, giving Carmel's bottom a little pat. 'I'll bring us up a cup of tea laced with whiskey to put new heart into us and then when we have that finished, I will warm you up properly.'

Carmel shivered and scampered up the stairs in delicious anticipation for the sex side of their marriage, though it wasn't as often as they might like, due to their working schedule, just got better.

The next morning, when Carmel opened her eyes, it was to see Paul sitting on the edge of the bed getting dressed. He smiled when he saw she was awake, leaned over and gave her a kiss.

'Happy Christmas, Mrs Connolly.'

'And the season's greetings to you, Mr Connolly.'

'Are you happy, darling?'

'Happier than I can ever remembering feeling,' Carmel answered sincerely.

Paul eyed the bed longingly and Carmel knew exactly what he was thinking, but they could hear that Chris and Lois were already up, and regretfully Carmel shook her head. 'We have to go down,' she said.

Paul sighed. 'I know, but later we'll make up for it,'

'You're on,' said Carmel, as she leaped out of bed and started to dress.

As soon as the debris from the breakfast had been tidied away, the girls began to prepare the mammoth dinner. They had just finished and gone back into the breakfast room to join Chris and Paul when there was a knock at the door. They were intrigued as to who would visit on a Christmas morning. Paul went to open it and came back with his father, who carried in his hands two bottles of champagne, both tied up with ribbon.

'My goodness,' he said as soon as he was over the threshold, breathing in deeply, 'something smells good. Magnificent, in fact.'

'That's Lois's dinner cooking,' Carmel said.

'You helped too,' Lois said.

'Ah, but I just did what I was told,' Carmel said. 'You did the planning and all.'

Jeff smiled. 'Lois, your father says that life has never been the same since you deserted the ship and went on to nurse. The woman that they have in to see to your mother is also supposed to cook an evening meal and James always says she isn't a patch on you. I know for a fact he often goes out for fish and chips when she has gone home. Anyway,' he said, beaming around at them all, 'you are in for a treat and I am not going to stay

286

here and let it spoil. I just came to wish you a very merry Christmas.'

'Thank you, Dad,' Paul said, taking the bottles from him. He felt bad about his father, caught in the crossfire between him and his mother. Lois and Chris had been to see their respective families already and taken cards and presents, but Paul had not been near his old home, though he had phoned the factory and wished both his father and brother a happy Christmas and a very prosperous new year. Lois told Carmel she didn't blame him one bit, and Paul didn't seem to care one way or the other, but Carmel couldn't help feeling sorry about it all. She saw now that Paul had some guilt about it too.

'Look, Dad,' he began, 'I feel really bad I haven't been round and—'

'Don't fret, son,' Jeff said. 'We know who is at fault here and I don't think your mother will ever change. But there is no need for us never to see each other. Maybe we can meet for a drink a time or two. I could sign you into my club with no bother, or maybe I can come and see you here.'

'You would always be welcome,' Carmel said warmly. 'In fact, we would love to have you visit.' The others endorsed that just as earnestly.

'Right then,' Jeff said, a big beam lighting up his whole face, 'I'll get your Christmas present. I have it in the car.'

'You have given us our Christmas presents,' Paul said. 'The champagne.'

'That was just to drink and enjoy,' Jeff said. 'This is something different and I might need a hand with it. The box is quite hefty.'

The box was indeed quite hefty, and a few minutes

later, when Paul and his father brought it in, the girls were nearly delirious with joy.

'A wireless,' cried Lois. 'Oh, Uncle Jeff, aren't you just the tops?'

'I take it you're pleased?'

'Much more than pleased,' Carmel said. 'More like delighted.' And, greatly daring, she stood on tiptoe and kissed Jeff on the cheek. Lois followed suit.

Jeff went quite pink and said, 'I'll bring presents more often if I get that sort of reaction.'

'Thanks, Dad,' Paul said again. 'It really is very good of you.'

'Well, there is great entertainment to be had from a wireless, right enough,' Jeff said. 'But the world is an unsettled place just now and it does no harm to keep abreast of things.'

It was as if a sudden chill fell over the room and Carmel shivered.

'You're cold,' said Paul solicitously. 'And no wonder. Between Chris and myself we have let the fire nearly go out.' He was poking up the fire as he spoke and then placed nuggets of coal on the embers. Carmel didn't bother telling him that it wasn't cold made her shiver but a sudden sense of foreboding.

Chris and Lois had placed the wireless on one of the shelves at the side of the fireplace and were twiddling knobs on it.

Jeff, noting the preoccupation of the others, said quietly to Carmel, 'How is your mother these days?'

'Oh, grand,' Carmel said.

'Charming woman,' said Jeff. 'Quite utterly charming.'

'I wanted to send a few toys to the children, for it is Christmas, after all,' Carmel said, 'but Paul convinced me that money to my mother was probably more beneficial.' She didn't say that what Paul had actually said was that for the children to have full bellies for once in their life would mean more.

'I'm sure that is right,' Jeff said. 'Your mother would have more of an idea of what they wanted.'

Carmel thought that what her siblings wanted didn't even enter the equation. She knew Jeff would have no concept of how they lived, but she was prevented from giving any sort of answer because Paul came forward with two glasses of champagne.

'You must have a Christmas drink with us at least, Dad,' he said, handing a glass to his father and one to Carmel. 'What I do know is that in order to secure this day together we will all be working flat out over the new year, so let us all raise our glasses both to Christmas and to 1936, and all it may bring.'

CHAPTER SEVENTEEN

On 20 January 1936, King George V died. Carmel
remembered the old and rather dour, heavily bearded
man whose pictures had been splashed all over the papers
the previous May at his anniversary. Apparently, though,
his son who would become Edward VIII was nothing like
his father.

'Now that is what I call handsome,' Aileen said, one
day in the hospital dining room. 'A real man.'

There were hoots of laughter around the table. 'Bit
out of your league,' Jane put in. 'Anyway, he's spoken
for.'

'You don't mean that Wallace Simpson?'

'Who else?'

'Well, he'll have to give her up now he's the King,'
Aileen said.

'Yeah, could you see us all accepting an American
divorcee as Queen?'

'He couldn't marry her, could he?' Sylvia said. 'Even
if she wasn't an American, I mean. He couldn't marry
a divorced woman and stay King because he will be Head
of the Church of England then.'

'But the Church of England allows divorce, doesn't it?' Carmel said. 'Isn't that one of the differences between that and the Catholic Church?'

'Ah,' said Sylvia. 'They might allow it, but it is frowned on a bit, isn't it? I mean, it isn't common or anything, and you can't have the head of the whole caboodle marrying a divorced woman.'

'Yeah, it would be like taking the mickey,' Jane said in agreement.

'So,' Lois said to Aileen with a smile, 'there is an opening, after all.'

'Yeah, hope for you yet,' another nurse put in, and there was laughter before the nurses dispersed and went to their respective wards.

Paul, however, was less concerned about the King than he was about Germany and its Chancellor, Adolf Hitler. Chris was just as bad, and they would often discuss things round the table on the rare occasions they could eat together.

Carmel couldn't quite understand their concern. 'Why should we care what is happening in Germany?'

'Sometimes we are forced to care,' Paul said.

'Paul, some of the people here worry themselves silly about getting enough to eat for themselves and their families,' Carmel said. 'That's the people I care about. Let Germany sort out her own problems. We have too many of our own to interfere, even if we wanted to.'

'Yes, but some of the tales coming out of there are so incredible ... well, they are almost unbelievable,' Chris said. 'I mean, I heard that Jews are being ousted from their jobs and some are just disappearing altogether. And I wish the Olympic Games were anywhere but Berlin this year.'

'It will be a farce, just like the Winter Olympics Hitler held in Bavaria in February, I bet,' Paul said.

'Yeah,' Chris said. 'Put on to promote the idea of the master race's superiority in everything.'

'Master race?' Lois repeated. 'What's that when it's at home?'

'Hitler's mad on promoting the Aryan race, tall, blond-haired, blue-eyed and athletic,' Chris said.

'Oh, so you're all right, Paul,' Lois said. 'You and this Herr Hitler bloke could be the best of buddies.'

'Huh, I don't think so,' Paul said, 'I'm more particular about the people I choose as friends. And this stuff about an Aryan master race is just crazy.'

'Yeah,' said Chris, 'but what is even crazier is the fact that the man proposing this master race is a shrimp himself – an Austrian by birth, black-haired and brown-eyed, and it seems no one in Germany has seen the anomaly of that.'

'All right,' Carmel said. 'So the man is an idiot, but he can't be any threat to us, can he? I mean, what have we ever done to him?'

'Nothing, but that might not save us,' Paul said.

Just before the Olympic Games began, civil war broke out in Spain in early July and the elected government found themselves fighting a group called Fascists.

'They are no better that the German Nazis,' Paul said.

It seemed Paul was right because, almost from the first, Germany sided with the dictator Franco, trying to oust the government. The British government elected not to get involved, which Carmel thought a very sensible thing. Spain was a long way away and what was happening there had nothing to do with them. She couldn't understand the British men who took themselves off to fight for the Spanish government.

'If they have enough energy to fight, then they should fight the poverty here first,' she told Paul fiercely a couple of days later. 'We had an old woman brought in today after she collapsed on the street. She was like a skeleton, virtually starved to death, so far gone that when we tried to get sustenance into her, her stomach couldn't take it. Think of that in this day and age. Daily I fight the illnesses often brought about by deprivation and poverty of our own people. It's disgraceful the way some people have to live.'

There really was no reply to what Carmel said. Britain was in dire straits and no one knew more about that than the four young people in the house, who were dealing, in the main, with the city's poor.

Just a few days later, as Paul and Chris prophesied, Hitler showed his racial policies to the world when an African American won four gold medals over Germany's white Aryan athlete Lutz Long, and Hitler refused to shake the winner's hand or place the medals around his neck, because he regarded the victor as racially inferior.

'Shouldn't have surprised anyone, really,' Paul said. 'What d'you think Hitler Youth is? Oh, the ideals are good, instilling national pride – and they tell them all about their culture, teach them nationalistic songs, taking them away to camp – but underneath all the fun are far more sinister motives. I mean, it isn't like the Boy Scouts here, for example.'

'I've heard that too,' Chris said. 'Maybe, though, the idea of national pride isn't a bad one in itself.'

'I dare say it isn't—' Paul began.

But Carmel cut across him, 'I would say it is very hard to feel pride in a country whose policies mean that you and yours are nearly starving to death and that no one seems to care enough to even try and find a solution. It won't go away on its own.'

Carmel, it seemed, wasn't the only one to think that something should be done. In early October two hundred men marched from Jarrow in the North-East, where unemployment was running at seventy percent, to London. They carried a petition with over eleven thousand signatures in an effort to bring their plight to the government's notice. There was a picture of them all in the paper, assembled behind the second-hand bus that was carrying all their cooking equipment, and the whole thing caught the imagination of the population.

As the Jarrow men trudged their way to the seat of government, Oswald Mosley, who was the leader of the British Union of Fascists, led an anti-Jewish march along Mile End Road in the East End of London, where many Jews lived or had businesses. There was much destruction as the premises were looted and ransacked, and any who protested were beaten up. Carmel, looking at the pictures in the paper Paul had brought home that night, felt sick.

Strangely, no repercussions followed. There were relatively few arrests at the time, and those responsible for the atrocities were never brought to book for it, including Mosley himself, although witnesses said he had incited the violence.

On the other hand, the Prime Minister not only refused to see any of the deputies of the Jarrow March,

294

but told the men unless they dispersed and went home, they would be arrested.

'It's because that Mosley is one of the toffs and the fellows from Jarrow aren't,' one of the nurses said in the dinner hall. 'My chap told me.'

'Mosley still shouldn't be above the law,' Carmel said.

'Are you kidding?' Jane answered scornfully. 'How many toffs have you read about coming up before the judge? The whole of this society hinges on class.'

Carmel cried at the pictures of those defeated, dejected men retuning home with no promise of a better life for their families or themselves, and they had set out with such hope in October. She knew what it was like to feel that yawning emptiness of acute and extreme hunger that lasted years, not days or weeks. She had seen, even through the grainy newsprint, the wasted look on the men's faces and read the panic and despair in their eyes.

'It's all corrupt, if you ask me,' Carmel said fiercely to the others at the house. 'Those poor, wretched men are harassed and threatened with imprisonment while Mosley and his cronies get away with mayhem and brutality.' She added, 'I know what it feels like to be beaten for nothing. The Jews must have felt like that, and what father could stand by and see his home destroyed and his wife and children terrified and not make some sort of complaint about it? And you know what really gets to me is that they didn't even have any redress in law, for the distressed Jews had been ignored just as effectively as the men from Jarrow.'

It seemed the last straw for Carmel when Edward decided that if he couldn't become King and also marry

Wallis Simpson and have her respected as Queen, he would abdicate in favour of his brother. The announcement of the abdication was scheduled to be broadcast at eleven o'clock on Friday, 11 December. In the end it was short and to the point as Edward said he would find it impossible to discharge his duties as King as he would wish to do without the help and support of the woman he loved.

Ruby came in to listen as she and George hadn't a wireless. When it was over she said, 'My George says it's a good job him leaving, like.'

'Why?'

'Because he is great friends with the Germans, ain't he?'

'Is he?' Carmel asked.

'Yeah, and if war comes, like . . .'

'There won't be a war, though, will there?' Carmel said. 'The Great War was the war to end all wars.'

'That's what they said,' Ruby said. 'Mark my words, we ain't heard the last of Germany, and if the balloon goes up, I want a man I can trust as King, not someone who is a friend of the enemy.'

Strangely, Carmel found many people, including Paul and Chris, felt the same as the Hancocks about the former King, and thought the new one was a man they could trust, though she thought him very uninspiring.

'He'll be all right, will George,' Paul assured her. 'He might not be as flamboyant and charming as his brother, but people will find he has far more integrity, especially if he can conquer that wretched stammer.'

The one who lamented the abdication of Edward was, of course, Aileen Roberts.

'I hear he is moving to a new country,' she said a few days later. 'Even if he stays, as he is sort of in disgrace, the papers won't be photographing him all the time any more.'

'If that woman had an ounce of breeding and any thought about doing what was right, then she would have gone right away from Edward and let him get on with the job he has been trained for from the cradle,' one of the other nurses commented.

'And what then?' Carmel said. 'People say Edward was too friendly with Adolf Hitler for their liking, and it could be awkward if later they became our enemies. So I'll stick with George. Better safe than sorry, I say.'

All four in the house were working over Christmas that year, which they thought only fair. However, they were off for New Year and the house fairly filled with friends to say goodbye to the old year.

They had the wireless on and when Big Ben began to chime the witching hour, glasses were raised and clinked together and there were hugs and kisses and cries of 'Happy New Year'. Suddenly, Carmel found herself pulled into the corner of the room by Paul and he hugged her tight.

'Happy New Year, darling,'

'And to you, Paul,' she said. 'To tell you the truth, I am glad to see the back of 1936 and I hope 1937 is better.'

At first it really seemed that things had improved for the four sharing the house. Now, with the men more senior doctors, their hours were more regulated and they were starting to have more of a social life.

Spring came early that year and towards the end of April, the days were definitely warmer and the evenings lighter. Everyone was looking forward to a temperate spring, leading to an even better summer.

Then, on 26 April, forty-three German aircraft attacked Guernica, a small town in the Basque area of Spain. Guernica was filled with its own people, refugees and those drawn in to shop, for it was Monday and market day. Those in the house heard about it first on the wireless and then read about it in the papers the next day. They saw the pictures of the mounds of rubble that had once been streets of houses, mixed with corpses and mangled, severed limbs, and the survivors traumatised and distressed.

The sight brought tears to Carmel's eyes, but Paul knew he was looking at a foretaste of what would happen in Britain if they went to war with Germany. He felt as if the whole world was in a spiral and the only outcome would be war, a war that would affect them all. He had talked over with Chris and his father what he intended to do if and when this happened. Jeff said he should try to prepare Carmel, but Paul hesitated to do that yet.

The new King, who would be known as King George VI, had his coronation on 12 May 1937, and although it was celebrated in the hospital as well as in towns and cities all over the UK, the rejoicing was muted compared to the anniversary celebrations for his father in 1935. The patients in the General, however, were happy enough with the festive food, the like of which few of them had seen for years, and the children were entertained with a puppet show followed by a conjurer, while the adults were treated to a concert.

The Prime Minister Baldwin retired not long after that and his place was taken by Neville Chamberlain.

'I don't know whether he is the sort of man this country needs at this time,' Jeff declared to his son one day.

Carmel didn't either. She had never been bothered about world affairs previously, but she had become interested in the talks around the table and gone on to discuss things with Lois and the others at work, where there was always a paper lying about in the rest room. As far as Carmel was concerned, the world was in complete disarray. In her opinion the country needed a strong man at the helm to steer Britain safely through the choppy waters.

'The world seems a really unsafe place at the moment,' Carmel told Paul one night as they lay in bed, as 1937 was drawing to a close 'I'm glad we made the decision not to have children, aren't you? I mean, this is no place to bring a child into at the moment.'

Paul murmured agreement and Carmel said, 'Do you think it will all calm down in the end?'

Paul sighed. 'I would like to say yes, to reassure you everything will be fine . . .'

'But it wouldn't be true,' Carmel said, 'and I am no wean to be fobbed off. I need the truth. Do you think it will eventually come to war?'

Paul was silent so long that it was answer enough.

'You do, don't you?'

'I think it may come to that, yes.'

'When?'

'Who knows that, pet? I'm not a world leader. They decide these things.'

'But you think it is inevitable?'

'Yes, in my heart of hearts I feel it is unavoidable. And when it comes, you know I will have to go. Everyone will have to do their bit.'

Carmel gave a sharp intake of breath, but she knew that already really. It was the type of man he was.

'But let us get it in perspective,' he went on 'It won't happen tomorrow, or the day after, and tonight I am sure I can think of something to take our mind off all this doom and gloom – for now, at least.'

Carmel submitted to Paul's embrace eagerly enough, though her mind was elsewhere, and she lay awake long after his even breathing told her he was asleep.

In March the following year, Hitler and his armies goose-stepped unopposed into Austria and took over its government in a pact with them known as the Anschluss. Then he turned his attention to Sudetenland, an area of Czechoslovakia where there were many German-speaking people, and which he said felt more German than Czechoslovakian.

The only cheering news at this depressing time was that British unemployment had eased slightly, and there were fewer clusters of dejected men hanging around the street corners.

'Why do you think that is?' Carmel asked Paul one evening.

Paul shrugged. 'Something to do with the new factories going up, I suppose.'

'So why weren't these factories erected earlier?'

'Maybe the powers that be thought we had no need for them.'

'Well, why do we need them now, all of a sudden?'

'Because every week and month that passes we are one step nearer to war,' Paul said. 'I would like to take a bet that most, if not all, of the new factories are concerned in some way with making armaments.'

It was a chilling thought. Yet just a few short months later, Carmel knew that Paul was wrong. Mr Chamberlain and Edouard Daladier, France's Prime Minister, had gone to Munich and seen Herr Hitler himself. Hitler signed a treaty of peace with both countries on the acquisition of Sudetenland. On 30 September, Chamberlain came back to Britain waving this piece of paper and declaring that there would be 'peace for our time'.

Everyone appeared to breath a sigh of relief, although both Paul and Chris said Britain was crazy to trust the word of Hitler and they should use this lull in hostilities to prepare for what they imagined to be the biggest onslaught there had ever been. But Britain seemed to hover in an uneasy belief in peace.

On 15 March 1939, when Hitler made a triumphant entry into Prague, Paul said it was only to be expected and he didn't think the man would be content until he had the whole of Europe under his jackboot.

'There's not much left of Europe, though, is there,' Carmel said, 'with Franco now in control in Spain and Mussolini in Italy?'

'Well, I think he will go for Poland next,' Chris said.

'What about "peace in our time"?' Lois asked.

'Not worth the paper it was written on,' Chris said, and Carmel, for the first time, faced the fact that war was inevitable.

It seemed too that the government had woken up. The following month the Territorial Army were mobilised, any serving abroad were brought back, and on 27 April there was an announcement that there was going to be conscription introduced for young men of twenty and twenty-one years of age to be brought into effect immediately.

That night, as they snuggled in bed, Paul drew Carmel close and said, 'This is it, pet.'

'But . . . what do you mean?' she cried. 'War hasn't even been declared.'

'It's only a matter of time.'

'Then why don't you wait until you have to go?'

'Because this way, I will have a choice,' Paul said. 'I want to join the Medical Corps of the Royal Warwickshires. You needn't worry, I won't even be in the firing line. Even if I am sent abroad you can imagine that their field hospitals will be some way from the battlefield, and they will be desperate for doctors now. Each of those conscripts will have to have a thorough examination to see if they are fit to be shot at. Chris is going too; we agreed to go together. In fact, at this moment he is probably telling Lois the same.'

Now Carmel understood the look that had passed between the men as they had listened to the announcement earlier and, gentle though Paul's voice was, Carmel heard the steel in it and knew he had already made his mind up. She could rant and rave, for all the good it would do. He had told her what he intended to do months before and now she must let him go and face life without her beloved Paul. The only consolation was that he would be safe, or as safe as anyone could be in a war, but she knew also that their lives might never be the same again.

Carmel and Lois decided that they would throw a party for the boys who would be leaving to join their regiments on Sunday, 14 May. The party was planned for the day before.

Carmel told Paul he had to tell his mother what he had done. Jeff was immensely proud of the decision his son had made and told him so. However, Jeff knew that Emma would hardly view it in the same light and agreed with Carmel that Paul had to see her and tell her face to face.

Matthew couldn't understand what had made him join up in the first place.

'I'd be conscripted eventually anyway,' Paul had said. 'Then I might have had no choice of where I was put or anything.'

'Couldn't you have claimed exemption as a medical man?'

'I don't know. I didn't try.'

'Well, I will,' Matthew declared. 'They will have to drag me away kicking and screaming. As the manager of an engineering factory, I'll probably be able to claim exemption.'

'What about Dad?'

'What about him?' Matthew said. 'By the time he arrives in the morning, he is usually in no fit state for anything much. Even if you don't live at home you must

303

be aware of how much he is drinking. He virtually lives at the club, though I don't blame him totally. The situation at home is bloody awful most of the time and I am out of it too, as much as I can be.'

Paul knew his brother spoke the truth. Whenever he met his father at his club, he had been aware how much he was putting away, though when he came to see them at the house, he was much more sober. Paul felt sorry for his father for he had told him things, once the beer had loosened his tongue, that he probably never would have told him sober. Paul thought he had had one hell of a life, one way or another.

'You're mad anyway to leave that pretty little wife of yours,' Matthew went on, bringing Paul's thoughts back to the present. 'I should think there will be plenty of offers to warm her bed at night once you are out of the way.'

Paul smiled. 'It isn't all about sex, Matthew. Carmel understands that I must do this.'

'Well, you go and do your bit, Paul,' Matthew sneered. 'I will employ my energies to staying out of the armed forces. It will be all right for you, safe in a field hospital miles far from enemy lines. I have no wish to end my life on the end of a German bayonet.'

Paul shrugged. 'You must do as you see fit.'

When the little maid of all work told Emma that Paul wanted to see her, her heart leaped with hope. When she had lost Paul to that little trollop, she felt as if her heart had been torn to shreds. None could take his place, certainly not his younger brother, whose presence in the house was an irritant rather than a comfort.

She even tried not to see her husband. It wasn't hard, for he was seldom in, even for meals, which suited both of them. In fact, evening after evening she had sat in isolated splendour in the dining room and eaten the meal the cook had prepared and then sat alone in the sitting room. She seldom met friends, for she often imagined them sneering at her. For years she had expounded the virtues of Paul and the marvellous future ahead of him, which Paul had thrown back in her face, and now she felt she was a laughing stock.

The exemption to this was Millicent Chisholm and her daughter Melissa. Emma and Millicent had planned for years that Melissa and Paul would marry. They had been together since babyhood with their mothers looking on fondly. It would have been so suitable, and Melissa had been more than willing. So had Paul been before that conniving little nurse had enticed him away. Emma couldn't bring herself to believe they could ever be happy together. How could they be when they were from two entirely different worlds?

Now Paul had come to see her and he'd come alone. Emma was convinced Paul had come to tell her he could no longer live with Carmel Duffy, that he had married her only as a stab of defiance against his mother and he realised he had made a mistake.

It was unfortunate that there was no divorce in the Catholic Church, but surely to God, one error of judgement shouldn't be allowed to blight a person's life for ever. Maybe they could get an annulment. Money could buy most things, Emma knew. They might have to pay dearly but, no matter, the money would be found to gain Paul's release.

However, the Paul that stood before his mother a little later didn't look at all like a man who was going to admit to some *faux pas* in his personal life. She had spent a lifetime studying the son she had loved so much, but she had seldom seem him look like he did that day.

Emma rose to her feet as Paul entered the room. She looked into his deep blue eyes and saw the challenge in them. She wasn't going to let him know that he was forgiven for upsetting her until she heard what he had to say and so she said in clipped tones, 'You wished to see me?' And then added before he could speak, 'Shall we take a seat and I am sure Mary won't mind making us some tea?'

'I'll stand, if you don't mind, Mother,' Paul said. 'This won't take long.'

'That sounds rather ominous.'

'That depends how you view it,' Paul said. 'The fact is, I have enlisted.'

It was the last thing Emma expected him to say. Now she understood the proud stance. Her dreams came crashing down around her head and her heart was pierced with the thought that her son was going to be in the carnage that everyone knew was coming. She was filled with sudden fear for him. She bent her head so that he couldn't see the anguish in her eyes as she reminded herself that once more he had shamed her. He was a doctor and didn't need to go anywhere. People said there would be air raids, planes dropping things from the sky, people hurt, maimed and killed, so why had he to go and enlist like some common nobody?

So the look she turned on Paul was as cold as ice,

her eyes like pieces of granite in a face screwed up with anger and disappointment.

'Why should I wish to know what you do?' she snapped. 'You threw away the values of this home long ago and then compounded the error by marrying that common little guttersnipe. From that moment you ceased to be a son of mine.'

Common little guttersnipe. The words burned in Paul's mind. 'How dare you call Carmel such names? What gives you that right? Do you know, I am glad that I am no longer a son of yours for I am ashamed that you were ever my mother.'

'There is nothing further I wish to say to you,' Emma said bitterly and added sneeringly, 'Go back to the vulgar strumpet you married and the slum you call home. You deserve them both.'

Paul held his mother's vindictive eyes. He had the urge to put his hands around her neck and squeeze tight. In fact, the urge to hurt the woman he now hated was so strong that he knew he had to get away quickly and stay away. He turned from her without a word.

Only when she heard the front door slam behind Paul did Emma allow herself to weep.

Paul gave Carmel an edited version of how his mother had received the news of his enlisting, but he told his father the lot later that same evening at the party.

'I wanted to hurt her,' he said. 'That's what I can't get over. I've never wanted to hurt another human being in my life and she is my mother.'

'I'm as easygoing a man as you are likely to get,' Jeff said, 'and the damned woman gets me the same way.

Why d'you think I spend all my leisure hours in the club and make sure I don't return home still she's in the Land of Nod and all I am good for is falling into my bed? Take my advice, son, drink enough tonight to forget your mother and enjoy the party.'

Paul took his father's words to heart and when Carmel noticed him knocking back the booze she wasn't all that concerned, knowing it might be all the alcohol he would get for a long time. The house was packed with friends from both hospitals and their partners if they had any, like Jane's fiancé, Peter Meadows, and Dan Smiley, his best friend, with whom Sylvia was going steady. Even Matthew had brought a girl with him, Carmel was glad to see. Then there were Jeff and James, and the Hancocks from next door, and Chris's parents, whom Carmel hadn't seen since the wedding.

It was a wonderful party but at the back of everyone's mind was the reason for it and all were determined to make it a memorable one for Paul and Chris. Carmel knew that Paul was looking for another memory to take with him, for she had seen it lurking in his eyes for the last hour or so and it had set the excitement mounting in her too.

Barely had the door closed on the last guest than Paul was tugging at her.

'Leave all the clearing up till tomorrow,' he said urgently. 'Let's go up.'

Paul was so drunk he had trouble mounting the stairs and Carmel found she was none too steady either. She was a very moderate drinker, as a rule, but had drunk far more than was customary that night.

Lois had told her not to worry. 'What can happen to

you?' she asked. 'You are in your own house so no harm can come to you and there is no work to get up for. Sometimes, Carmel, it does you good to let your hair down.'

And so Carmel had let it down good and proper, and was more than happy to fall on the bed beside Paul. Neither of them had any desire to sleep, though, and Paul's hands were all over her body, tearing at her clothes. Carmel helped him, knowing she was almost fully aroused already and wouldn't be able to wait long.

It was when they were both naked and Carmel was writhing and moaning on the bed that Paul remembered the johnnies and realised he hadn't any. He had intended going to the chemist on his way from his mother's house, but he had been so shaken by what he had wanted to do to her, that the trip to the chemist had gone out of his head.

'Carmel,' he said, his voice husky with desire, 'I haven't got anything. Know what I mean?'

Carmel was too far gone to care and so was Paul really. 'Come on?' Carmel pleaded. 'I need you now, quickly.'

Paul could no more have stopped then than he could have stopped the sun from shining. He had the vague idea he would pull out at the last minute, but that went by the board and sex that night was the best ever. It went on and on as Carmel had one orgasm after the other, until she felt she was drowning in rapture. Much, much later they fell asleep with their arms wrapped around one another.

Wakening next morning, hung over and feeling none too well, Carmel faced the fact of what they had done the night before. The thought of what might happen because of it forced her to heave herself out of bed, wash, get dressed and set off for nine o'clock Mass. She knew that she looked like death warmed up and some even asked if she was feeling all right. She wasn't, but she knew she had to be there and on her knees, pleading with the Almighty to let there be no repercussions from the previous torrid night. After Mass she lit a candle for good measure.

However, by the time Carmel, Lois, the Hancocks and various other neighbours were clustered around the wireless on Sunday, 3 September at 11.15 a.m. to hear that Britain was at war with Germany, Carmel knew without a shadow of doubt that she was pregnant. She knew it was the fault of both her and Paul the night of the party and she couldn't feel the slightest bit of excitement about it – more resentment that it should have happened at all.

Paul, when she wrote and told him, was at first frantic with worry. It was the very worst thing that could have happened, to leave his wife pregnant at the start of a war with him not even being there to give her support.

Others, however, did not feel the same. Lois asked her what she was worrying about and reminded her that she would be on hand and more use to her than any man. Her mother and Sister Frances, who had both been dropping hints about babies, were relieved.

'It mightn't be the best timing in the world right enough,' Eve conceded in the letter she wrote in response to Carmel's news, 'but babies have a habit of coming when they choose, and you will cope because you will have to. And thank God that you have good friends around you.'

Jeff was tickled pink, James a little jealous and Ruby Hancock had already started knitting. Jane and Sylvia, even knowing Carmel's views on having a family of her own, thought it the sweetest news in the world and they were both sure that she would love the baby to distraction when he or she was born.

CHAPTER EIGHTEEN

Birmingham at war was a totally different place, Carmel was finding, than Birmingham at peace. First there were the blackout curtains to fix in place each evening at the windows, which were already crisscrossed with tape as the government suggested, to protect against flying glass in the event of a raid. The curtains had been made up by Ruby on her treadle sewing machine with the material Carmel and Lois had lugged home from the Bull Ring way back in August. Not one chink of light could show around these curtains or an ARP warden would be knocking on the door and if you refused to comply, the fine was two hundred pounds.

With the blackout, and while any moon or stars not covered by clouds were often obscured by smog, once darkness fell, it was like a wall of black so dense you almost felt that it could be touched. Nobody could see a hand in front of them, and travelling any distance was a hazardous business. Everywhere you went you had to carry a gas mask. Carmel and Lois were so glad they lived just a few steps from the tram that dropped them right outside the General Hospital, but even so, Lois was

312

worried that Carmel might slip and fall and so kept tight hold of her.

Women and sometimes children had painted white lines along the kerbs, and around trees and lampposts. Some had painted them on the running boards of the few cars still left on the roads. They made not a scrap of difference. Each evening there were more reports of people injured or even killed in the blackout, until people began to wonder who the enemy was for there hadn't been the sniff of a raid. In fact, so uneventful was it that people were calling it 'the Bore War'.

It wasn't so quiet at sea. It depressed Carmel when she read of the ships sunk, often with vital foodstuffs on board, and sailors' lives lost.

There were fewer men about generally, and this was affecting everything. Jeff, on a visit to see if Carmel was all right, said that women had applied for some of the places at the factory vacated by the men, and he had asked men coming up to retirement if they could stay on a few more years. The same thing had happened to George Hancock, who worked on the railway.

'Should have retired next year,' Ruby said. 'Management asked him straight out if he'd stay put a bit. Point is, you've got to do it, haven't you? Everyone has to do their bit.'

There was less food in the shops too and if you complained you were reminded that there was a war on, as if you had dropped in from another planet and were taken unawares.

'People say there will be rationing introduced in the new year,' Ruby said. 'Fairer that way. In the last war, those who could afford it, the rich, like, would stockpile everything, even taking the carriages into the poorer areas and getting their coachmen to go and get the things, so there was little left in the shops for the ordinary people.'

'Doesn't surprise me in the least,' Carmel said, thinking that was the sort of stunt Emma would pull.

And then suddenly all the restriction and limitations of the war didn't matter, for Chris and Paul both wrote that they had leave and would be home on 4 October until the 7th. It was embarkation leave and heaven alone knew when they would be home again.

When Paul actually saw the slight swell of Carmel's stomach, he was overawed by the fact that inside Carmel was a part of him and a part of her and that between them they would produce another human being.

Carmel watched his face and knew how he felt, though he said nothing. She felt torn, for though she was glad she had pleased him, in another way she was irritated that her life was going to change so drastically and so abruptly.

'I'm only sad that you feel so upset about this,' he said at last.

'Well, I don't understand you totally,' Carmel said. 'You always said you weren't bothered about kids.'

'I know, but it has happened now,' Paul said. 'And I don't just want to accept our child as if it were some sort of duty. Whether it is a boy or girl I want it loved and cherished.'

'You have the luxury to think this way, darling, because your life will not change in any way,' Carmel said. 'I am now twenty-one weeks pregnant and Matron says I must leave at twenty-four weeks. So in three weeks' time it will be goodbye to the dream I have carried for years and God only knows if I will ever go back to it.

I mean, you are expecting me to get excited over something that was an utter shock to me. But never fear, I will look after this child well enough because it will be part of you and I might even feel differently once it is born. Everyone assures me I will. But let's not spoil one minute of this very precious leave on talking about a situation we are unable to change.'

Paul did see that it was totally different for him and he had no desire to argue with the wife he loved, who after this spot of leave he might not see for months – even, God forbid, years. Carmel had the same thought and they made the most of every minute, though Paul did make contact with his father and brother, which Carmel fully approved of.

Snow White and the Seven Dwarfs, a cartoon made by an American called Walt Disney, was still showing at the Odeon cinema in New Street, for all it had been released the previous year, and Chris and Paul were mad keen to see it. Neither girl was that struck on going, but found they were enchanted and enthralled by the cartoon, which they had never seen the like of before. The next day they laughed themselves silly at the antics of Max Wall, a comedian extraordinaire, who was appearing at the Hippodrome.

The nights, however, belonged to Carmel and Paul, and Carmel often wanted to stop time. She valued every second, and when Paul slept she would often lie awake and watch him, drinking in the sight and smell of him. She would feel the small mound of her stomach and regret that Paul might not see the child that she was carrying for some time. That saddened her, but there was nothing that she could do about it.

When the men returned to their unit, Lois and Carmel were glad that they had each other for company. They knew this wasn't the time to dissolve in despair and sadness, for this war couldn't be won if the women all went under.

Two days later, Paul and Chris were with the BEF, the British Expeditionary Force, which landed on the coast of France.

It was hard for Carmel not to feel upset on her last day at the hospital. She knew that as well as the work, which she still loved with a passion, she would miss the camaraderie of the girls, the room-mates that she had been friends with through thick and thin. She would even miss Matron, whom she had always got on well with. She faced the prospect that she was going to be downright miserable at home and this feeling was compounded by many of the patients, who said they would miss the sight of her cheerful face on the wards.

As they were due to make their way home on Carmel's last night, Lois asked her to go into the recreation room with her because she had to see someone.

Unsuspecting, Carmel followed her friend, but as Lois opened the door she said, 'There can be no one here, Lois. The room is in darkness.'

'Oh, I am sure there's someone here somewhere,' said Lois. She flicked the light switch and Carmel stared in amazement. As many of the hospital staff that could be spared were there – nurses and probationers, doctors she had worked with and the Matron, not to mention Jane and Sylvia, who had organised the whole thing. They all began singing 'For She's a Jolly Good

Fellow' as Carmel, with cheeks aflame with embarrassment, noted the streamers decorating the room and a small buffet set out on a table. She was almost overcome with emotion at it all.

'You're not crying,' Sylvia said accusingly, a little later, seeing Carmel surreptitiously wiping her eyes.

Carmel made a valiant effort to swallow the lump in her throat and said, 'No.'

'I've said it before and I'll say it again,' Sylvia said. 'You are one awful bloody liar.' Then she looked fully at her friend and said, 'Oh God, I am going to miss you.'

It was the sentiment expressed in so many ways by so many people that night, and Carmel wasn't the only one to shed tears. She even had a stiff and very proper embrace from the Matron and was given many gifts for the baby. She travelled home a little happier to await the birth of her child.

'I think that it is the lack of contact that gets to you in the end,' Carmel said to Lois on New Year's Eve. 'I mean, when Paul and Chris were at the camp we would write every week and they would write straight back. We don't even know if they received the parcels we sent them and that was ages ago.'

'Yes,' Lois agreed, 'though Uncle Jeff says he thinks a lot of units are in France and things might be more difficult if they are actually on the move.'

'I just don't know where he gets his information from.'

'Nor me,' Lois agreed, 'and he seldom will say, but it is usually right, isn't it?'

'Yeah,' Carmel conceded, 'and they could be in France. Could be in Timbuktu even, because when we do get a letter they can't give a whisper of where they are.'

'Tell you what, though,' Lois said. 'I'll be glad to see the back of this year, won't you?'

Carmel smiled grimly. 'In a way, but then I think 1940 might be worse and at the very least we will have to cope with rationing.'

'Oh God, so we will.'

Rationing came into force on Monday, 8 January, and affected bacon, ham and butter, of which each person's allowance was four ounces a week, and sugar, which was set at twelve ounces. In addition to this, Carmel, because she was pregnant, could be issued with a green ration card, which entitled the bearer to seven extra pints of milk each week, cod-liver oil and orange juice and extra eggs.

'You have to get a certificate from the doctor,' Lois said, reading the literature, which was issued with the ration books.

'I know. I read it too.'

'Well, did you get one?'

'No, not today I didn't.'

'Why not?' Lois demanded. 'You don't want to miss out.'

'I just didn't feel like it,' Carmel snapped

It was so unlike Carmel to speak that way that Lois said, 'You all right? Now I think about it you have been quiet all through the meal.'

'I'm getting pains,' Carmel admitted.

Alarmed Lois cried, 'What sort of pains?'

'Ruby said they are like the body practising,' Carmel said. 'I have had them for a few weeks now but though they are getting stronger, they usually go off after a while. Today, though, they were the most painful yet and still haven't gone off properly. The pain in my stomach is still rumbling away and it has also shifted around to the back. My head is a bit swimmy too, but I think that was queuing for so long in the cold, because the wind was like ice and it was snowing fit to bust.'

Lois's eyes were concerned. 'You shouldn't be standing in weather like that for hours on end. I think maybe you are doing too much. How about an early night?'

'Good idea,' Carmel said.

'Go on up then,' Lois said. 'I'll finish this washing up and bring you a nice hot cup of tea.'

Carmel nodded her head, too weary to argue. She mounted the stairs laboriously, for the baby lay heavily on her now. She had barely reached the bedroom when she felt the water gush from her and she let out a cry of anguish as a sudden pain caused her to collapse to her knees.

Lois galloped up the stairs to find Carmel in a sodden nightdress kneeling in a puddle of water and she knew, early or not, this baby was struggling to be born. She lifted Carmel to her feet as she cried out that it was too soon.

'Look,' Lois said, 'there is no help for it. Now I am going to get Ruby to sit with you and then I am away for the midwife, all right?'

Carmel nodded, knowing she would feel better with

Ruby beside her. Only a few minutes after Lois left, Ruby was in the door.

She put her arms around Carmel when she saw the tears on her cheeks. 'Don't take on so, ducks.'

'But it's far too early.'

'The babby don't seem to think so.'

'But will it be all right?'

'Course it will,' said Ruby confidently. 'But we got to give the little mite every chance possible. Now you come up and sit in this chair while I strip your bed and have it made up with the special sheets to protect the mattress.'

Carmel nodded again. The pains, each stronger than the last, were making talking difficult and she was immensely glad a few minutes later to sink back into bed and hold on to Ruby's stout hand. When Lois came back with the news that the midwife had gone out to a confinement and hadn't got back, Carmel was inclined to panic.

'Come on now,' Ruby said. 'What you getting in a state for? There wasn't never trained midwives in my day. You just had some neighbour woman who had done it a few times before and knew what was what. And I have attended enough births to know what to do, I reckon.'

'Are you sure?'

'Course I am,' Ruby said. 'And the first thing we want is hot water.'

'I'll see to it,' Lois said, glad to have something to do.

When the door closed behind Lois, Ruby smiled. 'You hang on, bab,' she said. 'We'll get through this together and I'll not leave your side until it is over.'

And she didn't, not once. Lois made reviving tea that

Carmel was glad of, and later sandwiches she couldn't touch, but Ruby sat beside her holding her hand, or wiping her brow with the cloth she had ready. As the night wore on Lois dozed in the chair by the bed. Sometimes Carmel would drop off from sheer exhaustion, to be woken by the pain minutes later, but always Ruby would be there, a constant by the bed. When Carmel cried out with it, Ruby was there to soothe and to comfort.

'Oh God!' Carmel gasped, when the pain was coming in relentless waves. 'How much longer?'

'Not long now,' Ruby said consolingly. 'You are doing fine.'

Carmel didn't feel as if she was doing fine. She felt as if she was being rent in two. By the early hours of the morning, she felt as though she had entered a tunnel of pain and there was no respite from it, and she screamed out against it and raised her knees to her chin.

Ruby swiftly roused Lois. To Carmel she said, 'I am leaving you for two minutes to scrub my hands. I want a take a look, all right?'

Carmel's face was bathed in sweat, she was panting like an animal and her eyes were pain-glazed. Lois approached the bed and, feeling immense sympathy for her friend, took up her hand and held it tight.

And then Ruby was back and had the bedclothes raised. Then she was saying, 'Push, bab. We're nearly there. Honest to God.'

It seemed to Carmel that Ruby, now at the foot of the bed, had said the same thing for hours. 'I have pushed,' she panted. 'I can't push any more.'

'Yes, you can,' said Lois, still holding her hand.

That angered Carmel. 'No I can't,' she declared. 'What the bloody hell do you know about it?'

The words had barely left Carmel's lips when she was assailed by the biggest contraction yet. She gave a sudden scream of agony and holding Lois's hand so tightly the bones crunched together, she gathered up every vestige of strength and pushed with all her might.

For a second or two there was deadlock and Carmel felt herself weakening. But Lois and Ruby wouldn't let her give up. Suddenly the pressure eased, she felt the baby slither between her legs, new-born wails filled the room and Ruby announced, 'You bloody clever girl, you. You have a beautiful daughter.'

Carmel took the baby from Ruby, who had wrapped her in a shawl against the chill of the room, and peeled back the covers and gazed at her, this perfect little person she and Paul had created. She had stopped crying and lay passive in Carmel's arms with her little fingers and toes and even tinier nails, her milky blue eyes trying to focus so that a little frown was developing in her brow at the effort. And Carmel realised she loved every bit of her and couldn't understand that she had ever thought she wouldn't be able to love this little mite, that she even might resent her.

At that moment she knew with certainty that she would tear limb from limb anyone who harmed one hair of her baby's head.

The birth was over and mother and child doing well by the time the midwife got there, totally exhausted because she had been up all night. She was full of praise for the

322

way Lois and Ruby had coped, and said although the baby was premature, she appeared healthy.

'She is a little sweetheart,' she said. 'Have you a name for her?'

Carmel nodded. 'Elizabeth,' she said. 'Though I will call her Beth, which I prefer to Lizzie, and then Eve for my mother.'

'Fine names both of them,' the midwife declared, and then gave a sudden yawn.

'You best be away to your bed,' Ruby said. 'You look all in.'

'I am tired,' the midwife said. 'Course, I have been at the other place all night, though I'll tell you, if the government hadn't had a rethink on the blackout and allowed shaded torches and shielded car headlights to be used, I reckon the woman would have had to manage on her own, because it was in an area I wasn't familiar with. My job was made very difficult for a few months unless the babies chose to be born in the hours of daylight, and you know as well as I do that they are not that accommodating.'

Ruby chuckled. 'Indeed not,' she said. 'They come when they are ready. This scrap, for instance, shouldn't be with us for a few weeks yet.'

Carmel had put the baby to the breast and her eyes were closed in blissful contentment.

The midwife said, 'Doesn't matter how many times it happens, it always strikes me as some sort of miracle.'

Carmel couldn't have agreed more and went over in her head the letter that she would write to Paul to tell him of this wondrous event.

※　　※　　※

323

The path to the house was nearly worn down by the wellwishers who called to see the baby, all bearing gifts. Jeff wanted to buy everything new and the best for his first grandchild, but Carmel told him not to.

'Ruby has everything kept from when hers were small, packed away in the attic,' she said, 'keeping it for her own children. But she said as they seem in no hurry to produce and the stuff is gathering dust, I might as well have the use of it. After all, will Beth mind one jot if her pram is brand-new or not?'

'No, but—'

'But nothing,' Carmel said. 'What I really would like is for Paul to be home beside us where he belongs. I know that cannot be, but my next desire, might be just as impossible.'

'And what is that, my dear?'

'It's to have my brother Michael and my sister Siobhan over here to be godparents to their little niece.'

Jeff was delighted there was something he could do for his daughter-in-law that would please her. 'You shall have that, my dear,' he promised. 'And I will go to Ireland myself to see to it.' And he felt a little thrill of excitement run through him at the prospect of seeing Eve again.

'Oh, but—'

'You must let me do this for you,' Jeff said. 'If Paul were here I am sure that he would attend to it, but I will deal with it in his stead. You arrange the christening and I will see that they will be there for it.'

Jeff didn't ask why Carmel didn't just write to her brother and sister and ask them to be godparents, which surely was the normal way of going about things.

Paul had described to him how it was in that household, and he had described the house too, but still Jeff was shocked. That Carmel had come from such beginnings and that her mother, the gentle Eve, who had made such an impression on him, should continue to live in such a place, shocked him to the core. He felt the bile rising in him for Dennis Duffy, who allowed his family to live in such a way

Eve had been amazed to see Jeff at her door. He had given her no notice that he was coming, for he couldn't risk being refused. But while she was embarrassed that Jeff should see how things were for her in her real life, Dennis was inclined to be belligerent. Jeff had expected this – again it had all been explained to him – and he watched the man's expression change and pass his tongue over his lips as Jeff pulled from his bag a large bottle of single malt whiskey.

'I thought you and I might wet the baby's head, one grandfather with another. What do you say?' he said to Dennis.

It cost Jeff dear to sit at that table drinking with such a man. Dennis Duffy was the very type of person Jeff despised: one who didn't want to do a decent day's work and yet would keep his family starving and not care a jot about it as long as he had his beer money. As for taking a drink with such a character! By choice he would rather take poison, though he liked a drink as well as the next man – more than like, if the truth was told, though from the time Carmel told him she was pregnant he had taken a grip upon himself, knowing that with

Paul away, he would have to keep a weather eye on Carmel and the child. Paul would expect it of him.

Jeff was aware too – sickeningly aware from the nervous, subservient attitude she displayed around her husband – that Eve was afraid of him. Later he was to see how terrified the children were. Even the times that he had returned to the house the worse for wear he had never raised his hand to his wife. His sons too had never felt even the flat of his hand as they were growing up. Their discipline, as every other aspect of their care, had been left to Emma and Jeff despised a man who beat his wife and children.

He would rather have laid his length on the cobbles outside the door than make a friend of Dennis, yet he knew that to get Dennis to agree to let Siobhan go to England – he imagined Michael would make his own deci-sion – he had to push down his natural instincts. So he sat on with Dennis, drinking one glass of whiskey after the other.

Dennis was well away by the time the two made it to the pub, where Dennis introduced Jeff as his daughter's father-in-law, over here to wet the wee baby's head, no less.

'He's a grand fellow altogether,' Dennis declared.

'The grand fellow' followed the same procedure for the next three nights, plying the man with drink until he had to help him home, though he took little him-self. At the end of the third day, he said that if Dennis allowed Siobhan to go to England he would lay down twenty-five pounds behind the bar for him. In Dennis's befuddled state, twenty-five pounds was the sort of money he had never seen – a fortune. By then he thought Jeff the best in the world anyway, and so he shook him by the hand and said he was a fine man, a true gentleman, and he could do what he liked with Siobhan.

Jeff accepted the acclaim and the promise, but trusted the man not a jot. So, as arranged, the following day he called for Siobhan while Dennis was sleeping off the excesses of the night before. He was to take her to Dublin where Michael would join them. He had arranged accommodation for the night. First, however, he wanted to get Siobhan some new clothes, and he also wanted her to have her hair done properly.

Before he left, he pressed twenty single pounds into Eve's hands, brushing away her protests that it was too much. 'It is nowhere near enough, my dear lady, and from now on I will send you money regularly, included in the letters Carmel sends you so as not to arouse suspicion.'

'You are very good.'

'Not at all,' Jeff said softly. 'I am not so good, but I am a very rich man. Twenty pounds is like a drop in the ocean for me, but I would like it if you will take it and try and make life easier for you all. I know you will do that for you are a loving, caring mother. That has been so apparent in just the few days I have been here.'

The tears were flowing freely down Eve's face and a lump rose in Jeff's throat as she turned those glistening eyes on him and said, her voice husky with the tears she had shed, 'You are the kindest man I have ever known.'

Jeff wished he could take her in his arms as he had

Carmel, and kiss her cheek, but he knew such behaviour would be inappropriate and could possibly be misconstrued so he contented himself with shaking her hand warmly.

CHAPTER NINETEEN

Siobhan and Michael were both enchanted by the baby. They arrived two days before the christening, which was to be on 21 January, when the baby would be twelve days old. Carmel noticed her sister's resplendent new clothes straight away and guessed they were a present from Jeff.

Jeff, watching the sisters greet each other, remembered Siobhan's almost speechless delight when he suggested taking her shopping in Dublin, and how thrilled and appreciative she was with everything he bought. It pleased him greatly to treat such a person and when she had been kitted out, it had surprised him how pretty the girl was, though not quite as stunning as her elder sister.

Once the meal was over, the child in bed and Jeff gone home, Siobhan asked to see over the house. She was astonished that Carmel lived in such a place, for though Michael and her mother had described it, seeing it for herself was something else entirely. Siobhan was full of praise, tinged with a little envy.

She had begun to think recently she would never leave home. In May she would be twenty-one, nearly on the shelf already, and as she had no chance of meeting anyone, little chance of marriage. She was also worried what her father would do to her mother if she were to leave.

In Birmingham, Letterkenny and its problems seemed far, far away and with her new clothes and with her hair cut stylishly, she decided to push the bad memories and thoughts what she would be returning to, to the back of her mind and enjoy the few free days she had.

The christening went without a hitch. The church was filled with friends, neighbours and other wellwishers, and Siobhan and Michael held the baby tenderly and gave their responses over a background noise of Beth screaming her head off, which amused everyone.

Afterwards, many piled into the house in York Road. It had been hard getting any sort of a party spread together with the rationing now of some goods and many others in short supply. However, everyone had helped, and with Lois being such a genius with food anyway, the table was respectable enough. Jeff provided the drinks and the christening party went with a swing.

Lois commented later how much she liked Siobhan. She was also a great favourite with Ruby Hancock. Carmel realised she had been wrong to be ashamed of her family. The star of the show, though, was of course the baby, who now some giant wasn't pouring water over her head behaved impeccably. She didn't mind at all being passed from one to another, and when she was eventually tucked into the cradle, she went to sleep like a dream.

In the days that followed, the weather wasn't conducive to exploring Birmingham. Every day snow tumbled from a sky the colour of gunmetal, and was whipped into drifts by the gusting winds, each night it would freeze over. It was far too cold and damp to take the baby far, though the day after the christening Carmel did manage to push the pram up Erdington High Street so that Siobhan could see the range and variety of shops on their doorstep. She was mightily impressed.

'You must come back in the summer,' Carmel said, once they were inside again. 'The weather will be better then and the baby won't need feeding every ten minutes.'

Siobhan laid the baby she had been holding back into the crib and said, 'You know I can't do that, as if I lived in a normal household where normal rules apply. I don't even know how I will be received when I go home, because although Daddy said I could come here, he was drunk at the time, and I was spirited from the house before he could wake and possibly change his mind. Now, if he is mad about that for any reason, I will catch it, and you know that as well as I. Surely to God you haven't forgotten how it is at home?'

'He'll not lay a hand on you,' Michael said. 'I told you.'

'And I told you that Daddy has ways and means and he is like they say elephants are,' Siobhan said. 'He never forgets or forgives a wrong he imagines have been done to him.'

'I'll put the fear of God into him. I have done it before for Mammy,' Michael said.

'D'you think it made any difference?' Siobhan said bitterly. 'Daddy still hits Mammy when you are not around. He just marks her in places she can hide and she says nothing because she doesn't want you to get into trouble. I would keep quiet if he hit me for the same reason.' The look on Michael's face was savage and Siobhan laid a hand on his arm. 'Don't feel bad, Michael. We need you with us, not in gaol someplace.'

'Huh, some good I am if I'm not allowed to protect you.'

'We need you for more than just protection,' Siobhan said. She turned to Carmel and said, 'Don't think you have to be entertaining me all the time either. At the moment I am enjoying the peace and quiet and I could cuddle your baby all the day. Sometimes,' she added wistfully, 'I don't think I will ever have one of my own.'

'Course you will,' Carmel said.

'There isn't any of course here,' Siobhan said. 'I never go across the door except to go to work or to Mass.'

'Well, that is one thing I can do for you,' Michael said. 'From when we leave here, the two of us will go to the weekly social. It will do me good as well.'

'But, Michael, my clothes . . .'

'The outfits Jeff bought you will do for now,' Michael said. 'We'll cross the bridge of getting more later.'

'Oh, Michael!' Siobhan said ecstatically, throwing her arms around her brother.

'You'll have me strangled, woman,' Michael said, though his face bore a huge grin. 'I gather you approve of my idea.'

Siobhan nodded enthusiastically. 'I . . . I don't really know what to say.'

'A speechless woman,' Michael said. 'Must be a first. A word of warning, though,' he added. 'Don't let the miserable bugger catch sight of those clothes or he might destroy them some way out of spite.'

Siobhan nodded. 'I'd already thought of that. I'll keep them in the cloakroom behind the bakery. No one will mind.'

Carmel listened to her brother and sister plotting against the man they all hated. She didn't blame them in the least and she knew one by one he would lose the stranglehold he had on the children as they grew, for even the youngest, Pauline, had been nine in December. It was only her mother who couldn't escape and that thought saddened her.

Once Michael and Siobhan had left, life settled down again to the horrible cold and wintry days. The only thing for Carmel to look forward to were the letters from Paul. Then from sometime towards the end of April, all communication ceased.

At first the two girls were unaware there was any sort of problem, because since their husbands had left the camp, they had experienced these silences before and then a batch of letters would arrive together. Lois was at work one day when Jeff called. Since he had broken off relations with his mother, Paul had always written to his father via the firm, and Jeff called down about the middle of May to see if Lois or Carmel had had any news.

'Why are you so concerned?' Carmel asked. 'I mean, this silence has happened before.'

Jeff thought of fobbing Carmel off with some reassuring nonsense, but he knew she was no fool. Nor was she a child and she deserved to know as much of the facts as he did. 'One of the chaps at work has this radio receiver,' he said. 'He gets messages from abroad and he says the word is that the whole of the Allied army is in retreat.'

'In retreat?' Carmel repeated. 'But they will be all right, won't they? I mean, there's that Maginot Line. Paul always said that that was unbreachable.'

'It is,' Jeff said, 'or at least without severe loss of life.'

'But?'

'What do you mean, but?' Jeff asked.

'There was a definite "but" in your voice,' Carmel said. 'I need to know about that "but".'

Jeff sighed. 'I know nothing definite, you understand, but that line was erected along the border that France shares with Germany, but it stops at the border France shares with Belgium and Luxembourg. The word is out that German paratroopers have landed and taken a Belgium fort thought to be impregnable and now the Dutch and Belgians are fighting for their lives.'

Carmel felt as if her veins were suddenly filled with ice and she looked at Jeff, horror-struck.

'But they will be all right, our husbands,' Lois assured her later, as they sat before the meal Carmel had cooked and she told Lois what Jeff had said. 'We're luckier than most, for ours are not fighting men.'

'I hope you are right,' Carmel said. 'We will just have to wait and hope to hear something soon. But I can't help remembering that Norway didn't hold out for long.'

'So what chance have Holland and Belgium got, you mean?'

'Yes,' Carmel said. 'I mean, the man and his armies

have just rode roughshod over every other country. It's as if he's unstoppable.'

The words hung in the air, because neither woman wanted to take that thought any further.

Then, just three days after Jeff's visit, Carmel and Lois were at home listening to the wireless when the programme was interrupted to report that both Belgium and Holland had been defeated. For a second or two, the women looked at each other and then Lois said, 'I bought a paper today and it has a map in the middle. Shall we have a look?'

What they saw horrified them, for it was plainly that if the Allies were retreating with the Germans on their tail, they had nowhere to retreat to but beaches.

'Jesus Christ!' Lois exclaimed. 'What can they do with the Germans behind them and the sea ahead of them? What bloody chance have they got?'

Then, on 31 May, the veil of secrecy was lifted and they heard of the thousands of Allied soldiers that the Royal Navy, with the help of smaller boats, were attempting to rescue from beaches at Dunkirk. There were pictures in the paper of the thousands of soldiers waiting their turn to be evacuated and the pier heads they had built out of discarded vehicles and equipment. There were many pictures of small boats of all shapes sizes and descriptions too of their lifting as many men as possible.

There were pictures of the returning soldiers, many wrapped in blankets, being given tea, sandwiches and cigarettes from the stalwart women of the WVS. Carmel and Lois scanned the pictures anxiously to see if they could spot their loved ones.

The telegrams began to arrive and on 3 June one was delivered to 17 York Road for Lois, who was on duty at the hospital. Carmel took it from the lad with trembling fingers and, lifting the child from her cot, she took her round to Ruby.

'I must take this to Lois straight away,' she said. 'And I would hesitate to take the baby because I don't know what it says . . . how she'll be, you know.'

'You go on, ducks,' Ruby said, lifting Beth from Carmel's arms. The baby loved Ruby and she gave her a gurgling smile and waved her podgy arms in the air as Ruby went on, 'Leave this little angel with me. Your place is beside Lois. She has need of you now.'

Chris was alive, but injured and at a military hospital in Ramsgate. Lois made immediate arrangements to go down and visit him. So Ruby knew Carmel was alone in the house when, as she dusted the front room, she spotted the telegraph boy stop again outside 17 York Road the following day.

She usually went into Carmel and Lois's house by the back door, but she didn't wait that day. Leaving her duster and polish, she scurried out the front way. The front door was ajar, but still Ruby had trouble opening it because the crumpled and unconscious form of Carmel was behind it, the telegram still clutched in her hand, the telegram that said Paul Vincent Connolly was missing, presumed dead.

By the time Lois returned the next day, confident that her husband was on the mend and would be transferred to a Birmingham hospital as soon as it could be arranged, she found Ruby rushed off her feet and worried to death.

Lois was devastated herself by the news of her cousin's death. She shed bitter tears and knew she would always feel the loss of him, a gap in her life that would never be filled. She was grateful to Ruby, who did not urge her not to cry, but seemed to think it perfectly natural she should. She held her tight and told her to cry it out.

Carmel, on the other hand, lay as one who had died herself, but her eyes remained open. She had not spoken nor eaten a morsel since she received the telegram, nor taken any notice of the child.

'I've had to feed Beth, you know,' Ruby said. 'I got bottles in and all because, well, I doubt Carmel could have fed her, even if she wanted to, for a shock that affects a person so deeply it would effectively dry up the milk, I'd say.'

But Carmel had given no thought to her child. Her mind was filled with thoughts of the husband she adored. The loss of him hurt her so deeply, she wondered how a person could be suffering so much pain and remain alive. She wondered bleakly what was there for her in life without Paul beside her. She wanted to be with him wherever he was. In one hand she clutched the locket he had given her for her twenty-first and with her other she held a photograph taken of him before he went away.

Ruby saw the despair in her eyes and the dejected slump of her body when she lifted her to try to coax her to eat a little broth or something similar. She would turn her head away from food, but would sometimes take a few drops of water.

'I am afraid to leave her and that is the truth,' Ruby told Lois. 'I would say she is distressed enough to do

337

something silly. Not that she needs to, because if she doesn't eat soon, she'll fade away. I mean, there wasn't much of her to start with.'

Lois knew every word that Ruby said was true and she was distracted with concern for her very special friend. She saw too that Ruby couldn't do it all and, anyway, Carmel shouldn't be left alone, so Lois went to the hospital the next day and asked to see the matron. The older woman, though pleased that Chris was on the mend, was distressed at Carmel's news.

'How is she managing?'

'She isn't. Not at all,' Lois cried. 'She lies in bed as if she is made of stone. She doesn't speak and hasn't eaten. Ruby, a neighbour, has been dealing with things while I have been away in Ramsgate. It can't go on, for there is the baby to see to as well and Ruby is frightened to leave Carmel alone for any length of time.'

'Does she think Carmel would do some thing silly?' the matron said. 'She never struck me as that type of girl.'

'Nor me, Matron, in the normal way of things,' Lois said, tears glistening in her own eyes. 'But . . . oh God, Matron, I have never seen Carmel like this.'

'What do you wish to do?'

'I must stay with her for now,' Lois said. 'For if anything happens to her then I would never forgive myself.'

The matron knew she had to release Lois to help her friend and so she said, 'Shall we say a week's leave for now, just to see how things go?'

'Oh, thank you, Matron.'

'Not at all,' the matron said. 'After all, I know the girl too, don't forget. When she is more herself, say I was asking after her.'

Lois was impressed by the matron's understanding, but as she looked at Carmel's prone form later, she did wonder if she would ever be able to pass on the matron's message. The only signs that Carmel was alive was the shallow sound of her breathing and her eyes, which were wide open and fixed on the ceiling.

Lois sat by the bed, eased the locket from Carmel's hand and laid it on the table beside the bed before covering that hand with her own, glad that Ruby said she would take care of the baby while Lois tried to break through to her friend.

'Look at me, Carmel,' Lois commanded, and when there was no response, Lois gave her hand a little shake and said sharply, 'I know you can hear me, so stop this and look at me.'

Carmel wanted to say that was almost too much effort but it took more effort to talk, and perhaps if she turned her head to look at Lois, she would then leave her alone. When Lois looked into Carmel's eyes fixed on hers, she was shaken by the level of pain she saw reflected in them. It was like looking into two pools of sorrow, and Lois knew Carmel wouldn't feel better until she had released the tears lurking behind them, which were making her eyes glisten.

'You really can't go on like this, Carmel,' she said quite sharply, sensing that Carmel needed to be shocked out of this trance-like state. There was no response and so she went on, 'Do you think Paul would like you to go on like this?'

Carmel gasped at the sound of Paul's name and, encouraged, Lois went on, 'I am sure he would be impressed at you lying in bed, neglecting your child, leaving her in the care of a neighbour and you not seeming to care whether she lives or dies.'

This time, Lois saw tears trickle from under Carmel's eyelids and slide down her cheeks, but she didn't let on she had seen. Instead she got to her feet, saying as she did so, 'Right I am away to fetch up some broth, and this is me you are dealing with, not Ruby, so we will have no nonsense from you. This time you will eat it!'

Carmel did eat it. She refused the bread and Lois didn't insist, but she drained the broth with a little persuasion and bullying, though she still didn't speak. But it was a start, and Ruby was delighted. It was that evening, as Lois sat feeding the baby, that she realised probably no one had been informed of Paul's death, for Carmel had been in no state to do so and Ruby wouldn't think to do it.

She would write to Carmel's family in Ireland that night after she had got the baby to bed, she decided. Her uncle would have to wait until the morning. She knew from what Paul and Jeff himself had said that he spent most evenings at his club and she could hardly trail him there. Women were not allowed in these bastions for men, anyway. Lois would have to tell her own family too and she knew she would have to call on the goodness of Ruby again in the morning while she undertook the unpleasant task of breaking the news of Paul's death to those closest to her.

When Lois told her Uncle Jeff about the telegram, she thought for a minute he was going to pass out. The colour drained totally from his face and he had to feel for his chair. Then he flopped into it as if his legs wouldn't hold him up any more.

'Uncle Jeff, are you all right?' Lois cried. 'Oh, what stupid things we say. I am so sorry. There is no way I know to soften news like this.'

'I'm all right, my dear,' Jeff said. He looked far from it. He appeared breathless, gasping for air, his voice was husky and his eyes unnaturally bright. 'If you would look in the filing cabinet there,' he said to Lois, 'top drawer, there is a bottle and a couple of glasses.'

Lois brought the whiskey and laid it on the table. 'You will join me, my dear?'

'No, thank you, Uncle,' Lois said for it was far too early in the morning for her, but she didn't begrudge her uncle taking comfort where he could. Jeff poured himself a good measure and downed it in one swallow. Lois was glad to see the colour return to his face and he seemed more in control of himself as he leaned towards her and said, 'Tell me everything you know.'

'That is precious little,' Lois said. 'I got word that Chris was injured first and that he was in hospital in Ramsgate and I set off to see him. He was in theatre when I arrived and, though I did see him for a few minutes later, he was too groggy to make any sense. I didn't know then about Paul, you see. Anyway, when they said Chris was going to be fine and that he was being transferred to a hospital in Birmingham later, I left because I was worried about leaving Carmel on her own. We all knew then about the rout of Dunkirk and because of Chris I knew the Royal Warwickshires had been involved but when I left she hadn't heard a word of how or where Paul was.'

'So she was on her own when she heard?'

Lois nodded. 'Ruby found Carmel slumped in a faint in the hall, the telegram still in her hand, saying Paul

341

was missing, presumed dead. She could barely open the door, she told me. She helped her to bed and she has been there ever since.'

'Ever since!' Jeff exclaimed, 'Why? When was this?'

'Three days ago. I came home only yesterday. Poor Ruby had too much to do looking after Carmel and Beth to think of informing anyone.'

Jeff nodded. 'I understand perfectly,' he said. 'She looked after the important things and that is all you can expect – more in fact than you can expect. You have a neighbour in a million there.'

'Don't I know it,' Lois said fervently. 'Without her I'm not sure what Carmel would have done. Will you go along and see her? She has always thought a great deal of you.'

'It's a mutual thing,' Jeff said. 'It will be no hardship for me to see her and, rest assured, you will have my constant support. Don't hesitate to call on me for anything.'

'Thank you, Uncle Jeff,' Lois said. 'What about Aunt Emma?' She had trouble saying the name without a curl to her lip when she remembered the way she had treated Paul.

She was mightily relieved when Jeff said, 'Don't worry about your aunt, my dear. Leave her to me.'

Lois hoped her sigh of relief wasn't audible as she said, 'Will you be all right? I have to go and tell my parents, and Ruby is once more holding the fort so I must get back as soon as I can.'

'Don't worry about me,' Jeff said. 'You already have enough on your plate. And I will be along to see Carmel as soon as I can manage it.'

He barely waited until the door closed behind his niece before buzzing his secretary. 'Find Matthew, would you, and ask him to spare me a few minutes?'

If the secretary was surprised there was no hint of it in her voice. 'Certainly, sir.'

Jeff poured another large glass of whiskey, which he again swallowed in one gulp. Then he leaned back in his chair and let the tears flow unchecked from his eyes as he grieved for the loss of his elder son, his favourite, if he was honest. He hadn't cried since he was five years old and his father had told him that if he wanted to grow up to be a big man, he hadn't to cry like a baby. As he wanted his father's approval above all else in the world, Jeff had adhered strictly to his rules and hadn't even shed a tear when the old man died.

But that day he cried for Paul, though he resisted the desire to wrap his arms around himself and howl like a wounded animal, for he ached so much inside it was as if Paul's death had carved a hole in his heart.

However, by the time he heard the sound of Matthew's voice as he accompanied the secretary to her office, he was calmer and he wiped the last of the tears from his cheeks and composed himself to tell Matthew of his brother's death.

Working in a different section, Matthew hadn't seen Lois arrive. When Jeff's secretary had found him and told him his father would like to see him, Matthew had been examining his conscience. Though they worked in the same firm, they seldom met on a regular basis and he knew there had to be some reason that he had been summoned to 'The Presence' like a naughty schoolboy, but he couldn't think of anything that he had done particularly bad – certainly nothing his father would think he had a right to interfere with.

The secretary claimed that she knew nothing of the reason, but Matthew knew that to be a lie. She knew most of what went on in that firm. In fact, she could keep the whole place running if his father was not there, and had often done just that, covering for the old man the mornings he had come in suffering so badly from the excesses of the night before that he was worse than useless for the first couple of hours.

When he saw the whiskey bottle and glasses set on the table Matthew knew that whatever it was all about was serious.

'You're starting early.'

'Will you join me?'

Matthew's eyes narrowed. His father's voice was husky, as if . . . as if he had been crying, and though Matthew had put the brightness of his eyes down to the booze, he saw now that there were unshed tears lurking there. There was just the one reason that his father might be moved to tears. Matthew's whole body began to tremble and suddenly a glass of whiskey seemed a very good idea.

He gave a nod to his father, who poured them both a stiff measure. Then Matthew sat in the chair opposite him and said, 'It's Paul, isn't it?'

Jeff nodded.

'Dead?'

Jeff shrugged. 'Missing, presumed dead,' he said. 'Means the same thing.'

'Oh Christ!' Matthew said. 'We had a few words when he came to tell Mother, you know, and I actually

344

sneered at him; said he would be in no danger. He would be well away from the fighting.'

'If I am honest, I thought the same,' Jeff said. 'I thanked God he wouldn't be in the front line, but in the débâcle of Dunkirk, everyone there would be in danger. Lois's husband, Chris, was injured too. It was Lois who came with the news just minutes ago.'

Matthew said nothing. He drank his whiskey and thought about his brother. He was shaken, but he didn't know how much he would miss him. They seldom met and, when they did, they had little in common. As a child he had longed to love him – he would have been easy to love, and a wonderful older bother to admire and respect – but his mother's blatant favouritism of Paul had driven away any love Matthew might have felt for him and replaced it with resentment. And yet he was sorry he was dead.

He said, 'What happens now then?'

'Well, I am away first to see Carmel, who has been rendered nearly senseless by this news. She was alone in the house except for the baby and her mind must have refused to take it. Anyway, I will see what's what and then I must be off to tell your mother. It might be best if you were in the house then too.'

Matthew drained the whiskey and nodded as he stood up. 'I'll see to it,' he said. 'I'll just finish what I was at and leave the foreman in charge.' He looked straight at his father and said, 'How do you think Mother is to take news like this?'

'I stopped trying to estimate your mother's reaction to things a long time ago,' Jeff said with a sigh. 'She doesn't seem to operate under the same rules or social mores as the rest of society. She had cast Paul completely out of her life and that saddened me, for if your mother loved anyone better than herself it was that boy.'

'Well, I know that,' Matthew said bitterly. 'Both you and I just had the leavings, didn't we?'

'We did, son,' Jeff said. 'And I often felt sorry for you.'

'I survived,' Matthew said lightly, though the hurt of rejection was still there behind his eyes. 'But however we feel about Mother, I know one thing: this news will hit her for six.'

Jeff knew that too. But before he faced his wife he went to see his daughter-in-law, the other one who had been hit for six. Lois hadn't returned by the time he arrived, but Ruby was relieved to see him.

'Go on up, Mr Connolly,' she said, adjusting the baby on her hip. 'As soon as I have madam here settled, I'll bring you a nice cup of tea.'

'Don't trouble yourself.'

'It's no trouble, honestly,' Ruby said. 'And maybe you can get Carmel to drink something. She plays up shocking with me at times. Lois can handle her better.'

'I'll do my best,' he said, chucking Beth under the chin as he passed and was rewarded by a beaming smile, Surely the baby was the only one to smile so readily in that house of sadness.

Jeff was glad he saw Carmel first on his own, for the sight of her lying so still, her open eyes fixed on some point on the ceiling, shocked him so much he was sure it must have been apparent. However, he recovered himself and, sitting on the chair beside the bed, he took one of her hands in his.

'Hello, Carmel,' he said gently.

Carmel hadn't been aware of Jeff entering the room. In fact she was aware of little. It was as if life just went on around her and she was outside of it. She turned her head and when she saw the sorrow etched so deeply on Jeff's face, which she knew must be mirrored on her own, she gave a sigh and said so softly it was little above a whisper, 'Oh God, Jeff, what am I to do?'

'Bear it, my dear,' Jeff said. 'There is no other option.'

'I can't,' Carmel said. 'Really I can't, the pain is too great.'

'Oh, my dear, dear girl . . .'

The sympathy in Jeff's voice was Carmel's undoing. She felt the tears that had threatened to fall for days begin to seep between her eyelashes and trickle down her cheeks and then this turned into a torrent and then a flood, and what Jeff originally saw as a good sign began to alarm him.

He glanced to the door, but there was no help from that quarter and in the end, he dropped Carmel's hand and, sitting up on the bed beside her, he put his arms about her shuddering body and held her against him while he stroked her hair with his other hand. 'Hush now,' he urged. 'You will make yourself ill if you go on like this.'

Carmel snuggled into the tweed of his jacket. She smelled tobacco and a whiff of whiskey, but it wasn't unpleasant; it was familiar. The heart-rending sobs eventually changed to hiccuping gulps.

Ruby, coming in with the tray of tea, was pleased that Carmel had cried at last. 'It was what she needed,' she told Jeff later as he was about to go. 'It was as if every-

347

thing was knotted up tight inside her and I think she needed your arms around her too. Having a stiff upper lip is all very well, but really it isn't much comfort when all is said and done and that is what you both needed if you ask me – a bit of comfort.'

Ruby was a very wise woman, Jeff thought. A little later, facing his wife across the room, he wished, whatever their differences, that he could gather Emma into his arms and they could comfort one another on the death of their son. However, he was unable to offer comfort because Emma looked at him coldly although her face was ravaged with wretchedness and heartache. Her voice when she spoke was strange and Jeff knew that it was sheer iron will that was keeping tears at bay.

But what she said in clipped tones was, 'I don't see why you think this should interest me.'

'Emma, for God's sake. He was our son.'

'He ceased to be my son when he married that little trollop.'

'She is no trollop,' Jeff said firmly. 'And you also have the dearest, cutest little granddaughter, if you could just bring yourself to see her. She is, after all, part of Paul.'

'And part of the woman he married,' Emma said stiffly. 'I want nothing to do with her. And now leave me, if you will. I want to be on my own.'

Jeff thought if he lived to be a hundred he would never understand his wife. But he also knew there was nothing to be gained by staying. He turned on his heel and went to find Matthew, who had returned home as he requested. Jeff had the urge to make a large hole in the brandy bottle and knew that for that day, at least, he would value Matthew's company.

CHAPTER TWENTY

While Jeff was talking to his wife, there was a surprising visitor to 17 York Road. Lois opened the door with the baby in her arms, and her mouth dropped open with shock.

'Matron!'

'Yes, don't look so shocked,' the matron said. 'I am here to see Carmel. Is this the baby?' She extended her hand for the child to grasp. Her face had softened and her voice was gentler with the child. Lois remembered someone saying how kind Matron was with the children in hospital and how they all loved her. 'It is just a pity,' said the girl who told her this, who was still recovering from a roasting Matron had given her, 'that her kindness doesn't extend to probationary nurses.'

'Yes, this is Elizabeth Eve,' Lois told her. 'She is called Beth for short.'

'And is Carmel still in bed?'

Lois nodded. 'There has been a breakthrough of sorts. No one had been informed, you see, and when I went and told Paul's father today, he came straight round. I wasn't here. I had gone on to tell my parents, but Ruby, the neighbour I mentioned, was, and she said Carmel started talking to Uncle Jeff. She could hear the murmur of voices, you know – Carmel hadn't spoken either since she got the telegram – and then, when Ruby went in, Carmel was crying so brokenheartedly Jeff had his arms around her. She needed those tears.'

'Oh, yes, indeed,' Catherine said knowledgeably. 'A person must cry before the healing process can really begin.'

She spoke as if she not only knew, but had experienced those things herself. And yet why wouldn't she? Lois thought. She must have been young once and probably had her moments.

'Is this Ruby with Carmel now?' Catherine asked.

'No,' said Lois. 'She has gone to make her husband a bite to eat and,' she added with the ghost of a smile, 'probably try and convince the poor man that she hasn't moved in here on a permanent basis.'

'So, could I see Carmel?'

'Of course,' Lois said. 'I will take you up now.'

Carmel was just as shocked as Lois had been at the sight of Matron in the doorway, and even more alarmed when Lois said, 'I will leave you to it, if that's all right?'

'That's fine,' Catherine said, and she sat on the chair by the bed. 'You are probably wondering why I have come to see you.'

Carmel gave a brief nod.

'Because I know just how you feel. Don't widen your eyes in such disbelief. My lover was killed in the First War. His name was Len Bishop and we were engaged and due to marry on his next leave. I was twenty-three and a nurse, but I was longing to be married and have a home and family of my own. But Len too was shipped to France and didn't return. I had just turned twenty-four when he died in 1915.'

Carmel's eyes were sympathetic, but Catherine continued, 'I don't broadcast this and I hope I won't have to ask you to be circumspect now. I don't want it to be bandied around the hospital, although you can tell Lois, if you wish.'

'What did you do?'

'I did just as you did, as you are doing,' the matron said. 'I retired to my bed. I felt my life was over. I wanted to die to be with Len. In the end, my distracted parents sent for the doctor. That man had the bedside manner of an alligator, which was probably good for me. He said that wallowing in grief would serve no purpose other than to worry those around me.'

'War is so dreadfully cruel.'

'It is,' Catheine agreed, 'and remember the war that Len died in was "the war to end all wars". I was quite resentful and envious of you and Lois the time you asked if you could nurse after marriage. I thought nothing could get in the way of your dreams. Even with Germany rumbling away, I never thought it would amount to anything and certainly not war.'

'Few wanted to believe it,' Carmel said.

'Well, it is here now,' Catherine said firmly, 'and, maybe even more than in the last one, it will be women that keep this country afloat. The luxury of lying in bed and letting the world go on around you is no attitude to have in wartime. If you don't want your man to have died in vain, this is a war we have to win and at the moment we have our backs to the wall.'

The matron looked at the sad eyes of Carmel and her voice was gentler as she went on, 'I know it's hard, my dear. Once Len was gone I knew I would never marry. He had been the one love of my life and I threw myself into nursing. You, my dear, have a child. I often wished . . . of course it could never be. Even engaged couples in those days did not indulge in such things and I would have been disgraced, I know, but it would have been nice to think that Len had left a piece of himself behind.

'The doctor said Len had been doing his duty and I owed it to his memory to get out of bed and do something useful with the rest of my life. Paul too had been doing his duty and you owe it to him to get up and care for your child. Isn't it what Paul would have expected of you?'

Carmel knew it was exactly what he would expect. She knew she would always miss him, but lying in bed thinking of him constantly would not bring him back, and meanwhile her baby was suffering.

Matron Turner left soon afterwards and Carmel called Lois and said she wanted to get up. Lois was delighted and Carmel was glad of her help for, once out of bed, she felt incredibly weak and the room listed dreadfully. But she persevered and made the stairs, then sat thankfully in the armchair and told Lois all that had transpired in the bedroom and what had given her the impetus to get up in the first place.

'She's right about the baby,' Lois said. 'Beth has been missing you. Both Ruby and I have noticed it, but I am so incredibly sorry for you, for me too, all of us, for Paul was such a very special person.'

*　　*　　*

352

Although Carmel forced herself to get up every morning and took on the total care of Beth, she felt numb and almost as if she were hollow inside. Nothing seemed to fill the gaping hole in her entire being and nothing helped or eased the pain lodged in her heart – not the letters of condolence and Mass cards arriving from Ireland, nor her mother writing to say that the family kneeled every night to say the rosary for the repose of Paul's soul.

Father Robertson came to see her. The man wasn't a very sympathetic person, but even he felt sorry for Carmel and knew that it would take her some time to get over such a tragic loss. He said he would remember her in his prayers and suggested a commemorative Mass, held both to celebrate Paul's life and mourn his death. Carmel was glad of Jeff's support there, for the Mass affected her greatly.

She was alone in the house and tidying up one day when she came upon the newspapers Lois had left out for salvage. She sat down and read what had been happening since Dunkirk when she had retired to her bed. Soon she realised that when Matron had spoken about Britain having its back to the wall, she had told the truth.

Nearly three hundred and fifty thousand Allied soldiers had been rescued from Dunkirk, which the paper acknowledged was an amazing feat. However, they had to leave behind them guns, ammunition and vehicles. Hitler, feeling sure Britain was finished, was massing his troops across the Channel, bent on invasion.

Carmel, like most others in the country, faced the possibility of defeat for the first time. If that happened she would feel that Paul had given his life in vain. A call had gone out for more Local Defence Volunteers and George Hancock was among the thirty thousand men in Birmingham alone who had rushed to join up. All civilians were urged to get involved and there were calls out to learn first aid, apply to be ARP wardens, or at the very least learn to operate stirrup pumps in the event of incendiary attacks.

Yet as Carmel pushed the baby out on those balmy summer days, it was sometimes hard to believe that there was a war on at all, apart, that was, from the notices appearing on hoardings. Travel was discouraged and one poster enquired, 'Is Your Journey Really Necessary?' Others reminded you that 'Careless Talk Costs Lives' and to, 'Be Vigilant! The Enemy Is Near'.

Lois had told Carmel that the road signs that had been removed and railway signs painted over to inhibit any potential invader, and people were also advised to disable cars not in use, to lock up or immobilise bicycles and hide maps.

Children evacuated to the south coast were being moved north to what were considered safer locations. Many children had already been taken home by their parents when the threatened bombing raids didn't materialise and more took them home now.

Ruby said she didn't blame them. 'If invasion comes,' she said, 'isn't it better for families to be together?'

Carmel supposed it was, but she had a horror of jack-booted Nazis marching down the streets of her adopted city, putting her life and that of her baby at risk.

'I worry about mine, for all they are big enough and ugly enough to look out for themselves,' Ruby went on. Carmel knew she had reason to worry. Ruby's two sons,

Bertie and Henry, had received their call-up papers and her son-in-law, Donald, was expecting his any day, as the battle began in the air.

The Germans began pounding the southern ports and attacking shipping prior to invasion, and Lois was very glad Chris had been moved, as Ramsgate was getting almost nightly raids. The hospital he had been sent to now was a new one, called the Queen Elizabeth, which had been built to replace the old Queen's. As many of the old Queen's staff had been transferred to the new hospital, Chris was well known there. That, together with the fact that he was a Dunkirk veteran, meant they could not do enough for him.

'He'll expect me to run around after him the same way when I get him home,' Lois grumbled, but she knew she wouldn't care a jot about that. Chris was alive and would be well again, and she knew how lucky she was.

So did Carmel. She still cried for the numbing loss of Paul some nights muffling the sounds in a pillow lest she disturb Lois. Sometimes, though she knew it was totally against the rules, she would take the baby into bed and they would sleep together.

Chris never spoke of Dunkirk and the first time Lois had asked him, his eyes had filled with tears so she was careful never to mention it again. This was what she told Carmel when she asked if he knew what had happened to Paul.

The day Chris came home, Carmel tried not to be selfish and begrudge Lois her happiness. But it did give her a pang when he walked through the door looking so hale and hearty.

He seemed happy to be back and he was totally charmed by the baby, but behind his eyes there was definite sadness. Lois asked about it when they were alone while Carmel was putting the baby to bed.

'I feel as if I have a heavy burden between my shoulder blades,' Chris said. 'And I need to speak to Carmel.'

Lois didn't ask why. She knew she would know soon enough and so, when Carmel came down, she used more of their precious tea ration and Chris ushered the two girls into the sitting room.

He waited until Carmel had the tea in her hand before saying, 'I was with Paul to the very end. I want you to know that. He was the greatest mate a man could ever have and there will never be another like him. I could weep now at the thought that I'll never see him again and I can only imagine your pain.'

Carmel noted Chris's glittering eyes, and though the tears were seeping from her own she was glad that Chris spoke about Paul so easily.

'Thank you for that, Chris,' she said through her tears. 'I know what good friends you were. You say you were with him till the end?'

Chris nodded. 'I could tell you about it, if it would help.'

'I don't know if it would help or not,' Carmel said. 'But I want to know it all.'

'We were in a little place between Lille and Wormhout,' Chris said, 'working in a field hospital together. Everyone was trying to make for Dunkirk, for the word was there was some sort of rescue operation being attempted from there and most of the wounded had been sent on. But Paul had four who were too ill to move and he was hanging on to the last minute, until the Germans were almost in sight, to leave them, believing then they would be taken care of.

'In the end, we had to go and we hadn't gone very far into this little wooded area when we heard German voices. We knew it was a scouting party going ahead of the main convoys and we were thanking ourselves for our lucky escape. Paul was saying that at least now the wounded would be cared for when we heard the machine-gun fire. Paul looked stricken for he knew that the Germans had shot the wounded men.

'He seemed to go a little mad then and he set off at a run back the way we had come. I went after him but when I reached him and tried to stop him he shook me off. His eyes were wild and I know he wasn't thinking straight. Neither of us had slept for days and hadn't eaten either for hours. What I mean is that he wasn't himself when he burst out of the shelter of the trees yelling that they were all murdering bastards. A single rifle shot brought him down and he sort of folded at the knees and then they shot him again and he slumped to the ground. I heard the Germans laugh as they kicked him into a ditch.'

Carmel was crying in earnest and Lois had her arms around her, but she was still glad that she had listened to Chris. Since Carmel had recovered from her collapse, she had harboured the idea that maybe Paul wasn't dead. The telegram had said missing, presumed dead. What if he was in hospital or a POW camp somewhere and he had lost his memory?

Now that theory was knocked flat. His best friend had seen Paul killed. She had to face that. It was no good hiding under dreams and fantasies. Paul was dead and gone and she had to face life without him for the sake of little Beth, who would depend on her. Lois too was upset, both by the story of the tragic death of Paul and also by the thought that in just a couple of days time, Chris had to rejoin his unit and could be in the thick of it once more.

All through the summer, the battle for supremacy of the skies raged on. The German airforce knew they had to annihilate the RAF before German landing craft could cross the Channel in safety.

The results of these attacks would be reported in the newspapers the next day. 'The Germans lost 217 planes to Fighter Command's 96' the papers would boast. Carmel wondered if it were true, or just written to raise morale, though it did nothing for hers. In fact she found it distasteful, as if the war was a kind of game. Yet every plane lost represented someone's life.

On 9 August a lone bomber attacked an Erdington suburb. What unnerved Carmel was the fact that everyone was so taken by surprise because no sirens sounded. The first people knew about it was when three bombs exploded. A number of houses were destroyed but it was amazing that only one person was killed. The victim was only eighteen years old and on leave from the army. Carmel knew nothing about the air raid until the next day, the rumbles far enough away for her to think it was thunder.

Birmingham was attacked again on 13 August, though it was a fairly localised assault on the aircraft factory at Castle Bromwich. After that the sirens sounded nearly every night but the attacks were light and sporadic, and concentrated mainly on the east side of the city. Although there were deaths and people injured and buildings destroyed, they were nothing like the blanket bombing the civilians had been half expecting.

Carmel and Lois had decided early on that they would sit out any raid that was close enough in the cellar, the garden being taken over with the motorbikes, which had been shrouded in tarpaulin and put aside for the duration, leaving no room for an Anderson shelter. People who had got shelters told Lois they flooded with just the slightest bit of rain, and Carmel thought them damp and dreary places to sit in hour after hour.

Paul had agreed with her, but had the man from the Ministry check the cellar out to ensure it was safe, before he enlisted.

'Perfect!' the man had declared. 'Some of these cellars need reinforcement to be of any use, but this now is very solidly built. You should be as safe as houses in there if Erdington is attacked in any big way.'

The girls, in cleaning out the rubbish in readiness, had unearthed the old paraffin stove. It still stank to high heaven when they lit it, but as Lois said, 'What is a smell compared to freezing to death?' Carmel just hoped she never had to put it to the test.

For a few days, it seemed as if she wouldn't have to, for the raids were too far away for the girls to seek shelter, but when the sirens did blare out a warning on the evening of 24 August, Carmel used the cellar, for the raid was more widespread.

Lois and George were both on duty so Ruby came into Carmel's cellar so that they could keep each other company. George had managed to pick up a flask from somewhere and Ruby had filled it with hot sweet tea before she came in. Carmel produced a packet of biscuits and, for a time, their refuge took on the air of a picnic.

However, the raid lasted seven and a half hours, and by the time the all clear sounded, both woman were worn out. Carmel's arms felt like lead from holding the sleeping Beth as there was nowhere to lay her down.

'We'll have to get organised,' Ruby said, 'get this place cosier, like, if we are to spend any time in here. I've got a couple of palliasses in one of the attic rooms, left over from when our lads were in the Boy Scouts. I'll get George to bring one round here when he has had a bit of a lie-in. Good job it's Sunday, eh?'

'I'll say,' Carmel said. 'I just hope her ladyship here lets me have at least a few hours. I feel I could sleep on a clothes line, I'm that jiggered.'

That evening when the sirens sounded again, Carmel groaned – and groaned even louder when she realised that the sound had woken the baby. She went upstairs and lifted her from the cot. She hadn't put up the blackouts and so she didn't put on the lights – the night was light enough anyway – and she took the baby to the window, rocking her while she patted her back rhythmically.

Lois tapped on the bedroom door before opening it and whispered, 'I'm off to work now. You all right?'

'Fine.'

'Are you going down to the cellar?'

Carmel shook her head. 'I will if it gets closer.'

It didn't get closer, but she couldn't sleep in case it did, and when she heard the sound of the back door opening and Ruby's voice shouting, 'It's only me,' she wasn't surprised.

She went on to the landing with the drowsy baby still held against her. 'Up here,' she said softly.

'George is away for a pint,' Ruby said as she laboured up the stairs. 'I came to see if you were all right.'

'Yes I am,' Carmel said. 'It is too far away to worry about it as yet, anyway. It is just that the siren woke Beth.'

'Looks like she's well away again now,' Ruby said. She looked out of the window. Darkness had fully descended now, although there was a strange crimson glow on the horizon. 'Some poor sods are getting a pounding, anyway.'

Ruby was right, for they could hear muffled thumps and crashes.

'I bet it's the city centre getting it this time,' she said.

'God, I hope not,' Carmel said. 'That's where Lois is heading.'

'Put the babby in the cot and let's go up the attics and see if we can see owt?' Ruby suggested. They did that, and saw the pall of thick black smoke before they saw the flames licking orange and red into the dark sky. They also saw the arc of the searchlights seeking the planes, and heard the tattoo of the ack-ack guns and, moments later, the ringing bells of the emergency services.

'Ain't it stupid?' Ruby said. 'Here they are worried about a chink of light showing and then the bloody German drop incendiaries before the other buggers and light the place up like bleeding daylight.'

361

'I know, and I just hope it wasn't the General Hospital they were targeting tonight.'

It wasn't the hospital, but it was the city centre, mainly the Bull Ring. Carmel had to wait until Lois came home to find out.

'Loads of us went for a dekko after work,' she told Carmel. 'We were getting the injured in all the time, see, and some of them were telling us bits while we patched them up, so we went to see for ourselves. The Bull Ring is just a mess,' she added sadly. 'The whole roof is off the Market Hall. Only the walls are standing, and they don't look too healthy. Someone said a man went back into the burning place and released all the animals from their cages.'

'That's good,' Carmel said. 'I did think about the animals. They might not have much chance on the street, but it has to be better than been burned alive.'

'I'll say,' Lois agreed with feeling. 'And everything else is gone. Even that magnificent clock, just cinders.' She gave a rueful laugh and commented, 'Huh, maybe there is some truth in the rumour of bad luck after all.'

'No,' Carmel said almost fiercely, 'it's not that. Our bad luck is that Hitler was born at all and then allowed to grow up.'

'You think he should have been drowned at birth?'

'Let's say it might have solved a lot of the world's problems if he had been.'

The raid the following night began just after midnight. Lois, who was not on duty, tapped on Carmel's door. She was awake, for she had been roused by the sirens, though she noted thankfully the baby slumbered on.

'Are you going down to the cellar?' Lois asked.

'I don't know,' Carmel said. 'I am worn out and loath to disturb Beth. She looks so peaceful and is the very devil to settle afterwards sometimes. Anyway, the raid might be too far away to bother about. I think I will wait and see.'

After a few minutes, when the drone of planes did not get any louder, Carmel said, 'I'll hardly sleep, though, because they could change direction in a few minutes.' She threw back the covers and said, 'Come here and keep me company.'

Lois slipped into bed beside Carmel, but they were too tired to talk much, though Lois did tell Carmel some of the gossip from the hospital, the life that she had once been a part of and that Lois knew she missed, much as she loved the baby.

Exhaustion had actually claimed the girls when the droning planes alerted Carmel again in the early hours. Lois was still fast asleep and Carmel left her, knowing she had to be up anyway in a few hours, but she lay and listened. The planes came no nearer and she snuggled down again, glad of the comfort of any other body next to hers. As dawn grew ever nearer, she eventually slept.

Carmel heard the report on the raid from Jeff, who called around later that day. Since Paul's death, he called to see Carmel at least twice a week and always gave her money to put inside the weekly letter she wrote to her mother.

Then, as soon as he judged Carmel was ready, he told her about the allowance that he and Paul had set up for her as soon as he had enlisted, payable if anything happened to him.

'It's money that would have been his anyway after my death,' Jeff said. 'I agreed to release the money now and set up a fund for you.'

'Oh,' Carmel said, taken aback. 'He was always adamant he would stand on his own feet.'

'And that was fine while he was alive and well,' Jeff said, taking hold of one of Carmel's hands as he spoke. 'But I know now, and will swear on anything you like, that Paul's dearest wish was for you and the child to be provided for. It was the one thing he was so worried about.'

What could Carmel say to that? Could she go against something her dead husband wanted so?

'You should still apply for widows' allowance, like,' Ruby said when she heard.

Carmel shook her head. 'I have no need of it. Let those not so well provided for have the benefit. I cannot spend all I am given now, or nowhere near it. There aren't the things in the shops to buy and whatever you get you have to have the ration for. Money alone is not enough.'

That was true. Ruby said nothing further and, every week, Jeff would call around with her allowance. She was always pleased to see him and the day after this latest air raid was no exception. Jeff immediately noticed the bags beneath her eyes.

'Well, no, I didn't sleep well,' Carmel said in answer to his enquiry. 'Who can really?'

'It was the city centre again last night.'

'We guessed as much,' Carmel said 'D'you know if there was much damage?'

'Hell of a lot,' Jeff said. 'From Snow Hill Station,

364

down Livery and Newhall Street as far St Paul's church and the start of the Jewellery Quarter there was a sea of fire, so I heard.'

'That's terrible,' Carmel cried. 'Aren't there a lot of wooden structures in the Jewellery Quarter?'

'I suppose that was part of the problem,' Jeff said. 'The way I heard it, the heat was so intense the roadway melted and tar was running like liquid fire, setting fire to more and more in its path.'

'Oh God,' Carmel said. 'Were there many hurt?'

Jeff shrugged. 'Bound to be some. Probably they were taken to the General, seeing as it is closest.'

'It's awful, isn't it?'

'Yes,' Jeff said grimly. 'And set to get worse before it gets better.'

However, while Birmingham was suffering nightly raids, so far London had got by virtually unscathed except for a few little skirmishes. But everyone, including Londoners, knew that their turn too would come. And then on, Saturday, 7 September, there was a report on the wireless.

'An armada of bombers protected by many fighters have been seen approaching the Kent coast.'

Carmel glanced at the clock. It was four o'clock and she shivered for those in London. There seemed little doubt where this large contingent was heading.

The Sunday papers that Carmel bought on her way home from Mass the following day told the whole, horrifying story. The bombers had been making for the London docks. As the sirens wailed, the people ran for cover and the docks were ablaze in minutes. By the morning, the estimated death toll was five hundred and the injured were well over a thousand. It made grim and harrowing reading. Carmel was well aware that a similar fate might be awaiting Birmingham and there wasn't a thing anyone could do about it.

The raids in London and Birmingham and many other cities continued, though Carmel sought the shelter of the cellar only twice, when the raids over nearby Pype Hayes she thought too close for comfort. Most of the them were over in two to four hours, although there was one in mid-September that lasted nine hours and the lack of sleep and disturbance was playing havoc with Carmel's nerves, especially when there were reports of barges and landing craft massing across the channel.

'Hitler has put back his invasion plans until 27 September,' Jeff said when he was visiting one Saturday afternoon.

'How do you know these things?'

Jeff put his finger to the side of his nose and then wagged it at Carmel. 'Ask no questions and you will be told no lies. But trust me. And if Hitler is going to invade then, which will be the last time really before the autumn storms, then he has to give the order by the seventeenth, ten days before.'

'But it's the fourteenth, now,' Lois said.

'Right, and the RAF is still there, so someday soon the Luftwaffe and the RAF are going to face one another in one hell of a showdown.'

Carmel shivered. She had no idea how and where Jeff got his information from, but wherever it was it usually turned out to be very accurate.

* * *

The following day was Sunday. Lois went on duty at lunchtime and Carmel turned on the wireless for company, only to hear of the major onslaught, the one Jeff had told them to expect, had begun that morning. Ruby came in later, after George had gone to the warden post, to find Carmel glued to the wireless.

'This is it, d'you think?' Ruby asked.

'Jeff said that if Hitler intends to invade this year, the order has to be in by the seventeenth.'

'Ooh,' Ruby said and shivered. 'Proper gives you the collywobbles, don't it?'

'I'll say,' Carmel said, and went on, 'I'll make us a cup of tea. That's always good for steadying the nerves.'

'God,' said Ruby, 'I think I need summat stronger than tea today. Still, a cuppa will do for now.'

When it was obvious that the RAF were victorious, Carmel felt almost light-headed with relief.

Ruby remarked, 'When old Churchill went on about "so much owed by so many to so few" back in August, he was right, weren't he? God, them lads must have nerves of bloody steel. I'll tell you summat else as well,' she went on. 'I'm telling George that we need a wireless. Plum daft it is these days to do without.'

Carmel didn't blame her and neither did Jeff when he called round later to find George and Ruby keeping Carmel company – only he went one step further. 'Let me buy it for you?'

'I wouldn't dream of it.'

'It would be the way of thanking you for all you have done for my daughter-in-law and granddaughter,' Jeff said. 'And it would please me so much if you would allow me to do this.'

'Well, put like that . . .' George began tentatively.

'Consider it done,' Jeff said, and he gave a huge sigh and said, 'That's it then. We are safe from invasion at least.'

'Maybe for this year,' Carmel said. 'What if Hitler tries again in the spring?'

'We'll be more ready for him then.'

'How come?'

'My dear, we are hardly recovered from Dunkirk,' Jeff said. 'More men were rescued that was thought humanly possible, but machines and equipment were left behind and we need that and more to fight a war and win. We really need more women in the workforce too, because every man is needed for the fight. Matthew got his call-up papers yesterday.'

'Matthew?' Carmel repeated in surprise. 'But I thought . . .'

'Oh, he tried to say he was in a reserved occupation,' Jeff said. 'But when they heard I was still alive and kicking and with my finger on the pulse, as it were, it didn't wash with them at all.'

'They do need them all,' Ruby said. 'My son-in-law's papers have come through too. My daughter came blarting on about it but I told her not to be such a silly cow. The man had no choice anyway. I mean, I know it's not going to be no picnic – and it's not for us lot left behind either – but we just have to get on with it. No good moaning about summat you can't change, I always say.'

'You're right there, old girl,' George said.

'Don't you "old girl" me,' Ruby retorted. 'I ain't fin-ished yet either. I was thinking myself of doing my bit as well, though to be honest I couldn't really see me in rollers making things in a factory, but her on the end, you know,' she said with a nod to Carmel, 'Tilly Dewhurst, with the two nippers, that lost her man at Dunkirk too.' Carmel nodded. 'Well,' Ruby said, 'she was thinking of taking a job. Says the widows' pension goes nowhere. Anyroad, she says having the two minded was dear so she is looking after someone else's babby instead so that she can go into the munitions and Tilly can earn a bit extra, and I reckon I could do the same.'

'Begod!' George exclaimed. 'Without saying a dickey bird to me.'

'How is it going to affect you?' Ruby demanded. 'When I haven't a dinner to put before you and a clean shirt to put on your back you can have your say. Till then, keep it buttoned. Did you ask me before you joined the Home Guard? Did you hell as like. You did it because you thought you should do summat and I will do this for the same reason. As I said, everyone should do their bit.'

CHAPTER TWENTY-ONE

'Everyone should do their bit.' Ruby's words haunted Carmel over the next few days. She began to feel she was doing nothing to help win the war for which her husband had given his life.

One evening she said to Lois, 'Do you think I should go into the munitions?'

'What about Beth?'

'If I could get her minded. What do you think?'

'I think you are clean barmy. Why go into the munitions when you are a qualified nurse?'

'Yes, but I have a baby now and Matron—'

'Look, Carmel, lots of the rules have had to be relaxed now we are at war and the men disappearing at a rate of knots,' Lois said. 'We have mothers working on the wards now, so if you are serious about this, go and talk to Matron. See what she says.'

'Well,' Carmel promised, 'I will certainly think about it.'

Jeff was totally against Carmel taking any sort of job. 'Why do you need to, my dear?' he said when she put it to him. 'If it is a case of money . . .'

'It isn't money,' Carmel snapped, irritated. 'I see now why Paul used to get so annoyed. Not everything revolves around money and not every situation can be changed by throwing more and more cash at it.'

'I'm sorry, my dear,' Jeff said. 'I have offended you.'

Carmel sighed. 'Not really,' she said. 'I'm sorry I snapped at you. I know in your world things are different.'

'How do you think Paul would feel about this?'

'How can we ever really know that?' Carmel said. 'It's unfair to lay that on me as well. I will tell you one thing about Paul, though: he might have wanted to keep me safe, but he would never stand against my doing something I knew in my heart was the right thing to do. He loved and respected me too much to do that.'

'I know he would be proud of you,' Jeff said. 'As proud as I am. And I will not harass you further. Your decision must be your own.'

Jane and Sylvia came to see Carmel one evening, as they were wont to do every few weeks, only this time both were sporting engagement rings. And when the rings had been admired, Carmel asked them if they had set the date for the weddings yet.

'I have,' Jane said. 'Well, not an actual date as such, because that will depend on when Pete has leave, but hopefully it will be in the spring. We were going to wait till after the war, but who knows when that will be? Anyway, we were sick of waiting and it was getting harder and harder, you know what I mean?'

'Only too well,' Carmel said with feeling, and Lois agreed.

'Anyway, we are going for it,' Jane went on. 'Nothing fancy, just do the business in the registry office and a bit of a buffet in a nearby pub. Then we are taking off to a hotel for the night. He will probably only have a forty-eight-hour pass, see.'

'Where will you live?'

'With his parents.' Jane made a face. 'I know it is not ideal, for all I get on with them well enough. But Pete thinks it would be better that I am not on my own and it will give us the opportunity to save for after this damned war.'

'What about you, Sylvia?' Lois asked. 'Have you set the date yet?'

'You kidding?' Sylvia said. 'Only just talked him into getting engaged.'

'Wasn't he keen then?'

'Not as keen as I was, but I told him straight, I can't keep hanging on for ever without some official under-standing between us. Course, at first he thought it gave him licence to . . . well, you know. I told him straight, none of that until the other ring is on my finger.'

'I have news too,' Carmel said. 'I intend to go and have a word with Matron as soon as possible about coming back to work.'

'What about the baby?' Sylvia cried.

'I'll have her minded,' Carmel said. 'Ruby next door has already offered. I've been thinking about this for a few days.'

'Won't you miss her?' Jane said. 'I don't think I could bear to leave a baby of mine.'

'Well,' Carmel said, 'the way I see it, Paul probably felt the same way. But he went to try and save or at least ease the suffering of the serving soldiers, and I want to do the same for the innocent victims in Birmingham. I will miss Beth, miss her like mad, but ultimately it is for her. This war is surely being fought to make it a safer place for her to grow up in. To win it, as we must, we all need to pull together.'

'Well, I admire you,' Jane said. 'And I will be more than glad to welcome you back on board.'

Matron gazed at Carmel over the desk and smiled. 'Before we go any further, can I say what a pleasure it is to see you looking so much better?'

'A lot of that was your doing,' Carmel said. 'And you were right, of course. There is no way that Paul would expect me to fold the way I did, especially when I had a child to see to. I miss him still and maybe always shall, but all the tears in the world will not bring him back. I know that now and I owe it to my daughter to be strong. I must be both mother and father to her.'

'I admire your courage, my dear,' Matron said. 'Your husband will always occupy a corner of your heart and no one can remove the memories you will carry.'

Carmel blinked back the tears and said, 'Thank you once more. You are so very understanding. I asked if you could see me today for a special reason. I want to return to nursing.'

Carmel could see by the surprised expression on her face that the woman hadn't been expecting that. She went on, 'Lois told me you have had to bend the rules since the war began.'

'She is right, but all the mothers we have employed so far have had their children evacuated, or they are older and more able to fend for themselves, whereas you . . .'

'Ruby will look after Beth.'

'But what about the night shifts?'

'We have talked about this. She only lives next door and she says that if I am working nights, Beth will sleep in her house.'

Matron still didn't look convinced and Carmel pleaded, 'Please let me try? See if it works for six months or so, because I must do something. I feel useless and want to play my part. I was thinking of going into muni-tions,' she went on. 'It was Lois said to come and see you.'

'My dear,' Matron said with a wry smile, 'what do you know about making guns and ammunition?'

'Well, not a lot, I suppose,' said Carmel with an answering smile. 'It isn't something that I have ever studied closely.'

'On the other hand, you are a first-rate nurse and Lois was quite right to advise you to come and see me,' Matron said. 'And the fact that you are now a widow changes things a little. I will take you on, but it will be on a three-month trial basis only. If at the end of that you feel you can't manage, or indeed the hospital feels it isn't working out, then the contract will be terminated.'

'Oh, thank you, Matron,' Carmel cried, leaping to her feet in excitement. 'You don't know what this means to me.'

'I can guess,' the matron said. 'Your face is very expressive. Shall we say you report for duty in a fortnight, Monday, 7 October? Is that enough time to get things organised?'

'Plenty of time.'

'Well, then, shall we shake hands on it?'

Carmel first sought out Lois, whom she knew was on duty, and told her, but Jane and Sylvia were on nights. Carmel knew, though, they would be told by someone. From her memories of the hospital, legitimate news, gossip and even unsubstantiated rumour flew around like wild fire. For all that, though, they were a friendly bunch and many she had worked with before said they were looking forward to seeing her back. She nearly floated home, fired with exhilaration.

There was a lull in the bombing until mid-October, just as Lois and Carmel were about to go off duty. Carmel was rather nervous when she heard the sirens. This was the first raid she had experienced since she had returned to work. She had practised the drill all the nurses were trained in when the sirens indicated a raid was imminent and for the first time she saw the system swinging into action.

Some nurses filled all the baths and sterilisers with water, in case the water supply was hit, while others led the patients able to be moved down to the basement. Carmel helped Lois erect steel cages around the beds of the bed bound and then tried to ignore the whines and crashes and booms all around them and dampen down their own fears as they soothed and comforted the frightened patients while the raid grew in intensity.

Before the all clear sounded, the ambulances were heard bringing in the wounded. Doctors and nurses worked through the raid tending them. At the same time, when the other patients were brought back from the basement, after four hours, all of them had to be made ready for bed. The nurses who would have taken over this task were dealing with those injured in the raid, so Lois, Carmel and the other nurses set to with a will to make hot drinks, help administer drugs, bring bedpans and bowls of water, and then tuck the patients up for the night before they left.

'You can't just walk out, can you?' Lois said as they made their way home. 'It just isn't that kind of job.'

'Never has been,' Carmel said, 'and I wouldn't want it any other way, but I must admit I will miss not seeing Beth tonight.'

She wasn't even in the house, for she had fallen asleep in the Hancocks' cellars and after the all clear, George had made a makeshift cradle from an old drawer and the child was fast asleep inside it.

'Didn't you bring her around here for the night?' Lois said. She had gone straight into the house to make them both a hot drink before bed.

'What would be the point?' Carmel said. 'She is fast asleep and warm and cosy. Why would I disturb her and lay her into a cold cot only to take her back to Ruby's tomorrow? It isn't as if they mind having her. They dote on her.'

'I know,' Lois said. 'Just seems mean that they see more of her than you do.'

'The war can't last for ever, Lois, and at least this way I feel that I am doing something useful. Tonight the hospital really did need every nurse on board.'

Lois couldn't deny that.

* * *

After that raid, there was a lull of nine days and though at first people waited for and expected the sirens to wail, they had begun to relax by the time the next raid happened. Carmel got in some much-needed sleep and time to spend with little Beth. She was home in time to bath her and put her to bed in her own cot, in her own house, and she spent much of her off-duty hours playing with her, or taking her for long walks.

Carmel thought her beloved baby looked more like Paul every day, and so did Lois and Jeff, who truly adored her. She had her father's blond curls, the same reflective deep blue eyes and sensual mouth that turned up at the ends as her father's had done, as if he was constantly amused. Even her laughter was reminiscent of Paul, and the fact that her beloved husband so evidently lived on in their child gave Carmel immense satisfaction.

When the sirens sang out again in the last week of October, there were some groans of 'Here we go again,' but everyone just got on with preparing for the air raid as usual.

The ferocity of that raid was stunning, though. The noise and crash of explosions across the whole city appeared relentless. The hospital was swamped with the wounded. Lois and Carmel worked on all through the night, as the casualties just kept coming in. Carmel no longer felt frightened but blisteringly angry that ordinary people should suffer so much.

She and Lois returned home the following morning and Carmel went straight round to Ruby's. Ruby looked at the girl, white-faced with exhaustion and with bags under her beautiful eyes, which were also filled with shock at the dreadful injuries she had seen and tended that night.

'Don't you worry about the babby none,' Ruby said. 'She's grand. I've put her down for a nap because we was up most of the night. Tell you the truth, I wouldn't mind forty winks myself now she is away and you should do the same.'

'Forty winks,' Carmel said with a wry smile. 'I think I'll need forty thousand winks before I feel anywhere near normal.'

'Well, you can make a start on them anyway,' Ruby said. 'Go on home and get your head down.'

Carmel did as she suggested, guiltily relieved that she didn't have to cope with an active baby.

The following evening they found out the extent of the damage of the previous night. Sylvia had bought an *Evening Mail* and read out bits from it at teatime. 'One hundred and eighty-nine fires were raging across the city by midnight,' she read. 'Marshall & Snelgrove is gone, and all down that side of New Street.'

'The Empire Theatre in Broad Street is gone too,' one of the other girls said. 'I treated a woman for burns and shock. She was walking past when the bomb hit.'

'Yeah,' Sylvia said, consulting the paper. 'And only efficient firewatchers saved the Hippodrome, but Tony's Ballroom was gutted. Shame, isn't it, because haven't we had some good nights there?'

There was a murmur of agreement. 'I sometimes wonder if there will be anything of Birmingham left after this,' Carmel said.

'Listen to this,' Sylvia said suddenly. 'The Carlton cinema in Sparkbrook was hit and nineteen people were killed, but this is the funny thing – they were all sitting in their seats still and hadn't a mark on them.'

'How come?' Jane said. 'How did they die then?'

'Says here their lungs were burned out.'

There was a collective 'Ugh' and shudder around the table.

'It doesn't bear thinking about,' Carmel said.

'Maybe it was quick,' Lois said. 'They probably died instantly and never felt it or anything.'

'They didn't all,' Sylvia said. ''Cos it's says here one young man talked to his dad in the hospital before he died. Name of Ted Byrne, and he was only fifteen.'

'What a shame!'

'It's all a shame,' another girl put in. 'A little girl about six years old died in my arms last night. She was in a public shelter in Hockley that took a direct hit, so the ambulance driver said. And this little one survived the bomb and then the bloody shelter walls caved in on top of her. The doctor hadn't even got round to examining her when she suddenly opened her eyes wide, gave me a lovely smile and just died. I put her down and cried my eyes out in the toilet block. I know we are not supposed to get involved, but there's some things . . .'

'No one would blame you for that,' Carmel said. 'I would have been exactly the same.'

'And me,' Lois said. 'It's all right this not getting involved business, but we aren't robots.'

'No we aren't,' Jane said. 'And if we didn't feel for people I don't think we would make very good nurses, would we?'

'No,' said the first girl. 'Of course we wouldn't. That's makes me feel a whole lot better.'

The sirens pealed out again that night and there was a collective groan from patients and staff alike. That raid wasn't as long or intensive, as the previous night's. However, the raid the following night was different and blitzed a vast area of the city.

The hospital was nearly bursting at the seams and Lewis's, seeing the problem, offered their basement for overflow. So did Ansells at Aston Cross, and a bevy of probationers, wearing the copious green overalls Carmel and Lois could well remember wearing, were dispatched to help clear and clean the areas. That showed more than anything that the hospital was expecting many casualties.

The sirens rang out every night. Sometimes Carmel and Lois were at home, and often in bed, and sometimes there were false alarms. Getting home itself was quite an adventure at times. They often had to go by vastly convoluted routes, or just get off and walk part of the way, for there might be a gigantic crater in the road, or the tar might have melted, slid into the gutters at the edge of the road and buckled the tram tracks. The girls had got used to the smell of gas, cordite and dust in their noses and throats, the clambering over piles of rubble that used to be houses or shops, often still smouldering, and pavements that ran with water fed by dribbling hosepipes snaking along them. And they stepped over many damp and seeping sandbags.

Carmel was weary of the daily strain and shattered by the sight of so many damaged buildings.

'Tell you, these raids are getting to me,' she admitted

380

one day to Lois as they ate their evening meal together. 'I feel worn to a frazzle, to tell you the truth.'

'Me too,' Lois said. 'And I will tell you what I find annoying and that is that they seldom mention Birmingham by name with regard to any attack, however severe, whether it is in the papers or on the wireless.'

'Yes,' Carmel said. 'I've noticed that too. The *Evening Mail* does sometimes, but most times it is referred to as "a Midland town". Why is that do you think?'

'Well, Uncle Jeff said Birmingham makes so much war-related stuff, they don't want Hitler to know he has reached his target, but it does seem strange when every other town and city is named.'

'Let's hope that whatever we are called there isn't anything to report tonight because I want to sleep the night through for once.'

'It's hardly likely,' Lois said. 'There is a full moon. I noticed it when I was putting rubbish in the bin. The night is cold and crisp and as clear as a bell.'

Hitler did not leave them alone that night. The raid was a bad one and extensive enough for the two women to rouse Beth and go down to the cellar. However, Hitler's real target that night was another 'Midland town', although Lois and Carmel didn't find that out until the next day, when the *Birmingham Gazette*'s headline was, 'Coventry Our Guernica'.

Rumours had been running around the hospital all day about some massive raid in Coventry and now there it was in the Birmingham papers. In fact, so successful was the Luftwaffe's near destruction of Coventry that the British papers claimed a new word had entered the

German language – 'Coventration', which meant the razing to the ground of a place.

That night, Carmel was hardly in the door after work when Jeff knocked on it.

'Come in, Jeff,' she said, but her heart sank when she looked at his face for she knew what he was going to say.

'Now then, Carmel, I let you go your own way when you decided to return to nursing. I said I wouldn't harass you and I haven't, have I?'

'No, Jeff. You have been very good about it.'

'Well, you must see that the bombing of Coventry has changed all that?'

'No,' Carmel said. 'You have me there, Jeff, for I don't see that at all.'

'What happened in Coventry will happen here sooner or later,' Jeff said. 'And I want you out of there. You, and Lois too, preferably,' he nodded across to his niece. 'But certainly you. I owe it to Paul and you owe it to that child you have just lifted from the pram.'

'And tell me, Jeff, when this dreadful raid happens and all these people are terribly injured and desperately needing care, who is going to treat them if all the nurses and doctors take off because they are scared?'

'I'm not talking about everyone, I am talking about you.'

'Remember, Jeff, nearly everyone there is special to someone,' Carmel said, but gently because she knew he was seriously concerned about her. 'I am not a special case and I am staying on at the General because that is where I am needed.'

'And you, Lois?'

'I feel the same.'

'Do you know the danger you are putting yourselves in?'

'We know it, Jeff,' Carmel said. 'We're not stupid. I won't pretend I'm not scared either, because I am often, but I will not turn tail and run away.'

In one way Jeff wanted Carmel to listen to him, to stay at home and bring up his granddaughter in relative safety, which Erdington was in comparison to the centre of town, but in another way he couldn't help but admire her courage and determination, and that of Lois too. It went against the grain with him to have women imperilled in any way and yet this war was not being fought on chivalrous lines. Civilians were often in as much danger as fighting men. If Carmel and Lois felt their place was with the wounded, he had to respect that attitude.

He spread his arms helplessly and said, 'You have me beat, the pair of you.'

Carmel laughed at the expression on Jeff's face. 'Come on,' she said. 'Don't take it all so seriously. Come and mind your granddaughter while I get things organised for a meal. Will you join us?' She saw him hesitate and went on, 'Don't worry about rationing because we have most of our meals at the canteen and so we stretch our allotment out quite well. Lois can work miracles with food, anyway.'

'If you are sure?'

'I am,' Carmel said. 'And now will you take this child out of my arms? She's trying to launch herself at you already.'

*　　*　　*

The raid of 19 November began at a quarter-past seven. Carmel and Lois had eaten and Carmel was getting Beth ready for bed. When the sirens began their unearthly wail she zipped Beth into a siren suit over her pyjamas in case they had to go down the cellar and said to Lois, 'Pop round to see if Ruby wants to come in with us. When I collected Beth earlier, she said that George was on duty tonight and so she will be on her own.'

Ruby was glad to be asked, though, as she said, it might all be over in an hour or two and she would be able to go back home. Carmel, though, had a funny feeling about this raid. She laid the child to sleep in the pram rather than putting her in her cot upstairs and she ran up for extra blanket, which she laid by the cellar door, but didn't suggest going down yet; the bombers were too far away.

They didn't stay that way for long. The women were in the cellar, with Beth fast asleep on the palliasse and the stinking oil heater lit, within an hour of the raid beginning. Carmel listened to the distinctive intermittent drone of the German planes, wave after wave of them, expelling their harbingers of death with crashes and booms, muffled slightly because of the stout cellar. She heard the rattle of the ack-ack response, which seemed to have little effect.

Suddenly she said, 'I think this is our Coventration.'

The other two women looked at her in fear and panic. 'He couldn't possibly raze a city the size of Birmingham to the ground,' Lois said.

'Maybe not, but he can have a damned good try,' Carmel said grimly.

'God,' said Ruby. 'My George is out in this.'

Carmel didn't try to say everything would be all right and George would be fine. Ruby wouldn't welcome empty reassurances from anyone, but she put her arms around the older woman's shoulders and held her tight.

The air raid went on hour after hour.

Eventually Ruby said, 'A cup of tea – that's what we all need. I am not going to worry about George one more minute unless I find there is something to worry about. Meeting trouble halfway, as my old mother would say.' Brave words, but her distressed eyes told a very different story. She bent her head to ferret in her shelter-bag for the flask. 'Filled up with hot, sweet tea,' she said. 'Just the job, 'cos a cup of tea can be a life-saver, I always think.'

It was half-past four in the morning before the all clear was blaring. By then the three woman were almost too weary to climb the stairs. 'Though I am tired, I am too hungry to sleep,' Carmel said, as she laid the slumbering Beth in the pram.

'I agree,' Lois said. 'Thank God tomorrow, or rather today, is a day off. Will you stay for a bit to eat, Ruby?'

'No, I won't take your rations,' Ruby said. 'Besides, I am that anxious about George. I will go down the warden post and see if I can find anything out.'

'I'll go with you,' Carmel offered valiantly, though her stomach growled in protest.

'You'll not,' Ruby said. 'You'll get something to eat and seek your bed. You might have the day off but Beth will likely be awake in an hour or two because she has slept the night through.'

Carmel knew what she said made sense and yet neither of them could let Ruby go out into that cold darkness alone. They prevailed on her to have at least a cup of tea and slice of bread smeared with margarine before she and Lois went together to see if they could find George or someone who knew where he was.

Carmel washed the few things up and then watched the clock tick round slowly, knowing she wouldn't sleep till they returned. When eventually she heard them at the door, it was almost half-past five. Ruby's feet dragged as she came in and her face was white and lined with strain.

'What is it?' Carmel cried. 'Has anything happened to George?'

'We don't know,' Lois said. 'There was no warden post left, just a pile of rubble where it had once stood.'

'But George probably wouldn't have been in there, would he?' Carmel said to Ruby.

'That doesn't help really,' Ruby said, 'knowing he was out in that raid last night.' She glanced at the clock. 'The trams start again at six. If I haven't had word by then, I am going to try the hospitals.'

The words were barely out of Ruby's mouth when there was a fearful pounding on the door. The three women looked at each other for a moment, faces full of fear and trepidation, before Lois, with a nod from Carmel, went to open it. Carmel instinctively moved closer to Ruby.

'George!' Lois cried as she opened the door.

And it was George. He was covered in brick dust, only his face clean, so they could clearly see the black eye and massive bruise on his cheek and the bandage wrapped around his head. There was another ARP warden with him and, mindful of the blackout, Lois drew them both inside where the man removed his helmet.

With a nod of acknowledgement to Ruby he said, 'George said we'd likely find you here. We have come from the General Hospital and they wanted to keep him in, but he insisted on coming home.'

'But what's happened to you, George?' Ruby cried as Carmel ushered them all into the breakfast room. Then, as George gave a shrug and appeared unable to answer her, she turned to the warden. 'What happened to him?'

'He don't remember owt about it,' the warden told her. 'He was caught in a blast from a bomb and blown right across the road. Most of his injuries are from masonry falling on him. Something caught him a right purler on the back of the head, near split it open and knocked him clean out. That's why they wanted to keep him in, like, 'cos he didn't come round proper till he reached the hospital. When he insisted on going home they said someone had to go with him in case he collapsed or summat, I s'pose, and I offered 'cos I live this way anyroad.'

'Why didn't you stay in, George, you silly bugger?' Ruby cried.

'Look, old girl,' George said. 'It was mayhem there. I have never seen so many injured, and a lot of them woman and little nippers too! Christ, it was terrible. I even felt guilty about taking up the attentions of a doctor, and all to examine me and the nurse to patch me up. I certainly wasn't taking up a bed that someone else more damaged than I was could make more use of. I can rest up just as easy here as there.'

Nobody spoke, not even Ruby, for she could see George's point of view perfectly.

Then he looked across at Carmel and Lois, and said,

387

'Your lot are run off their bleeding feet, and so brave as well, 'cos the bombs was falling all the time, you know.'

Carmel felt the tiredness drop from her and she looked at Lois and then back at Ruby. She didn't say a word and didn't have to.

'Get ready and get yourselves off,' Ruby said. 'From what George says, they need every hand on deck down there tonight. Beth will be all right with me until you get home, whatever time that is.'

'Don't know how you will get there, though,' the warden said glumly. 'It's bloody chaotic out there, and no trams are running until six. Someone gave us a lift or we would have had to walk.'

'It's nearly six now,' Lois said. 'The first tram passes here about a quarter past, which we've used many a time.'

'Yeah, but I don't know how far you will get, that's what I am saying.'

'Well, we'll find out,' Lois said quite sharply. 'And walk the rest of the way if we have to. But we are wasting time talking about it when we should be getting ready.'

'You are right,' Ruby said, taking hold of the pram. 'I'm off home. Come on, George. You need a bleeding good wash before owt else.'

Carmel and Lois went scurrying up the road just after five past six. There was dust swirling in the air. It couldn't be seen except sometimes in the beam of the torch Lois played in front of them, but it could be felt in the back of the throat and smelled, and there was a strange orange glow on the horizon.

They hadn't a long wait for the tram. When it trundled to a stop beside them the conductor called out, 'Where you bound for, girls?'

'The General Hospital,' Lois said. 'Apparently it is hell on earth down there.'

'So I believe,' the conductor said. 'And we can't promise to deliver you to the door but we'll take you as far as we can get. Will that do?'

'You bet.'

As the blacked-out tram trundled off, the conductor told them of the destruction he had witnessed as he had rode his bike to work that morning.

'Whole areas have been laid waste – streets and streets of houses and gigantic mounds of rubbish. A bloke down the garage was telling me they got a load of big factories, like BSA and Lucas's, as well as tons of smaller factories and workshops, all making stuff for the war effort. And then, of course, there will have been huge numbers of people killed and injured.'

'I know,' Carmel said. 'That raid must have been dreadful. We have a cellar we hid out in, but not everyone would have been so lucky. I am actually nervous of what I'll find at the hospital.'

'And did you notice the orange in the sky?' the conductor said, and the girls nodded grimly. 'That, I think, must be Birmingham burning.'

CHAPTER TWENTY-TWO

The tram could get Lois and Carmel no nearer than Aston and the two girls had to walk the rest of the way. Although the blackout was as bad as ever, and the pencils of light from their torches barely pierced it, the sky was alight with flames and in its light they saw with shock the extent of the damage.

They saw too what the conductor had spoken about: the vast seas of rubble tumbling on the pavement and road. Those roads themselves often had great craters in them, buckled tramlines, and lumps of melted tar that had slid to the kerbs. The girls slipped and slid over mangled iron bars, twisted and fractured beams and plaster boards, splintered slates from roofs and broken bricks, mixed with the crushed and ruptured contents of dwellings, factories or workshops, glass constantly cracking beneath their stumbling feet.

Some mounds were glowing, smouldering or flickering with small flames, wisps of smoke escaping into the semi-darkness to mix with the smell of burning, acrid stink of cordite, definite whiff of gas and the smell of the brick dust.

Others had people on top of them, searching for possessions or moving the rubble with the aid of the glowing sky and shielded flashlights, searching for survivors. They called to the girls, and when those nearest saw that they were nurses, a cheer of support was given by those weary people. It was so grim, so depressing and sad that the girls had few words to say to each other as they trudged along.

No one and nothing could have prepared them for what Carmel and Lois met that day in the hospital. The place was packed, the injured still coming in while others lay on trolleys, or sat on chairs awaiting attention. Some shambled around, shocked and dazed, their eyes filled with anxiety and fear as they waited for news of relatives or friends.

Most of them were covered in grey dust. It was coating their faces, their eyes rendered bloodshot because of it. It even gilded their eyebrows and eyelashes and was ingrained in their hair and clothes, which often were in tatters. The air stank too with that dust, mixing with the smells of vomit, blood and charred flesh overriding the usual odour of antiseptic. The fetid air reeked with human misery and helplessness.

There was also a cacophony of noise: heart-rending sobs, moans and groans. Some cried or screamed or shrieked out in pain, while others just wept wretchedly. Nurses didn't try to keep order, for it was futile. They moved amongst the patients, trying to soothe and reassure, and occasionally covering the face of one who had died before they could get even the offer of help.

Carmel knew exactly why George had felt guilty about the treatment he had received. She would have felt exactly the same. Though there were plenty of doctors and nurses, they were all needed. Many who should have gone off duty had stayed, and others had done what Carmel and Lois had, and come in regardless of their shift. Matron, whose shift should have finished at eight the previous evening, was still there and had no intention of going home yet, there was so much still to do. She was delighted to see the Carmel and Lois.

She moved her arms expansively as she told them, 'You can see how we are placed. Every hospital is the same and we have had to direct some to Lewis's basement or Ansells. You two will be a great help.'

Carmel and Lois worked as hard as any there, but there were just so many people to see to. Some of the injuries sustained and the courage and stoicism displayed reduced the nurses to tears, most particularly when the patients were children. Carmel dealt with victims of crush injuries and those with bad burns and lacerations, knowing that sometimes, if the internal organs were crushed beyond repair, the burns severe enough, or the lacerations deep enough, the chance of the patient's survival was remote. She saw and dealt with more deaths, often traumatic and painful, that day than she had seen in all her years on the wards.

She also had to deal with the aftermath, like the children orphaned, or people who would be disabled for life. There might be women mourning the loss of family members, perhaps badly traumatised by this, and also knowing they had no house for any of the survivors to return to, no clothes for them to wear for, no means of support and no idea what to do about any of it.

By five o'clock that evening, Matron had gone home

at last. Lack of sleep and sadness had drained Carmel. She knew she could be no good to anyone if she didn't get some rest. She was just about to suggest to Lois that they go home when the sirens blared out again. No one could quite believe it at first, and then terror and panic set in.

Carmel swallowed her own fear and helped console and reassure and ferry as many patients as possible down to the basement. And then, despite the explosions, the barrage of ack-ack fire, the ringing of the bells of the emergency services and the little yelps of terror or the keening of the already injured, exhaustion eventually drained her and she lay on the floor and slept. Lois, beside her, did the same.

They woke stiff and cold some hours later to the comforting sound of the all clear. However, as it was the early hours of the morning and no trams would be running, the two girls worked on until seven, settling people back in wards or in corridors and serving break-fast, before setting out for Aston in the hope of catching a tram to take them home.

The next day the girls were once more on duty, and though Carmel worked harder than she had ever worked, she felt it wasn't enough. Some of the people who had been incarcerated in the ruins of bombed buildings were only just coming in now, and some they had treated on the previous day were no longer there. The images of them rose up in Carmel's mind and she pushed them down lest she give way altogether. She knew she owed it to those who had survived to take a grip on herself.

Carmel and Lois's shift ended officially at six o'clock,

but there were so many to see to, neither felt she should just up and leave.

'Ruby will understand,' Carmel said. 'After such a devastating raid a few days ago, with so many injured and needing help, she'll know I can't just walk out because my shift is over.'

'Me neither,' Lois said.

So when the siren shrilled at seven o'clock that night they were still at the hospital, and again they sat the raid out in the basement.

It was six o'clock in the morning before the all clear sounded. Carmel declared herself too tired to be of any use to anyone and then she and Lois found they had to walk the entire way home as the bombing had made the roads impassable. Behind them as they walked, the sky was blood red with flames.

It was the next day before Carmel and Lois found out the extent of the damage. It was one of the ambulance men who told her.

'Whole city centre was blazing,' he said. 'Out of control, like. They drained the canal like they did on the nineteenth, but it weren't enough, because them buggers had hit the water mains, like, 'adn't they?'

'How d'you know all this?' Carmel asked.

'This fireman told me, d'ain't he?' the ambulance driver said. 'Three trunk mains on the Bristol Road got it and in places the tar was so bloody hot it went alight and they just had to let it burn. Let everything burn in the end. If the Germans come back tonight we've had it. Birmingham will burn to the ground 'cos this bloke reckoned it would take four or five days to fix the mains proper and they has had a pretty good pop at us already.'

The public were not told about the fractured water mains, and it was kept out of the papers, and yet everyone seemed to know. That night and the next they waited anxiously for the raid that they knew would wipe their city off the map. It didn't come. Hitler's forces began pounding the South Coast instead and Brummies breathed a little easier.

Eventually, though, while no one could get blasé about the raids, people began to feel that life had to go on. Carmel, feeling she had neglected her child for far too long, applied to have time off over Christmas and took holidays tagged on to it so she would be off straight through to New Year.

Lois did the same. Chris had a spot of leave due as well and he suggested spending the festive season at his parents'. He still felt awkward around Carmel, almost guilty to be alive when Paul was dead, and thought she might feel excluded and lonely, seeing Lois and him together.

Lois could quite see his point of view, but hesitated to leave Carmel alone at such a time and for the first Christmas after Paul's death, and she mentioned the dilemma she was in to Ruby.

'Well, ducks, you can go with an easy mind,' Ruby said. ''Cos Carmel won't be alone, will she? Fine neighbour I would be if I just let her rattle around in that house all by herself at Christmas. And your man has got a point. Carmel might feel it if she was to see you two together, because it is sure to bring back memories and that in turn will put constraints on you. Chris won't be at all happy with that, when after this he might not see you for some time. It would be better all round if Carmel comes in to us. It will be a full house too, for our Bertie has a spot of leave and our Chrissie will be on her own with her man away, so she is coming in as well.'

Ruby and George had another guest too they didn't anticipate and that was Jeff, who called round the week before Christmas and was invited to join them. He thought of the cheerless meal in the silent room that he would eat opposite his frosty wife, for Matthew either couldn't get leave or said he couldn't, and Jeff could hardly blame him; he didn't want to be there either and so took Ruby up on her offer.

'On one condition only,' he said, 'and that is that I bring the food.'

'You mustn't do that,' Ruby said. 'Not with rationing the way it is.'

'None of this food will be rationed,' Jeff said, with a large wink. 'And,' he went on, 'take that disapproving look off your face. Look at the way Carmel has been working just lately. How will it hamper the war effort if she has decent food for one day in the year? She looked absolutely worn out when I saw her the other day.'

He had been quite shocked. He hadn't seen her properly for some weeks as she had worked such long and strange hours at the hospital while the raids were at their height. At the times he had called she was usually working or asleep. Now he was determined to build her up over Christmas. On Christmas Eve he called around with food Ruby had hardly seen since the war began: a small turkey, sausages, bacon, best ham, a dozen eggs, a plum pudding, a Christmas cake and mince pies. Then there was a tin of sweet biscuits, and one of cheese biscuits and a large lump of Cheddar to go with it.

Ruby stared open-mouthed at the stuff Jeff had unloaded on the kitchen table, almost afraid to touch it. 'Where did you get it all?' she gasped.

'That would be telling.'

'Yes, but . . .'

'Look, Ruby, the stuff is all paid for and no one is going to come flying round here to take it off you.'

'I don't know how to thank you.'

'All I ask is that you serve me a meal tomorrow fit for a king,' Jeff said. 'And we'll call it quits.'

'You're on,' Ruby agreed.

The food alone would have ensured the day was wondrous. Although Carmel had met Bertie and Chrissie before, it had been fleetingly, and she found them very good company. They were both entranced by Beth and seemingly determined to make this a Christmas for Carmel and her baby to enjoy.

Carmel had been dreading it. She had spent the previous Christmas without Paul too, but he had been alive then. She knew this year would be worse because she had to face the fact that that was how it was going to be always, but for Beth's sake she knew she had to make an effort, though when she found herself laughing and joining in with the rest she felt a little guilty at first.

The good mood was helped by the chocolates, silk stockings and bottle of Chanel perfume Jeff presented to each woman, and the cigars and whiskey he had for the men. For Beth, the undoubted star of the show and impeccably behaved, he had a truckful of bricks. The child clapped her hands in delight. She had been crawling for a month or so and had just started pulling herself up on the furniture, and she knew just what to do with the truck.

'Before you say one word about spoiling her,' Jeff said to Carmel, watching the baby in delight, 'let me tell you the truck isn't new, as you can see, though as you said before, the child won't mind. I found it in this huge cupboard in the nursery and it is right she should have it because it probably was her daddy's once.'

'I wasn't going to say anything anyway,' Carmel said. 'Christmas is the time for spoiling children a little, if you have the means to do so. But whatever money you had at the moment, there is so little in the shops to buy that plenty of children will have a lean Christmas this year. And now,' she said, scooping the child up, 'this very lucky girl is going to be put up for a nap or she will turn into a weasel.'

Later, after a cup of tea and Christmas cake, and the King's address on the wireless, Carmel, knowing Ruby was becoming drowsy, insisted on washing up. Jeff offered to dry, a novel experience for him, but he wanted to talk to Carmel alone.

Barely had the door closed behind them that he said, 'You have been working too hard, Carmel. And in the teeth of those raids too. You have had me worried to death.'

'I'm sorry,' Carmel said. 'Everyone is the same and I know I need to be there. There is so much to do, so much suffering, you have no idea.'

'I do understand,' Jeff said. 'I just don't want you to become ill or injured yourself. What would Beth do then?'

'What she has been doing all the time I have been away,' Carmel said. 'And that is stay with Ruby. I do feel guilty about that. I worry whether I am doing the best thing for us both, because it breaks my heart to leave her sometimes. Then at the hospital I look at the wee children, not much older than her, who are so badly damaged or who don't make it at all, or who have lost all before them. I am so thankful for what I have – that Beth is in little danger here – that I feel I owe it to them, not just the children, but all the injured, to do to the best of my ability the job I am trained for.'

'Oh, my dear!'

'I'm all right, Jeff, really,' Carmel said. 'But there is one thing I do want to discuss with you. Maybe Christmas Day isn't the right time, but time of any sort isn't something I have a surfeit of just lately and it is important.'

'Go on.'

'During one of those devastating raids at the hospital I began to fret about who would look after Beth if anything happened to me. I wanted it to be Ruby, but knew, if she was agreeable, I would have to draw it up legally. Anyway, she was delighted and I went to the solicitor recommended by the hospital that lots of nurses use. In the event of my death, or if I am incapacitated to such an extent that I can't care for my child, Ruby and George will be her carers and you her legal guardian, if you wouldn't mind that?'

'Mind that?' Jeff said gruffly, strangely hurt that his daughter-in-law should look outside the family for this type of thing. 'I suppose I should be grateful that you thought of me in any capacity at all.'

'You're not offended?' Carmel said in surprise. 'Surely not? I am disappointed that you are looking on it that way. Look, I did this to protect Beth from my father and your wife, who would both harm her in their own way, and I thought you would see it that way too. I am trying to do the best for my child, and the way anyone else feels about it is secondary.'

Jeff hung his head. He knew that Carmel spoke sense and was ashamed of himself and his initial reaction. He said so and apologised.

'It's all right,' Carmel said, kissing him on the cheek as she dried her hands. 'I know how you love Beth, but I am relying on you, because if anyone tries to overturn this, then it will be your job to stop them. Course,' she went on, 'this is only if something happens to me and I haven't any plans that way. And if you have finished those pots, we will join the others and I will get her ladyship up from her nap or she will never sleep tonight.'

CHAPTER TWENTY-THREE

Despite the raid in the very early hours of 1 January 1941, as the winter turned into spring, people were becoming more hopeful, for there was a lull in the bombing and any raids there were, were light and sporadic, reminiscent of those early in the war.

'That's it, I reckon,' Sylvia said one day as the four friends sat eating their dinner in the canteen.

'What d'you mean?' Jane asked.

'Well, I reckon Jerry has finished with us now,' Sylvia said. 'Threw all he could at us and couldn't break our spirits.'

'I flipping well hope you are right,' Jane said. 'The last thing I want is for some raid to spoil my wedding day.'

'Yeah,' said Lois with a laugh. 'Maybe we should send a directive to Herr Hitler. Hold your hand on Saturday, 19 April, there's a good chap, because our friend Jane Firkins is hoping to become Mrs Meadows.'

'Oh, very funny.'

'We'll need one before that,' Sylvia laughed. 'We don't want him muscling in on the hen night either.'

'Oh, we are having a hen night then?' Lois asked.

'Course we are,' Sylvia maintained. 'However spartan and brief the wedding, Jane is going to be sent off by us in good style. What d'you say, Carmel?'

'I say, hear, hear,' Carmel said.

'You won't have any trouble getting a baby-sitter?'

'Are you kidding?' Carmel said. 'Both Jeff and Ruby will likely be fighting each other for the privilege. Between the two of them they would have the child ruined if I didn't put my foot down now and again.'

'And you missed out on your own hen night, as I recall?' Lois remarked.

'Yeah, well, if you remember, Mammy and Sister Frances had just arrived and we were all staying at the convent and I didn't think I could just go off.'

'You mean they would have taken a very dim view of you coming back roaring drunk?' Jane said.

'Yeah,' Carmel smiled. 'Something like that.'

'Ah, well, you'll have to make up for lost time then,' Sylvia said. 'What d'you want to do, Jane, a meal, a pub crawl or what?'

'Oh, I think both, definitely,' Jane said. 'If I can't have the fairy-tale wedding I wanted like Carmel and Lois had, then I am determined to have a send-off to remember.'

'If it is a good enough send-off there is a good chance you won't remember the whole of it at all,' said Sylvia with a sardonic grin.

The girls laughed together as Jane said, 'You're right, there.' She raised her cup in the air. 'Here's to oblivion.'

The cups clinked together. 'To oblivion,' they chorused.

Jane's eyes were suddenly moist as she looked around the table and she said softly, 'I would just like to say here and now, and when I am stone-cold sober, that you are the best and dearest friends I have ever had. And now,' she went on, dabbing at her eyes with a handkerchief, 'I best go back to the ward before I end up blarting my eyes out.'

Carmel knew exactly what Jane meant, for she too thought the world of the girls and regarded it a great thing that the first friends she had ever had should prove to be so stalwart and loyal.

When the sirens went again on 9 April at half-past nine at night, everyone went into air-raid mode without any sense of panic.

'He's giving out one of these every so often,' said Jane, as she began erecting the cages over the bed-bound patients, with Aileen. 'It's just in case we should get complacent.'

'Well, I hope he gets this one over early,' Carrmel said, as she began rousing the patients that could walk, many of whom had begun to settle down for the night. 'My shift should finish at eleven, and if Lois and myself are much later leaving here, we may have to walk home. It is quite a hike and not something I relish after a day here.'

'Don't blame you either,' Sylvia said as Lois and Carmel began leading the way to the basement where the people soon settled to play cards, or read, or sit chatting together and waited for the raid to pass. However, it soon became apparent that this raid was no short skirmish. The people in the basement began listening intently, glad of the depth and thickness of the walls that muffled the whine and whistle of the descending bombs, the crash and boom of the explosions and the barking of the anti-aircraft fire.

And then there was a sudden enormous crash just above them, the walls shook, bits of masonry from the roof spattered down on them, the light flickered and went out, and people began to scream and panic. Carmel couldn't blame them for being scared. It wasn't pleasant sitting there in the pitch-black, tasting the plaster and brick dust from the ceiling and wondering if the whole building was going to collapse and entomb them. She ferreted feverishly in her bag for her torch.

Other nurses were doing the same and soon thin pencils of light were piercing the gloom, showing the faces of the people petrified with fear. Carmel played her torch on the walls and roof and saw that they seemed solid enough. It seemed safer to stay where they were for the time being, at least. She said this to the patients and tried to calm them as Lois and others lit the hurricane lamps left in the basement for just such an event. Soon the area was dimly lit by the lamps' soft glow.

Carmel longed to know what had happened above them, but could hardly leave her distressed patients to go to find out. She would have to wait like everyone else.

After fifteen minutes or so, which seemed like an eternity, the door opened and a young nurse ran down the stairs, lamp held aloft. 'Are you all right down here?'

'We're fine,' Carmel answered. 'What's happened?'

The girl descended the stairs and Carmel saw the state of her: covered in grey-brown brick dust, her eyes full of tears in a face alive with terror.

'It's dreadful,' she said, placing her lamp on the floor.

'There was a bomb. Staff Nurse said she thinks it probably fell in Steelhouse Lane and we were caught in the blast. I was flung right across the room, but the others . . . oh God . . .' And the young nurse covered her face with her hands.

'What's happened to them?' Lois demanded.

The young girl raised her face and said, 'They're not there any more. One half of the room isn't there any more either. Sylvia was thrown across the room with me, but Jane and Aileen and all the beds that side of the room have just gone.'

'Gone!' Lois and Carmel said in unison as the other nurses in the basement crept forward to listen too.

The nurse nodded. 'They are searching the rubble for them now and they sent me down to see if you are all right here.'

'They will be all right, though?' Carmel asked the girl, seeking assurance. 'They are just buried, aren't they?'

The girl shook her head sadly and her eyes swam with tears. 'No, I'm sorry. I thought you understood. They don't expect anyone to have survived. I know that Jane was a special friend of yours and they brought her body out just before I came down here. She was quite, quite dead.'

Carmel just stared at the girl as if she couldn't believe what she had just heard. Numb with shock, she remembered that Jane had met her at New Street Station that first day, and how vibrant and full of life she was and the sense of fun she always had. And if the young nurse was right, there was Aileen too. Aileen who kept them constantly amused by the number of times she 'fell in love'.

Carmel was aware of Lois weeping beside her as she felt the enormity of the tragedy began to seep into her too. Poor, poor Jane, looking forward to her wedding day. And poor Pete too. What a terrible and tragic shock he was going to get. Yet she felt unable to cry, though she comforted Lois, who was crying as if her heart was broken.

Later, when the all clear rang out, Carmel worked like an automaton, finding beds in other parts of the hospital and helping to settle the patients down for the night. A whole wing of the hospital had been caught in the blast and under the rubble they had found the bodies of two doctors and two nurses, one of whom was Aileen, and numerous patients. There were many injured too, and they were sent to Lewis's basement, which is where Carmel and Lois found Sylvia.

They looked down from the top of the wide staircases, the steps full of bloodstained clothing. The pungent odour of blood permeated the air, and at the bottom of the stairs lay the injured, row upon row of them, on makeshift stretchers and covered with grey blankets so that only their faces, often powdered with brick dust, were showing. The keening and wailing of these poor people was constant and heartbreaking.

Sylvia, when they found her, looked not too bad when you discounted her panic-riddled eyes in a face as white as the bandage around her head, and the big black and blue bruise almost covering one cheek. She was pleased to see Carmel and Lois.

'What happened?' she asked.

'What can you remember?'

'Well, I know it was a bomb,' Sylvia said. 'I heard it

explode and then it was as if all the air was sucked from the room and next thing I woke up here.'

'You must have passed out.'

'I did. They told me that much.' Sylvia said 'That's why I was brought in. Was it a direct hit or what?'

'No,' Carmel said. 'The bomb fell in Steelhouse Lane. We saw the huge crater on the way here. Someone told us it had killed one policeman who was fire-watching on the roof, blinded another and nearly severed the foot of the chief inspector. The hospital was been caught in the blast.'

'A young nurse told us that you were thrown across the room,' Lois said.

Sylvia nodded. 'That's when I must have cracked my head. I think it was bleeding quite badly, because one of the nurses said it needs stitching when the doctors get around to seeing me, but he is so busy, as you can see. Apart from cuts and bruises I am all right really – a damned sight better than most of this lot, anyway. How are the others?'

Carmel couldn't prevent the shadow flitting across her face and Sylvia grasped her arm. 'Jane! Tell me Jane is all right?'

Carmel shook her head helplessly and Lois said gently, 'She didn't make it, Sylvia.'

Carmel took hold of Sylvia's hands, which were plucking agitatedly at the blanket as the horror of it all registered on her face. Tears began to trickle from her eyes as she repeated almost in a whisper, 'Not make it?'

'The whole side was blown out of the ward,' Carmel said softly, 'No one who was there could have survived it.'

'Are you sure?' Sylvia asked. 'Did you actually see for yourself?'

Carmel nodded. 'We saw Jane's body before we left. Aileen was there too, and all the patients, of course.'

'Jane was my best friend.'

'We know, love.'

'There will never be another like her.'

'We know that too.'

'Poor Pete.'

'Aye, poor Pete.'

The storm of weeping broke then within Sylvia. The tears flowed so fast and furious, it was as if a dam had burst. Lois took her in her arms and let her cry until she was calmer. Eventually the torrent of tears changed to hiccuping sobs and she pulled herself from Lois and wiped her eyes.

'Sorry.'

'Don't be,' Lois said huskily. 'It broke my heart too when I heard.'

'Will you let Pete know, and Dan?' Sylvia said.

'Of course.'

'My address book is in my handbag in the staff room.'

'We'll see to it, don't fret,' Carmel promised.

Carmel and Lois arrived home as a pearly dawn was lighting up the sky, worn down by sadness and weary, and footsore after walking every step of the way. Carmel had expected Beth to be asleep in Ruby's house and was surprised to see Ruby curled up on the settee in her lounge. She woke as the two girls came in and rubbed her bleary eyes.

'Ruby?' Carmel cried. 'What are you doing here?'

'Waiting for you,' Ruby said, and she withdrew the telegram from behind the clock. 'This came for you,' she said, 'but the raid was too fierce for me to leave the house.'

Telegrams seldom brought good news. Carmel felt as if she had had a surfeit of sorrow that day already and she sank into an armchair before opening the telegram with fingers that trembled slightly. It was from Michael.

'Daddy dead of heart attack. Details later.'

'My father's dead,' she said in a flat, expressionless voice. She passed the telegram over for Ruby and Lois to read. 'And don't even bother saying you are sorry. I'm not sorry, not one bit. I just wish he had done it sooner. And I don't even know why I am crying.'

It was more then mere crying; the trauma and tragedy of the day had caused more an outpouring of grief as she mourned the deaths, particularly of Jane. And she wept for all the other senseless deaths she had witnessed since the war began, indiscriminate killing of innocent civilians, the very old, very young and the vulnerable amongst them.

Her father's death was just one more, and why should she care? He was the one man in the world she had hated above all others and yet the tears continued to pour from her eyes and the sobs shook her whole frame. Ruby, her arms clasped around Carmel, was confused about the remorse the girl was showing over the passing of a man she never said a good word about when he was hale and hearty – until Lois told what had happened to them both that day, and then she understood Carmel's anguish.

'I can't possibly go, of course,' Carmel said to Jeff the

following day when he called round. She was holding aloft the letter that had arrived that morning, giving details of the funeral.

'Carmel, my dear, you can't not.'

'That man did nothing but terrorise me all the days of my life,' Carmel retorted angrily. 'I owe him nothing, but Jane, Jane was my friend.'

'This is not for your father,' Jeff said firmly. 'And you will go to your father's funeral and not shame your mother, and I will go too.'

'You?'

'I will go to represent my son,' Jeff said.

'You are determined about this?'

'Oh, yes, my dear girl,' Jeff said. 'Will you take the child?'

'Do you think I would be let in the house without her?' Carmel said. 'Mammy is dying to see her. But you know how Beth is now that she is mobile and taking life at a run. I think it will one body's work to watch her, particularly on that boat, and I would be glad of another pair of hands and a person who is firm with her when she needs it.'

Jeff chuckled. 'You know how hard I find that,' he said. 'For that cheeky little smile would melt a heart of stone. And yes, I know you go on all the time about my spoiling her, and within reason sometimes, I have to say, but in this instance I know what you mean and I will keep a weather eye on Beth, don't worry.'

'What shall I do about Jane and Aileen?' Carmel said. 'They are being buried on the same day as Daddy and I feel so bad I can't go and show my respects.'

410

'People will understand why you can't,' Jeff said. 'It isn't something you designed on purpose.'

Jeff was right. Lois and Sylvia both accepted that she had to attend her father's funeral, even though they knew what her feelings about him were. Lois said she knew Eve would value the support of her eldest daughter at the funeral of the man she had despised and feared.

'Your mother fully supported you when you wanted her to,' she pointed out. 'Look at the way she came hotfoot over here for your wedding. Now it is your turn, because this funeral is bound to be a strain on her.'

Carmel knew that every word Lois said was true, and she told Jeff to go ahead and book everything while she arranged time off from the hospital, and sent a telegram home detailing when they would arrive.

Michael withdrew all his savings from the Post Office and Jeff sent fifty pounds 'to help with things', and so Eve had herself and the children kitted out respectably for once in their lives for the funeral.

In fact, Eve displayed more grief when Carmel told her about the raid and the subsequent deaths of Jane and Aileen and the others than she had over her husband. She was genuinely very sorry about the deaths of the two girls she had met, and she remembered Aileen flirting with Michael at the wedding, to his obvious discomfort, and found herself smiling at the memory. Both Aileen and Jane had seemed so determined to enjoy life to the full and it was terrible that they had been killed in such a way. She definitely felt their deaths to be more of a tragedy, not to mention more of a loss to society, than the demise of Dennis Duffy.

Eve knew too the dilemma her daughter would have been in and was very glad that she had chosen to come to her father's funeral, rather than her friends', for she'd felt she needed her there. She also wanted to express in person how devastated they all were to hear of Paul's death. Wee Beth, of course, whom they all adored, was like the icing on the cake for Eve, and she hoped she had proved a consolation to Carmel when she had lost her soulmate.

She hadn't been that surprised that Jeff had come as well, ostensibly in place of his son, but really, Eve suspected, to give Carmel a hand and to see how she herself was coping. She didn't mind why he was there, she was just glad he was, because she liked him a great deal.

First, though, they all had to cope with the funeral. The church was quite full, the coffin by the altar covered with a black cloth bedecked with Mass cards. The Duffys and Jeff took up two complete rows and the younger ones, having been threatened by Michael what he would do to them if they should misbehave and shame their mother, were very subdued. The Requiem Mass was long and sometimes tedious, but no one shuffled or turned around or whispered. The priest, with the Mass nearly over, mounted the pulpit and described a man they had never seen, this devoted husband and father, and his family in mourning for him.

Carmel stole a look at her mother. Beneath the very proper and respectable widow's bonnet, Eve's eyes sparkled with relief and even happiness because she knew no one would ever hurt or terrorise her or the children again.

Carmel felt the same way and later, at the graveside,

rather than throw a clod of earth on the coffin she had the urge to leap on it and dance a jig of thankfulness that at last the man was dead and gone. She felt the pressure of Jeff's fingers on her arm and was grateful for the show of support. The moment passed and she felt the hate and resentment she had for her father seep away to be replaced by a feeling of peace.

There was no room for all the mourners back at the house. The landlord of Dennis's local, where he had spent considerable time and more money than he could afford, offered them the back room, and Jeff paid for food and drink to be laid on. There Carmel's hand was pumped up and down by men who might cross the street to avoid the living Dennis, but they declared the dead one to be 'a grand fellow altogether', 'one of the best' and one who they were sure 'would be greatly missed'.

'Aye,' Siobhan whispered to her sister when she overheard this remark, 'like I might miss a headache when it is over.'

'Who's the girl Michael seems so pally with?' Carmel asked, glancing across at her brother.

'That's Bridget McCauley,' Siobhan said. 'She's the daughter of the farmer Michael works for. Like to be more than pals, if you ask me. Anyway, now the old bugger is dead and gone, maybe Michael will feel free enough to have a life of his own.'

'And why not?' Carmel said. 'It's not before time, if you ask me. That bloody man tried to ruin so many lives.'

'You're right there,' Siobhan agreed with feeling.

Carmel moved closer to her mother. She had seldom left her side all day and was glad Sister Frances had offered to mind Beth until the whole thing was over, to enable her to do just that. She knew that her mother was finding it hard to respond in the way people expected when they expressed their condolence at her loss. In Eve's opinion, the whole thing was like a farce and she was being worn down by the total insincerity of it. When Jeff saw the jaded look on her face, he suggested to the landlord that he start to clear the tables so that people might take the hint the wake was over, and though some of the men elected to stay on at the pub, most began drifting home.

Siobhan was ahead with the younger ones, Jeff had gone with Michael to fetch Beth home from the convent, and Carmel found herself walking home with her mother.

She knew that such a situation might not arise again and there was something she had been worrying over and so she said, 'Mammy, how are you off for money?'

Eve smiled. 'You're as bad as Jeff,' she said.

'Jeff! What's he to do with this?'

'He asked me the selfsame thing.'

Carmel felt annoyed suddenly at his muscling in like that, and wondered if it was reasonable to feel cross. She knew, of course, that he had been sending Eve money weekly and that she had been glad enough to accept it, so maybe it was legitimate for him to ask such a question. But still she said, 'Jeff thinks every problem can be solved with money.'

Eve smiled. 'He is only trying to be helpful and it has oiled the wheels for me these past years.'

'Maybe, but between us we can look after you now.'

Eve laughed and Carmel realised that she had never

414

heard her mother laugh like that before. She smiled at her as she said, 'All right. What's so funny?'

'You,' Eve said. 'All of you. Look at me. I am not some decrepit old woman and I am quite capable of looking after myself and even earning my own living, if I have a mind. Your father took away enough of your freedom when you were growing up. You got away, but the others didn't. I will not chain them further by letting them think they have to support me now.'

'Michael said once you would be better off if Daddy wasn't here,' Carmel said. 'I just wanted to make sure, that's all.'

'Well, don't worry about me,' Eve said. 'I will be fine.'

She told Jeff the same when he asked again the day before he and Carmel were returning to Birmingham. 'Jeff, you are a good, kind man, but sure I will be in the lap of luxury now they are all working bar Edward and Pauline. With the keep they tip up and the widow's pension we will manage fine.'

'What about a better house?'

'I will be looking for one of those when I see what I can afford,' Eve conceded. 'I do know this one is a disgrace.'

'I could buy a wee place for you.'

'You could not,' Eve said firmly. 'What an idea, Jeff. And if I was daft enough to agree to it, what complexion would the townsfolk put on it? And don't say it doesn't matter what they think because in a small town it does matter a great deal. I know that they will view me with a certain amount of suspicion now I am a widow, and we have been the talk of the place for long enough. Even if I could cope with rumour and speculation, I would not have the children go through it again. Thank you from the bottom of my heart for the help you have given me so far, but from now on we will stand on our own two feet.

'I'll tell you what worries me more than anything else, and far more than concerns about money,' Eve went on, 'and that is where Carmel works. It could have been her killed just as easily as poor Jane and Aileen.'

'I know,' Jeff said. 'You saw where the General Hospital is when you were over, and most of the attacks have been centred around the city centre. You would see a very different skyline now if you came to Birmingham, for the place is bombed and burned to bits, and she is often in the thick of it.'

'Michael was for going over, you know, to see if she was all right,' Eve said. 'But she said she was grand and told me I was not to let Michael go over, for the raids were too bad and she couldn't guarantee his safety. What about her safety?'

Jeff shrugged. 'She doesn't seem to worry about it,' he said. 'Or if she does, she hides it well.'

'Could you not talk her out of it?' Eve said. 'Hasn't she done her bit for long enough now?'

'D'you think that I have not tried over and over to do that?' Jeff said.

'But she has a baby to see to now.'

'I pointed that fact out to her, but to no avail.'

Eve shook her head sadly. 'God, but she is an obstinate girl.'

Jeff laughed. 'All I can say to that, Eve Duffy, is that it takes one to know one. Carmel is in your mould, my dear, and you have taught her well, for the pair of you are as stubborn as mules at times.'

CHAPTER TWENTY-FOUR

Carmel returned to a hospital in mourning for the staff and patients killed. Lois said she had seldom seen anyone as distraught as Pete had been, and that without the support of his mate Dan, he would have collapsed altogether. Dan was tremendously affected himself and when he looked at the damage to the General Hospital and the death toll, he told Sylvia he wanted her out of there, and as quickly as possible. Sylvia was not fully recovered herself and, still grief-stricken over the death of her friend, clung gratefully to Dan, whom she wanted to marry more than anything in the world.

So, just a fortnight after Carmel returned to Birmingham, she and Lois were witnesses to the civil marriage ceremony in the registry office between Sylvia and Dan Smiley. There was no time for a honeymoon, or even a night away, but after the wedding, Dan intended installing his bride in his parents' house in a little village called Wilnecote, near the market town of Tamworth in Staffordshire. Dan said the village had never had the hint of a bomb of any sort and that, apart from rationing and the blackout, you could almost forget there was a war on at all.

'I will probably be bored to tears,' Sylvia told Lois and Carmel. She had been born and bred in bustling Birmingham and didn't know how she would take to village life at all. 'But Dan said that in his opinion I have done my share and he has enough to worry about looking after himself on the battlefield without fretting that I will be safe as well.'

'You can't argue with that really, can you?' Lois said.

'No,' Sylvia agreed. 'I do love him to bits and I have always got on with his parents.'

'Well then,' Carmel said, 'why the long face? After the war you will probably have the man you love by your side and a baby or two of your own to rear.'

Sylvia knew she had much to be thankful for, but she left the hospital and her friends with genuine regret, and Carmel and Lois knew that they would miss her greatly.

Afterwards, Lois said it was just typical that Sylvia had left to escape the bombing but that, after another fairly minor raid in May, there were just a few sporadic forays until July and then nothing at all.

'Seems as if Hitler has really finished with us at last,' Jeff told Lois and Carmel one evening in September.

'We all thought that before,' Lois reminded him.

'Yeah, I know that, but Hitler hadn't set his beady eyes on Russia then. Think he has bitten off more than he can chew there. Should have read his history books and learned what happened to Napoleon when he tried a similar tack. Anyway, it augers well for the rest of us if the Luftwaffe are concentrating their energies there. What's the news at the hospital?'

'The damage has nearly all been repaired,' Lois said.

'Well, what I mean is the ward is useable again, except one side of it, which has been sealed off. If we really are free from raids now they might have a chance to get it back the way it was.'

'I am out of all that now, anyway,' Carmel said. 'I have been transferred to Men's Surgical.'

'Oh, why is that then?'

Carmel shrugged. 'Short-staffed,' she said. 'And they are really rushed most of the time because as well as servicemen to deal with, they are having injured Germans in as well. It's no rest cure, I can tell you.'

By the early summer of 1942, everyone had began to relax, convinced at last the raids were definitely over. Added to that, after the bombing of Pearl Harbor on 7 December the previous year, America had officially joined in the war. GIs were becoming common on the streets of Birmingham. 'Overpaid, oversexed and over here' they might be, but most people thought having their support had to shorten the war.

There was a rumour flying around the hospital that a bomb had been dropped over Solihull way on the morning of 27 July, but few believed it because there hadn't been any sort of raid for almost a year.

However, there was no doubting the drone of enemy planes heard heading their way that same evening and then there were the first explosions in the distance.

'Where's the bloody sirens?' shouted one man. 'Are they all asleep or what?' The words were barely out of his mouth when the piercing sound rent the air.

And although the raid wasn't particularly long or fierce, the number of casualties was extremely high, partially because the sirens, warning people to take cover, had sounded too late.

Far more worrying, though, was whether the raid had been the forerunner of another blitz, especially when the sirens rang out again in the evening of 30 July, despite the fact that that raid was light and barely lasted any time at all.

The following day, Matron told Carmel she had a specific job she wanted her to take on with one of the patients.

'Yes, Matron?'

'His name is Terence Martin,' Matron said, 'and he was admitted after the first raid on 27 July. Some of the vertebrae in his back were crushed or cracked. Apparently he was helping people escape from a cellar and the lot collapsed top of him. He now has metal rods inserted in his spine. He is confined in a cage of sorts to prevent movement and it is hoped that in time the spine will heal and the bones knit back together. He's also had a neck brace fitted, mainly as a precaution. An added difficulty is that either because of shock or trauma he hasn't spoken one word since the accident. I thought you might understand how he feels better than anyone else. I am assigning Cassie Browning to help you. She is only a first-year probationer, but shaping up very nicely and it will be very valuable experience for her.'

Carmel had worked with Cassie on the wards and thought she had a lot of promise, and she was looking forward to being so involved with the total care of one particular patient.

'You will be directly answerable to Dr Stevens, who

operated on Mr Martin,' Matron said. 'However, you must report to me on his progress every day and especially if there has been any deterioration in his condition. Now, I am sure you will want to meet him.'

Mr Terence Martin was held rigid in his bed, his light brown hair flopping over his forehead, stubble covering the lower part of his pale face. In his pain-filled eyes, Carmel saw the misery and despair that had locked him away from everyone and everything. Oh, how well she remembered feeling that way, for she too had once been in that black pit of depression.

From the first she had felt drawn to help the desperately unhappy man, and by the end of the first week she had seen a slight improvement. It was small but significant. Every day, with Cassie's help, she would wash and shave the patient. She would be as gentle as she possibly could because his body was very battered and bruised, and she was aware too that sometimes she was washing very intimate parts of him, but he seemed unaware of it.

The second week, he began lifting his arms as they washed him and when Carmel thanked him, she knew he had heard and understood what she had said. His food had to be puréed, and each day Carmel would check it for lumps before either she or Cassie would spoon it into his mouth. He would purse his lips when he had had enough.

The first time he did this, Carmel, who was feeding him, smiled and said. 'Well, I don't see that you need much stoking, lying there all day and every day. When we have you on your feet and charging up and down the ward, I imagine that there will be no filling you. No, indeed, none at all. What do you think, Cassie?'

'I think you are right, Nurse Connolly,' Cassie said. 'I'll bet there will be little food refused then.'

Terry Martin wanted to smile. He often wanted to smile at the things Carmel said, and the way she had of saying them, and at the banter between her and the young one. From the beginning Carmel had been glad of the younger girl's cheerful disposition, for she found it was harder than she had imagined working with a silent and virtually unresponsive patient. As they weren't on the ward and were working so closely together, Carmel had allowed Cassie greater licence and so there was a lot of banter between them and some of it was amusing, but Terry had forgotten how to smile. He hadn't done so since that terrible day in November 1940, not that it did any good to remember that. It was like probing a sore tooth: better by far to push it down to the furthest recesses of his mind.

'Would you like a drink now?' Carmel asked, and she helped him take a drink out of the metal, lidded cup by his bed, which he had trouble using unaided without soaking the front of himself.

A few days later, Carmel was aware that Terry's eyes had left the point on the ceiling on which they had seemed fixed, and were following her and Cassie around the room and listening to their chat as they dealt with some aspect of his care.

That night, she wrote letters to her family in Letterkenny and to Sister Frances, telling them what she knew of Terence Martin and asking for him to be included in their prayers. She also sought out Father Robertson after nine o'clock Mass the following Sunday, which day she had off, and, after explaining, she asked to have a Mass said for Terry.

'I don't know if he is a Catholic, Father,' she said. 'I don't know if he is anything at all, if you know what I mean, but I thought God wouldn't mind that if he is in need.'

'No indeed,' Father Robertson said. 'I mean, Jesus didn't ask the blind man if he was a regular at the synagogue before he restored his sight, now, did he? Is this man very badly injured?'

'Yes, Father,' Carmel said. 'Though they say he will recover eventually. But it's his mind, you see. He is a poor tormented soul who doesn't feel worthy even of being alive.'

'But how do you know this, my dear?' the priest asked. 'I thought you said he couldn't or wouldn't talk.'

'Terence Martin doesn't need to talk, Father,' Carmel said earnestly. 'You can read all this in his eyes. They are dark grey and fathoms deep, but so expressive.'

'Rest easy, Carmel,' the priest said. 'I will say a Mass for this man of yours and pray for him each night. Between me, you and the Good Lord himself, the man will have no choice other than to get better and quick.'

Two days later, as Carmel gently spooned puréed stew into Terry's mouth, he suddenly pushed her hand away. He had eaten little and so Carmel asked, 'Have you had enough?'

He made no attempt to answer what Carmel asked. Instead, he held her gaze intently for a second or two and then said hesitantly, 'Why are you bothering with me?' in a voice husky from lack of use.

However, Carmel didn't care what the voice sounded like. Terry had spoken for the first time since the accident, and her heart soared in thankfulness. But she reminded herself he'd asked a question that needed addressing. 'Why wouldn't I bother with you?'

'You don't know me, what sort of person I am.'

'I know all I need to know – that you are ill and I am tending you because I am a nurse and that is what we do. So shall we go from that premise?'

'If you like.'

'So we will have no more of that kind of talk.'

'If you say so.'

'I do say so,' Carmel said with an emphatic nod of her head.

Matron was as pleased as Carmel was at Terence Martin's progress. 'The timing couldn't be better,' she said. 'Dr Stevens intended to see how he was getting on tomorrow anyway. This will be a bit of good news for him.'

Dr Stevens was pleased with everything, not least the way that Mr Martin's back was healing. He praised Carmel for keeping the scar so clean and infection free. He was nearly at the door when he suddenly turned.

'Connolly?' he said to Carmel. 'Were you married to Dr Paul Connolly?'

'Yes, Dr Stevens.'

'Heard he had married a nurse,' the doctor said. 'You have my sympathies, my dear. It was a tragic waste too, for he was a first-class doctor and a thoroughly nice chap into the bargain. I well remember when he was a student here.'

Carmel was too choked to make a reply and barely

424

had the door shut on the doctor than Terry called across, 'What happened to your husband?'

Carmel waited until she had crossed the room and sat on the bed, so that Terry could see her, which also gave her a few seconds to compose herself. Then she said, 'Paul was with the Medical Corps of the Royal Warwickshires and he didn't return from Dunkirk.' She left time for that to sink in, time for Terry to make a comment and when he didn't she said, 'Now my turn for a question for you. Were you in the Forces, Mr Martin?'

'No,' Terry said. 'I am a gas fitter, a reserved occupation. And what is all this Mr Martin business? I have a name and it's Terry.'

'I'll call you Terry when we are in here,' Carmel promised.

'Have you a name, or have I to call you Nurse Connolly?'

'My name is Carmel.'

'Pretty name. Unusual.'

'Not particularly in the North of Ireland where I came from,' Carmel told him. 'And while we can use our Christian names when we are in the room on our own, Dr Stevens and Matron might not like such familiarity so when they are here, I will be Nurse Connolly and you will be Mr Martin.'

'That's daft!' Terry said. 'Is that the rule for young Cassie too? She told me her name while you were on your break.'

''Fraid so,' Carmel said. 'We are supposed to treat you in a totally professional way. It is just more difficult in a situation like this. Anyway, your turn for a question.'

'Right,' Terry said. 'Did you and Paul have any children?'

'Just the one, a little girl that we called Beth. She is just two and a half.'

She saw the blank look suddenly flood Terry's face as if someone had turned the light off in his eyes, and was alarmed. 'What is it?'

'Nothing,' Terry said. 'It's nothing, but I don't want to play this game any more and I am too tired to answer any more questions.'

Carmel didn't argue. Terry certainly seemed suddenly very weary and she tucked the blankets around him and left the room, and so didn't see the tears seep from his eyes as he closed them.

When Terry woke up Carmel realised the shuttered look was still there on his face and he was exactly the same three days later. He answered anything asked him brusquely and sometimes not at all. No one else saw a problem, particularly the doctor, who had popped in a couple of times since Terry's silence had been broken and was delighted with him. Terry did whatever he asked him and answered his questions, and Dr Stevens remembered how unresponsive and uncommunicative he had been and thought Carmel had worked a miracle.

Carmel, however, wasn't happy at all. One evening she talked it over with Lois, and Jeff, who was round to see her. 'He makes all the right responses and that is it,' she said. 'There is no real communication. It's just as if he has pulled down the blind and effectively shut himself off. He reminds me of a hurt or damaged animal that has dragged himself away to lick his wounds in private. I'm sure inside Terry Martin is curled a tight knot of heartache.'

'Maybe this is his way of coping,' Lois said. 'Anyway, aren't we warned not to get personally involved?'

'That's what we're told, all right,' Carmel conceded. 'It is sometimes quite hard to put into practice. It is tough dealing with Terry physically, knowing that I can only do so much. Even when he recovers, he will still be carrying around emotional scars that will probably drag him down again.'

'Does he have visitors?'

'No,' Carmel answered. 'I spoke to the nurse who was on duty when he was admitted and those in the post-operative unit. They told me that no one had even been to enquire whether he was going to live or die, never mind visit.'

'Ah, that's sad,' Lois said. 'But I would still keep right out of it as far as you possibly can.'

Knowing Lois had a very valid point, Carmel said nothing, and things continued in the same vein day after day. When, after three weeks, the matron asked Carmel what she had found out about Mr Martin's background she had to say, 'Virtually nothing, Matron.'

'Nothing? You are with him day after day,' the matron said incredulously. 'Don't you talk together?'

'Not really,' Carmel said. 'I ask him questions if I have to and he answers, in monosyllables if he can.'

'I can scarcely believe this.'

'I think there is something in his past bothering him that I would hesitate to disturb because I think his mental state is very precarious,' Carmel said. 'When Terry, Mr Martin, first began to talk, Dr Stevens made some comment about Paul and when he had gone Mr Martin asked me what had happened to Paul and I told him. Then he asked me if I had any family and it was when I told him about Beth that he changed. He said he didn't want to answer any more questions. If anything, he has gone backwards since then.'

'Dear, dear, this will never do,' Matron said. 'Till Mr Martin spoke to you he hadn't opened his mouth and all we knew about him was the things the neighbours knew, and that too was precious little. No one has been in to see him or even enquire about him and my guess is no one knows where he is. Of course, it is quite possible that the man is alone in the world but we need to be sure. What would he do if you asked him direct questions again?'

'I don't know, Matron, but I have the feeling that he would become very distressed.'

'Would you try it?'

'Shouldn't the doctor ask him these things?'

'Maybe, because you have tasted tragedy yourself and he knows that and because Mr Martin spoke to you first, you would possibly have a better reaction,' Matron said. 'Anyway, isn't it worth a try?'

Matron's suggestions were really directives, as Carmel knew only too well. She very apprehensive as she returned to the room a few minutes later. Cassie went on her break and after she left, Carmel first busied herself in the room, tidying up and putting things in order and throwing the odd comment to Terry, which he chose to ignore. In the end, she decided she had dallied long enough and had to get started and so, feeling none too confident, she sat on the bed facing him and said, 'D'you remember the day I told you about my husband, Paul?'

Terry didn't answer but his eyes narrowed in suspicion.

Undaunted, Carmel soldiered on. 'Well, I'd just like you to know that that isn't information I share with patients generally. But you asked and I told you, but you didn't tell me whether you were married or not.'

Terry glared at her, but made no effort to speak and Carmel suppressed a sigh. 'All right then,' she said. 'Answer something else instead. Why did you ask me why I should be bothered with you, almost as if you didn't deserve to be helped?'

'Maybe that's what I think,' Terry growled.

'But why would anyone think like that?' Carmel said. 'If nothing else, people with your skills are badly needed. This is everyone's fight, every man's, every woman's and even every child's because we are fighting to make a safer world for them to grow up in.'

Terry's eyes suddenly filled with tears at Carmel's words. They poured from his eyes in a torrent and he sobbed and sobbed as if he never intended to stop, the weeping punctuated with gasps of sheer anguish that seemed to be tearing him apart. Eventually Carmel, alarmed by Terry's condition, could stand it no more and leaned right over him in the bed and held him tight.

She was heartily relieved when Cassie put her head around the door at that moment. 'Fetch Dr Stevens,' she said to the girl, who was staring almost transfixed at the man sobbing on the bed and Nurse Connolly nearly lying on top of him. Carmel, however, was too worried about

Terry to consider her incongruous position. 'Hurry,' she urged, and the girl almost ran from the room.

'Was that virtual collapse brought about by trying to talk to Martin about his past?' Dr Stevens asked Carmel after he had sedated Terry. He added, 'Matron said that you were going to try.'

Carmel nodded, feeling incredibly guilty that she had brought about such a paroxysm of grief, however inadvertently. She tried to remember the conversation before Terry had broken down completely and recounted it to the doctor as well as she could.

'D'you think that Mr Martin might have lost a child in one of the raids?'

'I think that is quite possible,' the doctor said. 'And if the man has been holding that inside himself all this time, when he comes around, he might well need help to deal with it. I will alert the Psychiatry Department.'

The next day, Carmel was summoned to Matron's office and was surprised to see Dr Stevens already there. 'Mr Martin was admitted to the psychiatric wing of the hospital last night,' Dr Stevens said.

Carmel was shocked. 'Was that necessary?' she asked and then blushed at her temerity. 'I'm sorry. I don't mean to tell you your job. It's just . . .'

'I know how you feel,' Dr Stevens said. 'This wasn't a decision I made lightly, I assure you, and I trust it will not be permanent, but I was too worried for his mental state. When he is more stable they will run some tests on him and maybe have some idea of the root of his problems.'

For three days Carmel and Cassie worked on the main

ward. Carmel worried and fretted over Terry, but no one seemed able to tell her anything. Visits to the psychiatric unit were discouraged and she felt helpless.

Matron was waiting for Carmel when she arrived at the hospital the following morning. 'Mr Martin wishes to talk to you. In fact what he said was you are the only person he will talk to. Though he is still in the psychiatric unit, he is in a private room so you won't be disturbed.'

After her last experience with Terry, Carmel was nervous of seeing him again on her own and she opened the door of his room tentatively, noticing straight away that his neck brace had been removed.

She sat on the bed so that she could see him. His face was white with exhaustion and there were black smudges under his eyes. She felt sympathy well up inside her and she felt bound to say, 'I am so sorry, Terry, that I upset you so much when I spoke to you a few days ago.'

'That wasn't your fault and I know you were trying to help,' Terry said. 'I had a few sessions with this psychiatrist chap and he said I had to talk to someone. "Release the demons," was the way he put it, before they destroy me. I knew he was right because the memories are ripping me apart and all this time I really thought I was coping.'

'Some things are just too hard to cope with alone,' Carmel said gently.

Terry nodded. 'I know that now and I wanted to talk to you first because you really seemed to care. You asked me if I was married. Well, yes, I was, to a girl called Brenda and we had two children, a son, Andrew, who was only six months old and a daughter called Belinda. She was as pretty as a picture and two and a half years old. God, when you told me your little girl was the same age, it was like a knife had twisted in my heart and I resented you for having a living child when mine was dead. I'm really ashamed now that I felt that way.

'We lived in a back-to-back house in Bell Barn Road down the Horse Fair way only a few doors from Brenda's parents. And since the raids started, we'd all had a bad time of it, living so close to the town.

'Anyway on this evening, 19 November, the sirens wailed out just as we'd finished our tea, like, and we got the kids ready to take them to the public shelter in Bristol Street like we'd done many times before. Brenda's parents and younger sister were waiting for us, and we all walked down together.'

'I remember that raid,' Carmel said with a shiver as she recalled the hospital packed with the injured, the maimed or those desperately searching for news of their loved ones. 'It was a dreadful night, that.'

'And it went on for hours and hours,' Terry said. 'And then about midnight a warden came in and asked for some men to help. A pub had collapsed, trapping people in the cellar, and they were being gassed to death. Naturally, I went and so did Brenda's dad. Some time later, after we got the people out and I had disconnected the gas pipe to prevent any explosion and we were on our way back to the shelter, we heard the planes coming closer. We both ducked into this entry. I was at the end of it, looking out into the street, and there were that many fires burning it was like bloody daylight. Brenda's dad had gone further in. Next thing I knew, I was blown to the other side of the street in the blast from the bomb that had landed on the entry and Brenda's dad had been killed. I was wondering how I was going to tell Brenda and her mother, sort of rehearsing it as I walked back, you know . . .'

Carmel wondered if he was aware of the tears that he was brushing impatiently away and she suddenly knew what he was going to say, but that didn't minimise any of the horror. With a grim and humourless laugh he went on, 'Huh, I needn't have worried. When I got to the shelter it was just a mound of rubble, sandbags seeping everywhere and people uncovering bodies and bits of bodies that were buried in the debris.'

Terry's eyes, which sought Carmel's, were bleak as he said, 'I never found any of them. The two babies, Brenda, her mom and sister were probably all cuddled together and were blown to pieces. I asked myself over and over, why them and not me? Why was I the only one in the whole family to be alive and everything I cared about taken from me?

'I knew I couldn't have stood seeing them in bits. I ran away from it and so now I don't even know where they are buried, nor Brenda's dad either. What sort of a useless person does that make me? I feel so bloody bad about that now, like I have let them all down.'

'Don't torture yourself,' Carmel said. 'You weren't thinking straight. God, you must have been in shock.'

Terry nodded. 'It was the house that was the last straw. Funny that, my family wiped out and when I found the house gone too, something snapped. Suddenly everything went black and I just fell in a heap across the rubble. I came to in a hospital bed the following day and after a couple of days, there was a pastor came round to talk to me and he sorted me out with a new ration and identity card because Brenda had them in her shelter-bag, and as far as I know that was never recovered. He got me some clothes too, and found the place that I am living in, and even contacted my boss at the Gas Board, who thought I had been killed.'

'They probably think that again this time,' Carmel said.

'This time I wanted it to be true,' Terry said.

'Don't talk like that,'

'It's true,' Terry said. 'Or it was. I just thought, what have I got to bloody live for? I was sort of holding part of this bombed house up so the people trapped in the cellar could get out and then I just let go and let the lot fall on me. I wanted to die. I had had enough, but there were people everywhere pulling at the rubble, trying to save the life I didn't want saved and I wanted to tell them that, but I found suddenly that I couldn't speak. I couldn't move either and that terrified the life out of me. I wanted to be dead, not paralysed.'

Carmel felt her stomach turn over for this poor tortured and very lonely man, and she had the urge to put her arms as tight around him as she was able to and hold him tight. She knew, though, she couldn't do that.

Instead she said, 'That is one of the most tragic tales I have ever heard and I feel touched that you have shared this with me. And now I am off to see if I can have you moved back to the surgical ward, because you certainly don't belong here.'

CHAPTER TWENTY-FIVE

'Are you sure that you are thinking of Terry as just a patient?' Lois asked Carmel one day.

'Of course.'

'Matron will have your guts for garters if there is the slightest hint of impropriety.'

'There isn't and, anyway, I know that, Lois. I'm not stupid and I do know how to behave as a nurse, thank you very much.'

'Don't go all mardy on me,' Lois protested. 'It's only you I am thinking of, and if you only knew how much you talk about him, how his name creeps into every other sentence . . .'

'I am with the man day in and day out – what do you expect?' Carmel asked testily. 'I realised only the other day that I know more about him than any man alive, including Paul, and that came as a bit of a shock. I also know every inch of his body, even the most intimate areas, because for some weeks the confines of the cage meant he was able to do little for himself. That is bound to make you closer to a person than the average nurse/patient relationship, but that doesn't mean I would forget myself entirely and leap on him in a fit of rampant lust.'

'All right, all right. Point taken,' Lois said with a grin. 'But, seriously, how does he feel? You know, even on the General Ward, many male patients fancy themselves in love with the nurses. I mean, does he—'

'Terry's fine,' Carmel said shortly. 'He knows the score.'

Lois wasn't convinced, but she knew that there was nothing to be gained by keeping on about it and she said nothing more.

Carmel was glad she had dropped the subject because she had been less than honest. Each day she longed to see Terry again, and when he smiled at her when she went into the room, she felt her heart turn somersaults. He brightened her day and her life. She felt like a young girl again. She had been brought up sharp the first time she had recognised that feeling. She had thought all emotion like that died with Paul, and she had never felt even mildly sexually attracted to anyone before, but she had been careful not to allow any glimpse of this to creep into the way she had cared for Terry.

Each day she would buy a paper on the way to work and either she or Cassie would read bits out to him. It was Cassie's idea because she said that time must hang heavy for him. He didn't even have visitors to break up the day and tell him what was happening outside the walls of the hospital.

Carmel thought it a very good idea and though she did most of the reading and discussing afterwards, Cassie was the best one to help him with the crossword. This was because at least a couple of the clues usually centred around the stars of the silver screen, or the title of the film they had starred in, and Cassie was never away long from the cinema.

Her favourite films were romances, so Carmel and Terry would hear about the elegance of Joan Crawford in *Mademoiselle France*, the glamour of Margaret Lockwood in *The Lady Vanishes*, the beautiful and sexy Veronica Lake and Marlene Dietrich in anything at all, and, of course, Clark Gable and Vivien Leigh in *Gone With the Wind*, which Cassie had seen three times.

Carmel, knowing of the penny-pinching of her student days, asked her one day where she got the money from.

'Oh, we don't pay,' Cassie said. 'One of my roommates's sister is an usherette at the Gaumont and she gives us free tickets, so I can go when I like usually.'

'No wonder you have all the answers,' Terry commented wryly from the bed. 'So come and help me with fourteen across.'

Soon, however, these sessions had to be severely curtailed, for Terry was on the road to recovery. Carmel went with him when they removed his supportive cage. When they started the intensive physiotherapy the treatment was explained to her, and she and Cassie worked together with him on the ward each day to strengthen his muscles.

It was Carmel who often had to bully him in the early days, despite feeling sympathy for the pain he usually endured afterwards. She would watch him as he lay back in the bed, knowing he would be aching all over, but she never let a hint of pity enter her voice or manner as she tended him, well aware that if he wanted to return to full health he had to suffer this.

Then came the day he was lifted to his feet where, supported by Carmel and a physiotherapist, Terry shuffled between two wooden bars. His excitement to be on his feet again brought tears to Carmel's eyes but she never let them fall. It would not help Terry to have people crying all over him, and she helped him progress first to crutches to get around and then eventually to sticks.

And now even the sticks had been thrown aside. He was completely recovered and fitter, he claimed, than he had ever been. Carmel knew that, happy as she was to see him so much better, there would be a big hole in her life when he left the hospital, which he was due to do the first week in November.

The morning that he was due to leave, he suddenly caught hold of Carmel's hand and said, 'I am really going to miss you. You have given me back my reason for living and I can't thank you enough for that.'

'It's my job,' Carmel said, trying to keep a lighter note in the conversation, because Terry's words were causing her stomach to turn over most alarmingly, and his holding her hand was sending a tingle running all through her arm.

'No,' Terry said. 'Nursing is your job. You have done far more for me than mere nursing. I don't know how you feel about me and have no right to say these things to you, but I think – no, I am sure – that I love you dearly.'

Carmel willed her voice not to shake as she said, 'It's a well-known fact that many male patients fall in love with their nurses.'

'This goes deeper than that,' Terry said earnestly.

438

'Can I – can I see you sometimes, when I am out of here?'

Carmel knew what he was asking, but she wasn't ready yet for any sort of relationship, so she said, 'Why? You're better now, you don't need the services of a nurse.'

'No, and it isn't the nurse I want,' Terry said. 'But I do want Carmel Connolly the woman.'

'No, Terry,' she said. 'It wouldn't be wise. I'll see you at Christmas anyway, won't I? By then you will feel differently. Trust me.'

'And if I don't?'

'I am still making no promises, Terry.'

She had worried how Terry would spend Christmas and with whom. She knew it was an intense and emotive time for many people anyway, and she didn't want Terry to slip back into depression again. Ruby fully understood her concern and said she should invite Terry to spend Christmas at her house.

When Carmel issued the invitation to Terry, just before he was due to leave, she knew by the look on his face that he was pleased beyond measure and that he had been worried himself.

'You're quite sure about this?'

'Absolutely,' Carmel said. 'There won't only be me and Lois – you know, my friend that I told you I share the house with. We always spend the day with next door neighbours, the ones who look after Beth in the day. It helps to pool the rations and then, of course, Jeff has all manner of contacts and we don't enquire too closely where he gets some of the stuff he brings.'

'Isn't Jeff your father-in-law?'

'That's right.'

'Won't he mind me muscling in?'

'No. Why should he?'

'Well, you know . . .'

'No, I don't know,' Carmel said. 'They know all about you anyway.'

That, of course, had been before he had made the declaration to her, but she had given him her answer. She had to be content with that and so had he.

Carmel couldn't seem to shake off the despondency that surrounded her after Terry left the hospital. It was almost tangible. Lois watched her pick at her food, her face become pasty white and her eyes develop blue smudges beneath them.

'What's up with you?' Lois demanded one night after Carmel snapped at Beth over nothing.

'What do you mean?'

'You know full well what I mean. You have been going around like Lady Misery for a couple of weeks and now you have started to take your bad humour out on Beth.'

'I'm just out of sorts,' Carmel said.

'What about?'

'Oh, I don't know, do I?' Carmel said impatiently. 'Why is anyone out of sorts?'

'Has the way you are feeling got anything to do with your Terry being discharged?' Lois persisted.

'No, of course not,' Carmel retorted quickly, almost too quickly. 'And stop calling him *my* Terry.' She was silent for a second or two and then said, 'I do miss seeing him at the hospital. I expected to and I expected to get over it as well, which I will do.' She hesitated and then

440

went on, 'If you want to know, Terry did say he cared for me, but as you once pointed out, many male patients fall in love with their nurses. Cassie has always said that he was sweet on me, but you have to take what Cassie says in that vein with a pinch of salt. As well as the numerous films she sees, she also reads these trashy romances and they fill her head with rubbish. She sees intrigue and passion around every corner.'

'Can't be bad,' Lois said, and was pleased to see the ghost of a smile playing around Carmel's mouth. 'Maybe, as she has done such a study of it, she is the very one to ask.'

'No, the very opposite,' Carmel said, laughing. 'She reminds me of Aileen in a way. Not that she falls in love herself every five minutes, but I think that she would like to arrange it that everyone else did.'

She shook her head and went on, 'To tell you the truth, I think Terry is still mourning the family he lost. And the feelings he said he had for me, well, they were more infatuation, mixed up with gratitude. He has no room in his head for further tangled emotions. I know that in my rational head. I'm sorry I have been such a grouch. I know it is my problem and no one else's and I intend to take a grip on myself. Don't worry, I'll have got myself sorted well before Christmas when I will see Terry again.'

Terry was also trying to work out his own feelings for the little nurse who had wormed her way into his heart. The love that he had once felt for his wife, his children and even Brenda's parents and sister had seemed to disappear totally when they died. He'd felt barren, emotionless, and

441

it was a young nurse who had made him feel again and taught him that his life had some meaning. She also taught him that though the memories of his loved ones would never leave him and would always hold a special place in his heart, he had to go back into the stream of life again because that is what they would have wanted him to do.

He had felt love for another human being stir in him again, as if it was being roused from a long sleep, and he knew he loved the little Irish nurse with the lilting voice who had pulled him back from the pit of despair.

After he left the hospital he felt cast adrift. He had got his old job back after the hospital had contacted the Gas Board, but his landlady had had to let someone else rent the rooms he'd had and had his belongings packed up ready for him to collect.

His boss was letting him sleep on his settee for the time being, but it was not suitable in the long term and Terry knew he would have to trail the streets once more, looking for someone with a spare room. In the meantime there was an ache in his heart every time he thought of Carmel. In the end the longing to see Carmel again got so great he knew he had to find her and tell her how he felt about her, and he set off after work one evening towards the end of November.

He had Carmel's address in advance of Christmas. Just forty minutes later, he was standing outside number 17 York Road, and before his courage could fail him he raised the knocker.

Carmel was just mounting the stairs to take Beth to bed when the knock came on the front door and so she opened it with the child in her arms.

'Terry!' she cried, but Terry didn't speak. He was startled by the sight of the child, though he could barely see either of them in the beam of his torch for Carmel had turned the light off before she could open the door. 'Come in,' she said. 'We're letting in all the cold air.' And then, as he stepped into the hall and Carmel was able to shut the door and turn the light on, he saw Beth clearly for the first time. She was gorgeous and as unlike his Belinda as it was possible to be, with her vivid blue eyes, her blonde curls and her little rosebud mouth. He smiled even though he felt a tug in his heart as he did so.

'Hello,' he said. 'You must be Beth?'

'Yes,' the child said and then, because she liked to get things straight, she said, 'What's your name?'

'Terry.'

'What are you doing here, Terry?' Carmel said. Then, with an impatient gesture, she said, 'Oh, don't bother telling me now. Wait until I get madam here to bed. Come through and meet Lois first, though, and have a hot drink at least. It is turning into a bleak old night outside, judging by the wind gusting around the house.'

It took Lois only a few minutes to realise that she liked Terry Martin very much and for her to note the love light shining in his eyes when Carmel came back into the room after tucking Beth up for the night. She also saw that Carmel was agitated and confused.

'Why are you here, Terry?' she said, sitting at the other side of the table opposite him. 'I thought we agreed.'

Lois looked from the lovelorn face of Terry to the flushed one of Carmel and thought to herself that Cassie might have got it right after all. She knew too her presence wasn't needed.

'If you will excuse me I have to write a letter to Chris.'

Terry threw her a look of gratitude, but Carmel didn't want her to leave. Couldn't she see she wasn't ready for this sort of thing yet? So she said almost accusingly, 'But you wrote to him two days ago.'

'Well, I am writing again,' Lois said firmly. 'There were things I missed telling him in the other letter,' and she slipped out of the room and left them to it.

Terry cleared his throat and, knowing it was no good beating about the bush, said, 'I came to see you, Carmel, because since I left that hospital, all I have done is think about you. You weren't able to express how you felt about me in the hospital, I know that now, and the last thing in the world I would do would be to make life difficult for you, but I need to know. If you cannot return my feelings then I will move out of your life and harass you no further.'

Carmel looked into the deep grey eyes that she had looked into so many times and saw real love there. Her insides had suddenly turned to jelly and she was glad that she was sitting down, for she doubted that her legs could hold her up. She knew that no way could she say that Terry meant nothing to her, now that she had allowed the feelings she had tried to crush to surface.

'You mean the very world to me,' she said simply. 'I think I have loved you from the first moment I saw you. I was worried that it was just a patient and nurse thing for you, mixed up with the grievous loss you had suffered.'

'I did worry that it might be too soon,' Terry said,

'even when I said those things in the hospital. I mean, it is only two years since . . . well, you know.'

Carmel heard the uncertainty in Terry's voice and reached out and caught his hand. 'These things cannot be planned,' she said. 'Neither of us went out looking for another. It just happened. Maybe we are both being given a second chance.'

Terry stood up and drew Carmel into his arms. 'Oh God, I never believed I would feel so deeply for someone again.'

'Nor me,' Carmel said, and when their lips met for the first time she let utter contentment flood through her body.

Lois and Ruby were delighted when Carmel told them how she felt about Terry, but she dreaded telling Jeff, wondering if he would see the relationship as a sort of betrayal. So she put it off. Then, in the second week in December, Lois had popped around to Ruby's and so Carmel was alone when Jeff turned up that evening. She knew she couldn't leave him in the dark any longer and, full of trepidation, she faced him and told him about her feelings for Terry.

Jeff wasn't totally surprised. She had told him lots about Terry anyway, while she was nursing him, and as the days passed into weeks, Jeff had seen Carmel's very expressive eyes shine when she spoke of the man.

'It isn't that I think any the less of Paul, you know,' she told Jeff anxiously

'My dear, I saw you with Paul,' Jeff said. 'I know how much you loved him and the sun rose and set with you as far as he was concerned. But Paul's body is in a foreign field somewhere, and you, my dear, have a life to live. Paul would not begrudge you this.'

'Ah, Jeff, you always make me feel so much better,' Carmel said, 'I have told Terry all about you and how much you mean to me and everything. You will meet him at Christmas at Ruby's and I'm sure you will like him.'

Jeff took to Terry straight away. He liked the firm hand-shake, the steady gaze in those dark grey eyes and the firm set of his chin. In Jeff's book these things marked Terry as a man of integrity and not one to be trifled with. Yet he saw the loving way he treated Carmel and how gentle he was with Beth, and thought the man would be good for both of them.

It was obvious what Beth thought of Terry, who always had time for her. That afternoon he had got down on the floor to help her play with the puppet show Jeff had brought her. He had got it from the toy cupboard in the old nursery, which he seemed to be systematically emptying, though Beth, of course, thought it came direct from Santa.

In fact everyone seemed to like Terry, including Ruby's daughter, Chrissie, who was also spending the day with them. Everyone went out of their way to make him feel welcome.

'He is really good with Beth,' Ruby remarked as the women were washing up after the mammoth dinner.

'Yes,' Carmel commented drily. 'Though did you see the delight on Terry's face at the toys? I don't know whether it is the man or the child getting the most enjoyment.'

'Well, they say that men never grow up.'

'This sort of proves it, doesn't it?' Carmel said.

'Oh, come on,' Chrissie said. 'Isn't it better he takes an interest than ignoring the child altogether?'

'Course it is,' Carmel said. 'I am only kidding.'

'Is he going back home tonight?' Ruby asked.

'No,' Carmel said. 'He can have the loan of our settee tonight. Make a change from the boss's.'

'What do you mean?'

'Well, he hasn't got anywhere to stay at the moment,' Carmel said. 'The landlady let his rooms while he was in hospital.'

'Bloody cheek!'

'He was in some weeks,' Carmel said. 'I expect she has to make a living, the same as the rest of us. Anyway, I don't know all the ins and outs of it, but I do know all his stuff was packed up for him and he was out on his ear.'

'But he needn't be any longer,' Ruby said. 'Haven't I two rooms above, just begging to be occupied?'

'Oh, Ruby, he will be delighted,' Carmel said. 'I know he worries about getting in the way where he is.'

'I'll put it to him over tea and see what he says.'

Carmel knew full well what Terry would say and she wasn't disappointed. On New Year's Day, he moved into Ruby's. Lois fully approved when she came back from Chris's parents, where she had spent the festive season, though Chris himself had had only a forty-eight-hour pass.

With each passing day and week Carmel's love for Terry seemed to deepen. It was different from the way she had felt about Paul. Of course she was a different person, older certainly, and one who had tasted tragedy in her own life and dealt with the aftermath of the tragedies of many other people.

Then Terry was different to Paul, both in looks and attitude. Carmel had thought he was more serious at first, but when she helped him shed the guilt he had felt burdened with, he emerged as quite a different person, with a wonderful sense of fun.

Beth accepted Terry as the father she had never had. She even called him 'Daddy', which gave Terry immense pleasure, though Lois had been quite shocked when she first heard the child use that term.

'It's all right, Auntie Lois,' Beth told her in explanation. 'I know that Terry isn't my real daddy, but he lives in Heaven now.'

'It was something she just started to do,' Carmel told Lois out of Beth's hearing. 'I have told her all about Paul and what happened to him, and I gave her a photograph to stand by her bed so she can see what he looked like. But, for God's sake, Lois, she is only three years old and has no concept of death. When I'd finished explaining she just said that if her real daddy couldn't live here, wasn't it good that Terry could. I was completely floored. I mean, what could I say to logic like that? And it isn't as if Paul can be hurt by her doing this, but I am sorry if it has upset you.'

'No,' Lois said. 'Don't be sorry. It's me being stupid. There is no reason on God's earth why Beth shouldn't call Terry "Daddy", and he is a father to her every way but biologically.'

However, despite loving Beth so dearly and getting on

well with all the others, Terry deepest love was reserved for Carmel. He wanted to take her out a time or two and court her properly. Carmel was in agreement with this and didn't want to rush into anything, for they had met and fallen in love in very strange circumstances.

Everyone else thought it sensible for them to take their time too, and so when Terry took Carmel to see *Casablanca* at the Palace cinema on Erdington High Street there was no shortage of people willing to baby-sit Beth, and it was the same when he took Carmel dancing one night in the upstairs room of the cinema.

'Are you sure this will be all right for you?'

'What?'

'Dancing?'

'I suggested it, didn't I?'

'Yes, but with your back, I mean.'

'Oh, Carmel, you can't be serious. I am a flipping gas fitter. That means I often have to climb into small holes or twist myself into unimaginable positions to reach the gas outlets. I don't sit at a desk and fill in forms all day, you know.'

'I know. I just—'

'Just wanted to fuss,' Terry remarked. 'Blimey, once a nurse always a nurse.'

'Oh, you . . .' Carmel cried, giving him a push. But Terry caught her hand and pulled her round to face him. Suddenly she could feel her heart pounding in her chest.

'I love you, heart, body and soul, Carmel,' Terry said seriously. 'There aren't words to say how much.' He kissed her gently on the lips and then his voice, still a little unsteady, said, 'Now let us away and teach them all how to dance.'

What a surprise awaited them, though, for they found that the waltzs, quicksteps and foxtrots that they had been practicing in the house were things of the past. There was an entirely new form of dancing now, brought over from the States and called jitterbugging. The music was jazzier and wilder. It was, as Terry said, 'foot-tapping music'.

Oh, how glad Carmel was that she had worn a dress with a full skirt as she saw most girls wore something similar. She hadn't any nylon stockings – few had, for they were like gold dust – but Lois had helped her coat her legs with gravy browning and then she had drawn a line down the back with an eyebrow pencil so that it looked as if Carmel was wearing stylish seamed stockings. With her hand in Terry's, she took to the floor with all the rest as the band started up again.

She had been nervous at first and hoped that she wouldn't make an utter fool of herself, but she found jitterbugging wasn't hard to learn at all and was the most tremendous fun. By watching and copying the others and also listening to the music, Carmel and Terry soon got the hang of it and were soon jitterbugging with the best of them and as if they had done it every day of their lives.

'You should have seen us,' Carmel said to Lois and Ruby, who had waited up for them. 'Like prize idiots, we were, expecting a slow waltz, or a fairly sedate foxtrot and this jitterbugging is just so . . . just so . . .'

'Unrestrained is the word I think you are searching for,' Terry said.

'Unrestrained!' Carmel mocked. 'Abandoned is more like it. Riotous even, and some of the girls were thrown about so much and twirled round to such an extent that their knickers were on show.'

'Could have been worse,' Terry said. 'At least they had knickers on.'

'Terry!'

'Only saying.'

'Well, don't bother.'

'So,' said Ruby, with a dry laugh, 'you'll hardly be going to this place of abandonment and riotousness again, then?'

'Are you kidding?' Carmel said. 'I'm up for it again next week, baby-sitters willing.'

There were things to do other than dancing, and the following week they queued outside the Odeon in what was left of New Street in the city centre to see *Gone With the Wind*, which Carmel had been wanting to see for ages, especially after Cassie had enthused over it so much. However, when they went to see *In Which We Serve* at the Palace the following week, mindful that Lois might be feeling a little pushed out, they asked her to go with them and Ruby happily baby-sat until they returned.

Sometimes, they sat in with Lois, just chatting or playing cards, or listening to a play or something on the wireless; sometimes Ruby would come in too, and George and Terry, and Jeff if he was there, would take themselves off to the pub while the women gossiped together.

The times Terry treasured, however, were the moments he had alone with Carmel, when they would sit, cuddled up on the settee in Carmel's sitting room, and Terry's hands would explore her body while his kisses and caresses caused her to groan with desire. However, much as she longed for fulfilment with Terry, she wanted to wait. He never pressed her to go further, for Carmel knew if they were to marry, she wanted her wedding night to be as special as the one she had shared with Paul.

At the beginning of April Lois went to see the doctor after work, to confirm really what she already knew – that she was at long last having a baby. Carmel had only to take one look at her face when she came through the door to know that the news was good.

'You are?' she cried, and Lois only had time to nod happily before Carmel caught her about the waist and the pair cavorted around the room.

Beth regarded such unbridled enthusiasm solemnly and then said, 'Why are you so sited?'

'Because your Auntie Lois is having a baby,' Carmel told her.

'Oh,' Beth said, her eyes lighting up. 'When?'

'Ages yet,' Lois said, and Carmel endorsed this. 'Not till the autumn. Lots and lots of big sleeps.'

Beth had no interest in things happening ages away. Even one day, one big sleep, was a long time to wait when you were only three, but for the two women their joy at the news did not abate and they spent the rest of that evening discussing names and ways of giving birth, and poring over baby books until the arrival of Terry put a stop to it. He was sincerely pleased for Lois, though. He remembered how excited he had been each time when Brenda had told him she was pregnant, but he didn't share this memory, knowing that it would put a damper on Lois's news.

CHAPTER TWENTY-SIX

In early May, as Carmel lay snuggled in Terry's arms one evening, he kissed her tenderly and said, 'Think 1943 is going to be our year. My ghosts are well and truly laid now, my darling, and it would be more perfect still if you would agree to be my wife.'

'Oh, yes,' Carmel said. 'Yes, please.'

The following Saturday, which Carmel had off duty anyway, Ruby minded Beth, and Terry and Carmel went into the city centre to choose the engagement ring. Carmel had already removed Paul's rings and put them away for Beth to have when she was an adult. Carmel would wear the diamond cluster Terry bought her with as much pride as she had Paul's. As she left the shop arm in arm with Terry that day, she gave a sigh of contentment and she thanked God for giving her this second crack at happiness.

Carmel's family had been told about Terry when he had been a patient of hers and they had all prayed for his speedy recovery. She had also told them what had happened to his family, and her mother in particular had been full of sympathy.

But now they were engaged and talking about wedding dates and so Carmel's family had to know how important Terry had become to her. She dreaded telling them because Terry wasn't a Catholic and had no intention of becoming one either. In fact, he went further and said after what he had seen happen to his family he wasn't at all sure there was a God and if there was, he had no intention of worshipping a deity that could allow such things to happen.

Carmel could see his point. There had been so many dead and dying and maimed, and she had seen and nursed such sickening sights. Oh, yes, she understood exactly what Terry meant. She had been a Catholic all her life and had never questioned it, but it was hard, even for her, to equate the loving father that God was supposed to be, with such carnage. She doubted, though, her mother would see it that way so in the letters home she side-stepped any reference to religion and just talked about how her feelings for Terry had changed from compassion to love and that they had become engaged.

The letters back were full of congratulations and delight from her mother, from all the family, but they wanted to see him, check that he was good enough to marry 'our Carmel'.

However, first there was the birth of Lois's son, Colin Christopher, who was born in a nursing home her father had booked for her, and on his due date of 11 September.

'I can't remember Beth ever being that small,' Carmel said as she held Lois's baby in her arms when he was just a few hours old.

'She was much smaller, as I recall,' Lois said. 'This big bruiser weighed in at eight and a half pounds, and

Beth, being premature and a girl as well, was far lighter. I remember being almost too frightened to pick her up at first, she looked so delicate.'

'They are all delicate and terribly precious,' Carmel said. 'Are you having him christened?'

Lois shook her head. 'Not till his father is home, and I don't care how long that takes. I want him to take some part in his son's life.'

'I don't blame you,' Carmel said. 'I wish Paul had got just a wee glimpse of Beth.'

'I'm sorry,' Lois said, flustered. 'How stupid and insensitive of me.'

'Not at all,' Carmel hastened to reassure her. 'The future is going to be wonderful for me now.'

'Carmel, I have thought about this over and over,' Lois said. 'What if Terry wants a child of his own?'

Carmel didn't answer straight away because she had faced that possibility already. At last she said, 'I have had that thought too and I would have another child if he wanted one so much.'

'You used to be so anti,' Lois reminded her.

'I used to be a lot of things that now don't seem important,' Carmel said. 'There has been and still is so much hatred in the world, death and injury and suffering, but a baby is so pure and innocent. Maybe it would do me good to focus on that. I'll tell you one thing, though, if I have another child, this time I won't give it to someone else to rear. I don't regret the decision I made when the country was in dire straits, and maybe if I hadn't returned to nursing I might never have met Terry at all, but I missed a lot of Beth's growing up because of it. I can never reclaim those years, and if Terry and I decide we want a child, I want to bring it up myself.'

'You wouldn't be afraid that Beth will have her nose pushed out of joint?'

Carmel smiled. 'No,' she said with confidence. 'That will never happen. The bond between Beth and Terry is just too great for anything to damage it. It might do Beth good, anyway, to have a half-brother or -sister. At the moment she thinks she is the most important person in the universe.'

'They all do at that age.'

'Maybe,' Carmel said. 'Anyway, how long are they keeping you in this place?'

'A fortnight, Daddy said.'

'Right. Well, I will make arrangements to travel to Ireland as soon as I can manage it and then I will be on hand when you are out,' Carmel said. 'Nothing will do for my family but they'll see Terry so they can approve or not.'

'They will be hard to please if they don't like Terry.'

'My mother won't like the fact that he is a Protestant.'

'Doesn't she know?'

Carmel shook her head. 'That wasn't something I wanted to write in a letter,' she said. 'I will have to tell Mammy face to face, so it suits me to go over now anyway.'

She gave the baby, who had begun to protest, over to Lois to feed and left to arrange time off from the hospital.

Carmel, Terry and little Beth travelled to Ireland on Wednesday, 15 September. When they set off in the pearly dawn of that early autumn morning, Carmel's concerns were for Terry when she remembered how sick Paul had been on the boat. She was glad that as the sun rose higher, the day turned out to be a mild one. At Holyhead the sea was calm and the waves more playful than boisterous, and they had a crossing with no ill effects for any of them.

The first member of the Duffy family that Terry met was Michael, who had come to meet them with Bridget McCauley, whom Michael had told Carmel was just a friend at their father's funeral. Evidently the friendship had deepened, for she saw the girl now wore an engagement ring.

'So,' Carmel said with a smile, 'you intend to try and make an honest man of my brother? I wish you well of it. You do know what you are taking on, I suppose?'

Bridget answered in like vein, 'Oh, yes. Don't you worry. I am well aware of it and I will have him licked into shape in no time.'

'Will the pair of you give over?' Michael said with a laugh. 'Maligning me in such a way . . .' He grasped Terry's hand. 'I am very pleased to meet you, Terry, for we need every man jack on our side to help us cope with the women of the house. And here's another one of them,' he went on, lifting Beth out of Carmel's arms. 'And the most important of the lot.'

That fact had never been pointed out to Beth before. 'I am?' she asked doubtfully.

'Well, course you are,' Michael affirmed. 'No doubt about it. Isn't that right, Bridget?'

'It is surely,' said Bridget, with a smile. 'They're never done talking about you, and your granny has been on pins all day waiting on you coming.'

Carmel smiled at the confusion on her daughter's face and knew any minute she was going to ask what her granny was doing on pins, but Michael forestalled her.

He set her down on her feet and said, 'Come on, Bridget's father has given me the loan of his car. Let us arrive at Mammy's in style.'

Carmel was anxious to see the house on Church Street that her mother had moved into as soon as she had got her job in Kilkenny's dress shop, not quite three months after her husband had been buried.

'Of course some townsfolk were scandalised by that,' Eve had written to Carmel, 'and thought I should be in mourning for a year. I haven't had one day, one hour of mourning for that vicious bully and I don't care who knows it. I am glad he is dead and I am just sorry he took so long over it.'

Carmel didn't blame her mother at all. In fact, she was proud of her and though she knew almost any house on the planet would be better than the shack in which she had been raised, she was impressed by the brick-built house with the slate roof that Michael drew up the car in front of.

Before the car was properly stopped the front door of the house was flung open and her mother flew down the steps, welcoming them all in a flurry of hugs and kisses and drawing them all into the house at the same time.

The kitchen that Eve led them to seemed full of people. Terry immediately felt nervous. Although he was introduced to all Carmel's siblings, he knew he would never remember them half of them. On the other hand, Beth was passed from one to another as they exclaimed about how she had grown while they hugged and kissed her. Revelling in the attention, Beth seemed to take it all in her stride. Then Siobhan brought her new fiancé, Tim McEvoy, forward to meet them. As Carmel shook hands with him, she was certain she had seen the man before but not sure where. Then suddenly she had it.

'Weren't you at Daddy's funeral?'

The man nodded. 'At the graveyard just. I went there to support Siobhan and because she asked me to go, but I would not go on to the pub. I know what happens when someone dies. Whatever they have been like in their life-time, that is all wiped out and they become some sort of saint. I couldn't have borne hearing what a "grand man" Dennis Duffy was when I know he had led Siobhan – all of you – one bloody awful life, begging your pardon, Mrs Duffy.'

Terry sneaked a glance at Carmel. She had told him all about her father after she had agreed to marry him, for she said he needed to know how it had been in the family if he was to join it. He had listened, appalled, to the account of a life of degradation and such brutality that he could scarcely credit it, and yet he believed every word. He had tried to be a good husband to Brenda and a good father to his children and he was, at any rate, a moderate drinker. That a man could abuse so cruelly the people that should be central in his heart was anathema to him, and he wondered how they had all got through it so well.

'Don't you worry about upsetting me, my lad,' Eve said. 'The words you said were but the truth anyway. Now let us all sit up to the table where I have a big feed ready for us all.'

The meal was like none that Carmel had eaten with her family. There was so much laughter and noise amongst them, she wondered if her father was turning in his grave, and she realised the tension had gone from everyone. Theirs had become a happy house, as it could have been years before with a different father at the helm of it.

Eve had changed beyond recognition. She was now a respected member of the town. She was independent and had no handouts, but earned money and paid her way. Her confidence had increased because of it, and it did Carmel's heart good to see her like that.

Eve liked nothing better than to have her family gathered about her, especially Carmel and her wee daughter, who lived so far away. So while the girls cleared away and the men sat around the range having a smoke, Eve drew Beth onto her knee while she sat on at the table with Carmel.

'It's a lovely house, Mammy,' Carmel said.

'Isn't it?' Eve agreed happily. 'I was lucky to get it. Of course Eliza Kilkenny spoke up for me. They have been very good to me altogether, both Eliza and her elder sister, Martha. I was at school with Eliza and, like everyone else, she was aware how things were at home, but she never looked down her nose at me like some of the others and she always said that there was a job in the shop any time I wanted it. There was no point in my trying to earn a penny piece while your father was alive, though, as you well know. Now, oh, now my life is just so happy.'

Carmel could see that for herself. There were no lines of strain on her mother's face, only laughter lines around eyes that sparkled and shone.

'Are you my granny?' Beth asked.

'I am indeed,' Eve said, 'and I am very glad to have you here.'

Beth, remembering the encounter in the station, suddenly said, 'Were you standing on pins?'

Carmel laughed. 'It's just an expression, Beth,' she told her small daughter. 'It means Granny was so looking forward to you coming that she could hardly sit still.'

'On pins,' Eve said. 'That's what it means all right.'

'Oh,' Beth said. She looked from one woman to the other and saw their eyes alight with amusement, and wasn't sure that she liked being laughed at. 'I think I'm going to sit with my daddy now,' she said, and sidled off Eve's knee and went towards the range where Terry sat. Eve's eyes opened in surprise.

'There goes one offended girl,' said Carmel with a chuckle. 'And straight to Terry.'

'She calls him Daddy.'

Carmel shrugged. 'It was her choice,' she said. 'She knows he isn't her real daddy, but Terry is here and Paul isn't, and, of course, it has helped Terry too.'

'He loves her well enough, anyway,' Eve said, looking across to where Terry was bouncing Beth on his lap, much to the child's delight.

Carmel nodded. 'The two of them are as thick as thieves.'

'You have picked another good one there,' Eve said.

'I know,' said Carmel. Then, because there was no point beating about the bush, she said quietly, 'But he isn't a Catholic, Mammy.'

'I thought not,' said Eve. 'There was some hesitation in your letters. I thought perhaps you weren't sure of

461

the man, that maybe you were marrying him because you felt sorry for him and that is why I was so anxious for you to come over so I could see for myself. I only had to see you together for a few minutes to realise how much you love one another, so that put my mind at rest at least.'

'And how do you feel about this, Mammy?'

'I don't know really,' Eve said. 'Why did you not say earlier? Did you think that I would disapprove?'

'Well, don't you?'

'Yes and no,' Eve said. 'I mean, I am bound to say that I wish you were marrying a Catholic man, but there is more to marriage than what religion a person is. What I am saying is that I married a Catholic and he led us all a dog's life. I'd not want one of mine to go through five minutes of what I spent half a lifetime enduring. In other words, I'd rather you marry a good Protestant than a bad Catholic. All I want for you is peace and happiness.'

Carmel felt love for her mother well up inside her and she leaned forward and kissed her gently. Then, grasping one of Eve's hands, she said earnestly, 'I will never forget what you have just said, and your blessing on my relationship and forthcoming marriage with Terry means the world to me, for no one else's opinion matters more than yours.'

And Carmel meant every word that she said. She knew the priest, Sister Frances and even some of the self-righteous townspeople would disapprove of her marrying a Protestant, but with her mother on her side none of that mattered.

Eve was too choked up to reply and then the girls,

having finished all the washing and tidying up, were in on top of them, laughing and chafing one another, and the moment was gone.

The wedding between Carmel and Terry was set for Saturday, 25 March 1944, because Carmel did not want to get married in the depths of winter. It was also going to be as different from Carmel's first wedding as was possible, much quieter, and this time none of Carmel's family was coming over for it.

One Friday evening in early March, Terry and George had gone off to sink a pint or two and Ruby was at her daughter's, so the girls were alone. Lois took the opportunity to air with Carmel all the concerns she had about the wedding.

'It's different the second time around,' Carmel told her. 'And I couldn't really ask the family, not this time.'

'I don't understand why not,' Lois said. 'After all, you said they liked and approved of Terry, for all he's a Protestant.'

'They did,' Carmel agreed. 'And he liked them, though he was a bit overwhelmed sometimes. He didn't say he was, but I saw it in his eyes a time or two when we met *en masse*, as it were.'

'Is that why?'

'No. Well, only partly,' Carmel said. 'Look, Lois, imagine I had a big flashy wedding. My family alone would probably fill two or three pews. Then there would be friends from the hospital, Sylvia and you, Chris and Dan, if they could make it, not to mention Ruby and George and some people I know from church. On Terry's side there might be a couple of workmates if he is lucky.

How would that make him look? Anyway, as I am marrying a non-Catholic, I can't have Nuptial Mass said, so the whole thing will only last about twenty minutes.'

'Is your mother upset over it?'

'No,' Carmel said. 'She sees the reasoning behind it. Then there's the problem of finding them somewhere to stay too, of course, and feeding a big party, with rationing the way it is.'

'I do hear all you say,' Lois said. 'Aren't you just the tiniest bit disappointed yourself, though?'

'No,' Carmel said. 'I want to be married to Terry quite desperately now, but how I am married, the pomp and ceremony of it, doesn't bother me. It is the being together that matters.'

'Oh, I do know what you mean,' Lois said. 'I long for this war to be over and for my husband to come home safe and sound and help raise our baby son.'

'The war is on the turn,' Carmel said soothingly. 'It really is just a matter of time now.'

'I have lost count of the people who have said that to me just lately,' Lois said. 'It doesn't really help.'

'I know that,' Carmel agreed. 'And listen to me. I am as bad as the rest.'

She felt sorry for Lois and guiltily glad that, once they were married, her husband would come home every night and be by her side, but it wouldn't help to say that either.

Instead, in an attempt to turn Lois's mind on to something else, she said, 'I'm giving notice next week, you know?'

'Giving notice? You mean you are not going back after the wedding?'

'No.'

Lois shook her head. 'My God! Those are words I never thought I would hear you say. What's brought this on?'

'A number of things,' Carmel said. 'First and foremost it's about Beth. She has a year, maybe less, before she goes to school, because if she doesn't start in January next year she certainly will after Easter, and I would like to spend some time with her before that. I mean, I felt I had to use my skill as a nurse when it was needed so badly, but the blitz seems to be over now and so it is the right time for me to leave. Added to that, Ruby and George have been marvellous, and I know Beth will always love them dearly – God, I do myself – but they are not getting any younger and Ruby in particular has not picked up since her daughter had that telegram to say her husband was missing, presumed dead, now has she?'

'No, you are right,' Lois said. 'She has never been the same since.'

'I have felt guilty sometimes that, because she has the care of my daughter, maybe she hasn't been able to support her own fully. That is a terrible situation to put her in.'

Lois had to admit it was and since she had been at home with Colin, she had seen how drawn Ruby had looked sometimes. She thought that Carmel had made the right decision, but she wasn't the only one involved and so Lois asked, 'What does Terry think?'

'Oh, he is all for it,' Carmel said with a smile. 'I think he imagines that if I have already left work, I can get on with the job of producing his son and heir all the quicker. He sort of sees it as one less hurdle to jump.'

'Son and heir, eh?'

'He wants a son,' Carmel said. 'What man doesn't, deep down? Terry, being Terry, would bite his tongue off rather than admit it, but I've seen the way he looks at your Colin. Point is, though, I am not a brood mare,' Carmel went on. 'We all know people who go on and on giving birth to one girl after another in their quest for a boy and that is one road I am not going to go down, and I have let Terry know that.'

'Well, I wouldn't call him an unreasonable man.'

'He isn't,' Carmel agreed happily. 'He is absolutely lovely and could quite see my point of view. But even I know that with two children to see to, it will be well-nigh impossible to nurse, the hours being what they are. So I will either have to give it up for many years, or train for something less demanding, or at least more fitted to family life.'

'Like what?'

'Like district nursing, or midwifery,' Carmel said. 'I would have to take a further course, but one of the doctors was telling me that once this new Health Service the government keep wittering on about really kicks in, which will be when this war finally grinds to a halt, there will be a greater demand than ever for services like that.'

'I can see that,' Lois said. 'I might make some enquiries myself.'

'Can't hurt,' Carmel said. 'No rush, though. This will all be years away yet, I should think. My more immediate problem for the future is finding something suitable to wear for the wedding, now that clothes are on ration and utility the order of the day. I don't want a fairy-tale wedding dress this time, and I don't mind something more practical, but I'd like something a wee bit different and I would love to be able to get my hands on something a bit bridesmaidy for Beth. I am finishing at two o'clock tomorrow. Don't suppose you would meet me after work and go round the Bull Ring and help me choose?'

'Course I will, you dope,' Lois said, her eyes shining with happiness for her dear friend. She knew that whatever dress Carmel wore, her wedding would be like a fairy tale, and she couldn't have been more pleased for her. 'In fact,' she added, 'you just try to keep me away.'

Despite Carmel's efforts to keep the wedding low key, that day there were far more thronging the church that ever she could have imagined. There were plenty from the hospital because Carmel was a popular nurse, and the whole romanticism of it appealed to the droves who turned out to support her. The romance element was fuelled by Cassie, who was claiming some of the credit for bringing Carmel and Terry together in the end.

'They were looking doe-eyed at each other for weeks,' she said to any who wanted to listen. 'Course, they had to keep it under wraps a bit because of Matron and everything, but as far as I was concerned it was a foregone conclusion once Terry was out of the place. Anyhow, I think it is dead romantic. Fancy falling for and marrying a doctor who is killed in France and then falling in love again with a man she has brought back from the brink of death. And she did do that, you know; he told me himself. "Gave me a reason to live, Cassie," he said, just like that. Isn't that the loveliest thing you ever heard?'

Most of the nurses agreed that it was, and inside her office Matron smiled to herself. There was little she missed and she had seen the way the wind blew between Carmel and Terry Martin long before Carmel had given notice and officially told her the name of her intended. It amused her that both probationers and nurses alike thought they had a secret and that the groups whispering together would disperse when they saw her approaching. Wait till she turned up at the church, she thought with a smile. That will set the cat among the pigeons right and proper.

Carmel, at the church door, with her arm tucked into George's, waiting for the Wedding March to begin, was glad to see that many guests had been directed to the other side of the church so that Terry, with his boss beside him as best man, were not sitting in isolated splendour. Then suddenly her eyes caught sight of Matron Turner sitting towards the back of the church. She'd never seen her in smart clothes before, but for all that she would have known her anywhere. Hearing Carmel's arrival, she turned and smiled at her, and Carmel felt sort of warmed from within. It was as if the matron was giving her a seal of approval.

Many turned to look as Carmel began her slow walk. She had on a costume of ivory silk, the jacket fitted to show off the sort of figure many would die for. The full skirt, falling halfway down her calves, rustled when she moved. The light brown hat, with the veil semi-covering her face, matched her shoes, and in her hands she carried a bouquet of silk flowers, the real thing being in short supply, due to many fields being given over to the growing of vegetables.

Beth, coming solemnly behind her, had a similar posy, which matched the Alice band attached to the small veil that topped her golden locks. Her dress of apricot satin was to the floor, and peeping from the edge of it was a pair of white patent shoes. They both looked gorgeous and Carmel knew few would guess that their outfits had come mainly from second-hand stalls in the Rag Market. The woman tending the stall had been delighted to see Carmel interested in the silk costume. It was beautiful and almost new, but she had thought she would have it left on her hands, for few woman were slender enough to wear it.

'You must have it,' she said, when Carmel tried it on. 'It's made for someone like you and doesn't it fit you like a glove?'

It was important to Carmel that she and Beth looked good, to prove this was no shabby hole-in-the-corner sort of wedding, which Father Robertson had intimated it was, as she couldn't have the sacrament of Nuptial Mass to bless the union. She had never before come up against the disapproval of the Church and it had affected her keenly.

Even at the six weekly meetings that they had to attend before the wedding so that Terry could fully understand what being married to a Catholic entailed, the priest's manner had been grim, almost disdainful.

As Terry had said as they returned home one evening, 'If anything could ever put me off joining the Church, then it is the attitude of that priest. The point is, if I was to go in next week and say that I had decided to join the Church he would pump my hand up and down and declare me a fine fellow altogether, and yet I would be exactly the same man with the same opinions and sets of values as I had the previous week. The whole thing is crazy.'

It was crazy, and they were both in it together. Even Sister Frances went on about it in her letters after Carmel returned home, for all she'd liked Terry when she met him in Letterkenny.

Carmel did feel bad about upsetting Sister Frances, for she knew that she owed her a lot. But when she wrote to her mother and said this, Eve's reply was swift.

> Remember you have to live with the man you choose, not any priest or nun. Follow your heart, my darling girl. True love is the only thing that matters in the end.

And then Terry turned and looked at her, his fathomless eyes so full of love, and Carmel knew her mother was right for her heart was filled with rapture that she was soon to be married to this wonderful man.

She gave her bouquet into the outstretched arms of Ruby, stepped away from George's side, and took her place beside Terry.

CHAPTER TWENTY-SEVEN

Being married to Terry, Carmel soon found, was nothing like being married to Paul. Paul had been filled with almost restless energy and so had she then. They needed that vitality to make the most of every second they could, to give them quality time together, for they'd both had to work long and gruelling shifts at the hospitals. In fact, she recalled much of their lives centred around rush and bustle and snatched moments together.

With Terry, each day was much calmer. She loved getting up in the morning to cook breakfast for him and then waving him off to work before listening to *The Kitchen Front*, which was on after the eight o'clock news on the wireless. This programme saved the sanity of many women, as it gave out recipes for foodstuffs that were usually available and the two girls would write down any of the recipes they fancied having a go at before toiling up to Erdington to fetch their rations and see if there was possibly some little delicacy off-ration that they could join a queue for.

They had been shielded from the true effects of rationing when they had both been nursing and getting many of their meals at the hospital – except for the time that Carmel had away from work waiting for the birth of Beth, when rationing was just kicking in – and rationing to them had been seen as a irritant more than anything. Lois had complained how difficult it was when she stopped work to await Colin's birth, but Carmel hadn't appreciated this until she experienced it herself. It was a nightmare, because as well as jiggling the rationed food, there were things on points and this effectively dealt with canned fish, meat, vegetables, fruit and condensed milk, together with ordinary milk, cereals, rice, biscuits and oat flakes, and everyone had just sixteen points a month.

They would pool rations as they always had and produce such delights as vegetable and oatmeal goulash, Woolton pie or curried carrots and rice to put before Terry when he came in after a hard day. He never complained, and if he had it wouldn't have made any difference. He always ate everything on his plate and complemented them both on it, however tasteless it was.

They did their best, often adding Bovril to a dish or making up a soup of whatever they had in the cupboard to pour over things to make it tastier. They were both mighty glad that dried egg had appeared in the shops. It was nothing like the real thing, but it wasn't that bad scrambled, or as an omelette, which was another meal, and if they had the sugar and butter enough to make a cake, dried egg could be used in place of the real thing. If they ever got hold of a real egg it was saved for Beth, or Colin, now he was being weaned, or occasionally for Terry. Both women knew though they were luckier than most, for because their children were under five, they had special green ration books that entitled them to extra milk, orange juice, cod liver oil and a packet of dried egg powder off points every eight weeks, and so they managed.

Terry said they should utilise some of the garden and, with Carmel's agreement, he had sold Paul's motorbike, which he said was not the vehicle for a family man.

'After the war I'll look around for a little car,' he told Carmel. 'No point now with petrol rationing the way it is, but afterwards won't it be just champion to take a run out on a Sunday, get Beth out of the streets to where the air is a bit fresher?'

Where Paul's bike had stood in the garden was a pile of mud, for any grass underneath it had died. Terry dug it over, tilled it and planted potatoes, carrots and onions. On the little lawn left he fashioned up a swing for Beth. Carmel had seldom known Beth so happy and contented, though she had always been a compliant child. She loved having her mother at home all day and told her often. However, when Terry came home, she turned into his little shadow, wanting to be with him wherever he was. It gave Carmel so much pleasure to see the bond between them grow deeper every day.

Even Ruby and George had taken their rightful place as pseudo-grandparents and now they hadn't the care of Beth, they were able to just enjoy her company. Ruby was able also to be some measure of support to her poor, bereaved daughter.

In fact the only thing that caused Carmel any concern at all was that she hadn't seen Jeff for some time. After discussing it with Carmel, Terry had told Jeff that, after they were married, Carmel would no longer need any financial contributions from Paul's estate, but if Jeff wanted to put the money in trust for Beth he had no objection to that at all and he had assured Carmel at the time that Jeff hadn't seemed upset or offended by anything he'd said.

Carmel had been so glad the matter had been resolved because she had felt guilty from the first taking money from her dead husband. There had been plenty of it too, far more that she had needed, and far more than she could ever spend in the current climate, try as she might. In fact, once she had begun nursing again, even paying Ruby for minding Beth, she had plenty left and now there was a sizeable amount resting in the bank.

'Keep hold of it, darling,' Terry told her one night, as they got ready for bed. 'I too have a fair bit stashed away. I wasn't sure how much until this legal chap at work sorted it all out for me, because there were insurance policies to redeem and all sorts, but I am saving it, because one day I want to buy us our own house. What d'you say to that?'

'I say that you are a lovely, wonderful man, and I am more glad every day that I married you,' Carmel said, with a smile.

'And I say words are cheap,' Terry said with mock severity. 'And people do say actions speak louder than any words, so how about it?'

'How about it?' Carmel repeated sarcastically, while at the same time lying back in the bed, gazing at him provocatively. 'I think that you are a sex-crazed beast and what's more . . .'

Carmel got no further as Terry's lips covered hers and she gave herself up to the pleasure of it. Again, sex with Terry was not like sex with Paul. It was slower and more controlled and more waiting until Carmel was fully aroused, absolutely ready, and then so tremendously fulfilling that she would cry out again and again.

One Monday in early June, Terry sent word that he had to work over on a difficult job and not to bother saving him any dinner, that he would get chips or something for himself. He didn't know how late he would be and Carmel let Beth stay up until eight o'clock to see if he would come in, before insisting that she go to bed.

She protested strongly, but Carmel was standing no nonsense because she knew from experience just how difficult Beth could be the next day if she had had insufficient sleep. So when she came down after putting her very disgruntled child to bed, Lois was smiling as she handed Carmel a cup of tea.

'There goes one very unhappy little girl.'

'I'll say,' Carmel said. 'And I know she is pulling out all the stops and employing all the delaying tactics she can think of, but she asked tonight why her Granddad Jeff doesn't come to see her any more and I couldn't answer because I have no idea. Do you know anything about it?'

'Not in so many words,' Lois said. 'I mean, no one has ever said, but I do know, for instance, that Emma is ill.'

Carmel sat back in the chair and stared at Lois. 'You are asking me to believe that because Emma has a cold, Jeff has sat by her side night after night, holding her hand, mopping her fevered brow and whispering sweet nothings in her ear? I think not.'

'It isn't a cold,' Lois said. 'It's cancer and she is dying from it.'

'Don't you dare try and get me to feel sorry for that bitch of a woman.'

'I'm not,' Lois protested with a smile. 'I am just offering it as a possible reason for Jeff not coming so often.'

'Even so,' Carmel said. 'I mean, I haven't seen him since before the wedding and that was nearly three months ago. That means Beth hasn't seen him either and that is a long time for a little girl especially—'

'Ssh,' Lois said urgently. 'Do you hear planes?'

'I do, and many of them,' Carmel cried, leaping to her feet. 'They are right above us. I'll get Beth, and I bet that cellar will be damp.'

'No, wait,' Lois said. 'These are our planes, I'm sure of it. Don't you remember the intermittent engine sound the German planes had?'

'Yes, of course,' Carmel said. 'But why would so many of our planes be flying overhead?'

'I don't know,' Lois said. 'But I aim to try and find out.'

'And I am coming with you,' Carmel cried.

The two made for the back door. They were not the only ones standing in their gardens. Most of their neighbours were out too in that unseasonably chill evening, watching in awe mixed with apprehension as plane after plane, squadron after squadron, flew above them.

'Maybe this is what Chris meant,' Lois said.

'What d'you mean?'

'Well, he said he heard a rumour there was something big planned for the summer,' Lois said. 'Didn't know what, of course.'

'It'll be this, all right,' Ruby said from across the fence. 'A woman was telling me two days ago about how the South Coast is out of bounds to civilians, like. I didn't right believe it, 'cos she's a dozy cow and has got things wrong afore.'

'Got it right this time anyroad, I'd say,' said the man the other side of Ruby. 'Here we go agen, another bleeding Dunkirk.'

Even in the half-light Carmel saw Lois's face blanch. 'It won't be like Dunkirk,' she said. 'They are better prepared.'

'Don't you think the Germans are too? Do you think they will stand on the beaches and hand out calling cards?'

'You don't even know Chris has gone this time,' Carmel said, putting her hand on Lois's arm. And then she was gently peeled from Lois as strong arms encircled her, for Terry had arrived home and Carmel leaned against him and sighed.

'I wanted to be here with you two tonight,' Terry said, his other arm encircling Lois. 'This is history being made. Soon we will know whether we are going to win this war, or fall under Nazi dominance.'

'I hope to God we win then,' Carmel said fiercely. 'Then Paul and thousands like him won't have given their lives in vain.'

The next day they kept the wireless news on after *The Kitchen Front*, and many houses and workplaces did the same thing, knowing eventually they would be told officially what had happened. When the news flash came it was from Reuters News Agency and just said that earlier that morning Allied armies began landing on the coast of France. Everyone knew that the next few days would determine whether this would be a massive defeat or the beginning of the end.

In the papers Carmel began to read avidly, she saw the scale of the invasion now known as D-Day or Operation Overlord, and she learned that while the Allies fought their way from the south, liberating besieged towns and villages, the Red Army were doing the same in the north. It was they that found the first of the death or concentration camps, many being in Poland.

The pictures and accounts of those places like Treblinka and Maidenek beggared belief, and the pictures of the bald and naked survivors, many like skeletons, and the mounds where thousands had been tipped into mass graves Carmel found almost too distressing to read about.

She had cheering news of her own, though. Just a few days after D-Day she too took herself off to the doctor's, but she said nothing to Terry until they were snuggled up in bed together that night and she left the lamp on as she wanted to see his face.

'I went to the doctor's today,' she said.

'Oh, anything wrong?'

'Not a thing.'

Terry looked at her shining eyes. He hardly dared hope. 'You mean . . .?' he began tentatively.

'I mean that your shenanigans just after we were married have borne fruit, darling,' Carmel said, her smile nearly cutting her face in two. 'I am carrying our child and he or she will be a Christmas baby.'

For a few moments Terry was stunned. Those were the

words than once he had thought he would never hear again, and then exhilaration surged through him and could not be contained. 'You bloody terrific lady, you!' he cried out. 'Having a baby! Oh God! Oh, what bloody marvellous news!' And he hugged Carmel tightly in sheer delight.

Samuel Terence Martin was born at three o'clock on 24 December at home and with no great drama. The midwife was in attendance and it soon became apparent that there was nothing remotely wrong with the child's lungs. Terry, pacing the floor outside, was allowed to see his wife an hour later, when the midwife declared her fit to be seen. As Terry entered the room, the midwife left it, knowing the two would want to be alone. Carmel looking thoroughly pleased with herself had the baby, his son, suckling at her breast.

The sight affected Terry so much, he felt his knees begin to tremble and he kneeled by the side of the bed and gazed into her eyes as he said earnestly, 'I can't tell you what this means to me.'

Carmel smiled at him. 'You don't have to,' she said. 'Your whole face says it all, and I feel the same, for I wanted this child so much – your child because I love you so very much.'

'Ah, Carmel.'

'Here,' Carmel said, removing the baby from her breast and wrapping the shawl more securely around him. 'Hold your son.'

Terry took him in his arms tenderly, overwhelmed by the power of his love for the little baby.

'You have given me the greatest gift of all, a Christmas baby.'

Carmel laughed gently. 'You might be thrilled by the thought of a Christmas baby, but young Sam could well feel that he is cheated as regards presents and all.'

'I never thought about that.'

'I bet he will when he is old enough.'

'I'll make sure he doesn't miss out, don't worry.'

'Well, Beth has a heap of toys she has grown out of, courtesy of Jeff, which he can start on,' Carmel said. 'She looks like she'll get no more, though, for we seem to be out of favour altogether.'

'It is odd when he was such a regular visitor before.'

'Are you sure he was all right when you discussed with him about the money?' Carmel said. 'It's all I can think of.'

'Yes, I told you.'

'Well, the whole thing is stupid and the man is too important to me, and young Beth as well, to just let things dwindle on like this,' Carmel said. 'In the new year, I intend to go and see him, not at the house where that woman, ill or not, is in residence. I will go and see him in the office.'

Suddenly, there was a terrific pounding on the door. 'Wonder who that is?' Terry said.

'Whoever it is, Lois will deal with it,' Carmel said, and then just moments later there was the sound of thumping feet on the stairs and then a rather timid knock on the door.

With a questioning look at Carmel, Terry crossed to open it, holding the baby against his shoulder. 'Jeff!'

'Lois has just told me about the baby,' Jeff said, twisting his hat nervously in his hands. 'Can I . . . would it be all right . . .?'

'Come in, Jeff,' Carmel called from the bed where she had pulled herself into a sitting position and raised her arms in welcome as he came in. As he took hold of her hands she pulled him onto the bed and said, 'You are a sight for sore eyes.'

'Do you mean that?'

'Yes, truly.'

'I have been a fool,' Jeff said miserably. 'Stiff-necked, nearly as bad as my wife. I took umbrage when Terry said about the money. I know now how unreasonable I was being. Can you forgive me?'

'Jeff, there is nothing to forgive,' Carmel said, and her eyes shone with tears of thankfulness. 'I am just glad you are part of our lives once more.'

'I am glad you feel that way,' Jeff said, 'though I hardly deserve it. I have a tricycle for young Beth in the car, a big one with a bread basket on the back for Santa to deliver tomorrow. It's old because it was Paul's and then Matthew's, but I had it done up and painted, and a new bell fitted, and it's like new now.'

'She will be thrilled,' Carmel said. 'But just as important as the things you give her is the time you spend with her. She has missed you sorely. In fact, in the new year I was going to seek you out.'

'You might be a bit of a granddad to the new edition too, if you like,' Terry said, lifting the child who had gone to sleep against his shoulder so that Jeff could see him. Jeff traced one finger gently around the baby's face and said, 'You are a lucky man, Terry.'

'I know it,' Terry said softly as he laid the sleeping baby in the cradle.

* * *

The war was over. Hitler shot himself in a bunker in Berlin on 30 April and his body was found by the Red Army who entered the city first on 2 May. Germany surrendered officially on 7 May and the following day was a national holiday.

Church bells pealed out the good news and street parties were hastily organised. No one mentioned bedtime and the children ran about in the streets till all hours, Beth along with the others. Carmel knew it was pointless trying to put her to bed as she would never be able to sleep.

Carmel couldn't blame the people for their slight hysteria. The war had been long and arduous, and many had suffered tragedy and trauma. Yet she knew whatever the cost in human life, war couldn't have been averted and, once undertaken, it had to be won, for the evil Nazi regime had to be stopped. She saw the relief on Lois's face that Chris had survived it all and would soon be home again where he belonged.

Each morning, when Carmel woke, she would be filled with contentment and she enjoyed the first summer of peace. Each fine Sunday, they would all travel to Sutton Park, Lois and Colin too. Petrol rationing was too restrictive yet to make a car a viable proposition, but Carmel at any rate loved the little steam train that took them nearly to the entrance.

The first time they had done this, she remembered her first experience of the park when Paul took her there the day they had become engaged. She had almost expected a pang of nostalgia, but there was none, just a warm memory that made her smile.

'What's up?' Terry asked with a quizzical look at her.

'Nothing.'

'Well then, why are you grinning like the Cheshire Cat?'

'I'm not, and anyway,' said Carmel archly, 'it's my business.'

'Oh, yeah? What about the obey bit in the wedding ceremony?'

'Doesn't say that you own me body and soul,' Carmel replied. 'And my thoughts are my own, so put that in your pipe and smoke it.'

'Why you!' Suddenly Terry reached out and caught Carmel up in his arms.

Lois was smiling at the pair of them and Beth caught her eye and then cast her own upwards as if to say 'they are at it again', for she was well used to the way her mother and father went on.

'Are you happy, Mrs Martin?' Terry asked, as he held Carmel close.

'Ecstatically so, Mr Martin,' Carmel replied.

'That is all the answer I need,' Terry said. 'And I will do all in my power to make sure that is always the case.'

Carmel knew he would, he had, and she thanked God nightly for giving her a second chance with this very special and wonderful man. She knew she had much to be thankful for and the only thing she had any concern about at all was that everyone would have Sam spoiled to death. Even Colin, little more than a baby himself, seemed to adore Sam, while Beth was his willing slave when she wasn't at school for she had started at the Abbey Infants in January.

In fact, everyone ran round for Sam – Ruby, George, Jeff, even Lois – and as for Terry, there was sometimes no reasoning with him where Sam was concerned. Only the other day Carmel had put her foot down about Terry buying Sam a train set for Christmas. Not that she thought he would be able to lay his hands on one. Precious few toys had reached the shops yet and this first Christmas of peacetime would be a lean one for many children, Carmel guessed.

It was Saturday, 13 October. Lois and Colin had gone away for a few days to stay with Chris's parents. Terry and Beth, who had been in the garden, had come in for a warm drink. Carmel had Sam in the highchair, feeding him, when there was a knock at the door. Leaving Terry to finish with Sam, Carmel went to open it.

The man was slightly stooped, his hair was pure white and he had deep score lines scarring his face. Yet Carmel had the feeling that he wasn't old and he was also familiar. Then the man spoke.

'Do you not know me, Carmel?'

Carmel felt her mouth go dry, while her heart hammered against her ribs and the scene swam before her, for though the man's voice was cracked and husky she would have known it anywhere.

'Paul?' she said, but hesitantly, and as if it were a question – as if she couldn't believe it and didn't want to believe it.

CHAPTER TWENTY-EIGHT

'Yes, it's me,' Paul said. 'And I know I'm no oil painting, but you should see the poor buggers who didn't make it.'

Suddenly there flashed through his mind the doctor in the military hospital he had been taken to in the British sector of Berlin, who had said he wasn't yet in any fit state to leave the hospital. 'Come now, Mr Connolly, you are a medical man yourself and you know that we haven't even had the results back of the tests we have run on you yet. My concern is about your lungs—'

'I'm sick of bloody tests,' Paul had said angrily. 'That's all you sodding well do. As for being a medical man, that was in a past life. All I have done for the past five years is try to survive, and the only reason I did that was the thought of my wife waiting for me back home.'

'Of course, we all understand that,' the doctor had said in the soothing, patronising tones he might have used to a half-wit. 'We will, of course, contact your wife as soon as you give us some more details.'

'Don't you understand anything?' Paul had roared in

frustration. 'Haven't you listened to a word I have said, you moron? I will never be well until I hold my wife in my arms.'

Excuses were made for Paul's outburst in the hospital, for they knew what he had gone through and they'd thought to treat his anger alongside trying to get him as well as he ever could be, considering how much he was damaged, which they would know more about when the results of the tests were in. The doctor certainly didn't want him to return as he was. He was nowhere near ready and he seemed to think his wife was in some sort of time warp, that things hadn't moved on for her too.

'Write to her,' the doctor persisted. 'Prepare her a little?'

'I don't want to write. I need to see her. What is there to prepare about a woman welcoming her husband home?'

He had left the hospital without their knowledge and, using someone else's clothes – for the ones he had been wearing when he was brought in were only fit for the incinerator and all they left him with was a hospital gown – he had taken five days to cross war-ravaged Europe. Always in his mind had been the picture of Carmel the day he had left her. He had thought that when she put her arms around him he would be at peace and healed by her love for him, but it had all gone wrong somehow.

Carmel was looking at him as if he was a ghost, and a very unwelcome ghost at that, and Paul knew that scenario being acted out at the door was the very thing the doctor had been worried about when he had advised him to write and prepare his wife. But, for God's sake, this was his home.

'Am I to be asked in then?' It was meant to come out in a fairly jocular way, but he had lost the art of doing that and, like most comments he made these days, it sounded aggressive.

'Of . . . of course,' Carmel said, opening the door wider.

And then, as Paul stepped into the hall, he saw the man behind Carmel. He had a baby in his arms and a little girl danced by his side as he said, 'His lordship is finished. Is he to have anything else?'

'Who is this man?' Paul asked Carmel, his voice unnaturally and unnervingly calm.

Carmel swallowed deeply. 'You must understand, Paul, we thought you were dead.'

Now it was the man's turn to look alarmed and astonished. 'Paul!' he repeated.

Carmel, perilously close to tears, cried, 'Oh, come in. None of this can or should be discussed on the doorstep.'

At first, it was little better in the breakfast room, for Carmel and Paul faced each other like two combatants. Terry took one look at them and disappeared into the kitchen, taking Sam with him. Beth gazed at each of them, feeling the tension but not understanding it.

Suddenly Carmel felt guilty. However she felt personally and whatever the outcome of this, it was a poor homecoming.

'I'm sorry, Paul,' she said, crossing the room. 'I was taken totally by surprise. It was the last thing that I expected.'

487

She would have put her arms around him then, but he stepped out of her reach and said again, 'Who is that man?'

'Paul, please . . .'

Paul slammed the table with the flat of his hand and Beth jumped and looked with sudden fear at the man who was bellowing at her mother. 'Tell me who he is, damn you.'

Carmel looked at the red face and eyes bulging with temper and the cruel twist of the mouth, and saw this man was not the gentle peace-loving Paul she knew.

Terry came in, still carrying Sam, and said to Paul, though his own heart was as heavy as lead, 'There is no need for any of this.' Then he turned to Carmel and said, 'There is a tray of tea in the kitchen. If you bring it in, I will put Sam to bed. There is some talking to be done.'

Carmel nodded and then she said to Beth, 'Do you want to go to Ruby's for a bit?'

Beth shook her head. What she wanted was to roll her life back by just a few minutes to the happy time before this strange man came to the door, upsetting everyone and shouting. But now he had come, she was being shunted nowhere until she understood why and who he was.

Carmel brought in the tray and sat at the head of the table. When Terry came back into the room he sat opposite Paul as Carmel said gently, 'This is going to be hard for you, Paul. God knows, it is going to be hard for all of us but Terry Martin is the man I married in 1943, after I thought you had been dead three years.'

Paul gave a sudden jerk in the chair. He wondered

why. He had known in his heart of hearts what she would say, but the actual words caused his innards to twist so painfully that he almost cried out against it. What he did instead was glare at Terry as he ground out, 'Don't matter what you both thought, I am not dead and as a woman can only have one husband, I suggest you sling your hook, mate.'

Before Terry had a chance to speak, Beth flew to Terry's side and said heatedly, 'Don't you tell my daddy to go away. It's you needs to go away.'

'Hush, Beth,' Carmel said.

Beth turned to her mother, her face full of distress, tears trickling down her cheeks as she cried, 'Make him go away, Mommy. He is horrible and we don't want him here.'

Carmel lifted Beth onto her knee and said to her, 'He belongs here, Beth. Paul is your real daddy.'

Beth looked at the old man with the lined face and white hair beside her, and remembered the picture beside her bed. She loved that picture, and the Paul in it had been happy and smiling and young and wearing uniform – and as unlike the man beside her as it was possible to be. So she said, 'No, he's not.'

Paul had almost forgotten about the child. Because she hadn't been born when he left, she had faded from his memory and when he had thought of home he had thought only of Carmel, but he remembered now that he had a daughter too. He tried to smile at her, but it came out like a grimace and Beth was repelled and snuggled further into her mother as Paul said, 'Oh yes, I am your real father.'

'Well, I don't want you to be, so there.'

'That will do, Beth!' Carmel snapped out and then to Paul, she said, 'All of us, Beth included, have a right to know where you have been for five and a half years and what has happened to turn you from a fit, vibrant young man into . . .'

'A shambling old one,' Paul finished for her.

He lifted the cup of tea and drained it as Carmel went on, 'I mean, I got the telegram and all, and then Chris said he saw you killed and tipped into a ditch.'

'And he would have been right if I hadn't been found by a French farmer and, I was to find out later, one of the Resistance,' Paul said. 'At great risk to himself and his family, he took me in and tended me. He said for weeks I hovered between life and death. When I recovered, there were plans to get me back to England and I had already got my false papers when the Gestapo swooped.

'If I would have spoken, given my name, rank and serial number, I still might not have survived,' Paul went on and added. 'The Gestapo record on taking prisoners is not good, but no one else would have survived either. Every man, woman, child and anyone else working on the farm would have been killed. But some mightn't be killed straight away. The Gestapo would know that I had to have help to get false papers and that would mean there was an active Resistance cell in the area. People would be tortured until they told what they knew; even I might have had the thumb screws applied.' Paul glanced at Carmel cuddling her daughter before he continued, 'And they would get the information, for if the men won't talk, they torture the children till the women speak, so I was told.'

Carmel instinctively held Beth tighter as she said, 'So you kept quiet.'

'Yes,' Paul told her. 'There was no choice. You know my French has always been good and it improved further in the three or four months I was at the farmhouse; was good enough, anyway, to fool the Germans. I was marched away with all the fit man of the area to one of the German labour camps and there was no way I could get word to you either then or later.

'Anyway, to tell you I was alive and well would have been a lie. Barely alive would have been more like it. We were set to rebuild roads and bridges and essential buildings the Allies had destroyed in bombing and so we worked in blistering heat, freezing cold and in pounding rain, and we were given just enough food to keep us alive. If you took a rest at any time you were whipped, the second time you were shot and any too sick to leave their beds received the same treatment.'

Paul's eyes were so full of pain as his story unfolded that Carmel's heart constricted in pity. She reminded herself that once she had loved this man more than life itself, and she longed to reach out and touch him, to cover his agitated hands with her own, but she was constrained with Terry there, who she could see clearly was suffering too. She knew whatever happened after this, someone was going to be so terribly hurt and she knew that would have to be her beloved Terry. How then could she comfort Paul in front of the man who was going to lose everything all over again?

Inside, Terry felt as if he was dying. Although he was moved by Paul's tale – and who wouldn't have been? – he saw the life he had built up, the second chance he had been given, crumbling away like so much dust before his eyes and he wanted to howl at the unfairness of life.

And so did Carmel, who felt as if she was being rent in two. 'I am so sorry, Paul, for all you have had to endure,' she said at last after the silence had stretched out uncomfortably between them.

'You don't know the half of it,' he burst out almost savagely. 'You looked out just for yourself there. We would be marching for days, sometimes in unrelenting heat on subsistence rations and a scant amount of water, and men would drop before you and you had to step over them and go on. The guards would pull them out of line and put a bullet through their heads and any who helped them, as they had in the beginning, were similarly dealt with. No one there could afford to have human emotions. We were treated like animals and in time behaved like them. I have seen men fight to the death over a slice of bread one has stolen from the other. Jesus Christ, it was hell on earth.'

'It's over now,' Carmel said soothingly, and then as Paul began to cry great gulping sobs of sadness, she put Beth down and put her arms around him. Her own eyes met those of Terry and she recognised the despair and helplessness she saw there.

'Is there no way around this?' he asked desperately.

'What do you suggest?' Paul asked sarcastically, turning his ravaged and red-rimmed eyes on Terry. 'That we share my wife – is that it? Maybe you should have her Monday, Wednesday and Friday and then my turn would be Tuesday, Thursday and Saturday, and Sunday could be turn and turn about. How would that suit?'

'Oh God, you know that isn't what I meant,' Terry

cried brokenly. 'Almighty Christ, I don't know how to cope with this.' He looked across at Carmel, her hands still on Paul's shoulders and saw her pain and knew her heart was being ripped in two, as his was. And if he stayed talking from now till doomsday, the end result would be the same, would have to be the same, and he would further upset Carmel and little Beth.

He swallowed the lump in his throat and said, 'There is no point prolonging this. I'll start collecting my things together.'

Carmel just watched him leave the room. She couldn't speak. What she wanted to do was hold him tight and beg him not to go and leave her with this stranger that she was almost afraid of, but she knew she could do or say none of those things and she sank onto the chair beside Paul and put her head in her hands. Beth stood sucking at the thumb she hadn't needed the comfort of for some time, her dress gathered into a bunch by her restless hands because everything had gone way past her understanding.

Terry could barely see for the tears falling from his eyes as he emptied drawers and his side of the wardrobe into his suitcases. He ached with pain and loss, and wanted to cry out with the injustice of it, but there was nothing that he or Carmel could do to fight against this. In the end the pain would be less for everyone else if he was just to walk away, and as quickly as possible.

Beth didn't see it that way at all and when he appeared in the doorway with his cases, she threw herself at him with a cry of anguish. 'Daddy, don't go!' she begged tearfully. 'Please don't.'

'Beth, I must,' Terry said, and he put the cases on

the floor and put his arms around the distressed child.

Paul lifted his head and growled out, 'Don't call that man Daddy. I am your daddy.'

'Paul, Beth didn't know you were alive till today,' Carmel chided gently. 'She is bound to take time to adjust.'

'She is being openly defiant,' Paul said, and he pulled her out of Terry's arms and nearer to him so suddenly neither could do a thing about it. Then he held on to her so she couldn't pull away.

'Paul . . .' Carmel said nervously, but Paul wasn't in the mood to listen to Carmel.

'If you call that man Daddy again, or refer to him as daddy when he has left here, you will make me very angry,' Paul said to Beth, and gave her a shake. 'Do you want to make me angry?'

Beth was very frightened and yet she found herself saying, 'I don't care about making you angry, because I don't like you and I wish you hadn't come back.'

The sharp smack across Beth's legs took them all by surprise and it would have been followed by more if Terry hadn't stepped forward and grasped the man's upraised hand as Beth's cries of outrage rent the air.

'Keep out of this,' Paul said to Terry. 'It really is none of your business how I chastise my own daughter.'

'It's mine, though,' Carmel said angrily, pulling Beth into her arms. 'And I have never found the need to smack Beth.'

'And this is the result,' Paul countered. 'A badly behaved and insolent child and one too used to getting her own way. I see I will have to instil some discipline here.' He cocked an eye at Terry and said, 'You still here?'

'I am just on my way,' said Terry miserably. He added to Carmel, 'If you want me, I will probably lodge at my boss's for a bit again. I'll give you the address.'

Carmel nodded, knowing that it would be untenable for him to stay with Ruby now, but Paul said, 'You will do no such thing. It is highly unlikely that my *wife* will need to call on you for anything. In fact, once you leave, I do not expect to see you ever again.'

'He must,' Carmel protested. 'There's Sam, for a start.'

'He will take his bastard with him.'

'Oh no he will not,' Carmel cried, bouncing in front of Paul angrily. 'And don't you dare call my son a bastard. Terry and I married in all good faith and he never laid a hand on me, in that way, until we were married.'

'Very laudable, but I still don't want the evidence of your infidelity, whether intentional or otherwise, before my face every day.'

'Paul, Terry can't look after a baby and I am the child's mother,' Carmel said. 'You can't do this.'

'Oh yes I can.'

'Please, Paul,' Carmel pleaded, putting a hand on his arm. 'This really isn't like you.'

Paul shook Carmel's hand off and growled, 'That Paul is dead and gone. This is the Paul you have to deal with now, but you are still my wife and what I say goes.'

'No,' Carmel said. 'Not in this. I gave birth to Sam and he is my child as much as Beth. If you will not allow him to stay here, then I will leave you and take the child with me, and Beth too.'

'Not Beth,' Paul said. 'I would fight you through the courts for Beth.'

He wouldn't win though, Carmel told herself. But could she take that risk? She turned stricken eyes on Terry.

'I am not having that man coming here ostensibly to see his son and really to see you,' Paul went on. 'And that is my final word on the subject.'

Then Terry knew what he had to do, for all it would break his heart. He had hoped at the end of all this he would be still able to see his son, be a father to the boy, take joy in his growing up, but all this he would have to give up for Carmel's sake.

'If I relinquish all ties with my son,' he said, though he was having trouble forming the words, 'will you allow him to stay with Carmel?'

'Ah no, Terry,' said Carmel, who knew what it had cost Terry to say that. She almost explained it to Paul, but she knew that this man who'd returned to her would have no sympathy for Terry under any circumstances.

Terry shook his head helplessly and said to Paul, 'Well, will you?'

'And you will have no contact with my wife for any reason?'

'None,' Terry said. 'You have my word.'

'Then yes, he can stay,' Paul said.

Carmel sighed with relief, for she knew it would tear the heart out of her to lose Terry and she didn't think she could bear to lose Sam as well.

In fact, when she watched Terry walk dejectedly away that day, she felt as if her heart had shattered into a million pieces. She was glad that Sam chose that moment to begin complaining and she was able to hide her tears from Paul, who wouldn't understand them and might become angry. She couldn't linger in the baby's room long, though, for she heard Paul shouting at Beth again.

Ruby had been unaware of the drama being played just the other side of her wall. It was Beth who told her in the end. Fed up with being shouted at, and frightened of the atmosphere presiding in the house, she took herself outside and sat on the swing Terry had made for her, swaying backwards and forwards, and letting the tears trickle down her cheeks unheeded.

Ruby, going out to her bin, heard the child crying and popped her head over the fence. 'What's up, bab?'

'Oh, Auntie Ruby . . .' Beth cried, relieved to see a familiar and safe face.

Ruby had seldom seen the child so downcast. 'Come on, bab, can't be that bad.'

'It can, Auntie Ruby,' Beth said. 'My real daddy is back and he is old and horrid and has made Terry go away.'

Whatever Ruby expected Beth to say, it was not that. At first she could barely take it in and stared at the child in stupefaction for a second or two before saying, 'Your real daddy, Beth? Are you sure that was what your mom said?'

Beth nodded. 'It's what she said. But he don't look nothing like the picture what Mom gave me.'

Ruby decided she had to find out what was what. 'How would you like to come round here and have a cup of cocoa?' she asked. 'You must be cold without your coat, and I'm sure I have some chocolate biscuits in the tin.'

'Chocolate biscuits,' Beth repeated. Now that Ruby mentioned it, she was cold, and cocoa and chocolate biscuits in a familiar house where no one was shouting was suddenly a much more attractive prospect than going back inside her own home. 'OK,' she said.

Ruby only waited till she had the child settled before she set off for Carmel's, only instead of nipping in the back, this time she went up to the front door and knocked. She hoped the child had got it wrong. She had nothing against Paul, but the man was dead and gone – or everyone thought he was – and Carmel had been that happy with Terry and her little family.

When Carmel opened the door, Ruby had only to look into her deadened and yet heartbreakingly painful eyes to know that Beth might be right after all.

Before either was able to speak, a haggard, white-haired man appeared by Carmel's side and snarled out while Ruby was coping with the shock of his appearance, 'Hello, Ruby. I wondered how long it would take you to come snooping around here.'

Carmel turned and looked at Paul, but said nothing.

Ruby, annoyed at the way he had spoken to her, said, 'I am not snooping. I came to tell you that Beth is in my house and she told us that you had arrived home, Paul, and I came round to see for myself as any concerned friend would.'

'Of course they would,' Carmel said in a voice thick with unshed tears. 'Come in, Ruby, and we will tell you all about it . . .'

Later Ruby said to George, 'The man has suffered, that much is certain, but he is changed and I don't mean appearance alone. He seems angry all the time and is that nasty to Carmel. Anyway, I'm going to listen out for the nippers tonight while they go and see the old man. Carmel wanted to go on her own, prepare him like, but Paul wouldn't hear of it.'

'And Terry?'

Ruby shrugged and sighed sadly, before saying, 'He had to go, didn't he? And Carmel is going round like she is encased in misery.'

Carmel wished Paul had been agreeable to her preparing Jeff. She thought he was going to collapse when he opened the door to them both. Like Carmel, he hadn't at first recognised the son, but then he was completely bowled over by the news. He put his arms around Paul's emaciated body and hugged him tight while tears rained down his face.

'Praise be!' he cried. 'Oh, thanks be to God! Come in, come in.'

Carmel stepped into the hall. She had been here just once before and she noted the house bore no resemblance to the last time she had seen it. Now it had an air almost of faded grandeur. Jeff led them to a small room he called his 'snug' and he explained he spent a lot of his time in there.

'Most of the house is shut up now,' he said. 'Emma is probably turning in her grave, but there you are.'

She could indeed be turning in her grave, because she had died in the spring when Sam had been only a few months old. If Emma had still been alive, Carmel knew she wouldn't have walked down the path, let alone gone inside. She knew Jeff had never liked the place and told her he considered it too ostentatious for his tastes and that he had not chosen it.

'I sometimes look back on my life,' he'd said, 'and see

what I have achieved. Through working myself into the ground I now have a beautiful mansion, a top-of-the-range Rolls-Royce and an extravagant way of living. I also have two sons I hardly know, a wife who can't bear me near her and a house that never has been and never will be a home.'

She had felt so sad and sorry for him when he'd said that, and now she looked across at him almost drinking in the sight of Paul, whom he thought he would never see again. She couldn't expect Jeff to share in her heartache at her losing Terry, for all he liked the man, and as he called to the cook to fetch champagne he poured himself and his son each a large Scotch and Carmel a sweet sherry, 'to be going on with'.

Jeff wanted to know, as Carmel had, what had happened to Paul, where he had been. Carmel let Paul's words wash over her and remembered Emma's awful funeral, which Jeff had inveigled her into attending.

'It wouldn't be right, Jeff.'

'Please, my dear?' Jeff had pleaded. 'I need someone on my side to cope with this, and Matthew can't get leave, or says he can't, which amounts to the same thing. It isn't as if she can hurt you any more.'

'Oh, Jeff . . .'

'It would mean so much to me if you would come.'

What could she say to that? She thought of the very many ways that Jeff had helped her and her family, and much against her better judgement she agreed to go.

Lois had been staying with her parents for a few days before the funeral so hadn't known that Carmel was going to attend until they got out of the cars at the church. Carmel saw Lois's eyes widen and then she felt herself begin to shake as she saw they were unloading a wheelchair and realised that Lois's mother was also going to be there.

There weren't that many, in all truth, for Emma had successfully alienated and ignored any friends she may have had long before she became too ill for visitors. Yet in the church Carmel felt uncomfortable and could almost feel the animosity around her and the malicious eyes boring into her back. At the reception, she saw all the Chisholm women glaring at her, and Lois's mother in black from head to foot, sitting in her wheelchair, looking ever inch some sort of murderous spider, her glittering eyes scanning the room, looking for her latest prey and coming to light on Carmel.

As Carmel saw the Chisholms approach her, she looked about for Jeff, but he was nowhere to be seen. Then the older woman, flanked by her daughters, almost spat out, 'This is all your doing, you know. Made Emma's life a misery.'

Carmel thought that was rich, but before she had chance to speak, Melissa said, 'We know the sort of place you were brought up. Had to have Paul, didn't you, and he had been promised to me for years. You are nothing but a dirty gold-digger.'

'Guttersnipe,' the older woman said. 'And no thought for Paul, dragging him down into the scum with you. No wonder you broke Emma's heart.'

'This is monstrous,' Carmel said, incensed. 'You have no right to call me names. All you are doing is cheapening yourselves and, as for Paul, I made him do nothing. You didn't know him if you think that.'

'Not know him?' Melissa scoffed. 'I have known Paul since the day I was born.'

'You knew Paul the boy, manipulated by his mother,' Carmel said scathingly. 'I fell in love with Paul the man.'

Before any could reply to this, Marjory Baker, whose chair had been pushed over to them by a waiter, suddenly said, 'Emma couldn't stand the girl.' She stared at Carmel with spiteful dark eyes. 'Said you were a trollop, and that you used to entice the men.'

'That will do,' Jeff said, coming upon them at that moment. 'I am surprised at you. Carmel had nothing to do with my wife's death and you all know it. She died of cancer.'

'That she was too heartbroken by that one's doings to fight,' Marjory Baker said.

'That's rubbish,' Jeff said. 'And now I think I will take Carmel to where the company is more congenial.'

'That means home, Jeff,' Carmel said as he swung her away.

'But, my dear . . .'

'No, Jeff,' said Carmel, and her voice was like steel. 'The very air is poisonous here and I have been away from my family long enough.'

Later, Lois told Carmel of a furious Uncle Jeff virtually throwing the Chisholm women out and wiping the floor with her mother, which left her dumbstruck, probably for the first time in her life.

'I just can't see why they all thought you had anything to do with Aunt Emma's death. I mean, you hadn't made a voodoo doll of her and gone round sticking pins in it, had you?'

'Lois,' Carmel said decidedly, 'if I had ever thought of

502

doing such a thing I wouldn't have waited so long about
it.'

The news flew around like lightning that Paul Connolly,
whom everyone thought killed in France, was home
again, large as life. A lot felt sorry for Carmel and Terry
and that lovely little lad they'd had, and owned that
coming back from the dead was not always the best solution for everyone, but really all this was nobody's fault.
All in all the general consensus was that war was a
bloody bugger.

The only one who didn't feel this was Father
Robertson. In his opinion the only true marriage was
the one he had conducted of Carmel with Paul, a
Catholic man to a Catholic woman, their union blessed
by the sacrament of Nuptial Mass in which the two had
taken Communion, as expected. That had no comparison to Carmel's hasty marriage to a man of another
faith, or even worse, no faith at all. Well, of course that
marriage didn't stand any more and it was the best thing
all round, in his opinion. This was actually what he told
Carmel that first Sunday after Paul's return, and she had
been so burdened with sadness at the loss of Terry, she
couldn't speak to him.

CHAPTER TWENTY-NINE

Paul found it hard to settle into the house and into post-war Britain. It was difficult to realise that people's lives had gone on and they hadn't just marked time while he had been away. He was furious that his motorbike had been sold.

'Paul, be reasonable,' Carmel pleaded. 'Terry didn't think that you would ever need it again. He didn't think you were even alive.'

'Huh. So you say.'

He didn't understand the shortages either, the make-do-and-mend culture ingrained in the people through the war. He just wouldn't co-operate with having five inches of water in the bath and refused to believe there was a shortage of coal and that that too was rationed.

He hated the food with a passion. Paul had never experienced a wartime menu and so he didn't see why he couldn't lather butter on the bread as he liked, though he detested the grey stodgy national loaf. Nor did he see why he couldn't have as many cups of tea as he wanted, though he didn't want national dried milk in it. He said he couldn't abide dried egg. He was a headache to feed but then he turned his nose up at or criticised most of the meals served up anyway.

This came to a head one day when he had been home a few days. For the evening meal, Carmel served sardine fritters, mashed potatoes, cabbage and turnip.

'What d'you call this muck?' Paul asked as he tasted a piece of fritter and spat it out on to his plate.

Carmel sighed. 'Sardine frittters,' she said. 'I hadn't points for anything else.'

Carmel looked from her daughter, biting her bottom lip in apprehension at Paul's raised voice, to her son in his high chair, battering the mashed potatoes on his tin plate with the spoon she had given him, and said, 'We have to do with what we can get, Paul, and it isn't always easy.'

'Not easy?' Paul shouted. 'This is bloody inedible. Shit! That's what it is.' And the plate and the dinner went sailing through the air to hit the wall with a crash. The baby began to wail and Beth to shake in fear as Carmel watched the potato slide down the wall in glutinous lumps to join the rest of the meal and broken pottery on the floor.

She had had enough and she stood up and yelled, 'What has that achieved, you bloody stupid imbecile, except make a mess for me to clean up and terrify the children? I just hope you are bloody proud of yourself.'

She saw the raised hand and side-stepped it. 'Don't you dare raise your hand to me!' she screamed. 'You are a bully, no better than Hitler. You have picked the wrong one to start that sort of caper with, for I will not stand it. You try that again and I will be over in Ireland with Mammy and both children before you can blink, so think on.'

Paul did think on. He was bitterly ashamed of himself. He had never raised his hand to Carmel before and had never imagined a time when he would even consider it. He knew that somehow he had to get a grip on the anger coursing through him.

Paul had been home a week or so, when Ruby saw him pass the house one morning and she took the opportunity to pop next door. Carmel was tackling a pile of ironing while Sam was taking a nap.

'All right?' Ruby asked.

'No,' Carmel admitted miserably, too dejected to keep pretending everything was fine. 'Ruby, I don't understand myself at all,' she said. 'For months and months I missed Paul so much and I would have done anything, literary anything, to have him walk through the door. I have told him this, but I doubt he believes me. He is Beth's father and yet he shows her no affection and I know she would open up like a flower if he did and be less afraid of him. But,' she said with a sigh, 'if I try saying any of this he says I have ruined her.'

'You have not,' Ruby said stoutly. 'Beth is a good wee girl and a little ray of sunshine into the bargain. I know that you'll have little Sammy the same before he is much older. What about any affection Paul gives you? One time he'd have taken the moon from the sky if you had wanted it.'

Tears stung Carmel's eyes. 'Don't, Ruby. Remembering how Paul was is like a dagger piercing my soul. Now . . . oh, he doesn't like me out of his sight, but that is more like a control thing than because he wants me near him. He is never out of the house for long and he sits there sort of brooding. I am almost afraid to speak, because I know he will find something to criticise.'

She looked at Ruby with tearful eyes and went on, 'I try not to think about Terry because that . . . that just hurts so very much. I have dealt that man such a damaging blow, I think sometimes maybe he will never get over it. No one should have to bear pain like that. I mean, neither of us planned to fall in love and both of us thought we were free.'

'I know that, bab.'

'Paul's like a stranger, Ruby,' Carmel said. 'And a stranger I don't much like, and together with the heartbreak over losing Terry . . . Oh God, Ruby, I am so bloody unhappy.'

Ruby knew that full well and wished she could put her arms around her friend, but at that moment they heard the front door open. Carmel immediately scrubbed the tears from her cheeks, adjusted her expression and picked up the iron again, while Ruby slipped out the back door, because though they hadn't spoken a word about it, they knew this new Paul wouldn't like them having a chat while he was out of the house.

Jeff came to see them one early afternoon, when Paul had been home a few days. He hoped that his son might have got over the awful shock he must have had arriving home to find Carmel married again, though he would know that Carmel would never have knowingly betrayed him. Maybe, he thought they had begun to gel back together again the way they had once been, but he was appalled at the set-up in that house that had once been such a happy place.

* * *

507

Paul took no notice of little Sam at all, and at coming up to a year old he was a delight. Jeff couldn't understand how anyone could be immune to his charms. On the other hand, Paul took almost too much notice of Carmel, either ridiculing her, or treating her in some other disdainful way. Jeff tried remonstrating with him and it seemed to make matters worse.

He returned home a worried man. He wondered if Paul just needed more time to adjust, or whether something should be said. He wished Matthew and Chris were home. He would value their advice and maybe one of them could have a word if they thought it necessary.

Carmel was so glad to see Lois and Colin back a couple of days later. At first Lois was overjoyed to see Paul, although Carmel had written to tell her the news. She declared it to be a miracle and she threw her arms around him, cried over him and kissed him and said Chris would be delighted. But she too very soon saw a vast difference in his manner.

'When I remember how you once were together, the change in him is incredible.'

'I know.'

'Can he still . . .? You know what I mean. Is he OK in bed?'

Carmel shook her head. 'He can perform all right, but sex between us used to be wonderful. At first, I did think that we might achieve some measure of closeness there, but now it feels like a nightly assault on my body, a stamp of ownership when he asks over and over if he is better than Terry. Oh, I don't know.' Carmel sighed. 'Dreadful, heinous things happened to him, things that

508

should never happen to a human being, and he did say that at the camp it was every man for himself. You couldn't allow yourself to care about anyone else and I suppose that would get to be second nature after four or five years.'

'So maybe Paul's emotions are just buried deeply and could surface again,' Lois said.

'Or perhaps snuffed out altogether,' Carmel said. 'And only time will tell which.'

By January, Paul's medical records had caught up with him and he had to report to the military doctor for a medical to ensure a proper discharge from the army. The doctor studied the notes sent on from the hospital in Berlin and knew Paul was a very sick man indeed. He ordered further X-rays to see if the shadow on his lungs had grown. He didn't tell Paul the level of his concern. Instead he said it was a routine procedure to clear up any minor problems. He also told him the results would be sent to his own doctor in about a fortnight's time and Paul had no reason to disbelieve what he was told.

And so a fortnight later he sat stunned in the chair and looking at the Dr Baxter as if he couldn't believe his ears. 'I wish there was better news I could give you, Dr Connolly,' the doctor said.

Paul stared at him. He had thought if they found anything wrong they could soon fix it. The doctor had intimated that with his 'routine' and 'to clear up any minor problems'. Paul hadn't any inkling the news would be so bad. He had heard that there were great strides made during and since the war in the curing of many diseases that had been killers in his youth and he'd always been a fit man. Hadn't he survived the labour camp when many hadn't? Many fell like flies and now here was this doctor telling him . . .

He wanted to rant and rail at the unfairness of life, to shout at this stupid doctor, throw things, smash up his goddamned room. But he did none of these things because, in his heart of hearts, he knew it would make no difference.

Yet he had to be sure. 'Are you saying that there is nothing in this God-awful world that you can do to get me right?'

The doctor's voice was soothing and his eyes sympathetic, but the words were exactly the same, 'I really am sorry. It is the very worst news a doctor has to give anyone, but the tumour on your lung is huge and completely inoperable. Haven't you found yourself breathless at times?'

'A bit,' Paul said almost impatiently. 'It was nothing to speak of.'

'Dr Connolly, you know yourself that the symptoms will only worsen. I could arrange for you to be admitted.'

But Paul had had enough of hospitals and their rules and regulations. 'No hospital,' he said to the doctor.

'But, Dr Connolly—'

'My wife is a nurse and I want to stay at home,' Paul said. 'How long have I got?

'Dr Connolly, it's impossible to—'

'No. it isn't,' Paul burst out, his eyes wild with fear and panic. 'You are not talking to an idiot here. You can have an educated guess.'

The doctor knew he couldn't tell the distressed man in front of him that his death could be imminent. He wished someone had come with him and so he said. 'I would say six to twelve months or so. Are you sure your wife will be able to cope?'

'I'm sure,' Paul said.

With months before he thought he had to worry about the death sentence hanging over his head, Paul resolved to shelve it and so when Carmel asked him what the doctor said, he said everything was fine.

'Not quite fit for work yet, but getting there.'

Carmel wondered if he would ever be ready. The doctors weren't there in the night when sometimes the rasping in Paul's throat and wheezing in his chest was so loud it kept her awake and she had noted how often he got out of breath. She had worried that it might point to something serious, and was relieved that it didn't.

'He will probably pick up in the spring,' Lois said, when Carmel expressed concern. 'Let's face it, these dark and freezing days would put years on anyone.'

She wasn't concerned much about Paul, though, and Carmel couldn't blame her, for Chris was finally due for demob on 20 February and Lois could hardly wait. As Matthew was being demobbed then too, Jeff suggested a celebratory dinner for them on Saturday 23 at Penn's Hall Hotel, a salubrious place in Sutton Coldfield in its own grounds. Chris's parents and Ruby and George were also invited, yet Carmel wasn't looking forward to it one bit, for Paul was so unpredictable.

She was nervous when Matthew came to greet her straight away, holding the hand of a pretty young girl he introduced as Alison Sheldon, his fiancée, and Carmel greeted the couple warmly. Jeff had noticed how nervous

Beth was around her father and though he was heart-broken over that, he had placed Beth opposite Matthew and Alison for the dinner and Carmel could see that both of them thought her delightful. Away from her father, Carmel saw a spark of the old Beth appear as she basked in their approval, while Sam had been fed and put to sleep in the hotel room they were using for the night.

Chris had been over the moon to hear of his friend's survival, but had been distressed by his manner to both Carmel and Beth in the couple of days he had been home. Lois had warned him how changed Paul was, but he hadn't been that concerned, convinced it was just that he needed to adjust.

However, he had soon seen that Paul's problems were more deep-seated than that. That evening, as Chris sat opposite him, he was upset by his friend's manner to Carmel, and by the end of the meal he decided enough was enough.

'Come on,' he said to Paul. 'I need a pint and I am sure it is your turn.'

This was the way they had always been together and Paul smiled as he said, 'No, I'm sure you are wrong. It's your turn.'

'We'll fight it out when we get there,' Chris said. 'Come on before I die of thirst.'

Once they had got the pints in their hands, however, Chris dropped the jocular tone and stance and said to Paul, 'We need to talk.' He led the way to a small table in a quiet corner of the bar.

Paul raised his eyes to the ceiling. 'Here comes the bloody lecture.'

'Not at all,' Chris said. 'Not yet, anyway. When I've

finished you may feel you deserve a lecture for I am going to fill you in first on what our wives, yours and mine, were doing with their time while you were sweating it out in a labour camp and I was working my fingers to the bone to save lives.'

'What are you on about?'

'You know the type of woman Carmel was and would be again if you would let her be without finding fault with her every five minutes,' Chris said. 'Honestly now, in a war of that magnitude, was she the sort to be happy knitting squares for blankets or rolling bandages when she could be applying them? She went back to nursing at the General Hospital and only the goodness of Ruby and George in taking care of Beth enabled her to use her skills in that way. You have seen the devastation of the city's buildings – well, they dealt with the city's injured and maimed and dying, often with bombs hurtling down around them. You have no idea what danger they faced day after day. In fact, the General was hit once, Lois told me, and they lost two good friends. You might remember their old room-mate Jane, and the flirtatious Aileen, as well as a number of other colleagues and patients.'

Paul was stunned. He searched the recess of his mind and could remember the two girls, especially Jane, and he shivered when he thought it could have been Carmel. All that time in the labour camp he had told himself that at least Carmel was as safe as anyone could be in war. There had been no bombing of civilians in British cities before he had sailed out with the BEF and he had been ignorant of what was happening to his own country. But when he had arrived in Britain and then went on to

513

Birmingham he had seen the ravaged destruction, almost obliteration of vast areas.

'I had no idea,' he said. 'Why didn't she say?'

'Maybe you have never given her chance,' Chris said. 'When do you talk to her, other than to bark orders at her? She had a virtual collapse after she received the telegram. She was so bad that Lois took time off to care for her and then I told her, in all good faith, that I had seen you killed. I saw the last vestige of hope that she had been clinging to that you were alive somewhere leave her face that day,' Chris went on sadly. 'To her you were dead and gone, finished, done, and she had to face life without you, knowing she had to go on for Beth's sake.'

'I sort of forgot about her,' Paul admitted.

'Beth?'

'Yeah,' Paul said. 'It was as if she wasn't a real person. Carmel wrote and told me when she was born and we were in the middle of it then, if you remember, casualties coming in thick and fast. You know as well as I do that after March it was hard to get letters through and by April impossible, so it was as if Beth didn't exist, wasn't a person at all. And then I came back and she was definitely a person and a person that doesn't like me one bit.'

'Now why should she?' Chris said heatedly. 'You tore her from the only father she has ever known and instead of trying to understand what she was going through, trying to help her, you set out to bully her. Think about it, Paul. We spent six years fighting a war against the bully boys of Europe and you come home and practise these tactics on your own wife and child.'

'You don't understand,' Paul said. 'All right, I am ashamed and should never have behaved as I did – as I do – but when I came home and saw that Terry Martin . . .'

'Oh, yes, let's talk about Terry Martin,' Chris said, 'who was an honest and decent fellow, by all accounts – and a brave one into the bargain. Carmel didn't go looking for another to put in your place. It actually was the last thing on her mind and Terry Martin has a tragic story of his own that you might like to hear . . .

While Chris was talking to Paul, the room was being cleared for dancing. Jeff had taken Alison up on the floor and Matthew sidled up to Carmel. He saw the nervousness in her eyes as he did so and he said, 'Don't get all flustered, Carmel. I have come to apologise.'

'Apologise?'

'Yes, apologise,' Matthew said. 'For the times I embarrassed you or was just downright nasty, and that one time I virtually attacked you. I have no defence, not even that I was drunk, because I always knew what I was doing. It was jealousy, plain and simple, and I just want you to know that you have nothing to fear from me any more.'

'Thank you, Matthew,' Carmel said. 'I would like it if we could be friends and I think that Alison is a lovely girl.'

Matthew grinned and said, 'She is and you are too, and generous not to hold a grudge over the way I treated you.'

'Life is too short to bear grudges.'

'That is what I learned in the army amongst all the

blood and guts and gore – that life too is infinitely precious and yet can be snuffed out in a minute – and I promised myself that if I survived that, I wouldn't always be blaming the fact that my mother didn't love me for the way I was, that a person has to take responsibility for their own actions when they are adult. I get on better with the old man these days as well.'

'I am glad. Jeff is a lovely person, Matthew.'

'Yeah, funny how you and he hit it off from the first,' Matthew said. 'If he tried to defend you at all, Mother used to go wild.'

'Your mother . . .'

'My mother was so eaten up with bitterness that it turned her brain and ate away at her mind just as the cancer ate away at her body,' Matthew said. 'Her love for Paul, I know now, was total and absolute only when he did things she approved of. He was cast aside the first time he stood up to her.'

'I know.'

'What I mean is, it didn't have to be you. In my mother's head she had a blueprint for Paul. She must have been shaken when he decided he didn't want to go into the business and the plans needed rearranging a bit, but anytime he would have gone against her, the situation would have been the same because Paul was all she had, all she wanted. She had successfully cast me out and she never had any time for Dad. Anyway,' he went on, 'she would turn in her grave just now, because we are selling the mausoleum.'

'Are you? I thought you would inherit that along with the business.'

'I don't want it,' Matthew said. 'Neither does Alison

516

and neither of us wants servants. In the army I mixed with all types and some of them, most of them, the salt of the earth and the ones you had to trust with your life. What gives me the right in civvy street to lord it over such people? Anyway, Alison was in the Land Army during the war and what she wants is a house in the countryside, just outside Sutton Coldfield with a bit of land that she can grow vegetables in.'

'Sounds lovely,' Carmel said. 'But what about the servants you have? What will happen to them?'

'They will be pensioned off, which should have been done years ago. Dad is seeing to all that.'

'And has your father plans?' Carmel said. 'Where will he live?'

Matthew looked at Carmel with a sardonic grin on his face as he said, 'I am surprised that he hasn't told you. He is buying a house in Letterkenny.'

Carmel just stared at him. 'You are joking?'

'No, I'm not,' Matthew said. 'Ask him yourself.'

The dance was over and Jeff approaching the table. Carmel said, 'Are you buying a house in Letterkenny?'

Jeff's amused eyes slid across to his son. 'Matthew has told you, then?'

'So you are?'

'Yes, it's time to hang up my hat,' Jeff said and added, 'I'm tired and now my son has finished conquering Europe, I thought it about time he did an honest day's work for once.'

'Cheek!' Matthew said in mock indignation as Carmel persisted, 'But why retire to Letterkenny?'

'Why not, my dear?' Jeff said, and then as Carmel seemed too nonplussed to reply, went on, 'We never

517

recognise the value of the place we grow up in and Letterkenny suits me fine. I want out of the city, out of the rat race, but I know I would be bored to tears in a village. Letterkenny is a thriving little town, surrounded by beautiful countryside, and if I should buy a yacht, as I am hoping to do, it is on the edge of Lough Swilly. It's just the perfect place.'

'Does Mammy know you are moving there?'

'I should think so,' Jeff said. 'She helped me find the house.'

'Oh,' Carmel said, slightly hurt that her mother had not told her.

'No, don't be holding that against her,' Jeff said. 'I told her to say nothing until it was finalised.'

'And now it is?'

'Yes. I will be staying on for a few months until Matthew is back in the swing of it again and then it is Letterkenny here I come,' said Jeff. 'Now that your curiosity has been satisfied, perhaps you can do me the honour of having this dance with me?'

Paul stood at the entrance to the bar and watched his wife dance with his father, noting that she was as lovely and slender as she had been the day he married her. He knew that he loved her just as deeply as he ever had and he could weep to think that they would not have much time together, for the bloody thing growing inside him would get him in the end. And how did he want to be remembered by his family – as a moody and angry malcontent that they were glad to see the back of?

Once he had said to Carmel's father that he would be ashamed to have his wife and children so frightened of

518

him, and now look at him: almost as bad. He was ashamed and knew it had to stop. As for Terry Martin, Paul had been shaken by the tale Chris had told him and the way Carmel and he had met, and he knew that the man had suffered enough. No wonder he had loved Beth so much, and Paul now saw that he had no right to separate Terry from his son. That had just been too cruel. The point was, he didn't know where he was now, but he would get on to his solicitor to see if the man could be found. But for now he had to try to repair the damage with his wife and child, and try to act as a proper father to Terry's son too for the time he had left. He owed the man that much.

He put down his empty glass and walked across to the table and asked Carmel if she would like to dance.

She danced with Paul a lot after that, but was not aware of the fact that Paul only did the slow, more sedate dances with her. He knew he couldn't have managed anything more lively, because as the night wore on his breathing got worse and worse, though he managed to hide this.

Jeff had paid for everyone to have rooms in the hotel for the night. When Carmel saw the lines of strain on Paul's face, she suggested they seek their rooms and he agreed thankfully. Carmel had sensed a softening within Paul since he had spoken to Chris and she had responded to it as she did to kindness. So when he put his arms around her as she sat on the chair before the dressing table, she leaned against him with a sigh.

'You are a very beautiful woman, Carmel,' he said. 'Once I told you I would love you till the breath leaves my body, and that is still true.'

Carmel wasn't sure that she loved Paul now, though she knew she had once. However, she knew it was what he wanted her to say, but she couldn't bring herself to utter those words as if they meant nothing and so she was silent.

And into the silence, Paul asked, 'Did you love Terry?'

'Please, Paul . . .'

'It's not a trick question so I can start getting angry and shout at you,' Paul said, 'and I have a reason for asking. Chris enlightened me about a lot of things this evening – about what you were doing in the war and how you met Terry, and I just wondered if you did actually love him, or just felt sorry for him.'

Carmel swung around in the chair, stood up and, taking Paul's hand, led him to the bed. There, sitting together, she took his face in her hands and said, 'Paul, I loved you heart, body and soul, and I wanted to die when I thought you had. When you have loved like that, you don't settle for second-best.'

'So you loved him?'

Carmel did not trust herself to speak and just nodded.

'And now?' Paul persisted.

Carmel swallowed the lump in her throat, lifted her head and said, 'Now I am married to you and this is my place and I will never leave you. Tonight I had a glimpse of the old Paul, the one I fell in love with.'

'Could you . . . do you think it is possible that . . . you could ever love that Paul again?'

'I don't know,' Carmel said honestly and then across her face flitted the ghost of the impish grin he had loved so much as she said, 'But I do intend to have a damned good try.'

Over the next three weeks, Paul deteriorated physically at an alarming rate and he tried to hide this from Carmel for he was making great strides with her emotionally. Jeff saw it, though, and Chris, who had treated cancer patients, asked him outright one day if he had cancer.

'How did you know?'

Chris shrugged. 'I know you too well, man. What treatment have they offered?'

When Paul didn't answer, but looked steadily at his friend, Chris burst out, 'Jesus, Paul, they must be trying something.'

'There's no point.'

Tears stood out in Chris's eyes at the thought that very soon, he was to lose his best and oldest friend. He thought that he had seen him killed in France and then, like a blessed bloody miracle, he wasn't dead, he had survived. And now this. What a bloody, shitty life it was.

'I struggled to stay alive in the labour camp to get back to Carmel,' Paul said. 'Many times I was so tired and in that much pain I wanted to sink to the ground, where a bullet would have finished me off. It would have been quick and clean and I wouldn't have come back to disrupt so many lives and make everyone so unhappy.'

'You weren't to know any of this, mate,' Chris said brokenly. 'All of us can be as wise as Solomon with hindsight. Oh God, I can hardly cope with this. To have you back for such a short time and then lose you all over again. Who else knows?'

'No one else.'

'Why in God's name not?'

'I don't want to be pitied, and patronised.'

'Who said you would be?' Chris said. 'But your family at least need to know.'

'Not Carmel.'

'Definitely Carmel.'

'No,' Paul said. 'I want her to love me as she used to, not feel sorry for me.'

'Do you love Carmel, Paul?'

'What kind of damn fool question is that?'

'Well, do you?'

'Course I bloody do.'

'Well, you sure as hell don't understand her,' Chris said. 'You *must* tell her.'

Chris took Lois to the pictures the following evening to give Paul and Carmel the house to themselves. Paul only waited until the children were in bed before putting his arm around Carmel and telling her what the doctor had really said to him. For a long time afterwards she just stared at him in shocked silence. She wanted to scream at him that these things were not true and what was he doing, telling her such things, but she didn't do this, because she really studied Paul's face and knew she was looking at a dying man. She had not seen this before because she hadn't looked, or maybe hadn't wanted to see, and she put her arms around Paul and they cried together.

Even when the tears were spent, Carmel felt such sorrow, such deep, deep sadness. She was just beginning to get to know this man again, come to love him for himself. Oh God, it was so cruel, so very, very cruel. She leaned across and kissed Paul gently on the lips.

'You once asked me if I could love you again,' Carmel said. 'I know now. This is not to be mixed up with pity or compassion. I know what both of those emotions are like, but this is love and it is for one man, my husband, Paul.'

Paul fell against her with a groan. 'Will you come to bed?' he said humbly. 'I can't make love to you as I would want, but I would love to just hold you.'

'Then you shall,' Carmel said and stood up, pulling Paul to his feet. Hand in hand they mounted the stairs.

Jeff and Matthew reacted with anger when they first heard the news the following day, for as Paul said, no one really knew how long a person had and he thought they needed to know. Jeff was all bluster to cover his distress, talking about second opinions and treatment abroad, until it was prevailed on him that it was too late for any of that and that all the money and influence in the world would not save his son this time. He cried then in grief-stricken helplessness as he had when Lois had brought him news of the telegram.

Matthew has never seen his father cry so openly, not these gulping sobs of anguish that were causing tears to prickle behind his own eyes.

'What's it all about anyway?' he asked Carmel later. 'I mean, why was Paul's life saved on the battlefield only for him to develop this thing eating away at him?'

Carmel shook her head helplessly. There were no answers.

CHAPTER THIRTY

Gradually the tragic news of Paul filtered through the neighbourhood and people called to offer support or extend their sympathies for them all. Ruby, George, Jeff and Matthew, often with Alison, were regular visitors. Paul and Carmel were at one with each other and Paul was working to really get to know Terry's son and his own daughter, and possibly spend some quality time with them before he became too sick. Sam was easy, for he would love indiscriminately anyone who gave him attention. Beth had no yardstick to measure Paul by, however; she couldn't remember a time when he had been nice, only when he had been horrid, and was much harder to win over at first, but she took the pattern from her mother and in the end she began to thaw towards him.

The day that she climbed on his knee, wound her arms around his neck and said, 'I love you, Daddy,' he felt as though his heart would burst from unadulterated joy and love for this child.

He had the urge to put his head in his hands and cry his eyes out that he would not live to see her grow up.

He controlled himself with effort and gave Beth a squeeze, for all it hurt his chest, and said brokenly, 'And I love you too.'

Over a fortnight later, a Saturday, Beth asked Paul if he would push her on the swing. Carmel didn't want him to. The March wind was fierce and his cough and breathing had got much worse, but Paul's relationship with Beth was too fragile and tenuous to start refusing to do things with her and he said he would be fine. He would wrap up.

They hadn't been in the garden long, however, when Beth's screams sliced through the air. Carmel reached the garden first to see Paul in a heap on the ground, his face chalk white and scarlet blood pumping in a stream through his blue-tinged lips. She was rooted to the spot, her hands covering her mouth as Chris burst past her.

'Almighty Christ!' he exclaimed, running to his prone friend. He checked that he was still breathing before lifting Paul in his arms, for there was no weight to him now, and carrying him inside.

Dr Baxter wasn't at all surprised by Paul's collapse. 'He refused hospital care,' he said. 'The tumour has burst now. I was afraid of this happening because it was so big.'

'How long as he got, Doctor?' Carmel said. 'Please be honest with me.'

'My dear, I would be surprised if he lasts twenty-four hours,' the doctor said. 'I have given him morphine, because he must be in pain, although he hasn't complained.'

He complained about nothing and Carmel sat and

held his hand. She leaned over and kissed him lightly on the cheek. 'I love you, Mr Connolly,' she said, and saw his drugged eyes light up and then close in sleep, and she advised Chris to bring in Jeff and Matthew.

Darkness fell. Paul's father and brother had been to see him and were now in the breakfast room waiting. Lois had put the children to bed and Carmel was glad someone else was caring for the children. Her place, she felt, was by her husband's side. From time to time Lois, Chris, Ruby and George or Jeff came to keep her company, but she sat on in the same position hour upon hour and held Paul's hand.

In the dark hours before dawn she felt the change in him, a slackening of the hold, and she had sat with enough dying patients to know this was it. He opened his eyes, suddenly so clear, and said in a whisper that she had to bend her head to hear, 'It was good between us, wasn't it, Carmel?'

'Very good, darling.'

'Can you put your arms around me?'

Carmel's arms encircled him, nestling his head in the crook of her arm, and he sighed and smiled at her. Then he closed his eyes, let his head fall back. She knew he was gone and she kissed his cheek for the last time.

Paul's funeral was huge. There were representatives from the Royal Warwickshires, and the friends he had made during the war; those who remembered being treated by him, either in a military or civilian capacity, and a sizeable contingent from both hospitals; people from Jeff's club, Ruby and George, of course, and hundreds more friends and neighbours, including Sylvia and her husband, Dan.

There were even photographers from the papers flashing away. Paul's family was not only rich, but many, Jeff said, would be interested in the story behind his son's funeral.

'I'll have copies made of the articles and any good photographs so that you can have a record of it to show Beth when she is older, if you like.'

Carmel felt as it she was in a daze, 'Yes,' she said. 'Thank you, Jeff.'

'And look,' Jeff suddenly said. 'Here is your dear mother coming.'

There was Eve and all the clan, but it was Eve whom Jeff was looking all misty-eyed at, and Carmel knew she would have to buttonhole her mother at the first opportunity and ask what was going on. She was delighted, though, to see each and every one of her brothers and sisters. They gave her so much moral support through that sad time.

'Your poor daddy has gone to Heaven,' Eve told Beth.

'I know,' said Beth, 'but it is all right because he has been before.'

Carmel choked back the laugh, knowing if she gave way to it she would never stop, for she was verging on hysteria. Jeff saw this immediately and had his arm around her in seconds. Instantly she felt calmer and he led her into church like that.

But as they reached the door a sudden movement by the gate caught his eye, and as he left Carmel in the seat, he said, 'If you will just excuse me, my dear, there is something I must attend to. I will be back directly.'

Jeff wasn't away long at all and Carmel was glad of his solid presence beside her, though Jeff was so overcome with sorrow himself, he wondered who was comforting who.

The Requiem Mass was over, the clods of earth dropped onto the coffin, and all retired to the Lyndhurst pub. There Carmel was able to have a quiet word with her mother.

'I know that this is neither the time nor the place,' she said. 'But I have to know, is there something going on between Jeff and you?'

'Not yet.'

'Mammy!'

'Carmel, we are both free agents,' Eve said. 'And we like one another and have done for some time, so we are going to see. If it develops, then it does, and if it doesn't, there's no harm done.'

No harm done of course, and Eve looked happy and relaxed, though she said the whole family had been devastated by Paul's death. 'It made me think that you have to grab every moment when you can,' she told her daughter.

It was good advice but not anything Carmel seemed able to take on board straight after the funeral. She was irritated by this attitude and often told herself to count her blessings. She had two beautiful children, was surrounded by good caring friends, had a supportive family in Ireland and yet she was crushingly lonely. Everyone but her, her mother included, appeared to have someone special in their lives.

When the spring gave way to summer, it was worse. The streets seemed full of lovers walking along, entwined or hand in hand, and there were more in the parks, and mothers and fathers playing together with their children. Inside Carmel felt dead, like a dried-up shell, who could give nothing and accept nothing.

Paul had been dead for four full months when the letter for Carmel came from Fanshawe and Bone, Solicitors in Bennett's Hill in the city centre.

'They want me to go and see them at two-thirty on Monday,' Carmel said to Lois, 'but they were Paul's solicitors, not mine. I've never had any reason to have a solicitor.'

'You'll have to go just the same.' Lois said. 'Do you want me to come with you?'

'No,' Carmel said, 'I'll manage, but I'll not want to take Sam or Beth with me. Would you see to them for me?'

'You don't need to ask,' Lois told her. 'Aren't the two boys as thick as thieves anyway, and as it is the holidays I will have Beth here to keep them in order. What could be better?'

'Mr Connolly left instructions that four months after his death I was to deliver a letter to you,' Mr Fanshawe told Carmel that Monday afternoon. He withdrew an envelope from a file and handed it to her. She saw immediately that it was Paul's writing, and she suddenly shook all over.

The solicitor was sympathetic. 'Always upsetting, getting something from the grave, as it were,' he said. 'I will let you read your letter in peace and make us some tea.'

Carmel was grateful for the solicitor's sensitivity and

she waited until the door closed behind him before she slit the envelope.

Dear Carmel,

If you are reading this then I am dead and gone and I would like to apologise for the way I behaved when I first came home. I did both you and Terry Martin a severe disservice that time, and I wish I could go back and put it right, but I know that is impossible. Sister Frances told me that you would have made a very bad nun and she was right, for you are a beautiful and sensual woman who has a heart full of love for all mankind. I have never stopped loving you from the moment I first saw you.

Do not feel bad if you find someone else to share your life. You have my blessing, for my dearest wish is for you to be happy.

Goodbye my darling.

All my love,

Paul

Carmel could barely read the last words, her eyes were so blurred with tears, and she dabbed at them with a tissue as Mr Fanshawe came in with a tray of tea and said, 'Have you read the letter?'

'Yes, yes, thank you,' Carmel said. She folded it up and put it in her bag.

'Now there was another charge your husband laid upon us,' Mr Fanshawe said, handing Carmel a cup of tea. 'If you will just wait here for one moment . . .'

Carmel sat and sipped her tea and wondered what

other shocks were in store. Then Mr Fanshawe came back in and there, framed in the doorway, was Terry.

He was the very last person that Carmel expected to see and she went into complete shock. The tea slopped in her saucer so badly as her whole body began to quiver that Mr Fanshawe took it from her and placed it on the table. Then Terry was across the room and Carmel rose to her feet, mindful that she hadn't seen the man for months and her mind was teeming with questions.

'How did you know to come here today?' she asked Terry. 'Have you been around all the time? No one has seen anything of you. This is just, well, it's just like a miracle.'

'It needed a little mortal intervention, I believe,' said the solicitor. 'Take a seat and I will tell you how it was.'

Carmel and Terry sat down, Carmel so agitated she was rolling her handbag strap over and over in her fingers.

The solicitor smiled. 'Try to relax, Mrs Connolly,' he urged. 'Your late husband asked us to try and find Mr Martin, but he had successfully gone to ground. You were working in London, I believe.'

Terry nodded. 'Plenty of work for a gas fitter in that blitzed city, and I couldn't stay here,' he said, turning to Carmel. 'I might bump into you, or the children or Paul. I didn't want to make things more difficult for you and I knew it would be worse seeing Sam and not being allowed to touch him, hold him, be a father to him, you know?'

Carmel nodded, well able to understand that. 'So how did you get in touch?' she asked the solicitor.

'We didn't,' Mr Fanshawe said. 'Your late husband's father contacted us with Mr Martin's address.'

'Jeff? How did he get involved?'

'Despite what I said about not wanting to see Sam regularly,' Terry said, 'I became desperate just to see what he looked like, see how he had grown – just from the distance only. So when I read the details of Paul's funeral in the paper, which shocked me to the core, I must say, I took a train up.'

'You wouldn't see Sam. We left him, and Lois and Chris's son, Colin, with an obliging neighbour,' Carmel said.

'Yeah, I gathered that after a while,' Terry replied. 'The funeral was no place for them anyway. I did see Beth, but she didn't see me, but Jeff did and came out and had a word.'

'Oh, that was it,' Carmel said. 'He said he had something to attend to and left the church for a while.'

'Yeah, he came to see me outside,' Terry said. 'I couldn't stay then, see. I had taken a day's holiday to come up in the first place and had a job and digs to go back to and it wasn't the right time to see you, anyway, at your husband's funeral.'

'No, I suppose not,' Carmel said. 'But why didn't Jeff say something then? I could have written to you.'

'I asked him not to,' Terry said. 'I honestly didn't know whether I wanted to go through it again. I was very ill when I left that first time, and the thought of that again . . . I didn't think I could stand it, Carmel. It was only the thought of Sam that stopped me knocking the whole thing on the head anyway and taking off for Australia. Anyway, when Jeff told me about this arrangement Paul had of contacting you after he had been dead a certain length of time, I said I wasn't sure I wanted to get involved. I suppose he didn't say anything to you then in case you were disappointed. Anyway, here I am.'

'Did you only come back because of Sam?'

'Yes . . . I mean no. Oh, I don't know,' Terry said. 'Hell, Carmel, I didn't know how you would be feeling about me, did I?'

'Paul changed, you know,' Carmel said. 'It was when he realised how ill he was, I think. He became a quieter version of the Paul I once knew.'

'Jeff told me a little of how he was,' Terry said.

'He left a letter for me,' Carmel said, extracting it from her bag. 'You should read it, because it concerns you too.'

Terry read it and gave it back to Carmel.

'Where do we go from here?' Though his words were nonchalant, his eyes were full of trepidation and doubt, and Carmel knew she had never stopped loving this wonderful man and father of her son.

She stood up and pulled Terry to his feet. 'I say we go home,' she said. 'Unless of course you have a better idea.'

'There isn't a better idea than that,' Terry said, taking Carmel's hand. 'Good afternoon, Mr Fanshawe, and thank you.'

'Oh, don't thank me,' the solicitor said. 'We did very little and, to be honest, I haven't had such an entertaining afternoon in some time. May I wish all the very best to you both?'

'You may indeed,' Terry said, and he swept Carmel out of the office and into the street, where they kissed soundly, but very sweetly.

'That kiss was for my wife-to-be,' he said. 'For as

soon as it can be arranged we are going to do the whole thing all over again. That is, if you still want to be my wife?'

'The answer to that is yes, yes and again yes,' Carmel said. 'And now let's go home and tell the children.'

ACKNOWLEDGEMENTS

Those of you who know my books well will be aware of how much I strive for accuracy and so, when I first had the idea for this book, I naively thought that it would be relatively easy to research the training of nurses in the 1930s. After all, the internet is a marvellous tool. It is, but in this case it was no help at all.

As I said in the book, Birmingham then had two teaching hospitals, the Queens, which was the forerunner to the Queen Elizabeth, and the General, both totally funded by voluntary contributions. I have spent a fair amount of time at the General as a patient, though not in the 1930s I hasten to add, but I have never been into the Queen Elizabeth. So, the General was the hospital I wanted to concentrate on, especially as it is on a direct line to Erdington, where my characters were going to be based. The problem here was that the General Hospital is now Birmingham Children's Hospital and so much of its history has been either lost or filed away in some obscure place that no-one seemed to know how to access.

In desperation, I took a trip to Birmingham in the autumn of 2005 and visited the Central Library's Local History Department because the staff there have been so helpful in the past and I found a book called *QE Nurse*

1938 – 1957, compiled by Doreen Tennant, Jeffrey Wood and Ann-Carol Carrington and edited by Collette Clifford. It is a brief history of nursing at the Queen Elizabeth and was a very interesting and illuminating read as well as a valuable resource for me. Despite the title, the book actually went back to 1931, detailing the difference in training at that time and later. It also stated that the training of nurses in the two hospitals was virtually identical and in fact in later years the probationers of both hospitals often had lectures together. I thought I would have to photocopy great swathes of it, but the library staff said they thought it was still in print and phoned up the publisher for me to check this and so I was able to order my own copy.

There were other important books I used when writing about this period, some of which I have used before like *Ration Book Recipes*, part of the English Heritage series compiled by Gill Cordishley. I also bought a copy of *Catholics in Birmingham* by Christine Ward Penny, which gave me a valuable insight into the history and rise of Catholicism in the city and Carl Chinn's book *Our Brum* gave me details of the music halls and theatres and the dance halls, so prevalent at the time. Carl is a quite amazing person, who does all he can to promote my books, so a special thanks to him too.

A motor bike rally organised on the sea front, less than five minutes from my home came at just the right time. As enthusiasts, those owning vintage bikes were only too anxious to tell me about them and extol their virtues and so I was able to choose suitable bikes for my young doctors to ride.

We visited Ireland in the very early spring of 2005 to collect information for this book and I was grateful once more to the staff at the County Library at Letterkenny for their help, advice and their stock of very important

OS maps and I used Niall Nói-giallach's book *Our Town* again detailing Letterkenny. More general thanks to all the Irish people we met and talked with, who not only are proud of their history and heritage, but know all about it and are quite willing to share it with anyone showing a spark of interest. I need to make a particular mention here of my cousin Eddie Mulligan from Donegal, who is full of suggestions for promoting my book in Ireland.

My family are very important to me and I value their support and their interest in what I write about and this was shown in the summer of 2004, when on a visit to Devon, my eldest daughter, Nikki and friends Amanda, Bernadette and Caroline ended up brainstorming the ending of this book, which was then just an unfolding idea in my head. It was terrific fun, but the book would have had a different slant altogether if I had taken on board some of their more bizarre suggestions. But thanks anyway girls, it was great.

Thanks must also go to others who have helped and championed me from the beginning, the lovely Judith Evans at Birmingham Airport and my dear friend and confidante Judith Kendall, who does so much for me and is so appreciated.

As always, a special thanks has to go to my marvellous husband Denis, who organises the trips to London and then to Ireland and Birmingham for research and promotional purposes, where he drives me wherever I wish to go and without a word of complaint. As this is just a small amount of what he actually does for me, I really think he could do with a gold star.

And then there is the stupendous team at HarperCollins. Peter Hawtin, who I actually managed to see this time I was in Brum, which is surely another notch to your belt, Peter. My editor, Susan Opie works so hard for me that the published book would not be half as good without her input and I am always incredibly grateful. My publicist, Becky Fincham is fairly new to HarperCollins and me, but she is just terrific. There is also Clare Hey and I cannot finish these acknowledgements without special 'hi' to Maxine Hitchcock.

My agent, Judith Murdoch is a wonderful lady who always looks out for me and always listens to my point of view, though she is not above a little gentle bullying, which is probably good for me in the long run. All in all, I feel fully supported in all I do with a strong team surrounding me and helping me in all ways and I am incredibly grateful for this.

Last, but by no means least, are you, the readers; those who choose my books and hopefully enjoy them. Some of you write or email to tell me so, which always means a great deal to me.

And so I will use that overworked word again, but no less sincere for all that: thanks a million times to each and every one of you.